He liked that she kissed with everything she had...

...and the little noise she made. He liked how her breath caught when his hand found a sliver of flesh beneath her shirt, as though the contact was new and unexpected. The woman was a breath of fresh air, even if she did drive him crazy sometimes.

Then she yanked herself away and pressed a hand to her mouth while her chest heaved in deep breaths.

"Jesus, Joseph, and Isaac Mizrahi."

Yeah, ditto to whoever that last guy was.

ALSO BY ERIN KERN

Champion Valley Series
Winner Takes All
Back in the Game

Trouble Series
Looking for Trouble
Here Comes Trouble
Along Came Trouble

CHANGING THE RULES

ERIN KERN

Champion Valley #3

FOREVER

NEW YORK BOSTON

Copyright © 2018 by Erin Kern
Excerpt from *Winner Takes All* Copyright © 2016 by Erin Kern

Cover image © Tim Robbins—Mint Images/GettyImages. Cover design by Elizabeth Stokes. Cover copyright © 2018 by Hachette Book Group, Inc.

Forever
Hachette Book Group
1290 Avenue of the Americas, New York, NY 10104
forever-romance.com
twitter.com/foreverromance

First Edition: March 2018

Forever is an imprint of Grand Central Publishing. The Forever name and logo are trademarks of Hachette Book Group, Inc.

The publisher is not responsible for websites (or their content) that are not owned by the publisher.

The Hachette Speakers Bureau provides a wide range of authors for speaking events. To find out more, go to www.hachettespeakersbureau.com or call (866) 376-6591.

ISBNs: 978-1-4555-3601-6 (mass market), 978-1-4555-3602-3 (ebook)

Printed in the United States of America

OPM

10 9 8 7 6 5 4 3 2 1

CHANGING THE RULES

ONE

Audrey Bennett had been on the road for almost seven hours. The two extra double-shots she'd hastily tossed back with a chocolate scone at daybreak had long since worn off, leaving her with the jittery aftereffects of a caffeine crash. As a rule, she usually avoided caffeine, simply because her nerves were almost always edging on this side of shot. Not that Audrey had issues with anxiety. Usually. But, thanks to both her parents being type A personalities with a bit of OCD thrown in, Audrey rarely understood the meaning of calm, cool, and collected.

So yeah. Coffee had been a bad choice.

Audrey glanced in the rearview mirror at her passenger, who'd been alternating between sleeping and talking to her stuffed cat Jellybean, which had long since turned from its original pink to a questionable brown. Audrey had meant to wash it, but Piper had yanked the cat from Audrey's hand with a trembling lip that had cut straight to Audrey's already broken heart. Because Piper had been through so much lately, the loss of her mother to cancer and being forced to move away from her home to live with an uncle she'd never met, Audrey had let the subject of washing the putrid stuffed animal rest.

A sign for the Blanco Valley city limits came into view, and Audrey practically cried tears of relief. Or maybe pain, because her legs had gone numb about an hour ago.

"Are we almost there?" Piper asked from the backseat.

Audrey glanced in the rearview mirror and offered a comforting smile. Piper had Jellybean wrapped in one small arm, and the other was playing with the hem of her shorts.

"Almost, sweetie."

"I'm bored," Piper announced.

Audrey ground her teeth together and reminded herself to be patient. The poor girl had been in the car as long as Audrey had: a miserable seven hours.

She made a left turn and followed the directions toward the high school football stadium. "Why don't you watch your movie again?"

"I don't want to," Piper answered.

"Okay," Audrey said, searching her brain for something for Piper to do. "What about one of the books you brought?"

"I already looked at all them," Piper offered.

Well, shit.

"Audrey?" Piper asked.

Audrey's heart cracked open again at the child's soft tone. Piper had been through a whirlwind of emotions the past few weeks, alternating between crying and asking when her mommy was coming back. Audrey had cried with her and tried answering her question as best she could, but how could a six-year-old understand about death? Did she understand it was permanent? Did Piper know she'd never see her mother again? Never hear her voice, or hug her or hear Dianna tell her little girl everything was going to be okay?

Audrey gripped the steering wheel harder at the unfairness of the situation. Piper was a sweet, loving, outgoing girl who'd lost her only parent and would be forced to live the rest of her life wondering why. Why she didn't have a family. Why she didn't have a mom to tuck her in at night or teach her how to wear makeup. Piper deserved the very best. She deserved to feel safe and loved and whole.

"Is my uncle Cameron nice?" Piper asked when Audrey hadn't responded to her.

Audrey swatted away the fresh tears that almost fell. "I don't know, sweetie. I've never met him."

"Why can't I stay with you?"

Audrey sighed at the question Piper had asked a dozen times already. As much as she'd love, and give anything, to keep Piper with her, it just wasn't possible.

She spared the child a glance in the rearview mirror. "Honey, we talked about this, remember? Your mom wanted you to stay with family."

"But you're my family," Piper argued.

The statement pulled a smile from Audrey. "Not in the way your mom meant."

The poor girl didn't understand any of it. She didn't understand why her mom had died, and she didn't understand why she had to live with an uncle she'd never met. But Dianna had been explicit in her wishes. She'd awarded custody to her half brother, Cameron Shaw, and she wanted Audrey to deliver Piper. To help make the transition easier, she'd said. Audrey didn't understand it either, but Dianna didn't have any other family, and Piper's dad had never been in the picture. Audrey's job was simply to deliver Piper to her uncle and stay until Piper was comfortable with the man.

But what kind of man was he? Audrey's brow furrowed as she came to a red light. From what she knew, Dianna and Cameron hadn't had much of a relationship. Dianna had been tight-lipped about it, only saying Cameron's father had left his mother and remarried, and Dianna had been born several years later. She said she'd met him a few times when she was little, but as she'd gotten older, Cameron had stopped coming around. Audrey suspected that maybe the mysterious Cameron Shaw had resented his much younger half sister, even though Dianna had never said as much. Audrey hoped that wasn't true, because what kind of asshole would resent his little sister for a situation that wasn't her fault?

In any event, if Dianna had entrusted the life of her little girl to Cameron, then he couldn't be that bad.

Right?

But if Audrey even sensed a flicker of something not right with the guy, she'd whisk Piper away so fast, his head would spin. She'd fight for custody of the little girl herself.

"Why don't you read one of your books to Jellybean?" Audrey suggested. "We'll be there in a minute."

Silence filled the car, followed by a muffled, "'Kay."

The light turned green at the same time that her phone vibrated in the cup holder. Probably Evan, Audrey's boyfriend of three months, who hadn't been comfortable with her driving. She blindly reached for the phone just as she heard a loud *pop* and the car jerked wildly to the left, almost veering into oncoming traffic.

From the backseat, Piper yelped, and Audrey barely stifled a curse as she gripped both hands around the steering wheel. She knew a popped tire when she heard one and cursed her shitty luck after already having been on the road for half a day.

"Audrey?" Piper called out with fear lacing her voice.

"It's okay, honey," Audrey soothed, while trying to keep herself calm. She jerked the car into the next lane, ignoring honks and other drivers whipping around her. The shredded tire, which sounded like it was in the back, thudded around the rim and bobbed the car all over the place. She managed to pull the SUV over while narrowly missing a handful of bikers. The thing jerked to a stop, then rested crookedly, hanging halfway in the bike lane and half into traffic, where impatient drivers were forced to maneuver around her.

With a sigh she tossed the gear in park and leaned back on the headrest.

"What happened to the car?" Piper asked from her car seat. "Is it broken?"

Audrey blew out a breath and opened her eyes. "Audrey really wishes she could curse right now," she whispered to herself. Then she pasted a smile on her face, for Piper's benefit, and turned to face the girl. "The car's not broken. I just need to take a look at the tire."

Piper blinked and hugged Jellybean closer. Her chubby cheeks were red, and her once neat ponytails were loose, allowing the girl's blond curls to stick to her cheeks.

"It sounds like the car broke," Piper said again.

"It's not broken." She reached back and rested a comforting hand on the child's knee. "But I need you to stay in your seat while I get out and look at the tire. Okay?" When Piper nodded, Audrey grabbed a book from the seat and dropped it in Piper's lap. "Here, read this to Jellybean. I think she's bored too."

Piper picked Jellybean up and bounced the stuffed toy on her knee. "Jellybean was asleep, but the broken car woke her up. She was dreaming about jelly beans."

Of course she was. Jelly beans were Piper's favorite thing in the whole world, aside from her stuffed cat.

Audrey got out of the car and ignored the glares from other drivers. Like it was her fault her damn tire blew and forced her off the road. Thank goodness her father, a dentist, had shown her countless times how to change a flat tire. He'd said he never wanted his little girl to be unprepared should she ever find herself in a situation such as this.

Audrey yanked open the back hatch to start removing suitcases to get to the spare tire and her other tools, mentally cursing all the way.

Piper stuck her head over the backseat. "Are you gonna fix the car?"

Audrey grinned and ignored the bead of sweat rolling down the middle of her back, even though the temperature was in the sixties. "You bet, sweetie."

Piper bounced in the seat. "I'm hungry."

Of course she was. Next thing, she'd have to go to the bathroom.

Audrey set the jack on the ground and dug around for a snack. She handed the girl a plastic bag of Goldfish crackers and a Fruit Roll-Up.

"Stay in your seat, please," she reminded the six-year-old. Piper, God love her, had the attention span of a puppy.

Audrey had just set the jack and wrench on the ground in front of the flat when a deep rumbling behind the trailer caught her attention. A shiny yellow Camaro slowed to a stop; then the rumbling quieted and the driver exited the car.

Great. Probably some guy who thought she didn't know shit about changing tires. Just because she was just shy of a hundred twenty and average height didn't mean she didn't know how to handle things herself. Men always underestimated her.

"Need a hand with that?"

The voice was deep and low and tickled long-forgotten places. Places Evan had yet to discover. Strange. This guy pulls over to offer help, mutters five words, and all of a sudden sparks were igniting all over the place, like she was some nun who'd never heard a sexy voice before.

Audrey jabbed the wrench on the first lug nut and twisted. The thing didn't budge. "I've got it," she responded with a glance at his brand-new AND1s.

The stance of his feet widened. "Looks like you're struggling."

She spared him a glance... way the hell up because, *damn,* he was tall. But she couldn't get a good look at his face because the bright afternoon sun shone just over his shoulder and blinded her. Her only impression was long legs and wide shoulders. Oh, and don't forget that voice. "I know how to change a tire," she told him.

"I never said you didn't," he responded, and squatted next to her.

She continued to work on the lug nut, finally loosening the first one. She kept at it until the nut came all the way off and fell to the pavement.

The dude next to her tensed. Audrey wasn't sure how she could feel the tension in him, but somehow she just knew. Sort of like how the air shifts when someone enters a room. He wanted to correct her. He probably thought she was doing it wrong. He had another think coming if he thought he was going to tell her how to change a tire.

Audrey was a bit of a perfectionist who liked to do things herself. She was independent like that.

"You should loosen all the nuts before you take them all the way off," he told her.

Audrey's mouth quirked as she loosened the next lug nut. "I appreciate your help, but—" Holy hell, were all the men in Blanco Valley walking Calvin Klein ads? Audrey had just meant to toss him a dismissive glance, long enough to convey her message that she didn't need help. But the overwhelming hulk of a man who'd hunkered down next to her had captured her attention. No, not just captured. Commanded. Deep blue eyes, sort of like staring down into the deepest part of the ocean, held her gaze from beneath the bill of a Blanco Valley High baseball cap. The shadow from the hat slashed across his straight nose, which was perched above a mouth so firm and full that Audrey actually felt a flutter somewhere in her belly.

Shit, what had she been saying?

Oh, yeah. She'd been about to tell the guy to take a hike when she'd been rendered speechless by a pair of dreamy blue eyes and a mouth that probably delivered toe-curling grins.

One of his dark brows arched. "But...?" he prompted.

She blinked and tried to regain the composure she had had before he'd shown up and tied her tongue in knots.

"But I know how to change a tire." Hadn't she already told him that? To prove her point, Audrey went back to loosening the lug nuts. The second one was proving to be trickier, which was just her luck. She turned the wrench, with no progress.

The guy, who'd yet to give a name, so Audrey had decided to dub him Gorgeous Baseball Cap Guy, reached out to take the wrench from her.

She shot him a look, and he held his hands up.

"May I?" he asked.

Audrey spotted Piper bobbing her head up and down in the window. She probably had to go to the bathroom, in which case she needed the tire fixed stat.

Reluctantly, she passed the wrench over and moved aside for him. Mr. Gorgeous Baseball Cap Guy took her place in front of the tire and worked the lug nuts with ease.

"I take it you're one of those independent types," he commented while loosening one nut after the next.

"It's faster if you take each one off first," she pointed out instead of confirming his observation.

One side of the full mouth kicked up. "It really isn't." He loosened the final nut and slanted her a look. "You have control issues as well?"

Audrey opened her mouth to argue, because that was always her first reaction to everything. Correct. Control. It was sort of a vice for her and one she'd been trying for way too long to fix. And it was also probably why she hadn't had a relationship that lasted longer than three months. She'd come to learn that men didn't take well to their girlfriends constantly correcting everything they did. She had a coping mechanism for when she felt her anxiety skyrocketing and the urge to nitpick came clawing to the surface. Unfortunately, reciting designer labels alphabetically tended to annoy people just as much as her control issues. But Evan didn't seem to mind. Evan was a sweet guy.

"I'm not controlling," she found herself saying, and ignored the look of disbelief that flashed across Mr. Gorgeous's blue eyes. "It's just that when I see something that I feel could be done better, I say something."

"But you weren't doing it better," he pointed out.

"In your opinion," she argued.

He nodded as though he understood. "Controlling," he

said again, and any forgiveness she had been about to offer him was obliterated.

She reached for the wrench. "I think I can take it from here."

"Just give me a sec." He placed the jack under the car and raised the thing as though it were nothing more than a child's toy.

"Okay then." Audrey attempted to shoulder him out of the way, but it was like trying to move a cement statue. She had a brief impression of a solid shoulder underneath his hooded sweatshirt before backing away. Her first thought was, why would a man like him hide all that goodness beneath a bulky sweatshirt? But her second thought of *Hello, boyfriend* immediately smacked away any improper thoughts.

"Impatient little thing, aren't you?" he asked with a smirk as he removed the lug nuts.

She narrowed her eyes at him. "Maybe I'm not the only one with control issues."

His smirk turned into a full-blown grin, and holy Alexander McQueen, the man had some serious wattage. "So you admit you have control issues."

Was he for real? And in the time he'd been distracting her with his pearly whites, he'd removed the tire and re-placed it with the spare, in probably half the time that she could have done it. But still. There had been nothing wrong with the way she'd been removing the lug nuts.

"I could have done that," she told him.

"Yeah," he agreed as he replaced the lug nuts and tightened them with little effort. "Except you were doing it wrong."

His grin widened at the same time that his gaze dropped to her chest. It took a second of heat flaming Audrey's cheeks for her to realize that he was checking her out. But because it had been so long since a man of his…caliber had shown any interest in her, Audrey could do nothing more than stare and blink. Yeah, real sexy. No wonder she went a year in between boyfriends.

Gorgeous Baseball Cap Guy handed over the wrench with that maddening smirk still causing all sorts of flutters in her belly.

Focus. You're here for Piper, not to get noticed by hot Good Samaritans.

She took the wrench from him, and they stood at the same time.

He braced a hand on the roof of her car and leaned forward. Was he meaning to crowd her? Intimidate her with those wide shoulders and eyes so blue it was like staring at a crystal-clear lake? Except Audrey didn't feel intimidated. The spark that flamed to life took her off guard because…well, had she ever felt anything like that before? She couldn't remember.

"You know, it's customary to say thanks," he pointed out.

"Thanks," she offered.

His grin turned to a chuckle as his gaze dropped to her chest once more. He dropped his hand from the car and gave her a mock solute. "Have a good one. Try not to shred any more tires."

Then he strolled away, moving with a grace that kept Audrey riveted in her spot for longer than it should have. Did Evan walk like that? Like he owned the ground beneath his feet? Better yet, why did she keep comparing the two men? Evan and Gorgeous Baseball Cap Guy were nothing alike. Evan was shorter and not as…overwhelming? Yes, that was a good word for the man. Overwhelming. Evan made her laugh and held doors open for her. Gorgeous Baseball Cap Guy was bossy and too big.

Too big?

Women drooled over men like him, and all Audrey could think about was how he'd taken over and kept looking at her boobs.

He also helped you out when no one else would stop.

Audrey blinked and realized she was still standing by the car, and Piper had once again pressed her face to the window. Audrey cleaned her tools up and replaced everything in the back of the SUV. When she was back inside the car, Audrey's phone kept beeping. Then she remembered she'd received a notification when her tire had blown.

"Put your seat belt back on," she instructed Piper as she started the car and pulled out into traffic.

"Did the car get fixed?" Piper questioned.

Audrey glanced over her shoulder and changed lanes. "Yep, good as new."

"I have to go potty."

"We'll find a place to go at the high school."

Piper was silent a moment. "Why are we going to a high school?"

Audrey picked up her phone as it beeped again. She thumbed the screen while navigating traffic. "We're meeting your uncle there."

Piper fell silent again as Audrey pulled up a text from Evan. She grinned as she thought about his deep brown eyes and silly sense of humor. He probably would have called a tow truck for her and then made sure Piper was taken care of. Evan was a gem of a guy who—

This relationship isn't really working out for me.

Audrey scowled and scrolled through the messages,

looking for the *It's not you, it's me,* pushing past the hurt knifing through her chest.

A second later, her phone buzzed again, and another text came through.

It's not you, it's me. You're a really sweet girl, Evan wrote. *But I can't be in a relationship right now. I need to focus on me.*

Audrey stopped at another red light and resisted the urge to toss her phone out the window. Dumped via text message. She'd expected better from Evan. Evan was supposed to be the real deal. Guys like him didn't come along very often, and now she was filing yet another relationship into the Said and Done part of her life.

She huffed out a breath and leaned her head against the headrest. Of course she was hurt. She'd liked Evan. She could have even grown to love him if he'd given the relationship a chance. Maybe it was her. Maybe she had "damaged goods" stamped across her forehead. Why else couldn't she pin a guy down longer than it took for the leaves to change color in the fall?

Audrey's eyes jerked open when someone honked. The light had turned green, so she pressed forward and turned right toward the high school. It didn't matter. Evan was just another guy in a long string of men who hadn't been able to stick. All that mattered now was Piper and easing her transition into her new life with her uncle.

Except she was reasonably attractive, right? Yeah, Audrey was pretty sure she could hold her own. Guys liked blondes, and five-six was a decent height. She stayed in shape by jogging every morning. Audrey gave herself a once-over, glancing from her jeans to her button-down and giving herself a nod of approval. Then she did a double take as she pulled into the high school parking lot.

"Shit," she whispered to herself.

Maybe dressing in the dark hadn't been such a good idea after all. The gaping hole her missed button had created had afforded Gorgeous Baseball Cap Guy a straight shot to her hot pink bra.

She only hoped Cameron Shaw wasn't anything like him.

TWO

There's a woman with a kid here looking for you. Why didn't you tell me you had a baby mama?

Cameron Shaw sat on the edge of his destroyed bed as he thumbed through Blake's text messages, ignoring the baby mama thing. He didn't have one, that he knew of. Yeah, pretty sure.

His phone had started vibrating about twenty minutes ago, then turned to beeping when he'd been too preoccupied to answer. Blake was a needy bastard sometimes.

Cam thumbed his reply.

What the hell? Who are you talking about?

And why had she gone to the high school instead of his house?

Although, considering what he'd been doing twenty minutes ago, Cameron was glad the mystery woman hadn't come knocking on his door. He'd been too busy digging his fingers into Tessa Monroe's hips as she rode him.

Cam slid a glance at Tessa as she shimmied into a pair of black leggings, then snatched her bra off the floor.

"I have to go out of town next week," she informed him.

Cameron's phone buzzed again as Tessa continued dressing.

How the hell should I know? Some woman with a kid. Just get down here, practice is about to start anyway.

Yeah, practice. He knew he needed to get his ass moving. He'd gone out to run errands, then swing by home to pick up a few things. He'd been on his way home when he'd spotted the woman with blond hair struggling with her shredded tire. His first instinct had been to press harder on the gas and go about his day. But something about her caught his attention. Maybe it was the sight of her struggling with the wrench. Maybe it had been the way those jeans had fit over her very fine ass. Either way, he'd found himself stopping.

Christ, she'd been something else. First she'd pinned him with a pair of brown eyes that had dared him to tell her what to do; then she'd opened her mouth, and Cameron couldn't decide if he wanted to strangle her or kiss her. She probably would have clocked him good.

But he'd seen the way the pulse at the base of her neck had fluttered when he'd grinned at her. Then the way her cheeks had flamed when he'd gotten an eyeful of a pink bra cupping a generous breast. She probably didn't even know she'd missed a button.

Highlight of his day. Hell, his whole week.

Then Tessa had shown up and hadn't wasted any time shoving him into the bedroom and stripping his clothes off along the way.

"Cameron, are you listening?" Tessa lowered herself to the bed and pulled her boots on.

Cam sent his reply to Blake.

On my way.

Tessa stood from the bed and jammed her hands on her slim hips. "Cameron?"

He tossed his phone on the dresser. "What?"

She rolled her eyes. "You haven't heard a word I said, have you?"

He stood also and pulled his Blanco Valley Football shirt from the dresser. "I'm sorry, what were you saying?" He'd been too busy thinking about a woman with a pink bra. He should feel like a bastard for thinking about the tire girl when his sheets still smelled like sex and Tessa. But he couldn't muster any guilt. It's not like Tessa was his girlfriend. She'd made it clear in the beginning that she wasn't looking for anything serious or even exclusive, and she knew full well he didn't want anything more either. She was just someone who occasionally scratched an itch whenever she happened to be in town.

Tessa ran her gaze over him. "I said I'm going out of town for a little while. My sister had a baby, and I'm going to visit her for a few weeks. So I won't be around."

Cameron tugged his shirt on, then swiped his cell off the dresser. "All right." He grabbed his wallet and keys and pocketed them as well.

"Think you can get by while I'm gone?" she teased.

"I think I'll manage," he told her.

One of her brows arched. "Because you have a list of women you can call up, right?"

Was that jealousy he heard? "No questions, Tess. That was your rule, remember?"

She rolled one of her shoulders as though it didn't matter either way. "Yeah, I know." She dropped a kiss on his cheek. "I'll call you when I'm back in town."

Then she was gone, and Cameron stared after her. He hoped she wasn't developing feelings for him. This arrangement between them was supposed to be casual. No expectations, no questions, and no attachments. Just sex.

Because that was the only thing Cameron had to offer a woman. He'd learned the hard way not to jump headfirst into anything. He'd been there, done that, bought the whole damn T-shirt factory, and it had bit him in the ass big-time. Since then he'd kept his relationships strictly casual. He didn't take women on dates, and he definitely didn't fall in love. He gave orgasms. That was it. And he was damn good at it, if he did say so himself. If he wasn't, Tessa wouldn't come knocking on his door every time she came into town to show a house to a potential buyer.

He was sure Tessa understood that, but if she had other plans, he'd have to set her straight.

Cameron turned to yank some socks out of his dresser drawer, and his gaze fell on the offer letter from Denver. A position as head coach for a 5A school. He'd received the letter a few weeks ago after interviewing with them over the summer. Their current coach had one year left on his contract; then he was retiring.

The letter had been set aside when the Bobcats' season started a month ago, but the issue had been in the back of his mind. Every time he set foot on the field, every time he lectured, reamed, or pep-talked a player. He'd see their sweat-drenched faces and feel their frustration during a difficult game, and the nagging doubt would start.

Don't abandon them, it would say. *Those kids need you.*

But Cameron wasn't built to be an assistant, even if it was for his best friend. He wanted to go back to running his own team.

But at what cost?

Leaving his home? His friends?

Those questions had been keeping him up at night and pushing aside the initial need to strike out on his own.

Cameron folded the letter back up and headed out the door for practice.

Audrey had never liked football. Not only did she not like the grunting or the head-smashing, but she also didn't understand anything other than get the ball to the end zone. She didn't understand flags, or penalties, or gaining yards. Rushing was another foreign concept. If the team's objective was to outrun the other team to the end zone, shouldn't they be rushing anyway?

Give her a Jimmy Choo sale any day over this.

Watching a high school football practice for the past twenty minutes and waiting for Cameron Shaw to show himself hadn't made her love the game any more. When she'd arrived, she'd approached a coach she'd immediately recognized as Blake Carpenter, the former NFL quarterback, and almost swallowed her tongue. She'd remembered hearing about his retirement, that he had accepted a job as a high school coach, but she hadn't realized it was for this high school.

When she'd inquired about Piper's uncle, Blake's eyes had briefly narrowed, then flicked to Piper. For a moment Audrey had thought maybe Blake assumed Piper was Cameron's kid. She'd resisted the urge to correct him, and then her frustration grew when he'd replied with a gruff, "He's not here yet."

Audrey had grabbed his arm when he turned back to his team. "Well, how will I know which one is him?"

Blake had chuckled. "Just look for the big surly guy."

Um...okay?

So she'd been sitting on the bleachers for the past twenty minutes and looking for anyone who could be Piper's uncle. Then ten minutes ago, the bleacher had tilted under her rear end when Gorgeous Baseball Cap Guy had come strolling onto the field with the same confident, loose-limbed grace he'd had earlier. He'd exchanged his worn blue jeans and sweatshirt for athletic pants and a black Bobcat Football T-shirt. A whistle hung around his neck, and the same ball cap was pulled low over his blue eyes.

Shit, there was no way that was Cameron Shaw. Just. No.

But Audrey's gaze kept flickering back to him, alternating with annoyance and . . . well, something close to *damn*.

Because wouldn't that be a perfect cap to a shitty day? Flat tire. Dumped via text. Then the man whose gaze had flickered to the gaping hole in her shirt while he argued over how to change a tire turns out to be Piper's uncle.

The universe could not be so cruel.

Audrey turned around to the two women seated behind her. "Excuse me?" When they ceased their conversation to look at her, Audrey continued. "Can you tell me which coach is Cameron Shaw?"

The woman with teased auburn hair pointed toward the field. "That one standing on the forty-yard line."

"The one with the ass like cement," her friend quipped.

Yeah, as she feared. Gorgeous Baseball Cap Guy. Audrey laughed and turned back to the women. "That can't be him."

The brown-haired woman leaned forward. "Honey, I would know that backside anywhere."

Meaning what?

The other woman nudged her friend's shoulder. "My cousin Becky says he has the stamina of a porn star."

Audrey resisted the urge to cover Piper's ears, even though the child was too busy playing with Jellybean to pay attention to anything else. Or maybe Audrey should just cover her own ears.

Of course someone who looked like Cameron Shaw would be a god in bed. Did she expect someone who looked like an underwear model to be anything less?

Practice eventually ended, and she and Piper exited the bleachers, with Piper dragging Jellybean along with her.

Piper gazed up at Audrey with eyes so green, like her mother's, that Audrey felt the familiar pain in her chest. "Are we going to meet my uncle now?" the little girl asked.

"Yes, and he's going to love you," Audrey assured her.

Piper bit her lip and hugged Jellybean tighter. "I'm scared."

Audrey forced the lump out of her throat and tried not to think about having to leave Piper. She loved that little girl as she would her own, and the idea of being away from her tore her guts up. There would be no more makeovers, no more whimsical stories, and no more sticky kisses. She took a deep breath, dropped to her knees, and forced herself to be brave—for Piper's sake.

"I want you to listen to me for a minute," she told Piper. "You have nothing to be afraid of. I'm sure your uncle Cameron is a good guy, and your mom trusted him, so that means we can trust him, right?" At Piper's hesitant nod, Audrey continued. "I know you're worried, sweetie, but I promise I won't let anything bad happen to you. Okay?" Audrey stroked Piper's soft cheek and had to remind herself that Piper was just a little girl who didn't know where she was or who she was going to live with. Just another reason to get those lustful thoughts of Cameron Shaw out of her head.

"'Kay," Piper answered. "But what if he doesn't like me? What if he doesn't want me to live with him?"

Audrey shook her head. "That's not possible. I know he'll love you." Audrey moved herself and Piper out of the way of people who were leaving the bleachers. "Do you remember when we went to the zoo last year and you didn't want to feed the giraffes because you were too scared? Then you put your brave face on and walked up to the giraffe, and he took a leaf right out of your hand?"

Piper smiled, then giggled. "Yeah. He licked my hand with his tongue."

Audrey grinned with her. "That's right, he did. And you had nothing to be afraid of, right?"

Piper hesitated, then nodded.

"I need you to be that brave girl again," Audrey told her. "Can you do that for me?"

Piper glanced at her feet, then at Audrey. "'Kay."

Audrey stroked Piper's hair, loving how soft and fragile the curls were. Then she pulled the child into a tight hug, reminding herself of how small and vulnerable Piper was, how much she depended on Audrey to keep her safe because Audrey was the only person in the world Piper knew anymore. Dianna hadn't been close to any of her extended family, and her mother had died several years ago. Piper's grandfather had been too old to care for a child, and hadn't been that close to Piper anyway. Audrey was it, and she'd be damned if she'd let the kid down. She'd made a promise to Dianna, and she'd see it through to the end.

She let go of Piper and led the girl onto the field. Now wasn't the time to think about wide shoulders or sexy voices or how Cameron Shaw awakened things inside her that had been dead for years. She was here for Piper, and it needed to stay that way.

When Cameron turned around and pinned her with those dark blue eyes, her stern talking-to evaporated.

"Did you come by to give a heartfelt thanks?" he asked, then strolled right past her.

Wait, what?

Audrey spun around, still holding Piper's hand, and hurried after him. "Excuse me?" she called. But he didn't listen. What a shock. "Can you please wait? Or at least slow down, because I'm wearing heels."

He paused and glanced at her over his shoulder, while flicking a brief glimpse at Piper. "Look, I don't remember you, but I always use protection." Then he turned abruptly and kept walking.

Audrey could only stare because *what?*

Was this guy capable of saying anything polite?

Audrey stuffed back the bout of serious annoyance and plowed after him. *Alexander Wang, Anna Sui, Bill Blass . . .*

She reached him right as he approached the fence and stopped him with a hand on his shoulder. His very bulky and muscular shoulder . . . No, she wasn't supposed to allow those thoughts to interfere, and she definitely shouldn't be thinking about how solid he was after what he'd said to her.

"*What* is your problem?" she demanded. "Piper isn't your daughter, you ass; she's your niece."

Cameron turned fully to face her and jabbed his hands on his hips, and gave Piper more than a fleeting look. He gazed down at the child as though mentally trying to work through the knowledge in his head. "Come again?" he questioned.

Audrey stepped closer so Piper wouldn't overhear. Unfortunately, all that did was give her a whiff of some seriously delicious stuff. Woodsy and spicy. "Your sister, Dianna—"

"I was sorry to hear that she passed away," he admitted. Something flashed across his eyes. Regret maybe? Audrey couldn't be sure, because it came and went so fast that she almost forgave him for his shitty attitude. "Dianna and I weren't that close," he went on.

She'd known Dianna and Cameron hadn't had much of a relationship because Dianna had said as much. But he'd known he had a niece, hadn't he?

Cameron jerked his head toward Piper. "How's she holding up?"

His concern for the girl managed to break through the gruff first impression he'd given. Though Audrey wasn't ready to let him off the hook just yet. She spared Piper a glance; she'd tugged Jellybean even closer. She was practically strangling the cat. "Pretty good, considering." She reverted her attention back to Cameron. "Dianna left her with you."

Cameron blinked; then he scratched his square jaw, which was edging just past five o'clock. "Me?" he repeated. "For how long?"

Audrey paused before answering, preparing herself for whatever reaction he'd have. "Forever. You're her guardian now."

Cameron blinked again, and Audrey had the urge to knock her knuckles on the side of his head to see if he had anything going on up there. Then he laughed. As though he hadn't been a big enough of an ass, he had the gall to actually laugh. That shouldn't have been sexy but, dammit, it was. And a part of Audrey was more irritated with herself than the man towering over her with his form-fitting shirt, lean hips, and arrogant approach.

"That's funny," he stated. "But no."

"What do you mean *no*? Dianna signed guardianship over to you, so it's legal. Piper's yours."

"She can't be mine now," he argued.

"Well, she is," Audrey insisted.

Cameron scrubbed a hand down his face, the sounds of his whiskers grating along his palm giving Audrey goose bumps on top of goose bumps. "I don't understand," he finally said. "Why would Dianna do this? We didn't even know each other."

Audrey had wondered the same thing for weeks. But she'd been too grief-stricken to question anything other than why Piper had been left motherless. "I don't know," she answered. "But she made her wishes clear. She wanted Piper to stay with family. She never told you?"

Cameron's dark blue gaze bore into Audrey's, making her squirm in her Manolos. He flicked another glance at Piper. "No. Isn't there any other family who can take her?" he asked in a low voice. "Maybe someone who knows more about kids than I do?"

"There isn't anyone else."

"What about the kid's father?"

Audrey peeked at Piper, who was picking at Jellybean's ears. "He's a shithead who took off when he found out that Dianna was pregnant. She didn't have any siblings, and your father—"

"I know all about my father," Cameron growled.

The ticking in his jaw gave Audrey the hint that his parent-son relationship with his old man was a sore one. Given how Dianna had come into Cameron's life, Audrey wasn't surprised.

"Okay, then," she replied, trying to regain her train of thought.

Cameron blew out a sigh. "Look, I can't have a kid in my life right now. You need to find someone else to leave her with."

"I'm getting the impression that you think I'm asking you to take her," Audrey snapped. "See, I have a document signed by Dianna and notarized stating you are Piper's legal guardian until she turns eighteen. I don't have the authority to 'leave her,'" she said, using air quotes, "with anyone else. And even if I did, I couldn't, because there isn't anyone else." She poked him in the chest with her index finger. "You're it."

"I'm sorry, but no," he finally said.

Oh, dear God, the man was going to be the death of her. Like slow, painful, agonizing death, and he'd probably watch her go down with a smile on his too masculine, too handsome face.

Audrey pulled a deep breath and forced herself not to strangle his thick neck. "Calvin Klein, Carolina Herrera," she whispered to herself, hoping the gods of fashion could steady her boiling blood. "Christian Dior, Christian Lacroix..."

"Uh-oh," Piper whispered.

Cameron shot an alarmed look at the kid. "Uh-oh, what?"

"You upset her," she told her uncle.

Cameron scratched the side of his face. "I what?"

"Christian Louboutin, Coco Chanel..." Audrey went on.

"She says people's names when she's upset," Piper explained.

Cameron turned his narrowed gaze on Audrey. "You know, most people just count to ten."

"I'm not like most people," she told him.

One of his brows quirked. "I'm starting to realize that."

They stared at each other for a moment, like two cage fighters waiting for the other to go down, the air around them crackling with the kind of crazy tension that would send some people running. Audrey had never been one to admit defeat, and she was starting to realize Cameron wasn't either. So where did that leave them? Audrey couldn't return to Boulder with Piper, and the little girl didn't have anywhere else to go. Somehow she needed to convince Cameron to accept her.

He flicked a glimpse at his sports watch. "Look, I'm late for a meeting. Why don't you give me your number and I'll text you later."

Audrey recited her number while he punched it into his phone. "But don't text me. Just call."

Cameron slid his phone away. "What kind of phone doesn't have a texting feature?"

"Mine does," she said. "I just don't like to text."

"But texting's easier," Cameron pointed out.

"I don't like typing with my thumbs. It's annoying. Just call me."

One side of his mouth twitched. Was he laughing at her? "So what do you do when someone texts you?"

"I call them back." Why was this a hard concept to understand? Then she stuck out her hand, determined to bring some sort of civility to this encounter. And also because she'd neglected to introduce herself or Piper. "I'm Audrey, by the way. I would say nice to meet you, but it really hasn't been all that nice."

Cameron glanced at her hand, as though he didn't want to touch her, and after he wrapped his larger palm around hers, Audrey understood why. Holy mother of all tingles. The man had a firm grip with long fingers and a rough palm that scuffed against the softer flesh of her hand. While he held on longer than necessary, Audrey combated images of his hands sliding into her hair, or maybe skimming down her arms. Yeah, he probably knew how to use his hands to his advantage. Make a woman's breath hitch, or her eyes drop closed.

Stamina of a porn star.

The women's conversation slapped Audrey with a reality check. The fact that two strangers so freely discussed Cameron's bedroom performance spoke to what kind of man he was. A man whore, as her best friend Roxy would say. As in, trouble. As in, Audrey needed to stay the hell away.

But how was she supposed to when he looked at her like he wanted to smear whipped cream all over her?

"No, you're right," Cameron responded, shattering Audrey's thoughts. "It hasn't been nice."

Audrey gritted her teeth against his sarcasm and shifted her attention to Piper, who'd been unusually quiet. "And this is Piper." And then she added with a whisper, "Don't talk about her mom."

Cameron squatted to Piper's level. "Hi, Piper," he said to the girl. "I'm your uncle Cameron." Piper nodded, and Cameron reached out to finger Jellybean's scruffy leg. "And who's this?"

Piper hugged the stuffed cat closer. "Her name's Jellybean. She's a cat."

Cameron offered a smile, and Audrey's heart just about flipped out of her chest. "Is she your travel buddy?"

Piper nodded again. "She's my best friend."

Audrey's heart went from tumbling all over her chest to constricting with pain. Jellybean had been with Piper since she'd been a baby, and now was the most constant thing in the child's life. The knowledge that a stuffed cat was Piper's best friend only reminded Audrey of how much the little girl had lost. Her mother, then moving away from her neighborhood and friends. Now her only friend in the world was a stuffed cat that smelled like chicken nuggets.

No, she has you.

"She keeps you safe, huh?" Cameron questioned.

Piper blinked those big green eyes, then gave a tiny nod.

Cameron pinched Piper's chin. "She's a special cat, so keep her close."

Piper nodded again, and Cameron stood. But the man didn't just stand. He unfolded with a gentle grace that shouldn't exist in a man of his size. His muscles shifted and flowed with his movements as easily as water cascading over a boulder.

And why did she keeping thinking things like that instead of reminding herself of how annoying he was?

"I'll be in touch," he informed her before turning and stalking away.

Audrey stood on the now empty field, gaping after the man who'd visibly softened for his niece, giving her a moment's hope that he wasn't the ogre she thought he was, then dismissing them with a single curt statement. The man was probably used to giving orders and people jumping to do his bidding. She had no such plans to do any bidding for Cameron Shaw. The only thing on her agenda was getting Piper settled with him so the girl could work on healing and realizing she still had family who loved her.

She took a hold of Piper's fragile hand and led the two of them off the field. "See?" she asked the girl. "That wasn't so horrible, was it?"

But Piper didn't respond, and Audrey had the feeling that she'd been just as horrified as Audrey had.

THREE

Cameron Shaw sat on the other side of the desk from the athletic director, Drew Spalding. The two men hadn't bothered to hide the loathing that had gone all the way back to their competition on the high school football field.

After high school, the two had gone their separate ways, and Cam had been happy to leave the prick behind. But a few years ago, old animosities had resurged when Cameron had an affair with a woman he only later realized was Drew's wife. She'd worn no wedding ring, made no mention of a husband. Needless to say, the second he'd learned her identity, he'd immediately broken things off, despite her desperate pleas otherwise.

A few months later Drew's marriage had ended, and he'd blamed Cameron for its demise.

That, in a nutshell, explained why Drew tried to drill lasers into Cameron's head every time the guy looked at him, as though he wanted Cameron to drop dead.

Drew hung up the phone call he'd been on and leaned back in his chair. He pinned his dark, soulless eyes on Cameron, probably trying to intimidate him. "I don't like you bringing JV players to the varsity team."

Okay, then. Guess they weren't going to beat around the bush. Fine with him. "Your displeasure is noted," Cameron commented.

Drew stared for a moment, then apparently decided to try a different tactic. "Do you think it's in the team's best interest to be starting younger players?"

In the beginning of the season, a few of their starters had injured themselves, forcing Cameron and Blake to be creative with their backups.

"I think it's in the team's best interest to have our best players starting," he informed Drew. Cameron placed his hands on the arms of the chair and motioned to leave. "Is that all?"

Drew held his hand up. "Not so fast. I have a message here from a man named Heath Junger. I believe you're familiar with him? He called to discuss your current contract."

Well, shit. Heath Junger was the athletic director in Denver who'd offered Cameron the coaching position. But they'd already offered him the job, meaning they'd already checked references. Drew knew Cameron was contemplating leaving, so the news was no surprise to the man. In fact, Cameron wouldn't be surprised if Drew had gone out and bought himself a cake to celebrate.

Cameron bided his time and waited for Drew to get to the point. "Apparently they're so desperate to have you, he doesn't want to wait until next season. He wants to bring you in now."

What the hell? "Why didn't Heath talk to me about that himself?"

Drew gave a careless shrug. "He wanted to see if I'd release you from your contract early. I haven't called him back."

"But their current coach isn't retiring until the end of the season," Cameron pointed out. And why wasn't he more excited? This was what he'd wanted, to get out of Blanco Valley and coach his own team. What did it matter if he left now or later?

Audrey and Piper flashed through his mind, whispering that he couldn't just up and go. Dammit, this was why he didn't want anybody depending on him. He wasn't in a place in his life where he could care for a kid. He lived for himself, and he liked it that way. Somehow he needed to make Audrey understand that.

"All you have to do is say the word, and I can have you gone," Drew offered.

Yeah, he just bet Drew would do everything he could. Problem was, Drew was a slimy bastard and Cameron didn't trust the guy as far as he could throw him. Drew would find a way to sabotage the opportunity for Cameron, then turn around and fire him at the end of the season, and Cam would be up shit creek.

"Don't do me any favors," Cameron told him.

Drew's eyebrows flew up his forehead. "Sure? It's really no trouble."

Slick asshole. Cameron stood, then leaned over Drew's desk and got in the man's face. "I would love nothing more than to stay for the rest of the season and make your life a living hell."

Drew's face turned a nice shade of strawberry red. "Be careful, Cameron. I can ruin this opportunity before it even gets handed to you."

Cam stood and shrugged off Drew's veiled threat. Drew

wasn't going to do shit, because he wanted Cameron gone too badly.

"Am I going to go with my uncle now?" Piper asked as Audrey parked the car in front of a place called the Bobcat Diner, where Cameron had asked her and Piper to meet him for dinner.

The thread of fear and uncertainty in Piper's voice tugged at Audrey's heart. Since Dianna had died, Audrey had tried her best to cocoon Piper from more grief and insecurity. Sometimes she felt like she was fumbling around in the dark, because Piper would look up at Audrey with such unadulterated trust. But the thing was, Audrey didn't know what the hell she was doing. Sure, she'd been around Piper enough in her six short years, but raising a kid? Being with one all the time, taking care of her every need? The whole process was still a learning curve for her, but she didn't want to let Piper down.

Audrey got out of the car and opened the back door. "I told you I'd be with you a little while longer, and I meant it," she assured the girl as she unbuckled Piper's seat belt and helped her climb out of the car. "Hey." When Piper glanced up, Audrey pinched her chin. "You trust me, right?"

Piper hopped out of the car and nodded. "Yep."

"I'm not going to go home until you're comfortable with your uncle Cameron."

They entered the diner, which was about half full of people eating an early dinner. It was just past five o'clock, and Cameron was already there. Audrey attempted to steady her pulse as he watched them approach from his casual sprawl in a booth. One heavy arm was draped along the back of the booth, and one hand was loosely cradled around a glass of soda. He'd removed his ball cap, revealing rich, too-long dark hair that made Audrey's fingers itch just looking at it. His gaze tracked hers with a steady perusal that made her feel like an organism under a microscope.

The man had some serious intensity that probably drilled fear into the hearts of his players.

As they approached the table, his attention briefly touched on Piper. His eyes softened for a second, but long enough to have Audrey wondering. Maybe he wasn't the hard-ass he wanted her to think he was? Maybe there was hope for him after all?

"Have any trouble finding the place?" he asked as he lifted his glass for a sip.

Audrey opened her mouth to answer, but was momentarily distracted by his throat muscles. How could a throat be sexy? She'd never noticed a man's throat before. But something about the way Cameron sipped his drink, slow and unhurried, carefully swallowing each sip before taking another. Yeah, something about that was just...worrisome for her.

One of his dark brows lifted when she didn't answer. "Audrey?"

She blinked herself out of her trance. "Sorry. And no, it was no trouble."

Cameron chanced another look at Piper, who'd crawled into the booth after Audrey, dragging Jellybean with her. "The two of you hungry?"

"No—"

"I'm hungry," Piper cut in as she bounced in her seat. She pinned an excited look at Audrey. "Can I have pizza with garlic bread? And I want a Shirley Temple with extra cherries."

Audrey glanced at Cameron to find his mouth curled

in a half smile. Did he think the whole thing was funny? "Uh…"

"They don't have pizza here, squirt," he quipped. "But I'm sure they can whip up a Shirley Temple."

Piper bounced in her seat some more. "Well, what do they have?"

Cameron set his drink down and reached for a plastic menu at the end of the booth. "Let's see…" His dark blue gaze moved over the menu. "They've got grilled cheese, chicken nuggets, and a cheeseburger."

Piper made a face. "Ew, I hate cheeseburgers."

His mouth quirked again. "What about a grilled cheese? They use the really good bread."

Piper shook her head. "I don't really like cheese."

Cameron shot Audrey a quizzical look, but she just shook her head. "Don't ask," she said.

"Chicken nuggets it is, then," Cam said as he tucked the menu away.

"I want jelly beans with my nuggets," Piper announced.

Audrey patted Piper on the head. "Restaurants don't serve jelly beans, sweetie."

Cameron looked at Piper, then back at Audrey. "What's with the jelly beans?"

"They're her favorite thing," Audrey explained.

Cam stretched his arm along the back of the booth, revealing a thickly muscled bicep. "I thought the cat was her favorite thing."

Audrey smiled. "And the cat's name is Jellybean."

Piper held the cat up. "Yeah, and Jellybean loves jelly beans too. That's why I need some with my dinner. She's hungry."

"Why don't we stop at the store after we leave, and I'll get a bag of jelly beans," Audrey suggested.

Piper considered that for a moment, scrunching her face up in thought before nodding. Audrey couldn't help but smile because the kid was so damn cute and full of expression.

A dark-haired waitress approached their table. Cameron ordered Piper's nuggets, then glanced at Audrey in question. She shook her head, mostly because her stomach was tied in too many knots to eat, partly because the big man seated across from her kept stretching his long legs against hers, and partly because she knew she had a battle ahead of her. He thought he couldn't take Piper in, because for whatever reason he'd convinced himself he was no good for kids. Maybe Cameron was one of those people who didn't give themselves enough credit. Maybe he thought he wasn't good enough for Piper.

Either way, she needed to change his mind.

"Here," he said abruptly, bringing one hip off the bench seat to retrieve something out of his pocket. He tossed a small folded piece of paper on the table. "For your trouble coming down here."

A punch of nausea settled in her stomach as she stared at the folded check. He couldn't be seriously thinking he could just pay her to go away. Did Piper mean that little to him? What about his sister? Was their relationship so meaningless that he couldn't give his own niece a chance?

With reluctance, Audrey grabbed the check and opened it. He'd left the *pay to the order of* blank, and filled in the amount for one thousand dollars. Never mind the fact that Audrey could use the money to dump back into her home staging business, the very idea was so beyond insulting that she couldn't even think of a decent response. All she could do was set the check down and glance around the crowded diner.

"What're you doing?" Cameron wanted to know.

"Looking for the hidden camera to see if I'm being punked," she answered.

She heard his heavy sigh before settling a glare on him. "Audrey, I'm serious."

"And I'm not?" she tossed back. "You think this isn't serious?" she questioned with a gesture toward Piper, who'd pulled out one of her books to read.

Cameron held up a hand in defense. "I didn't say that."

She crossed her arms over her chest just so she wouldn't reach across the booth and strangle his sexy ass. "Why don't you tell me what you *are* saying?"

Audrey felt a moment of mild satisfaction when Cameron opened his mouth to respond, only to shut it again. Had she rendered him speechless? She should only be so lucky.

"I'm saying what I've told you from the beginning. I. Can't. Take. Her." He probably thought spacing out his words all dramatic and stuff would really drive his point home. Like she was supposed to collect Piper and head out of town. Fat chance.

"And I'm. Not. Leaving." Yeah, he wasn't the only one who could do the theatrical word spacing thing. She could match him. "You think I've been annoying so far?" She resisted yanking him by the collar when he snorted. Man, she had some major self-control tonight. "You haven't seen annoying yet. I'll continue to show up at practices. I'll be at your house, all your dates—" Because she was sure he had tons of those. "Everywhere you turn, we'll be there."

"You will, huh?" He made a show of taking a long, drawn-out sip of his soda before replacing it on the scarred Formica table. "You don't know where I live."

That's all he had to say? "I'm sure I can find it." When

he didn't respond, because he was just smirking at her like the whole thing was a big joke, Audrey leaned forward. "You have no idea how much she's been through," Audrey whispered, fighting to keep the tears back that had morphed from anger. "You seriously can't be that heartless."

Cameron gazed at her, his dark blue eyes, once hard and unforgiving, now searching and full of...sympathy? Was that what she was seeing? Audrey couldn't be sure because he was a difficult man to read. Unless he was undressing her with his eyes—then she knew good and well what was on his mind.

Piper's food was delivered, saving Cameron from having to respond right away. And dammit, she didn't want to give him a chance to calculate his answer. She wanted some impulse and passion.

"Where're you staying?" he finally asked.

Audrey blinked. "The Sunset Inn."

Cameron made a face. "You can't stay there; the place is a fleabag."

She wasn't going to argue with him on that. "It's what I can afford." Actually, she could afford way better, but she tended to be frugal about anything not having to do with fashion. Or her business.

Cameron switched his attention to Piper, who'd emptied half the bottle of ketchup on her plate before digging into the nuggets. "I have a guesthouse," he blurted out.

Say what?

Cameron gazed at her while turning his drink in slow circles. "You can stay there until we figure something out."

"What's there to figure out besides which of your bedrooms she'll be taking?" Yeah, good argument.

Cameron lifted a brow at her. "You want to work something out, you can stay with me."

She didn't want to stay with him, because being in that close proximity to him wasn't something she was prepared for. At least in the motel room she had a place to retreat and gather her thoughts. Regroup after having all her senses shaken up by the man leaning so casually across from her. Yes, Cameron was definitely dangerous. He'd touched on a weak spot that had been tucked away for years. Audrey wasn't sure what to do, because it had taken months of self-evaluation to refocus her priorities on something else. She needed to steel herself against him and his compelling stare.

"I've already unloaded all our stuff into the room," she pointed out.

"So come by tomorrow," he said with a shrug, as though it didn't matter one way or the other to him.

Audrey glanced at Piper as the child inhaled one nugget after the other. She made a play of feeding a nugget to Jellybean, then put the same nugget into her own mouth. Yeah, the motel was going to take a sizable chunk out of her savings, but it helped her maintain independence. A lot of people wondered why she didn't go to her father for money. Richard Bennett ran two successful dental practices, so Audrey had never wanted for anything growing up. They'd lived in a large home and taken expensive vacations every year. But Audrey preferred to make it on her own.

On the other hand, staying in Cameron's guesthouse would give Audrey the opportunity to see what kind of man he was, and Piper would have an easier time developing a relationship with him before Audrey had to return to Boulder. And that was more important than Audrey's need for independence or fending off her reaction to Cameron.

Before she could answer, he snagged a napkin out of the holder and jotted something down with a pen he'd made appear out of nowhere. "Here's my address," he commented as he slid the napkin across the table to her. "You can come by anytime tomorrow. I have practice first thing in the morning, then again after school. I'm usually home by five-thirty or six."

Audrey took the napkin, unable to squash back the surprise at how neat his handwriting was.

He's offering you a place to stay and all you can think about is his handwriting?

"I'll leave it unlocked for you," Cameron added.

"Okay," she answered with a nod. "Thank you. But just so you know, I'm not going anywhere anytime soon."

His mouth curled in a smile meant for dark corners and salacious whispers. "We'll see about that, Audrey."

FOUR

Cameron had expected Audrey to turn down his offer flat. She'd probably enjoy giving him the big, fat no too. Nothing about their encounters so far had indicated she was anything other than bossy and way too opinionated. So when he'd stood in his kitchen window at lunchtime the next day and seen Audrey and Piper open the front door of the guesthouse, Cameron had been amused. Surprised, definitely. But amused because he had a feeling that taking his offer went against everything she stood for. He couldn't help but feel triumphant at the knowledge that he'd stuck it to her something good.

He watched as Audrey and Piper disappeared inside the house for a moment before walking back outside, Piper dragging that dirty-ass stuffed cat with her. Then Audrey left Piper on the front porch while she returned to the car, turned it around so the trailer backed up to the house. He should probably offer to help her because it looked like she had a lot of stuff. Instead he just stood there and observed the way she moved. She flowed in an economical way that wasn't typical of a woman. Especially a woman who looked like her. She didn't stop to adjust her clothing or mess with her hair. She didn't check her reflection in the rearview mirror or double-check that everything was in the right place. It defied everything he knew about women, which wasn't surprising because he'd already spent enough time with her to know that Audrey wasn't like most women.

Audrey rounded to the back of the trailer and opened the door just as Piper jumped down from the porch and began running around the backyard. She pumped her little legs, Jellybean flying behind her, from one side of the yard to the other. Every so often she'd toss a wary glance at his house, as though she was still undecided about being there. Or about him personally.

Yeah, she wasn't the only one who was wary.

His thoughts were interrupted when his cell rang. He answered just as he saw his mom's name on the caller ID.

"Hey, Mom." Piper ran across the yard again, then stopped by some bushes to watch a butterfly.

"Okay, what's wrong?" she asked instead of returning his hello.

And how could she tell he was distracted? "What makes you think something's wrong?"

"Your voice has that tone. Like something's on your mind." Pamela Shaw was way too observant for his liking. "Tell Mother about it," she insisted when he didn't answer.

Cameron switched his attention to Audrey, who was carrying a box up the porch steps. With a deep breath, he recounted the last twenty-four hours, from the time Audrey had shown up at the school until meeting her at the diner last night.

"Well, then," she stated after he finished. "I bet you didn't see that one coming."

"Not funny, Mom. I don't know what to do with this kid."

"She probably doesn't know what to do with you, either," she pointed out.

Cameron closed his eyes and leaned his forehead against the sliding glass door. "You're not helping."

"But I'm being serious. This little girl just lost her mother and is probably just as scared and uncertain as you are."

Logically, he knew that. The way Piper kept shooting unsure glances at him touched a place deep inside his chest that hadn't been touched in a long time. A part of him wanted to help the kid, to place a hand on her skinny shoulder and assure her life wouldn't always be so shitty. Problem was, he wasn't sure she'd believe him, because he hardly believed it himself.

"You remember what it's like to lose a parent," Pamela pointed out.

Cameron opened his eyes and saw Audrey accept a yellow flower Piper and picked off a bush. Cam's gaze fell to Audrey's seriously slamming ass as she went back to the trailer. "Having a parent die from cancer isn't the same as one leaving," he reminded his mom.

"I realize that," his mom agreed, because she didn't need reminding of what they'd gone through when his douche of a father had walked out on them. "But my point is, you were a vulnerable kid once. You know what it's like to have your family fall apart."

Okay, he'd give her that.

"And," his mom went on, "after your dad left, you still had me. She has no one, honey. She didn't ask to be put in this situation, so it isn't fair for you to take your anger for your dad out on her."

Cameron turned from the door. "That's not what I'm doing." Was he, though? Cameron liked to think he wasn't that much of a shithead, even though sometimes he could be. His resentment for his old man walking out had become so ingrained that he no longer knew how to separate it from everything else.

"Maybe not deliberately. But I know you. When you see her, you're reminded of everything you felt when your dad left us. I don't even think she has much of a relationship with your dad, does she?"

"I think Dianna was all she had," Cameron admitted; even saying the words pinched his chest, because his mother was right. Cameron had been that kid once. After his father had ditched them, Pamela had been all he had. She'd been the rock, making sure Cameron had everything he needed, loving him enough for two parents. There was no way he'd have made it through those first few years without her. His world would have ended if he'd ever lost her.

Cameron turned back to the backyard and watched as Piper plopped down on the grass and talked to her stuffed cat. The thing was a mess, discolored and tearing at the seams.

She's my best friend.

The girl's small and quiet voice floated around in his head, solidifying what he hadn't seen before. She really was alone, except for Jellybean. And Audrey. She had Audrey too, who was willing to slay dragons for the kid. As annoying as she'd been yesterday, Cameron respected her for the way she'd taken Piper in and protected her.

"Cameron?" his mom said when he'd been silent.

"I don't know what to do with her," he admitted.

Pamela laughed softly in his ear. "You think I knew what to do when you came along?"

Cameron smiled, despite himself. "Yeah, but you planned me."

His mom made a sound of agreement. "True. But Piper didn't plan this either. I think you're both probably going to have to feel your way around each other."

"Yeah," he agreed absently as Audrey reappeared through the front door of the guesthouse and went to the trailer.

"Listen, I've got to run. I'll see you for Sunday dinner next month."

They disconnected the call and, without really thinking, Cameron slid open the back door. Piper jerked her head up when she heard him and clutched Jellybean tighter. Shit, she wasn't afraid of him, was she? Had he been that much of an ogre? He didn't think so. In fact, he'd been more preoccupied with Audrey and ruffling her feathers than anything else. But maybe that was the problem. Maybe he hadn't been attentive enough.

Maybe he should, like, try a smile. Or something.

Piper watched him with those deep green eyes; then her face softened a fraction when he grinned at her.

"Catch any good butterflies?" he asked. Audrey had walked back inside the guesthouse.

Piper set Jellybean down on the grass. "No, they're too fast for me. I was trying to catch one for Jellybean because she loves butterflies. Now she's sad because she doesn't have one."

Cameron thought Piper was the one who was sad, but he kept that to himself. He glanced around and spotted a yellow ladybug on a bush near his feet. He squatted, collected the insect, then walked over to Piper. Her gaze tracked his movements when he lowered himself to her level.

"How about a ladybug? You think she'd take that instead of a butterfly?"

Piper observed the ladybug crawling over Cam's hand. "Jellybean doesn't like ladybugs."

"What about you?"

Piper chewed her lip. "Ladybugs scare me," she admitted.

"Naw, ladybugs are harmless," he told her. "Hold out your finger." Piper hesitated and Cameron lowered himself to a sitting position next to her. "I promise it won't hurt you. See?" He held out his own hand to show there was nothing to be afraid of.

Piper finally stuck out her index finger, which was pale and skinny. Her worried expression turned into a giggle when the bug crawled from Cameron's finger to Piper's. She turned her palm over to track the insect's movements, and her grin widened.

"It's tickling me," she marveled. She let out a squeal when the ladybug started crawling up her arm. But the fun was over when it unfolded its wings and flew away.

For a second, Cameron thought Piper was going to burst into tears, because that's what kids did, right? He braced himself for the barrage and let out a sigh of relief when she just blinked at him. "Can you tie my shoe?"

He hadn't been expecting that, but he glanced down anyway as she stuck her little foot out. Her white-and-pink sneakers were dirty with the pink sparkly shoelaces loose and untied. Holding back a grin, Cameron tied them as tight as he could, then patted her knee.

"All set," he told her.

"Can I go sit in your swing?" she questioned as she pointed to the wooden swing on the back porch.

"Sure," he told her. Then she was gone, snatching up Jellybean and bounding up the porch steps.

Cameron stood, then paused when he spotted Audrey, standing next to the trailer watching him.

He approached her, taking in her tight skinny jeans, knee-high boots, and flannel shirt. The sleeves were rolled to her elbows, revealing pale, delicate forearms. And why was he even looking at her forearms?

"How long have you been standing there?" he asked.

Audrey shrugged, sending her high ponytail swishing along her back. "Long enough to know what a sucker you are."

That's really what she thought of him?

Audrey took another box out of the trailer. "But seriously, that was a really sweet thing you did. She'll remember that for a long time."

Cameron just shrugged. "It was nothing."

"That's right, because you don't even like her."

He narrowed his eyes at her. "I never said that."

Audrey hefted the box higher in her arms. "But you don't want her here."

Cameron took the box from her, ignoring the exasperation that swam in her eyes. "I never said that either," he told her as he climbed the steps and entered the guesthouse. The place wasn't that big, just two small bedrooms, with one bathroom, and an L-shaped kitchen with a love seat. There wasn't even a place for a table, so Cam had stuck a couple of stools under the bar top so his guests would have a place to eat.

"Okay, so I'm the one you don't want here," Audrey remarked as Cam stuck the box on the couch.

He straightened and considered her. "I didn't say that either."

"But you haven't exactly been very welcoming."

Okay, that was true. "Cut me some slack here. You show up on my doorstep with a niece I've never met and expect me to know exactly what to do."

Audrey crossed her arms over her chest and seemed to think about that. "Okay, I'll give you that. But technically I didn't show up on your doorstep."

He tucked his hands in his pockets and scanned his gaze over the freckles lining her nose. "Are you always such a stickler for details?"

She offered a coy smile, which was like a punch to his gut. "Always."

He nodded. "I'll try to remember that."

She regarded him for a moment, as though she didn't know what else to say. Cameron understood her confusion, because he didn't know what to say around her either. Something about her muddled his brain as though she were a mesh of contradictions that he hadn't figured out yet. As he took a step closer, Cameron reveled in his *aha* moment when her pupils dilated. Yes, she had a weakness, another side she kept hidden from the world, him included.

She wanted him. And she didn't *want* to want him. She probably hated herself for wanting him.

The control she prized so much wasn't able to stop the quickening of her breath when his attention zeroed in on her mouth. It was a kissable mouth, with full lips that were bare, perfect for capturing and moistening with his tongue. They'd probably swell when kissed hard enough, and they'd be unbelievably responsive, just like the rest of her. Cameron liked a woman who was responsive and owned her body.

She cleared her throat, abruptly ending the moment. "So, this is a cute place," she commented.

Maybe they should chat about the weather too. "It was here when I bought the house," he replied, without taking his attention off her. "It came furnished too." No one had ever actually stayed here. He'd christened one of the bedrooms with an old girlfriend, but he wasn't about to tell Audrey that.

A red flush bloomed up her neck. "Do you use it a lot?" she asked, as though sensing his thoughts.

"You're the first," he replied. "It needs some repairs, but it should be sufficient for the two of you."

Audrey nodded and bit her lip.

Nervous much?

Cameron embraced the swell of gratification at the knowledge that he made her fidgety. "Do you need some help getting the rest of your stuff unloaded?"

"No, I've got it. And why are you here in the middle of the day? I figured you'd be at the school."

She was right. Normally he worked through lunch, but today he'd decided to come home. *Yeah, right. You just rushed over to see if she was here.* "I came home to grab some quick lunch."

Just then Piper ran through the door, dragging Jellybean behind her. "Audrey, I have to go potty."

Cameron glanced at the kid, taking in the rosy cheeks and messy hair. He pointed down the hall. "The bathroom is across from the first bedroom."

Audrey clasped Piper's hand in hers. "I have to take her. She's terrified of toilets."

"She won't go to the bathroom by herself?"

"Nope."

He didn't get it. "What's so scary about a toilet?"

Audrey leaned closer, giving him a hint of lemons. Made him think of lemonade. Which made him think of hot summer days. Which made him think of sex in the sun. "Probably because she used to watch her mother throw up from chemo treatments."

Ah, shit. Wasn't he the big asshole?

He peered down at the girl, noting the way she clung to Audrey's leg like she was about to be dragged off for surgery. But instead of prying Piper away, Audrey embraced her, cupping one hand over the girl's head and the other running in circles over her back. They were good together, the two of them. Cameron suspected they needed each other, possibly filling a void that nothing else could reach.

"The football team's having a pancake breakfast on Saturday," he blurted out. First he hadn't wanted Piper in his life, and now he was inviting them to team functions? "It's a fund-raiser," he added.

Cameron waited for a reply, kicking himself for tossing it out so casually. Then Audrey smirked, and he got the impression she was laughing at him. "Are you asking if we'd like to come?"

Yeah, Cameron, are you?

"It would be a good way for Piper to see what I do," he answered, because that sounded way more reasonable, as though the initial invitation had more to do with helping Piper's transition. Which was strange, because he still wasn't sure he wanted the girl here.

Audrey looked down at Piper. "What d'you think? Want to go have some pancakes on Saturday?"

Piper looked up at Audrey, then switched her gaze to Cameron. "Can they make them into a Mickey Mouse shape?"

Cameron held back a grin, thinking about the reaction he'd get by asking tough seventeen-year-olds to put Mickey

Mouse ears on pancakes. "I'm sure we can make that happen."

Piper offered a shy smile, cutting through the brash exterior he'd been throwing out since meeting them. How could one girl make him question his own solitary existence? And how had his life changed so much in twenty-four hours?

"I don't want these anymore."

Audrey paused in the act of dialing a number on her cell phone and glanced at Piper. For lunch she'd asked for chicken nuggets, so Audrey had hastily thrown a handful on a plate while she'd been on the phone with the elementary school. Piper was supposed to start kindergarten this year, and school had been in session for almost a month already. Instinctively she knew inquiring about school was something Cameron would overlook, so she'd taken the initiative.

Audrey set the cell phone on the kitchen counter. "But that's what you asked for."

Piper glanced at the plate and spun back and forth on the barstool. "I don't like them anymore."

Audrey bit back a groan and reminded herself that Piper was a fickle six-year-old who constantly changed her mind. But ever since Dianna passed away, Piper's indecisiveness had worsened, especially when it came to food. She'd ask for a corn dog, take one bite, then ask for something else. It had been a learning process for Audrey, one that was rife with frustration and lots of designer label counting.

"So what would you like?" she asked the girl.

Piper thought for a moment. "Popsicles," she announced.

In the two days they'd been there, Audrey had unpacked

everything and run to the store for necessities. Unfortunately, Popsicles weren't a necessity.

"We don't have any Popsicles," she told the girl.

Piper dragged Jellybean off the bar top and hugged it close. "Do we have any ice cream?"

They did, but she wasn't about to tell her that. "You can't have ice cream for lunch."

"What can I have?" Piper asked with a blink of her big green eyes.

Audrey pointed to the plate of food. "You can have the nuggets you asked for."

Piper stuck out her bottom lip and pushed the nuggets around the plate.

"You just had nuggets a few nights ago," Audrey reminded her. "What happened?"

"I just don't like 'em anymore."

Audrey picked up her cell again and rounded the bar top. She dropped a kiss on Piper's clean, blond hair. "Well, that's what we have so if you're hungry enough you'll eat them."

Piper bounced in her seat. "Jellybean's gonna eat them instead."

Whatever. Usually what Jellybean ate, Piper ended up eating too, so Audrey wasn't going to argue. She left the girl to her food and walked toward the front door. When she'd gotten up that morning, she'd propped the door open to let in the early-morning cool breeze. The brisk wind had felt good on her face, reminding her of how much she loved Colorado. The sky was clear and the mountain peaks soared around them. She'd reveled in the quiet of the day with a cup of coffee in her hand and the birds chirping around her. With Piper still asleep, she'd taken advantage and sat on the porch steps, making sure to avoid the bottom one since it had a broken board.

But when she'd sat, she'd noticed a yellow piece of paper stuck to the wood, flapping in the breeze. Audrey had set her mug down and glanced at the Post-it note.

Fixed the porch step this morning. C.

Just looking at Cameron's handwriting had brought all sorts of tingles along her spine. Even now, hours after finding his note, Audrey stole a glance at his house. She knew he wasn't home, but that didn't stop her from taking in every detail of his property. The craftsman-syle log home was beautiful with a manicured lawn full of trees and flowers. The guesthouse sat behind the home, giving her a perfect view of the back porch, kitchen window, and sliding glass door. She and Piper hadn't seen that much of Cameron since they'd arrived two days ago. He'd been gone all day yesterday and hadn't arrived home until almost seven. Then he'd been up and out the door by the time she'd gotten out of bed.

But not before fixing the broken step.

It was such a minor thing, repairing a piece of wood, but Audrey felt a tiny flutter in her belly. He could have left the step the way it was. After all, he didn't intend for Piper to stay, right? So why go to the trouble for them?

Underneath the grunts and steely glares was a man with values and honor. Of course, she hadn't really known him long enough to make such an assessment, but she trusted her instincts, and her instincts said that Cameron wouldn't turn Piper away.

She also suspected underneath was a body made for Under Armour commercials and loincloths. He probably had ridges in places most men didn't. Ridges that were perfect for a woman to run her tongue over.

Audrey smiled while simultaneously telling herself to put a halt to her fantasies. Cameron was bad news all around, and if she was going to keep her wits about her, she needed to stop imagining the stuff underneath those sweatshirts he wore.

Audrey tossed a glance at Piper over her shoulder. She was still feeding nuggets to Jellybean, holding the food to the cat's mouth, then setting it back on the plate. She then dialed her business partner's number.

She and Stevie had started their home staging business five years ago, contracting out to real estate agents who needed to quickly spruce up a house before putting it on the market. When Audrey had graduated from college, she'd planned on being an interior designer. She'd stumbled on the staging business by default when she'd done a favor for a Realtor friend by redecorating a living room. A few months later, she and her friend Stevie, whom she'd met in college, had poured every bit of blood, sweat, and tears into starting their business. It had been tireless, thankless work, and they hadn't broken even until two years later. Things had picked up and they'd finally turned a profit this year. Stevie hadn't been happy when she found out how long Audrey planned on being gone.

Her friend answered on the third ring. "How's it going?" she asked, knowing the uphill battle Audrey had ahead of her.

"As expected," she answered with a sigh. "Difficult."

"How's the little one?" Stevie asked, referring to Piper.

Audrey smiled because, as capricious as Piper could be, she always warmed Audrey's heart. She'd lost her mother, but her strength and resilience astounded her, especially since Audrey knew how it felt to lose a mother. "Coping." Audrey paused. "Actually, she's doing pretty well considering. I got everything unpacked yesterday and made a call about enrolling her in school this morning."

"You unpacked all your stuff in the hotel?" Stevie questioned.

Shit. Audrey hadn't even realized her slip of the tongue. Now her friend would ask all kinds of questions, and Audrey didn't want to talk about Cameron. "Yeah," she answered slowly. "Piper's uncle has a guesthouse."

Stevie was silent a moment before answering. "This guy offered up his guesthouse after you just met him?"

"You should have seen his reaction when we first got here. He wanted me to take Piper and go back to Boulder."

"You're kidding!" Stevie exclaimed. "What an ass. So what made him change his mind?"

"I'm not sure he has," Audrey admitted.

"You think he'd send his own niece away?"

Audrey watched as a squirrel dragged an acorn across the grass. "I don't think he would. But he's not pleased we're here. He keeps saying he doesn't know what to do with a kid."

Stevie snorted. "Most bachelors don't." There was a beat of silence. "He is a bachelor, isn't he?"

Audrey opened her mouth to answer a confident *no*, but now that she thought about it, she wasn't sure. She knew there was no wife, and he hadn't mentioned anything about a girlfriend, but that didn't mean he didn't have one. Or a string of women panting after him. The thought of leaving Piper with a man who had a revolving door of women made Audrey uncomfortable. She'd have to clear that up with him later. He had to understand that Piper's needs and welfare had to come first.

"I think so," she finally answered.

"You're not sure?" Stevie asked with a disbelieving laugh. "What *do* you know about this guy?"

Not much. "Midthirties, coaches high school football."

"Yeah? Is he hot?" Stevie wanted to know.

An automatic fire leaped into her face, spreading back to her hairline and blooming across her chest. In Cameron's case, *hot* was an understatement. The man was in a category that hadn't even been invented yet. "What does that have to do with anything?"

Stevie was silent a moment, as though trying to read too much into Audrey's response. "I'd say everything, judging by your tone. Now give me the lowdown on this guy."

Audrey picked at the splintered wood of the step, unable to control the heat still filling her cheeks. "I already told you about him."

"You gave me his stats," Stevie complained. "Now give me the goods. What's he look like? How tall is he?"

"I don't know. Six-two maybe." Tall enough to make her feel all fragile and feminine. Towering over her like some...big man. *Good one, Audrey.*

"And is he in good shape? Or is he kind of dumpy?"

Audrey's grin widened. What was she, some teenager crushing on her lab partner? "There isn't anything dumpy about him."

"Yeah, baby," Stevie responded, with a smile lighting up her voice. "Now we're getting somewhere. So who's he look like?"

Audrey's brow furrowed. "What do you mean?"

"Compare him to someone."

"Like, someone we know?" Stevie would be hard pressed to get a decent answer. Cameron wasn't like anyone Audrey knew.

"No, like a celebrity. I'm trying to get a picture of this guy in my head."

Audrey blew out a breath and racked her brain. "I don't know. He kind of reminds of Taylor Kitsch a little bit. But with less shaggy hair. And maybe not as broody." Even though Cameron could brood with the best of them.

Stevie whistled. "Damn. No wonder you ran to his guesthouse."

"That's not why." Except it totally was.

"Okay, then," Stevie answered with a snort.

"So how're things up there?" Audrey asked, desperately needing to change the subject.

"Crazy busy," her friend automatically answered. "Do you know how much longer you'll be? Because I can only handle all this work for so long."

"I can't leave until I'm sure Piper is completely settled."

"That could be months," Stevie complained.

Audrey guessed technically it could. And maybe a subconscious part of her wanted to drag it out because the thought of saying goodbye to Piper gutted her.

"I don't think it'll take that long," she assured her friend.

"But it could," Stevie argued.

She guessed it could, but she knew, realistically, she couldn't be gone from her business that long.

"Just try to make it as quick as you can," Stevie went on.

"I promise," Audrey answered. *Why are you making a promise you're not sure you can keep?*

They said their goodbyes, and her phone vibrated almost the second she disconnected.

Bring Piper to practice after school today.

Audrey blinked at the words and stuffed back her annoyance. He knew good and well not to text her, and he'd done it anyway. Probably to piss her off. No please. No *Hey, if you're not doing anything…*

He just demanded and assumed.

Two days ago when he'd helped her move boxes, she thought she'd turned a corner with him. The way he'd interacted with Piper, so gentle and understanding, then attempting a halfway civil conversation with her that didn't involve grunts and one-word answers. Sure, he'd invaded her personal space and sent her pulse skyrocketing, but he'd been sort of decent. Almost…nice.

Probably because he was having an off night.

She suspected Cameron rarely let anyone have the upper hand. Probably one of his defense mechanisms. Well, she knew all about defense mechanisms and could give as good as he could.

She dialed his number and pressed the phone to her ear. The other line rang, while behind her, Piper stepped through the front door.

Audrey peered at her to see Jellybean dangling from one hand and ketchup smeared across one cheek.

Cameron's voice mail picked up after the fourth ring. Damn, even his clipped tone telling people to leave a message sent chills through her midsection.

"Piper and I will have to check our schedules," she told him. "We're busy people, you know," she added, just to get his hair up. "By the way, I know you texted me just to get under my skin. It won't work."

She hung up and turned to Piper.

"Did you finish your lunch?" she asked the girl.

Piper nodded. "I have to go to the bathroom now."

Ten minutes later, after she took Piper to the bathroom and hovered over her to assure her nothing bad was going to happen, her phone vibrated.

And her back teeth ground together before she even checked the message.

You don't have anything else going on, Cameron's message said. *And we both know I'm totally under your skin.*

Audrey closed her eyes and took a deep breath. "Diane von Furstenberg, Dolce and Gabbana..." She made it all the way to Emilio Pucci before she realized Piper had already flushed the toilet and left the bathroom.

FIVE

Audrey found herself watching high school football for the second time that week. For someone who didn't even like the sport, she'd sure dedicated a lot of time to it so far. Piper had been preoccupied with her My Little Ponies, which she'd set up in a circle underneath a shade tree in the backyard. She'd been in a stubborn mood all afternoon, and Audrey had had to bribe her with frozen yogurt after practice just to get the kid in the car. They'd been late, thanks to Piper's unwillingness to leave her ponies.

Now she was busy with some coloring app on Audrey's phone, with Jellybean propped on the bleacher next to her. She'd been relatively quiet, leaving Audrey to study the action on the field. And by "action" she most certainly did not mean Cameron, who'd been alternating between yelling at the players and pulling them aside to give them instruction. Audrey had tried paying attention to the practice, which was a jumbled mess of players gathering in small groups to work on different exercises. She thought maybe she'd be able to use the opportunity to learn more about the sport, so she wouldn't seem like such a clueless nitwit in front of Cameron. Not that she cared what he thought.

"Is it just me, or does Cam seem distracted today?"

Audrey's ears perked up at the two women seated behind her. They'd been engaging in casual conversation for most of the practice, bouncing from a honeymoon one had just taken to morning sickness the other had been dealing with.

Of course she hadn't been trying to eavesdrop, but her attention had snapped to them when they'd mentioned Cameron's name. Something about the way the one woman had said it, with a thread of familiarity, had sparked Audrey's interest. They knew him, possibly as more than a friend.

"He seems like his usual grumpy self to me," the other woman chimed in.

Yeah, they definitely knew him.

"I don't know, something about him seems off," the conversation continued. "He's tense."

For a flicker of a moment, Audrey thought about introducing herself and taking credit for said tension, but something held her back. She wasn't sure why, but she had a feeling Cameron wouldn't appreciate her broadcasting his situation with Piper to random people, even if these women did know him. So she kept her mouth shut, her eyes on practice, and her ears behind her.

A second later one of them tapped her on the shoulder.

Audrey turned and clapped eyes with a beautiful woman with long, thick, dark hair and bright blue eyes.

"I'm sorry to bother you," she said with an open smile. "But are you Audrey?"

Was she supposed to know them? Had Cameron already told people about her and Piper? "Yes," she answered with hesitation.

The woman slid her friend a look. "Told you."

Her friend leaned forward. Her hair was a few shades lighter and pulled back into a high ponytail. "You'll have to excuse Stella. Nothing is off-limits to her." She stuck out her hand, and Audrey shook it. "I'm Annabelle Carpenter. Blake is my husband."

Ah, Blake Carpenter, the coach. That would explain how they knew about her.

"Stella West," the other woman offered.

Stella shook her hand as well, while assessing the two of them. They were both young and gorgeous with friendly smiles, though neither of them looked pregnant.

"Blake told us about you and your little girl," Annabelle continued.

"Oh, Piper's not my daughter. She's..." Audrey's words trailed off, because she didn't know how much they knew. The only interaction she'd had with Blake Carpenter was the day she'd arrived in town and asked if he knew where to find Cameron. Had he assumed Piper was his love child? If so, what had he assumed about Audrey?

"She's Cameron's niece," she finally explained, deciding it was better to just be out with it.

The two women flicked a glance at Piper; then the woman who introduced herself as Stella ran her gaze over Audrey. She glanced at the field, then back at her. "Something tells me you're not Cam's sister." Stella leaned forward when Audrey had only gaped at her. "I don't know if you've noticed, but he's been too busy sliding glances your way to coach his players. And no man I know looks at his sister like that, if you know what I'm saying." Stella arched a brow. "And if he did, he'd be in some serious need of therapy."

Um...

"Stella," Annabelle chastised.

But Stella just shrugged, totally unaware of the fact that Audrey had just swallowed her tongue. "Just saying," she replied.

Annabelle offered a comforting smile. "Like I said, you'll have to excuse her."

Audrey managed a smile, which was pretty difficult considering her tongue was lying at the bottom of her stomach. Had Cameron been checking her out? How come she hadn't noticed?

"It's all right," she offered. She opened her mouth to say something else, maybe something witty to offset the fact they'd noticed Cameron looking at Audrey. An excuse, or something equally reasonable, like maybe there was a giant clock mounted outside the announcer's box and he didn't want to lose track of time. And *that* was why he kept turning his head in her direction. But she had nothing. Literally nothing.

Stella considered Audrey for a moment, as though trying to work the facts out in her head. Audrey wanted to put a screeching halt to it, because these women not only knew Cameron, but they were also way too observant for her comfort.

"So you're not his sister," Stella commented. "And I know you're not involved with him, because you're way too nice." She paused, then added, "Cam has awful taste in women."

"He really does," Annabelle agreed.

Good grief, had she stepped into an episode of *The Twilight Zone*?

Audrey had no clue how she was supposed to respond.

"I'm just here for Piper." There. Nice and safe.

The two women just blinked at her. Were they expecting more?

"I'm sure Cameron will fill you in eventually," Audrey continued.

Stella laughed. "I wouldn't count on that. The man is annoyingly secretive."

Annabelle placed her hand on Stella's arm. "But we understand if you're not comfortable talking about it."

Stella tossed her friend an exasperated look. "Speak for yourself. I want the dirt."

"How long are you in town?" Annabelle asked, probably in an attempt to hold her friend back.

"I'm not sure," Audrey answered. "A month or so."

Annabelle pulled a granola bar from her pocket and opened it, making Audrey wonder if she was the pregnant one. "Where are you staying?"

Now, this was a tricky question. Given the way the conversation had gone so far, Audrey didn't want Stella to take the information and run with it. So far the woman had proved too observant and canny for Audrey's comfort.

"I was at the Sunset Inn," she answered, and left it at that.

The horrified look on Stella's face told Audrey the woman was all too familiar with the Sunset Inn's shortcoming. "Nice call relocating. That place is a dump."

Annabelle took a bite of granola. "So where are you now?"

Audrey racked her brain for something, *anything*, other than *so let me explain...*

But Stella, the human lie detector/psychic took advantage of Audrey's silence to draw her own conclusion. She placed a hand on Audrey's shoulder. "Wait, don't say it; let me guess," she quipped. "Cameron offered you his guesthouse."

"No way," Annabelle said with a shake of her head.

Stella nodded. "Yep, he did, didn't he?"

"So, let me explain," Audrey blurted out, just as she had told herself not to.

Annabelle swallowed. "He seriously offered to let the two of you stay with him?" At Audrey's weak nod, Annabelle shook her head. "I need to have a talk with that man."

About what?

"Don't you dare," Stella ordered. "He has a nice, attractive woman who will hopefully rub off on him, and you'll ruin it."

Audrey ignored the "rubbing off" comment, because she didn't want to do any rubbing of any kind with Cameron. Rubbing turned into other things that led to heavy breathing and panting. Okay, she knew Stella's words were figurative, but that didn't stop the graphic image that formed in her mind. The two of them rubbing, hands roaming all over. Mouths seeking each other. It would be hot and sweaty and messy. But good. It would be too good for Audrey to remain objective about her mission, and she needed to keep her mind clear.

"He's just trying to do me a favor," Audrey explained. "It was an economic decision. Plus it'll help him get to know Piper better."

Both women's attention switched to the child, who was still engrossed in her coloring game.

Annabelle nodded as she finished her granola bar. "Okay," she responded.

Hoping the subject was now dropped, Audrey glanced at the field to spot Cameron talking to a man dressed in slacks and a button-down shirt. Cameron's back went straight as they talked, but his gaze remained firmly on his players. For some reason he didn't want to give the other man the time of day, and Audrey's interest was more than a little piqued.

She turned back to Stella and Annabelle. "Who's that man talking to Cameron?"

"That's Drew Spalding, the district's athletic director," Annabelle answered. "He and Cameron don't exactly get along."

Stella snorted. "They hate each other."

Audrey glanced back at the field to see Cameron had moved away from Drew. "Why?" she asked the women.

Stella and Annabelle exchanged a glance, silently communicating something that Audrey couldn't pick up on. Finally, Annabelle answered, "That's something Cam should tell you about."

Audrey highly doubted he'd open up to her, especially about something so personal. Whatever story there was between the two men, Audrey couldn't help but wonder if it was part of the reason Cameron held himself so aloof. A handful of friends, maybe one or two family members. Probably his mom. Automatically, she thought of the way he'd talked to Piper the other night in the backyard. He'd been sweet and patient with her. He hadn't talked down to her or ignored her like a lot of adults did. He'd gotten down to her level and engaged her. For some reason she felt the need to credit his mom for that. She bet the two of them had a close relationship.

"He doesn't like to talk about it," Annabelle expanded, reminding Audrey what they'd been talking about. "Cameron's..." Annabelle tilted her head to the side, as though trying to pin down the most accurate way to describe the man.

Audrey could come up with a few words, but they probably wouldn't be the same words Annabelle would use.

"Private," Stella concluded.

Annabelle nodded. "Yeah, that's a good way of putting it. He likes his privacy."

"But don't let him fool you into thinking he doesn't like to get close to people," Stella went on. "Because he does. You just have to chip through the wall he likes to put between himself and everyone else."

Audrey had a feeling that would be easier said than done.

Cameron's niece, whom he'd only known for two days now, already had the ability to calm the simmering storms that sometimes threatened to take over. He'd finished practice with the overwhelming urge to commit bodily harm to anyone who so much as looked at him the wrong way.

Damn it, why did he always allow Drew to get to him?

Now he was sitting in a brightly lit frozen yogurt shop, watching Piper pick the gummy bears off her birthday cake–flavored yogurt. At first, he'd turned down their invitation for yogurt, because he'd been in a shit mood and only wanted his rifle and a set of bottles to blow up. But then he'd gotten a second look in Piper's deep green eyes and found himself saying, "Sure, just give me a minute."

He'd ignored the surprise on Audrey's face, which had mirrored his own shock, and met them at Yo-Yo Fro-Yo. Frozen yogurt had never been his thing, but the stuff was cold and sweet, and Piper seemed to love it. She'd dragged the cat with her, as she had everywhere else. The thing even had its own chair and an empty cup, which Piper would occasionally dip her spoon into to feed the cat.

Cameron switched his attention to Audrey, who'd been too busy swirling her spoon around her yogurt to actually eat it.

"Something wrong with your yogurt?" he asked her.

Audrey blinked up at him. "No, it's good."

She was distracted. He knew this because she'd yet to seize an opportunity to either drive her point home about Piper or make his pulse fly off the charts.

"I called today about getting Piper enrolled in school," Audrey announced.

Shit, he'd spoken too soon.

"Okay," was all he said. Because how else was he supposed to respond? One of the reasons he'd offered his guesthouse was so he'd have more of an opportunity to convince Audrey he couldn't take Piper. Didn't she see how unfit and clueless he was about kids?

"I need some kind of proof of residency," she told him. "A mortgage statement or utility bill."

"Isn't she a little young for school?" Cameron hedged as he dug into his yogurt.

"She's six," Audrey answered. "She's supposed to start kindergarten this year, and school's already been in session for a month. I don't want her to fall too far behind."

Perfectly logical argument, but Cameron couldn't bring himself to agree. Instead he remained silent and took another bite of yogurt.

"You don't still think I'm going to take her back to Boulder, do you?" Audrey questioned.

Well, yeah, he was kind of hoping...

Audrey shook her head. "We'll talk about it later."

Gee, could they?

"I met some friends of yours at practice," Audrey said.

Yeah, he'd seen Audrey deep in conversation with two women who'd made it their life's mission to marry Cameron off to a "nice woman." Actually, he loved Annabelle and Stella. They were fearless and gutsy and perfect matches for Blake and Brandon.

Audrey leaned forward with a half smile curling the corners of her mouth, one he'd been thinking about kissing. "Are you going to tell me not to believe anything they said?"

Cameron set his empty yogurt cup aside. "Depends on what they said."

Audrey's grin widened. "They said you're grumpy and surly and private."

Cameron couldn't help his own smile. "In that case, believe it."

One of Audrey's brows arched. "But see, I already knew that about you."

Beside him, Piper fed more invisible yogurt to her stuffed cat. "And yet you want to leave a six-year-old with me."

Some of the light in Audrey's eyes dimmed. "Not me. I told you, that was Dianna's decision. I'm just trying to fulfill her wishes." She leaned her elbows on the table. "But something tells me you won't be like that with Piper. You have a soft spot for her."

The thing was, he didn't want to have a soft spot for the kid. Yeah, she was cute, and her smile was pure, and sometimes when she looked at him he saw...

To be completely honest, sometimes he saw himself. The same grief. Confusion. Uncertainty. Cameron knew better than anyone how that could shake a child's world. Make them feel alone. Scared. In his case, the fear and loneliness had turned into anger and resentment. Some people would probably take any opportunity to go back and change things, to make things perfect, but not him. All the raw emotions that had swirled around him as a kid, that had clouded his dreams and shattered his sense of stability, had shaped him into the man he was today. He liked his solitary life. He liked being able to bring women to an empty house. He wasn't ready to give up his no-strings-attached lifestyle. Not for Audrey or anyone else.

He didn't respond to her observation. Yeah, he did have a soft spot for Piper. But that didn't mean he was fit to raise her.

He blew out a sigh. "Look, Audrey..."

Audrey shook her head. "Don't you dare."

Cameron blinked.

"I've been on the receiving end of enough 'Look, Audreys' to know it's never good. I can't legally take her back to Boulder with me," Audrey informed him. "She's supposed to stay with you."

"I know," he admitted.

The surprise that flashed across Audrey's eyes matched Cameron's. Oddly enough, the words hadn't struck him dead when he'd said them.

"But you have to understand," he went on, "I don't know anything about kids."

"Neither did Dianna, but she adapted and was an amazing mother."

Cameron shook his head. "It's different for women."

Audrey gazed at him for a moment, then leaned back in her chair. "Huh. Annabelle and Stella didn't mention how sexist you are."

"I'm just stating a fact," he argued, because, shit, he didn't want her thinking that about him. "Plus, women have nine months to prepare themselves."

"So you're just going to give up without even trying?" Audrey pushed. "Funny, but I wouldn't have pegged you for a quitter."

Dammit, he wasn't a quitter. "I've never been a quitter," he told her. "But I'm just trying to be realistic here."

"Yeah, you're probably right," she said with a shrug. "I doubt you could do this. You'd probably screw her up anyway, so you should go ahead and admit defeat."

Okay, wait a minute.

"I never said that," he argued, even though he knew damn good and well what she was up to. Audrey Bennett was a crafty little thing who'd picked up on his pride and used it against him. And he hadn't even seen it coming. "I could do this," he told her.

She considered him for a moment, running her light brown eyes over him and touching on places that felt like more of a stroke. "I don't think you can," she finally said.

Piper scraped the bottom of her yogurt bowl and licked her spoon, totally unaware of the tension brewing like a late afternoon thunderstorm.

Cameron leaned forward and pinned her with the most threatening glower that always had his players shaking in their cleats. "You think I don't know what you're doing?" His attention involuntarily dropped to her mouth. How had he not noticed how full her lips were before now?

She offered a shrug, as though she were totally unaffected by his scrutiny. But her dilated pupils gave her away, offering Cameron a moment of triumph. "I'm not doing anything," she hedged. "Just pointing out the obvious. It's okay to admit you're not good at everything. We all can't be winners."

Okay, she wanted to play? Cameron knew how to play like an Olympic champion. In fact, he'd practically invented the game. He'd play her so good that she'd never realize the games were finished. He'd be strumming her like a guitar.

Only Cameron didn't play fair. And he didn't intend to

play the same game as she was. She thought she knew what she was getting into, but she didn't have a clue.

"Cameron," Piper said. The kid was bouncing in her seat and had dried yogurt smeared across one cheek. "Can Jellybean have the rest of your yogurt?"

Cameron picked up his empty cup and showed it to her. "It's empty. See?"

Piper pointed to the empty cup. "But there's enough left for her."

Cameron tossed a confused glance at his cup, then realized Piper had spent the last thirty minutes feeding imaginary yogurt to her stuffed cat. "Have at it," he told her. "I even saved some jelly beans for her."

Piper's face lit up like a kid at Christmas. "Those are her favorite!" she exclaimed.

"I know," he said with a wink.

A glance at Audrey showed her grinning at him as though to say, *Aw, I knew you could do it.* He half expected her to give him a gold star. Maybe a pat on the head.

It was so game on.

SIX

Piper polished off her third pancake, shoving a huge bite in her mouth and getting more powdered sugar on her shirt than down her throat. Audrey nudged a napkin across the table, knowing the kid would just swipe the mess away with her hand. Her *Sofia the First* T-shirt was beyond help, but the mess of butter and white powder on her cheeks was salvageable. Audrey grinned when Piper used the napkin but missed half her face.

"Here." Audrey gave her a hand, ignoring the kid's protests. Heaven forbid she should be too clean.

Plus, and Audrey didn't have the faintest idea why she felt this way, she wanted to make a good impression for Cameron. When he'd invited them to the football team's pancake breakfast, she'd taken it as a token of peace. Like an olive branch or something. So she'd helped Piper dress, even though she normally exerted independence by throwing on whatever mismatching thing, and slicked her hair back into a pair of twin braids. When they'd left, Piper had looked like she belonged on the cover of *Parenting* magazine. Now, with one braid coming loose, her shirt in ruins, and a grape juice mustache, she looked like...well, she looked like a kid. And the happiest Audrey had seen her in a long time.

"Can I have some more?" Piper questioned as she wrapped an arm around Jellybean.

Audrey leaned forward and brushed more sugar off the kid's shirt. "Are you going to eat them or feed them to Jellybean?"

Piper shook her head. "Jellybean's not hungry."

Of course she wasn't.

Audrey stood and took Piper's hand in hers. "Can we go say hi to Cameron after this?" Piper was bouncing up and down, flopping Jellybean all over the place.

The gym was so crowded with players, parents, and fans that she and Piper had only caught fleeting glimpses of Cameron. The first time she'd spotted him, he'd been surrounded by people congratulating him and the other coaches on the team's win the night before. He hadn't spotted them, as least she thought he hadn't, but just the mere sight of him had sent her stomach quivering. The place was noisy, but it hadn't been noisy enough to drown out his deep laughter, which had danced down her spine like the feathery touch of fingertips.

Piper tugged on Audrey's hand. "Audrey?"

The kid was impatiently waiting for an answer to her question. "Uh..." When she looked back at Cameron, he'd already diverted his attention elsewhere. "He's busy right now. Maybe when you finish eating, we can find him."

Piper pouted for about two seconds before they reached the long table where players were cooking up pancakes. Then she was bouncing on the balls of her feet again.

Audrey ordered another plate of pancakes, when someone bumped her left shoulder. She turned to excuse herself, but she bit her tongue when she got an eyeful of a gigantic, teased beehive.

Did people seriously still style their hair like that?

Apparently this woman, who looked like she hovered around the five-foot mark, thought the thing had never gone out of style.

"Excuse me," Audrey finally said.

The old woman blinked her rheumy gray eyes. "Do I know you?" she asked.

Audrey's brow furrowed. "Nope." She turned to tug Piper back toward their table, when the old woman grabbed her arm.

"Yes, you're that woman. The one with the kid." Her sharp gaze dropped to Piper, who was hiding behind Audrey's leg. Then the lady leaned forward, overwhelming Audrey with a cloud of Aqua Net. "Cameron Shaw's baby mama," said announced in a loud whisper.

Come again?

A wave of heat ambushed Audrey, which she hoped to hell didn't show on her face, even though she didn't have a single thing to be embarrassed about. She'd been in town less than a week and people thought Piper was Cameron's love child? And Audrey was...what? Just one of many? Was she supposed to be some poor jilted ex-lover who couldn't get over Cameron? Was that what his dating life was like? People saw her and Piper and assumed she was another one of his notches?

"Tell me something," the woman went on.

Yeah, I'd rather pour a jug of syrup over my head.

She leaned closer, giving Audrey an up-close-and-personal glimpse of sun spots and deep grooves around her eyes. "How'd you get him to stick?"

Oh, dear God.

"Lois, will you leave her alone?"

Audrey melted with relief when Annabelle Carpenter rescued her from the nosy woman and her horrifying questions.

"Well, honey, we just want to know," Lois said to Audrey. "You're a looker, and the women of this town have been trying to pin that man down for years."

Annabelle rolled her eyes. "It's nobody's business, Lois. But if you must know, Piper isn't Cameron's daughter; she's his niece." Annabelle slid an arm around Audrey's shoulders. "Now, will you let them finish their breakfast in peace?"

Lois pinched her thin lips and leaned heavily on her cane. After a moment of thought, she shrugged her shoulders. "That's all right. I'll just get another shot of him mowing the grass." Then she chuckled to herself. "The man can never keep his shirt on."

Audrey opened her mouth to say something. Anything other than *What the hell?* But Annabelle was scooting them away, back toward the tables and far from the curious old woman whose beehive was almost as tall as Piper.

Annabelle sat beside them. "Go ahead and ask. I'm sure you have tons of questions."

Yeah, but most were about Cameron, and Audrey didn't want the other woman to think Audrey had taken an interest in him. "What's with the hairdo?" she asked instead, because it seemed like the safest question.

Annabelle giggled and watched as Piper cut into her pancakes. "She's part of the Beehive Mafia. She and her three friends do their hair the same way and go around causing trouble. It's all harmless," Annabelle expanded when Audrey looked confused. "They're mostly just busybodies."

"What did she mean by getting a shot of Cameron mowing his grass?"

Annabelle's laughter grew. "The Beehives take up their spare time by taking pictures of the young, good-looking men in town and posting them on their Tumblr page. Most of their obsession has bounced back and forth between Stella's husband, Brandon, and Cameron. But when Brandon and Stella got married, Cam got the full force of their efforts. Most of their shots are of men without their shirts on."

Audrey resisted asking for the name of the Tumblr account. The last thing she needed was an image of Cameron in the buff. Her imagination was enough for her to handle, thank you very much. "Is that legal?" she asked.

Annabelle lifted her shoulders. "Like they care. The four of them are overgrown teenagers, if you ask me." She shifted her focus to Piper, who'd already dusted half her powdered sugar on her shirt. "Are you enjoying your pancakes, Piper?"

Piper nodded because she was too busy shoving food in her mouth.

"Where's your syrup?" Annabelle questioned.

Piper shook her head and brushed her hair out of her face. "Jellybean doesn't like syrup. She only likes powdered sugar."

Audrey rolled her eyes. "Her diet is based solely on what the stuffed cat likes."

"Is that what it is?" Annabelle wondered. "I thought maybe it was a raccoon. I guess I need to learn this stuff."

Audrey thought back to her conversation with Stella about morning sickness. "Are you expecting?" she asked the woman.

Annabelle folded her arms on the table and nodded. "I'm due in May."

Audrey offered a grin because, even though she'd just met Annabelle, it seemed like the woman would make a good mother. "Congratulations."

Annabelle smiled her thanks, and Audrey tamped down the hint of jealousy. Why should she be jealous? Annabelle was a lovely woman who'd befriended her. And it wasn't like Audrey was dying to have kids right now, anyway. Hell, she didn't even have a man. And maybe that was the problem. Annabelle seemed to have it all together. A hot husband, a baby on the way, a network of friends. What did Audrey have? A thriving business, that was true...but what else?

No man, at least not one who could stick for more than three months. An estranged brother she never talked to, a workaholic father who was emotionally distant, and a mother who'd disappeared without a trace and left her family permanently fractured.

There'd been Dianna, whom Audrey had loved like a sister, but...

Now she was gone too.

So yeah, she was a little jealous. Annabelle was blessed in a way she probably didn't realize with a life like the one Audrey had had when she was young; now she was just by herself.

Audrey blinked when she realized Annabelle had been talking.

"...So now I just have to figure out how to put together a nursery," Annabelle finished.

"Do you have a theme or focal point?" Audrey blurted out before she could stop herself. *Don't get emotionally involved with these people.*

Annabelle scrutinized her for a moment. "Are you an interior designer?"

A sliver of discomfort bloomed inside her chest, because Audrey knew where the line of questioning would go. She should have kept her mouth shut, but the altruism in her didn't know when to stop. "Not exactly," she answered. "I went to school for interior design, but now I do home staging."

Annabelle tilted her head. "Home staging? Is that like when you're trying to sell a house?"

Audrey nodded. "Right. We contract out to Realtors who bring us in before a home goes on the market. We generally bring in our own decorative items to make it look like a model home. They usually sell better if they looked unlived in."

"But...you can pull together a room and make it look good, right?"

"Yes, but—"

"I would really love if you could give me a hand," Annabelle said with urgency. "I'll pay you whatever your going rate is."

Audrey shook her head. "I couldn't. I don't know how long I'll be here, and you still have a while before you have to worry about your nursery. Don't you want to know what you're having before you decorate?" Geez, she was grasping at straws and sounded completely desperate doing it.

"Oh, we're not going to find out the sex beforehand," Annabelle answered with a shake of her head. "And see, I'm a planner and have some mild control issues. I need to get this done before anything else."

Audrey opened her mouth and closed it again.

"And you don't even have to do anything. Maybe you could just come by and give me pointers." The desperation in the woman's eyes pleaded with Audrey to help. "Just point me in the right direction."

"Maybe..." Audrey's words died off because she honestly didn't know what to say. "Maybe I could come by and take a look at the space. Do you have a room picked out?"

A sigh of relief caused Annabelle's shoulders to sag visibly. "It's our office right now, but I'm making Blake move all the furniture into the other bedroom." She placed a soft hand on top of Audrey's. "You have no idea what a help this is. The paint color alone was overwhelming me."

Most people really don't know anything about putting a room together that flows, one that isn't overwhelming or disjointed with too many themes or colors going on. That's why she and Stevie did such a good business. They came in and cleaned things up, made the homes look professional and uncluttered.

"How're things going with Cameron?" Annabelle asked, throwing Audrey's thoughts in a jumble. Decorating rooms was a much safer, and less stressful, train of thought.

"Good," she lied. Okay, maybe it wasn't a total lie. The situation they were in was odd, to say the least, but they got along okay. And by "got along," she meant they kept their conversations to a two-sentence maximum, ensuring no arguing, ego matching, or sexual tension that felt like a barbed wire around her throat.

Annabelle narrowed her eyes, as though she didn't believe Audrey.

Hell, Audrey wouldn't believe her either.

"I don't know," Audrey admitted. "He's great with

Piper," she said with a glance at the girl, who was scraping the last of the powdered sugar off her plate.

"But not with you?" Annabelle pondered.

How was she supposed to describe her relationship with Cameron when she didn't know what it was?

"No, he's...he's fine, I guess." Audrey tucked a strand of hair behind her ear. "I don't know," she said again. "He's a hard man to read."

Annabelle nodded her understanding. "Cameron's one of a kind, that's for sure. But don't let him push you away. He's a good guy."

Of course, she sensed that about him. He couldn't be so kind and gentle with Piper if he didn't have a streak of chivalry somewhere underneath that death stare of his. But how was she supposed to bring it out in him? If Piper was going to live with him, he needed to open up. Soften the edges a bit.

"He wants me to take Piper back to Boulder with me," she admitted.

Annabelle watched Piper for a moment, as though pondering their situation. "He won't do that. He may be gruff and rude sometimes, but he's loyal. And that's his blood. He'll do what needs to be done."

"But see, that's the thing," Audrey added. "I don't want him to take Piper out of obligation, and then end up resenting her. He needs to develop a relationship with her."

"He will. Just give him some time." Annabelle shifted in her seat. "Cameron's been burned in the past. He holds himself back out of self-preservation."

Yeah, she'd kind of figured that.

"So how do I get through to him?"

Annabelle twisted a glance over her shoulder to where Cam was joking around with some players. "Something tells me you already have. You just have to get him to admit it."

Cameron had wanted his Sunday morning to himself. A cup of coffee, the sunrise, and the Sunday paper. Then maybe he'd kick back in his chair and catch something on ESPN. Blake Carpenter, the bogarting bastard, had swooped in and sent Cameron's serene morning into oblivion. He'd waltzed in with game film and a lopsided smirk that had Cam's back teeth grinding together. The only reason he'd forgiven his friend was the giant pink box of donuts. Blake had even brought Cam's favorite: coconut.

So he'd abandoned his ESPN for game film, which had spanned the last three hours.

The only thing that had kept Cameron from losing his mind was the fact that Audrey and Piper had made themselves scarce today. He'd seen Audrey leave this morning, then return about two hours later. Then, he'd gotten a glimpse of Piper running around in the backyard, trailing that damn stuffed cat after her. But the weird thing was that, other than the fact that Piper's shenanigans had made him smile, he missed them. But how could that be? They'd been here less than a week, and he didn't even like them.

Okay, he liked Piper. It would be impossible not to like that kid. But Audrey? She was a whole other story. She bothered him. Like hot and bothered him. Like sweaty palms, tongue-tied bothered. She probably thought he was avoiding her, and she'd be right. Because every time she looked up at him with those golden eyes, he saw something other than the bristly, bossy woman. He saw vulnerability. He saw fear. But mostly he saw concern for Piper. Worry for her.

Audrey didn't trust him. He'd figured that out pretty

quickly. To be honest, he hadn't really gone out of his way to prove she could trust him with his own niece. Because he hadn't cared. He'd taken one look at Piper and wanted to turn the other way. But his mother's words kept chipping away at his resolve. And then he'd looked at Audrey and seen the way she looked at Piper, and he'd realized how personal it was for her. Audrey loved Piper, probably like her own daughter. Cameron had yet to understand that sort of love, because he'd always lived for himself.

"Yo," Blake snapped.

Cameron blinked from his kicked-back position on the couch.

"Am I doing this alone?" Blake wanted to know.

"Sorry," Cam muttered.

"You distracted or what?" Blake asked as he paused the game film.

Distracted? Like Blake wouldn't believe.

Blake nodded toward the backyard, where Audrey and Piper were lazing around on the hammock. "How's it going with them?"

Cameron blew out a breath and stacked his hands behind his head. "Shit, I don't know. They've been keeping to themselves, mostly. But the whole thing was sprung on me with no warning."

Blake gazed outside. "She's a cute kid," he observed.

Cameron shook his head. "I don't know what the hell to do with her. She looks up at me with these big green eyes like I'm supposed to make it all better, and it kills me. The kid's been through a lot, and the last thing I want to do is let her down. She's already lost too much."

"Strange that Dianna never told you," Blake commented.

Cameron just shrugged. "Dianna and I were never that

close. She knew the issues I had with our dad, and it affected our relationship."

"But you're going to do it, right?" Blake wanted to know. When Cameron just looked at him, Blake continued. "Let her stay?"

"I have to." It was the first time he'd said the words out loud. Funny enough, a bolt of lightning hadn't incinerated him. "If I turn her away, then I'm just another person who's abandoned her. I can't do that to her."

"Yeah, we all kind of knew you wouldn't," Blake surmised. "You're not that much of a dick."

Cameron's brow arched. "Gee, thanks."

Blake's attention returned outside. "What about the other one?"

Cameron feigned ignorance. After all, it was better than saying, "All I want to do is screw her brains out," which was normally what he would do. Cameron rarely met a woman he'd been able to say no to. So he had a healthy sex life—so what?

The thing was, just being around Audrey made him feel like it was wrong, like he was a dirty bastard who wasn't worthy of her. She was far too good for him, with her open smile, bright eyes, and the unconditional love she had for a child that wasn't even hers. Hell, she probably volunteered at soup kitchens and belonged to a knitting club. Her Saturday nights were most likely spent reading something like *Little Women* while she sipped on a hot cup of tea, maybe soaking in a bubble bath. With candles. All naked and slippery and . . .

Shit!

Even his fantasies were unworthy of her.

He lifted a shoulder. "Fine," he answered.

Blake narrowed his gaze, and Cam knew his friend saw

through his bullshit. "Think you can keep it in your pants around her?"

Cameron's gaze narrowed even more. "You're a shit-head, you know that? Besides, she's not my type."

Blake let out a bark of laughter. "Yeah, she's nice and wholesome. Definitely not for you. How's it going to work with Piper if you end up not staying in Blanco Valley?" Blake questioned.

Shit, he hadn't even thought about that.

"I guess I'd take her with me," Cameron answered.

Blake nodded. "And Audrey's okay with that?"

Audrey didn't even know about Cameron's offer to coach in Denver. "It's not her decision."

Blake gazed back at him. "Don't you think that's something she'd like to know?"

Possibly, but that was the least of Cameron's worries right now. "I don't even know if I'm going to go yet. They gave me until the end of the season to decide."

"Do yourself a favor and give her a heads-up now," Blake suggested. "Don't let that shit blindside you."

Just then, the sliding glass door opened and Audrey let herself through, followed by Piper, who was clinging to Audrey's legs. The kid's inquisitive gaze was locked on Blake as though she didn't know what to make of him. Cameron had already learned that his niece was painfully shy around people she didn't know. And Blake was a giant of a man with extra wide shoulders and a penetrating stare. Of course, Cameron was just as big, but for some reason Piper had an easy time around him.

A set of grocery bags dangled from Audrey's fingers. "We were hungry for an early dinner."

Cameron shoved down the powerful kick of warmth that flooded his system. Her hair was pulled into a messy ponytail, and several fine strands had slipped free and brushed her face when she moved. The slight caressing of hair only emphasized her glowing, makeup-free face and made Cameron want to skim the pad of this thumb along her jawline. He bet her skin was soft. Touchable. He'd never thought of a woman having touchable skin because he was usually too busy worrying about unsnapping her bra.

She took a step forward, and Cameron used a nanosecond to assess her skinny jeans and long-sleeved T-shirt. She looked like she had a perfectly pinched waist that he could get both hands around. A seamless indentation for his palms.

Blake cleared his throat, and Cameron glanced at him in time to catch his friend's eye roll.

"You want to go somewhere?" he asked Audrey.

"No, I was going to cook," she told him.

"Here?" Because, for some reason, having her and Piper in his house was so...personal. Sort of like sealing the deal. Even though he suspected it was already sealed.

Audrey gestured toward the guesthouse. "Unless you'd rather do it over there."

Hell, he'd *do it* anywhere with her.

"Here's fine," he said. Then he shifted his attention at Piper, who was still eyeing Blake. "Did you get some good nap time in on the hammock?" Why couldn't he ever think of anything to say to the kid?

She gave a slight nod, without taking her eyes off Blake.

Cameron looked at Blake, then back at Piper.

Thankfully, Audrey jumped in and saved him. "Piper, do you remember Mr. Carpenter? He coaches the football team with your uncle Cameron."

Uncle Cameron. The words still created a shiver of uncertainty through his system. He'd never been anyone's uncle or anything else to anyone.

Piper nodded again, and Blake lowered himself to the kid's level.

"You can call me Blake," he told Piper. "What's your friend's name?" he asked as he fingered one of Jellybean's ratty, discolored ears.

Piper hugged the stuffed cat closer. "Jellybean," she muttered in a soft voice.

"She keeps you safe, huh?" Blake guessed.

Piper hesitated for a moment, then nodded.

Blake ruffled the kid's hair, which was already a mess of tangled blond waves, then stood as his phone vibrated. He withdrew the device and thumbed the screen. "I've gotta run. Annabelle wants pizza." He leaned toward Audrey. "Be careful with this one," he warned with a pointed look at Cameron. "He's OCD about cooking." Blake's mouth turned up in a wicked grin.

"Piss off," Cameron told his friend.

Audrey placed her hands over Piper's ears. "Child present."

Cameron cleared his throat, not used to having to censor himself. Was *piss* a bad word to say around a six-year-old? "Sorry."

Blake collected the game tape and with a quick "See ya in the morning," he was gone, leaving Cameron alone with two females who'd upended his life and were currently looking at him with mixed expressions.

Cameron gazed down at his niece, wishing he knew what made her tick. He wished like hell he understood her more. What went on in her head? Was she still grieving for her mother? Obviously she was; after all, Dianna had only been gone for about two months. But from what he could tell, Piper had adapted well. Cameron understood loss. He knew how it felt to have everything come crashing down. But this was different. His father had chosen to leave, because he'd been a weak, selfish bastard. Dianna had been taken from Piper, leaving her little girl with no one, except one fiercely protective temporary guardian and a clueless uncle.

He gestured toward the bag Audrey was holding. "What do you have in there?"

Audrey watched him for a moment, as though she didn't fully trust him. Then she lifted the bag and opened it. "Bacon, eggs, and a pancake mix."

"A *mix*?" he questioned. Who the hell made one of the greatest breakfast staples from a damn mix?

Audrey blinked, as though she didn't understand the question. "Yeah. What's wrong with using a mix?"

Cameron snorted and led her toward the kitchen. "It's artificial, that's what's wrong with it. If you're making pancakes in my kitchen, we're doing it from scratch."

Audrey set the grocery bag on the counter. "I have a feeling you're more than OCD about food," she speculated.

"I like my food made a certain way." He jerked his chin toward the bag of food. "None of that artificial stuff." When his father had cut out, his mom had taken two jobs to provide for both of them. She'd worked nights, leaving Cameron on his own and fending for his own dinners. Not that he'd ever resented his mother for how often she'd been gone. Pamela Shaw had busted her ass to provide for her only son, and Cameron loved the hell out of her for that. Because he'd been on his own so many evenings, he'd learned the art of food, how to play around with recipes and to make do with what was in the pantry.

Cameron turned to Piper. "You and Jellybean want to have a seat at the bar? It's the best seat in the kitchen."

Piper nodded, then climbed onto one of the wooden stools. She arranged Jellybean on the stool next to her so the cat could watch too. Cameron turned back to the food in time to see the slight tilt of Audrey's mouth, as though he had her approval.

Which was all fine and stuff, except he didn't need her approval.

Okay, but you totally do.

Whatever. Let Audrey think what she wanted to think.

Cameron rustled around in the pantry and fridge for the necessary pancake ingredients. He'd just set the flour on the counter when he stopped Audrey in the process of placing the bacon in a pan.

"Whoa, what're you doing?"

She blinked at him with a strip of limp bacon hanging from on hand. "Making the bacon?"

Cameron resisted an eye roll. Typical amateur cook. "Bacon doesn't go in the fraying pan. It goes in the oven."

"The oven," she repeated.

Cameron turned the oven to 400 degrees, then took a baking sheet out of the bottom drawer. "It cooks more evenly and doesn't make a huge mess," he told her as he took the strips of bacon out of the frying pan.

"But it tastes better when it cooks in its own grease."

Cam lined the baking sheet with parchment paper. "It'll still cook in the grease, only it won't splatter everywhere."

"Who cooks bacon on parchment paper?" she questioned.

Cameron slanted her a look. "People who know what they're doing."

Audrey narrowed her eyes and folded her arms, which

only enhanced the plumpness of her breasts. The first day they met, he'd gotten a nice view of the goods underneath, cupped nicely in a pink bra. Yeah, she had a nice rack. But when she crossed her arms like that?

Daaaaaamn.

Cameron almost dropped a slice of bacon.

Audrey waved her index finger at him. "I'm not sure about his whole setup."

"Then feel free to take a step back and let me do the cooking."

She shook her head, sending her ponytail sliding over one shoulder. "Nuh-uh. I came over here to cook the dinner, not to let you take over." She yanked a piece of bacon out of his hand. "Give me that."

"Not too close together," he instructed, then backed off when she shot him a withering look over her shoulder.

It was safe to say they were both OCD about how they liked things done. Great makings of a relationship.

Relationship? Had he lost his mind? There was no such thing in the future for them. She was here for Piper; then she'd be gone.

"By the way, I've decided to stay until the end of the football season," she announced, as though reading his mind. "Which has sent my business partner into fits, but it's best for Piper."

He lifted a brow at her as he started tossing pancake ingredients together. "Because you're not sure you trust me yet?"

Audrey finished with the bacon and set the pan aside while the oven continued to preheat. "I don't know, can I?"

"She's my niece," he pointed out.

"I'm aware of that, but..."

Cameron tossed baking powder into the bowl. "But I

didn't make the greatest first impression." Yeah, he was man enough to admit that.

She offered a tight smile. "You were insistent on me taking Piper back to Boulder with me, so...not really."

Okay, he'd give her that.

"Cut me some slack," he told her. "I wasn't exactly prepared for...all this."

Audrey lifted a brow.

Yeah, I mean you too, sweetheart.

The oven dinged, so Audrey slid the pan in and set the timer. "Well, all things considered, I'd say you're not doing too bad."

He smiled despite himself. "Gee, don't be too nice."

"Cut *me* some slack, okay? I'm just trying to protect Piper."

Cameron whisked the ingredients together, then set the bowl aside. "Okay, I'll give you that."

"How magnanimous of you."

Cameron leaned a hip on the counter, deliberately crowding Audrey. She smelled damn good. Like cinnamon and peaches. Last time he was around her she smelled like lemons, but both scents were intoxicating and reminded him of summer. Hot afternoons. Hotter sex.

And he really needed to stop thinking about sex around her.

"Why are you always so suspicious?" he asked her.

Audrey's shoulders went stiff when Cameron entered her personal space, close enough that he could see a faint scar that bisected her chin. But she didn't back up. Not that he expected her to. No, Audrey wasn't the sort of woman to back down from anyone. She'd stand her ground, chin lifted and spine straight, a trait that he admired.

Hell, it turned him on.

"Not suspicious, just...cautious," she answered.

He took a step closer so that his hip rested near hers against the counter. She sucked in a deep breath, which nudged the tips of her breasts against his chest. Cameron knew the second she noticed the contact because her eyes went wide, and her pupils filled her golden irises.

Damn. If such a brief glance could make his pulse elevate like that, what would happen if they really touched?

He cupped her chin and stroked his thumb across her scar. "And why are you so cautious about everything, Audrey?"

He liked the way her name sounded on his lips. Natural and sweet. Kind of like her.

"I've learned from experience that things rarely ever work out the way you plan."

"You sound more jaded than cautious," he pointed out.

Her tongue swiped across her lower lip. "If that's what you'd call it."

"I'm asking what you'd call it."

"I already told you," she murmured.

He wasn't so sure about that. In fact, Cameron would bet all the money in his bank there was a lot she hadn't told him. A lot she no doubt wouldn't want to tell him. And it seemed as though they both had trust issues. Cameron didn't trust people to do what was right, and Audrey...well, he had a feeling that Audrey didn't trust anyone.

Where did that leave them?

More important, where could they go from here?

Audrey's gaze dropped to Cam's mouth as he shifted his thumb to graze along her lower lip. She was soft and full and everything a woman should be, and how was he supposed to keep his distance from her?

It would be a completely shitty thing to sleep with her. She was here for Piper; then she'd return to her life in Boulder. And all Cameron could offer a woman was a good time between the sheets. It was all he wanted to offer a woman, and Audrey didn't strike him as the type who was into recreational sex. Plus, it would make the situation too awkward, and he needed to start thinking about Piper.

Audrey shifted closer, as though she wanted to test the waters. Maybe place her mouth against his? Yeah, he wasn't opposed to trying things out either.

But a faint buzzing interrupted the moment, sort of like having a bucket of ice water dumped over his head.

Audrey jerked back as though she'd been burned and glanced at her phone. "I need to answer this," she muttered; then she hightailed it out of the kitchen as though her ass were on fire.

Cameron glanced at Piper as she girl's gaze followed Audrey out the back door, before placing her wide green eyes back on him.

"How do you like your eggs, Piper?" Cameron asked, because it was better than apologizing for damn near molesting Audrey in the middle of his kitchen.

SEVEN

Audrey closed the sliding glass door with a trembling hand and tried desperately to calm her thudding heart.

Cameron had been about to kiss her. And more horrifying than that realization was the fact that she'd wanted him to. From the second he'd crowded her against the counter, she'd recognized the look in his eyes and the low timbre of his voice.

Worse yet, she'd been turned on as hell, even though she knew this kind of seduction game would never end well.

Luckily she'd been saved by her ringing phone. And like the coward she was, Audrey had run away.

But what had burned her more than anything had been the smirk on Cameron's face. The half tilt of his mouth had only heightened the burning sensation in her cheeks. He'd known exactly what he'd done to her and the fact that she'd wanted it just as much as he did.

But her focus needed to be on Piper, not a hunk of a man who could melt her bones with a simple stroke of his thumb.

Audrey jerked when her phone rang again. Whoever was trying to get hold of her had hung up, then immediately starting calling again. She stole a glance in the house and spotted Piper still on the stool and Cameron pouring pancake batter into a hot pan.

Audrey was about to answer her phone when a flash of blue out of the corner of her eye caught her attention. She recognized the elderly woman in the blue polyester pants and towering beehive from the pancake breakfast, the one Annabelle had told her belonged to some group. What was it she called them?

The Beehive Mafia.

If Audrey didn't know any better, she'd say this lady was spying on Cameron.

Even though Cameron was the last person who needed a protector, Audrey felt like she should put the woman in her place.

"Can I help you?" she asked Lois.

The elderly woman waved a hand in the air, then produced a phone. "Just pretend I'm not here. Trying to catch a shot of the guy, because he's so damn crafty."

"I'm pretty sure it's not legal for you to be snooping around someone's house and taking pictures," Audrey pointed out.

Lois pursed her lips as she tried to see inside the kitchen window. "Oh, Cameron won't turn me in. He tries to pretend he's a bear, but really he's just a big old softie."

"Does Cameron know you sneak around his house with a camera?"

Lois tossed Audrey a look as though she'd lost her mind.

"Well, of course he doesn't. The man would flip his lid if he found out."

Audrey arched a brow at her. "I thought you said he'd never turn you in?"

"And I don't think he would. But that doesn't mean he'd be pleased to find me here. Ever since that debacle with the married woman, the man's been intensely private."

Say what? "Married woman?" Audrey repeated.

Lois slanted her a look as she tried to get a better glimpse inside the kitchen window. "You didn't hear me say anything."

What the hell was that supposed to mean? Had Cameron been involved with a married woman? He didn't strike her as the type, but then again neither had Rick, her boyfriend before Evan, and he'd turned out to be a two-timing douchebag.

But Cameron was different. She'd sensed from the very beginning that he was honorable, even if he was a bit gruff and rough around the edges. Was she wrong about him? What if he turned out to be like every other shallow ass-wipe?

For some reason the very idea made Audrey uncomfortable, even though it shouldn't have bothered her. In two months she'd be gone. But it would matter to Piper, and Piper mattered to Audrey.

"Got one!" Lois exclaimed as she pumped her fist in the air. "Nothing sexier than a man who knows how to cook." She shot Audrey a triumphant grin. "Our followers are going to love this one."

"I really don't think you should be posting pictures of Cameron without his knowledge," Audrey warned her, even though she knew it wouldn't do any good. The woman was in her own world.

Lois only offered a shrug of her frail shoulders. "Oh, he'll have knowledge of it eventually. See ya."

And then she was gone as stealthily as she'd arrived, slipping around the corner of the house.

Audrey blinked after her, warring between Cameron's invaded privacy and the whole married woman thing. She supposed she could just ask him, but something told her he wouldn't confide in her.

She shoved the subject out of her mind, for now anyway, and reentered the house, sure of herself that her pulse had calmed down enough. But as she entered the house, the sight in the kitchen brought her to an abrupt halt.

Cameron was at the stove, and Piper was seated on the counter next to him as she poured pancake batter from a measuring cup.

Her little legs were swinging back and forth and her teeth were digging into her lower lip. She finished pouring and set the measuring cup on the counter.

"I think it's time to stir the eggs," Cameron advised. He handed Piper a spatula. "Remember how I showed you?"

"Yep," Piper answered. She stuck the spatula in the pan full of eggs and whipped the thing around.

"Be sure to scrape the bottom real good. We want them nice and fluffy." As Cameron gave the instructions, he dropped a handful of shredded cheese into the eggs.

Piper giggled. "More cheese," she demanded. "Cheese is my favorite food."

Audrey resisted the urge to remind Piper that she supposedly hated cheese.

Cameron chuckled. "I thought jelly beans were your favorite food?"

Piper swung her legs back and forth harder and thunked against the lower cabinets. "Nope, it's cheese."

And tomorrow it would be hot dogs.

Cameron took the conversation in stride, as though six-year-old speak were an everyday occurrence for him. It had taken Audrey forever to acclimate herself to the way Piper's mind worked. She bounced from one subject to the next, asking nonstop questions and making strange observations. One minute she'd say how she wanted to be a unicorn when she grew up, and the next she'd be yammering on about a puppy she saw on TV.

Cameron didn't break his stride from cooking to scratch his head at Piper's conversation. He'd grunt and nod at the appropriate times. He even laughed and ruffled her hair when she cracked a lame joke that didn't even make sense.

Audrey's ovaries clenched.

She cleared her throat, and they both turned to look at her. One fixed inquisitive green eyes on Audrey and the other raked his blue gaze in slow perusal that had her breasts tingling.

Her body really needed to stop clenching and tingling around him.

"Sorry for leaving you with dinner duty," Audrey said. She held up her phone. "That was my friend Roxy." Whom she now needed to call back.

"Not a problem," Cameron grunted.

"We're makin' eggs," Piper announced. She stuck the spatula back in the egg pan and gave them another stir. Next to the stove was a plate full of pancakes and another filled with bacon slices.

Audrey set her phone on the counter and walked across the kitchen. "Yes, I see all the cheese you dumped in. I'll be sure to have 911 on speed dial in case my arteries clog."

Piper blinked, and Audrey knew she didn't get the

joke. Obviously Cameron didn't either, because he just looked at her.

"You joke now, but wait until you taste them," he told her.

"By the way, there was a woman named Lois in your backyard taking pictures of you."

Cameron didn't stop cooking. "Yeah, she does that."

"You're aware that she sneaks around your house and takes illegal pictures of you?" Audrey questioned. Why wasn't he more outraged?

But he just snorted. "Illegal?"

"Well, yeah." Why was she the only one who had a problem with this? "She puts them on some social media page for people to look at."

Cameron shut the burner off and moved the egg pan to a cooler part of the stove. "Tumblr," he informed her. He shot her a look as he took three plates down from the cabinet. "The Beehive Mafia is harmless."

"She's invading your privacy," she told him.

Piper hopped down from the counter and ran to the stool she'd been sitting on earlier.

Cameron picked up a giant spoon and scooped eggs onto a plate. "Are you going to fight my battles for me, Audrey?"

She crossed her arms over her chest and watched while he stacked a pancake next to the eggs. "Sounds like someone should."

"Be my guest," he told her. "I've been trying to get them to leave me alone for years. They're tenacious as hell." He dropped one slice of bacon on the plate, then delivered the plate to Piper.

The kid swiveled back and forth on her stool, then smiled her thanks.

"You could call the police on her," Audrey suggested.

Cameron snorted again as he grabbed another plate and heaved a heaping spoonful of eggs. "And what? Have her arrested? She's a hundred years old."

He had a point, but still. "Maybe they could get her to leave you alone."

He slanted her a look, and they both knew she was kidding herself.

"All right, fine," she replied with a nonchalant shrug. If he didn't care about having himself posted all over some senior eye-candy page, then it was no skin off her back.

"This is killing you, isn't it?" he questioned.

Audrey watched while he added three slices of bacon to the pancakes and eggs. "What's that?" she asked as she took the plate from him and wondered how she was going to eat all the food he'd given her, even though it smelled delicious, like one of her childhood Sunday mornings.

"Not taking your advice," he finally answered.

"Not even a little," she lied.

He watched without responding while he ate from his own plate, standing at the kitchen counter instead of sitting. Why did he always have to look at her like that? Like he was waiting for her to reveal some ulterior motive? What kind of women had he been with in the past? She got the feeling that he was always waiting for the other shoe to drop.

Immediately, her thoughts went to the comment Lois had made about the married woman. Of course, it was none of her business, but Audrey couldn't help but wonder if Cameron had gotten himself into some nasty situation that had left him jaded about future relationships. Audrey could certainly understand the feeling of once bitten, twice shy.

Even though she was dying to ask, she kept the curiosity to herself.

"What?" he asked.

Audrey crunched into a piece of bacon. "Nothing."

"So you met Lois, huh?" he commented.

"Actually I met her at the pancake breakfast. But Annabelle came to my rescue."

One side of Cameron's mouth quirked. She'd learned really fast that he was good at smiling without really smiling. Although she wasn't sure how he did that, it was sexy as hell. It softened his features and created little shivers in her belly.

"Lois cornered you, did she?"

"She thought I was your baby mama," Audrey commented as she cut into her pancakes.

Cameron shook his head. "Beehive Mafia. It's probably all over town by now."

"I thought you said they're harmless," she pointed out.

"Normally, they are. But usually it's pictures, not speculation over my personal life."

Audrey set her empty plate on the counter. "You don't like that, do you?"

"What?"

"People getting in your business," she guessed.

Cameron pinned her with an unreadable look. "I like my privacy."

"So I've been told."

Cameron set his plate on the counter next to hers and put his hands on his lean hips. "You say it like it's a bad thing."

Audrey only shrugged. "Just making an observation."

Again, he just watched her. Audrey didn't like people getting too close either. People were unreliable. From her mother disappearing when Audrey was eight, her estrangement from her brother, and the men who'd come and gone, Audrey learned it was better to keep herself at a distance from people. If she stayed isolated, she couldn't be hurt anymore. Even Dianna's death had left her hollow.

"Why are you always looking at me like that?" she blurted out.

"How would you like me to look at you?" he countered.

Don't answer that. It's a trap.

She opened her mouth to form some really witty reply, because that was the only way to keep this man at a distance, when Piper saved her.

"Can I have more eggs?" she pipped.

Cameron gazed at Audrey for a moment longer. Then she breathed a sigh of relief when he redirected his attention to the six-year-old bouncing on her stool. This was why she carefully thought everything through. Blurting things out like that always got her into trouble, but she had to remember that Cameron was different. He saw her differently than everyone else. She hadn't been around him enough to identify what exactly that was. But it was definitely a threat, a threat to the isolation she'd built between herself and the world.

"Here you go, kiddo," Cameron said as he dumped another spoonful of eggs on Piper's plate.

"By the way," Audrey announced as she pulled a folded piece of paper from her pocket, "I have a list of school supplies Piper needs." She handed him the paper, but Cameron just set the thing down on the counter.

"If you leave that there, you'll forget about it."

He gave her a look like she'd lost her mind. "No, I won't."

She didn't believe him. So far, she'd been the only one to make an effort to get Piper into school. "Better to put it in your pants pocket."

"My pockets have giant holes in them. It'll just fall out."

Audrey's gaze dropped to his pants, as though she could see the holes through the material. But all that did was draw attention to his thighs and how, even through the loose cotton, she could tell how big they were. Strong. An image of those powerful thighs pinning her to a mattress sent a shiver down her spine.

"Why are you always looking at me like that, Audrey?" he questioned.

Yeah, touché and all that. He had her on that one.

"Good one," she answered with a tight smile. She picked the paper off the counter and folded it back up. "Just take it."

When he only stared at it, she shoved it against his chest. Colossally big mistake. The tips of her fingers got an instant impression of carved muscle, of grooves and dips that outlined what had to be seriously fantastic pecs. She'd always been a sucker for a man's chest perfectly sculpted for a woman to trail her fingers over. And judging by what she'd felt just now, Cameron had one in spades.

"You should really stop doing that, Audrey," he warned in a low voice.

Yeah, she knew, but she had to ask anyway. "Doing what?"

He wrapped his warm palm around hers, which trapped her against his chest. He was warm and solid and so undeniably male that Audrey almost whimpered. Why did it have to feel so good to be pressed against him? Why couldn't he smell like he hadn't showered in a week, instead of being all spicy and woodsy and stuff?

"Looking at me like you're trying to picture me naked," he murmured against her ear.

This time she actually whimpered.

"All you have to do is say the word."

She shifted her eyes to his and found them dark and smoky. Intent. On her and her only.

"What word?" she asked like the idiot she was.

He inhaled deeply and pressed his mouth harder against her ear. "Yes," he whispered.

If only it were that easy. If only she could toss all her structure and self-imposed rules to the wind and just go for it already. Couldn't he tell how hard it was for her? He seemed to be able to read her so easily, to see through everything she said. How could he not see how it was killing her not to drape herself all over him?

Just when she was about to give in and utter the single-syllable word that would destroy her, Audrey pulled away. She shoved the paper harder against him.

"Just take the damn list." With a good yank, she was free and striding across the room, away from him and everything he represented. "And fix your pants."

EIGHT

Audrey took Piper to the Bobcats' next home game. Luckily, Annabelle and Stella had saved a seat for her, because the stands were packed. She'd shared a brief introduction with Stella's hunk of a husband, Brandon, while carrying Jellybean under one arm and holding on to Piper with the other hand.

The child had been particularly cantankerous all day. First, she'd thrown a fit when Audrey hadn't let her have popcorn for breakfast. They'd compromised on s'mores Pop-Tarts, and she gave Piper a bowl of popcorn an hour after breakfast. But at least she'd had breakfast first, so whatever.

Then Piper had folded her arms and pouted when Audrey had mentioned taking her school shopping for clothes and supplies.

"I hate school!" Piper had screamed as she'd run into her room and thrown herself on her bed.

Audrey hadn't bothered to point out that Piper hadn't even been to school before, so how would she know? Dianna had opted not to send Piper to preschool because she'd been on the downhill slide of her cancer battle and wanted to spend as much time with her daughter as she could.

Two hours later, she'd finally gotten Piper out the door, but only because Audrey had told the kid that Jellybean wanted to look at new toys.

When in doubt, use the stuffed cat. Worked every time.

She seemed to calm down after that. But it had been short-lived, when Audrey had mentioned the football game. Piper had shut herself in Audrey's bedroom and refused to go, and hadn't opened the door until Audrey had promised ice cream on the way home. Every mom in America would probably smack her wrist for using bribery, but it had worked, so win for her.

So here they were, both tired and cranky and wanting to go home. But she was here for Cameron and Piper and furthering their bond, and all that sappy shit. Yeah, she was in a bad mood, but not all of it was because of her day with Piper.

No, most of it was last Sunday's encounter with Cameron in his kitchen. He'd gotten to her. Again. And she'd allowed him.

Yes.

He'd whispered it into her ear with such passion. Such conviction. For a flicker of a second, she'd contemplated saying yes in return and allowing him to whisk her away and do delicious things to her body. Of course, it would have been a mistake. She'd known that even as she'd stood in the cradle of his thighs while he'd skimmed his lips over her ear and inhaled the scent of her shampoo.

The man was good. He'd had her whimpering and reduced to a puddle of mush without her even realizing what had happened. That made him dangerous. Then again, she'd known that about him since clapping eyes on his blue gaze shaded by a low baseball cap.

The game moved on to the fourth quarter, and Piper started griping about how bored and tired she was. Normally Audrey wasn't a huge fan of giving a kid an electronic device for entertainment, but she decided to make an exception. She passed her cell phone over, and Piper pulled up a coloring app.

"How's she adjusting?" Stella asked.

Audrey ran a hand over Piper's downy soft hair, trying to remind herself how little she still was. It was easy to get caught up in the everyday activities of settling into Cameron's guesthouse and worrying about Piper starting school that sometimes Audrey forgot to cut Piper more slack. She was such a sweet girl who'd taken everything in stride. Sometimes Audrey would catch a flash of grief in the little girl's eyes and it would take all of Audrey's strength to hold herself together.

"Today's been tough, but overall she's been an angel," she answered Stella.

Annabelle spun around on the bleacher. "Cameron's never really talked about his sister before."

Audrey shrugged and tried to follow the action on the field. "They weren't very close. She was a lot younger than him."

"His dad taking off probably had a lot to do with that," Brandon commented.

"To be honest, Dianna was pretty tight-lipped about it," she told them. "She was really close with her mom, but she and her dad . . ." Audrey shook her head. "I don't know, they had a complicated relationship. Her dad wasn't your typical affectionate, hands-on type. And then when she found out she had an older brother, it changed their relationship."

"She didn't find out about Cameron until later?" Annabelle wanted to know.

"No, she always knew about him. From what she told me, he'd come to visit once every few months when she was little. But by the time she was eight or nine, he stopped coming around." Audrey glanced at Piper to make sure she wasn't paying attention to the conversation. "She told me she thought Cameron was a distant relative or maybe just a family friend. Her dad didn't let the cat out of the bag until she was a teenager."

"Guy was a selfish asshole," Brandon commented.

Stella ignored her husband's comment. "So you and Dianna were friends, but you never met Cameron?"

"I didn't meet Dianna until high school, and by then Cameron had been out of the picture for years. All I knew was that she had an older half brother who lived hours away." She shifted a look from Stella to Annabelle. "She never talked about him."

"That had to have been really hard for her," Annabelle commented.

Audrey pondered Annabelle's words for a moment. "I think she felt like she'd been cheated. I mean, she had this whole other family that her dad had kept from her. She and Cameron could have been really close if the situation had been handled better. But instead she died never really knowing him. He wasn't even at her funeral."

"That's not Cameron's fault," Stella pointed out.

"Oh, I know," she agreed. Then she blew out a weary breath. "Actually, at first, I did sort of blame him. I kept thinking, 'What sort of brother doesn't come to his own sister's funeral?' I hated him on principle because I'd see Piper crying herself to sleep with no other family to comfort her. All I could think was how unfair it was." Audrey wrung her hands together, trying not to go back to that dark time. "But then the fog of grief lifted, and I realized that it was probably just as hard on him as it was on her."

Annabelle placed a comforting hand on her knee. "Piper's really lucky to have you."

"What about Piper's dad?" Stella wanted to know.

Around them, the crowed went crazy as the Bobcats scored a touchdown, bringing them ahead of the other team. Audrey clapped on cue, but didn't stand with the rest of the fans. "He took off when he found out Dianna was pregnant. He's never expressed any interest in Piper."

"What about Cameron's dad?" Annabelle questioned. "Is he still around?"

"Yeah, but his health is really bad. He's on oxygen and lives on state assistance. And Dianna's mom died a few years ago, so Cameron's really the only family Piper has."

"That's not true," Stella said as she nudged Audrey's thigh. "She has you."

Piper would always have Audrey no matter how far apart they were, but her heart still squeezed at the thought of leaving. She loved Piper and wanted what was best for her. She didn't want to think about going to bed without reading a bedtime story first or getting five drinks of water. Or checking in the closet for monsters. Or leaving the hall light on.

"I think you've been good for her," Stella added. "Just look how well she's adjusting."

Audrey exhaled. "The real test will be after I leave. I feel like I need to leave Cameron an instruction manual."

Annabelle chuckled alongside Stella. "Don't let his brooding nature and animal grunts fool you. Cameron's smart, and he's a good guy. I think he's probably catching on faster than you realize."

Cameron was good with Piper, despite Audrey's doubts when she first arrived. He got down to her level and talked to her, instead of talking around her. He didn't constantly ask if she was okay, like most people had after Dianna had died. Getting back to a normal routine and not having people tiptoe around her had been good for Piper. Cameron got that. Audrey had a feeling a lot of that had to do with his dad leaving. He identified with Piper's grief and confusion, and part of Audrey kind of loved him for that.

"He kept trying to get me to take Piper back to Boulder with me," Audrey admitted.

"Not surprising," Stella agreed. "But that was because he was scared. Once you have Cameron's loyalty, you have it for life. He won't let Piper down now."

"Even if he does end up moving," Brandon cut in.

Audrey's head jerked toward the big man who'd just been elbowed by his wife. "I'm sorry?" she demanded. "Moving?"

Stella opened her mouth to cut off Brandon, but he beat her to it. "I wouldn't worry about it. Even if he does leave, he'll take Piper with him."

"Do you have a death wish?" Stella hissed at her husband. She turned to Audrey and placed a soothing hand on her arm. "I'm sure Cameron's not going anywhere. He loves Blanco Valley too much."

"But he's thinking about it," she concluded as she tossed a desperate look between Stella and Annabelle.

Stella only stared straight ahead, as though she was suddenly interested in the field action. Annabelle opened her mouth, then shook her head as she shut it again.

"I've spent the entire day with a cranky six-year-old," Audrey asserted. "If someone doesn't start leveling with me right now..."

Annabelle turned all the way around. "I'm sure it's nothing."

Audrey waited for her to continue. "But?" she prompted.

"But..." Stella began. "I think maybe Cameron was toying with the idea of relocating. But I'm sure he's changed his mind now that he has Piper," the woman concluded in a rush when she got the look of panic on Audrey's face.

Of course, Audrey didn't have a say in it. But Piper had been uprooted too much, had been through too much to move again. Another new neighborhood. Different friends. Different school. The girl needed some continuity in her life. But what could she do? Demand Cameron stay put forever?

And maybe it wasn't even true. Annabelle and Stella seemed unsure, and Cameron would have said something if he had plans to move. Wouldn't he?

"In all honesty?" Annabelle went on. She must have taken Audrey's silence as distress. "I don't think Cameron has confirmed anything. And I think it was more him just exploring some options rather than making plans. If you're that worried about it, you should ask him."

But would he give her a straight answer? He was mysterious and secretive to a fault, and he'd have to know that Audrey wouldn't take well to him moving Piper again.

Why did this whole thing have to be so exhausting? Every time she thought she had Cameron Shaw figured out, he threw her a curve ball.

Cameron stood at his back door and watched as Audrey sipped wine straight from a bottle. She was perched on the top step of the guesthouse, with the light of the full moon shining down on her loose blond hair and highlighting her cheekbones. She really was beautiful. Cameron was used to being with beautiful women, and yet Audrey was different. Something in the way she held herself, and the wary way she watched everyone around her, as though waiting for the bottom to fall out.

He knew that feeling all too well. But everything else about Audrey was a total mystery to him. What bothered him even more was his desire to figure her out. She wasn't going to be in his life very long, so why should he care? Why did he want to know the story behind the shadows in her eyes? Who had wronged her? And why did he want to beat the shit out of them?

Audrey lifted the bottle of wine to her lips. Cameron tightened his grip on the sweatpants dangling from his hand.

When he'd returned home from the football game, which they'd won, he'd found his sweats folded in a neat pile on the kitchen counter. On top of them was a yellow Post-it with Audrey's neat handwriting informing him she'd mended them. As he'd stared down at her note, something had shifted inside his chest: an unfamiliar tightening around his heart that he didn't recognize. They were just sweatpants, for chrissake. But for some reason, it felt like more.

A peace offering?

That had been his first thought. His second thought had been why the hell the gesture meant so much to him. So she'd mended his pants. So what? His mother used to mend his clothes all the time, and he'd never had the wind knocked out of him.

He should go out there and thank her.

Except ever since that night in his kitchen, when they'd almost kissed, he'd tried to keep a respectful distance, to give her the space she seemed to need around him. He'd needed the space too, because inappropriate thoughts were always crowding his mind. Like how it would feel to shove her against the wall and explore her mouth with his tongue. Or maybe tunnel his hands in that silky hair, to feel the cool strands sifting around his fingers. She'd be soft and curvy where women were supposed to be soft and curvy. The polar opposite to his hardness and scuffed hands and scabbed knees.

His phone vibrated, and Cameron withdrew it from his pants pocket.

I'm back in town. Want to hook up this weekend?
Tessa.

Normally he'd text back for her to stop by whenever, because why not? He was single, she was single, so why not indulge? But as he shot a quick glance at Audrey, something stopped him. His thumb hovered over the keypad as multiple responses tumbled around his mind. Finally, he answered without giving himself too much time to ponder it.

This weekend isn't good. I'll call you later.

With that, he tucked his phone away and opened the sliding glass door. Audrey's head jerked up at the sound, tracking his movements as he set the sweatpants down on a porch chair and crossed the yard.

"Have room for one more?" he asked.

She blinked at him, then scooted over. He sat, ignoring the groaning of the wood beneath his weight.

"I see you got your pants," she observed.

He grinned at her. "Yeah. Maybe I should hire you to mend the rest of my clothes."

Her brows knitted together. "Are all your clothes in that sorry of shape?"

Great. Now he sounded like a bum. "No. I just don't shop that much."

She slanted him a look as she lifted the bottle of wine to her lips. "Somehow that doesn't surprise me." He watched her throat work, thinking how he'd like to place his lips there. She lowered the bottle and offered it to him. "Want some?"

He gazed at the opening of the bottle and thought, *Yeah, her mouth was just on that.* Then he thought, *What the hell? Close enough.*

Her brows lifted when he pulled a sip. "What?" he asked after lowering the bottle.

"I just wouldn't have pegged you for a wine drinker."

"I'm not." He handed the wine back to her

"But you'll make an exception for me, right?"

His mouth twisted. "Actually, I was thinking free booze."

She shook her head at him. "I should have known you'd be that simple." They passed the wine back and forth in silence, until Audrey cleared her throat. "Congratulations on your win," she told him. "So what's your goal? To win a big playoff game or something?"

A playoff game? Cameron slanted her a look. "The state championship," he corrected. "And yeah, we'd be pretty happy with that."

"No need to be sarcastic," she chastised. "I know as much about football as you probably do about home staging."

"Home staging?" He couldn't even make a guess at what that was.

Audrey took another swig of the bottle and handed it to him, while taking the opportunity to explain her business.

"And you make a living doing this?"

She chuckled as though he'd underestimated her. "We do okay."

"It's not an easy thing to run your own business," he pointed out. "Your parents must be proud."

Something dark flashed across her eyes as though he'd touched a nerve. "It's just me and my dad, and we..." She paused as though searching for the right words. "We have an odd relationship."

He waited, giving her an opportunity to explain if she felt comfortable.

"My mom disappeared when I was eight, and ever since then my dad has spent most of his time in his dental practice. I don't see him that much."

"What do you mean, disappeared?" Cameron wanted to know. "Did she leave?"

Audrey shook her head. "No, my mother never would have left us. My brother and I were her world. She went missing during a camping trip she and my dad were on." She gazed out over the moonlit lawn. "Every year, my parents would go camping in the Rockies for their anniversary. Like, seriously roughing it. Nothing but a tent, some sleeping bags, and food. My dad said he woke up one morning and my mom was gone. She'd taken her backpack, rolled up her sleeping bag, and gone for a hike." She glanced out of eyes full of grief. "At least that's what my dad told the police."

His gaze dropped to her mouth. Dammit, he should not be thinking about kissing her while she was confiding in him. "You don't believe him?"

She opened her mouth, then let out a humorless laugh. "I honestly don't know. I mean, my dad would never have hurt my mom, but there were things about that morning that didn't make sense. Like, she'd left her compass and her cell phone. And she never would have just up and gone hiking that early in the morning without my dad and leave her compass behind. That was totally out of character for her."

"You said your dad threw himself into his work. He was never arrested for anything?"

"No, the police had almost no evidence to go on. There were no signs of violence, no trace of her body, no witnesses, no nothing. Plus my dad had no reason to want my mom dead. They weren't going through a divorce, there was no life insurance, and my dad makes six figures a year, so there was no financial motive." Audrey pulled in a deep breath. "It's like she just got up one morning, walked away, and vanished." She turned to gaze at him. "How does that happen?"

Unable to help himself, Cameron tucked a strand of hair behind her ear. "I don't know. Maybe she really did go on a hike, somehow fell and hurt herself, then succumbed to the elements."

Audrey's brows twitched as though picturing the scenario, and Cameron wanted to kick his own insensitive ass.

"My mom was a skilled hiker. She never would have gone without her phone and compass. The lead detective once told me he'd never had a case keep him up at night like my mom's."

"They never solved it?"

She shook her head and spun the wine bottle around in between her legs. "No, it's still an active investigation. They think…"

He waited for her to continue, but she only bit her lip. "What?"

She exhaled a shuddering breath. "They think she left and started a new life somewhere."

"But you don't believe that," he guessed. Hell, he wouldn't have believed it either. Not all parents were worthless asswipes like his old man.

"No way," she said with conviction. "Setting myself aside, she and my brother had a really special relationship. She never would have abandoned him. Especially since he and my dad didn't get along. My mom was the only reason they tolerated each other."

"Your brother has a different dad," he guessed again.

Audrey nodded. "Yeah, he's eleven years older than me. He's my mom's son from a previous marriage. But after my mom went missing, his relationship with my dad completely unraveled. He told every news station and reporter within a fifty-mile radius that my dad murdered our mom and buried her body in the mountains somewhere. And when I didn't take his side, our relationship fell apart."

Damn, and he'd thought his childhood had been messed up.

Audrey's gaze lowered to the wine bottle. She lifted it to her lips, but Cameron couldn't help but notice how the bottle trembled in her hand. She chugged deeply, closing her eyes as though trying to get some relief or maybe rid herself of nasty childhood memories that had put shadows in her eyes.

Cameron reached out and took the bottle from her. "Easy. You'll make yourself sick."

Her tongue swiped across her lower lip and damn if he didn't want to wipe it clean himself. But how much of an asshole would that make him?

"I'm sorry for making you talk about it," he confessed.

She moved her shoulders, but they only rubbed against him again. "It's okay. I mean it's not *okay* okay. It is what it is." A nervous laugh popped out. "What I'm trying to say is, it's not your fault. Most people are careful never to mention it."

Yeah, Cameron got that. "What was your mom like?"

For the first time since he'd stepped outside, she smiled. "My mom was the most amazing woman. She was tall with long blond hair, but she was the most dedicated mom. She spent all her free time either volunteering at school or with me and my brother. She loved family vacations, and we always had family movie nights every Sunday. She'd make us a bowl of popcorn; then we'd share a blanket and watch whatever my brother and I wanted to watch."

Something inside Cameron's chest grew tight when Audrey talked about her mom. Her voice was soft and wistful, but absent of grief. She was speaking like a child who had an unadulterated and pure love for someone who'd been taken too soon.

"You're right," he said. "Doesn't sound like she would have left you."

They were both silent a moment, finishing off the bottle of wine and watching the changing shadows over the yard as the moon slowly moved higher in the sky.

"Piper likes you," Audrey said in a quiet voice.

Cameron glanced at her, trying to read between the lines, determine whether she might be setting him up to stumble over his own words. Was she fishing for something? "She's a good kid."

Audrey nodded her agreement. "Dianna did a wonderful job with her."

Okay, now she was definitely fishing. If she wanted to know about his relationship with his sister, why didn't she just ask?

"Don't break her heart," Audrey warned.

What kind of asshole did she think he was? Okay, so he

hadn't made the best first impression. Telling her to take Piper back to Boulder probably hadn't gone very far to instill much confidence.

"Do you always assume the worst in people?" he countered instead of responding to her warning.

"Yeah, it's kind of my default nature," she admitted. "Sorry," she added. "I didn't mean to imply you'd mistreat her or anything. It's just that she's been through a lot, and she can't take any more letdowns."

"And you think I'll let her down?" While he understood her reasons for being cautious and protective of Piper, Cameron still couldn't help but feel...annoyed? Which was strange, because Audrey's opinion of him shouldn't matter.

"I think you like your life the way it is," she pointed out. "And I think you've made plans that may or may not include her."

What the hell was she talking about? Cameron shook his head. "Audrey, you're going to have to be a little clearer. I don't understand subtlety."

She watched him carefully, and Cameron just knew she had more on her mind than she was saying. For some reason she held herself back.

"All right, look," he went on. "I'm doing the best I can here. You're going to have to understand that this whole thing is new to me. But I'm trying."

"I understand that," she replied after a moment.

"Do you?" he questioned.

She drew back as though he'd insulted her. "Of course. I just..." She twisted her hands around and blew out a breath. "I want her to feel like she's number one."

"She will," he assured her. "But it might take me a while to get there."

"Even if you end up moving?"

Huh? "What're you talking about?"

She did that careful watching again, as though waiting for him to confess something. Had she found something out about his offer to coach in Denver? But she couldn't have. Not unless Blake or Brandon had opened their big mouths.

"So you don't plan on going anywhere?" Audrey pressed.

He couldn't help but laugh. "Not right now."

"I'm being serious."

He blew out an exhausted sigh. "Audrey, if there's something you want to know, why don't you ask me?"

"I don't want Piper uprooted again," she said in a rush.

"I understand that would be a concern to you, but that's not really your call anymore."

She gripped his forearm with a fierceness that had his brows rising. "She can't handle any more change."

Cameron glanced down at her fingers and tried not to focus on the gold-painted nails. "I don't think you give Piper enough credit. She'll adjust no matter what."

The grip on his arm tightened. "Promise me you won't move her again."

"Audrey—"

"Promise me," she urged.

He stared back at her, noting the plea in her eyes that not only spoke of her love for Piper but also felt like a hand squeezing his heart. Despite that, he wasn't sure how to respond to her request.

Demand is more like it.

"I can't," he finally said.

Her brows twitched as though she were trying to keep from crumbling. He knew that wasn't what she wanted to hear, but what did she expect him to say?

She averted her face, turning it up toward the moon. He thought he heard her release a shuddering breath, but it was so minimal that he couldn't be sure. She wasn't crying, was she?

"Audrey," he said. He tried craning to see her face, but she kept her attention on something far away.

"Giorgio Armani, Gloria Vanderbilt," she recited.

Shit, she was doing that thing again. Piper had told him she said people's names when she was upset. How was he supposed to get her to stop? Would she sit there and keep talking to herself if he left her alone?

He touched her bare arm. "Audrey?"

"Hattie Carnegie," she whispered.

Maybe he was making it worse.

He gripped her chin between his thumb and index finger and slowly turned her face to his. "Audrey," he whispered. "I'm going to need you to stop doing that. Because it's kind of freaking me out."

Her eyes dropped closed. "Hedi Slimane."

Before she could utter another clothing designer, even though he'd only heard of one of them, Cameron leaned forward and pressed his lips to hers.

And yeah, that did the trick. Not only did it shut her up, which had been his only intention, but it also solidified what he'd suspected the whole time. Her lips were soft and yielding and warm enough to set off sparks. The sparks may have only been in his head, but *damn*. The split-second decision to kiss her, and yeah, okay, probably not his smartest move, had been only to calm her down, to take her mind off the weird conversation they'd been having and the fact that he'd somehow managed to upset her.

But then she softened and sighed against him, and suddenly his original purpose had gone up in smoke. Now it was about the contact, the warmth suffused by the touch of her lips and the hand curling around his shoulder. She was even more responsive than he expected her to be, leaning into him and probing his mouth with a searching touch of her tongue.

He answered back, because it was too good and hot, and her grip on him tightened. And yeah, she didn't want him to pull back either. She leaned closer to him and moved her hand from his shoulder to the back of his neck. Cameron couldn't be sure, but he didn't think a woman had ever dove her fingers into his hair like that. Usually they were trying to unbutton his shirt or shove their hands down his pants.

He liked that she kissed with everything she had and the little noise she made. He liked how her breath caught when his hand found a sliver of flesh beneath her shirt, as though the contact was new and unexpected. The woman was a breath of fresh air, even if she did drive him crazy sometimes.

Then she yanked herself away and pressed a hand to her mouth.

"Jesus, Joseph, and Isaac Mizrahi."

Yeah, ditto to whoever that last guy was. "You're supposed to stop doing that."

She refocused her dilated gaze on his. "Was that why you kissed me? To calm me down?"

The lady didn't miss much, did she? "At first," he admitted.

Her tongue darted out and swiped across her lower lip, which was still swollen and moist. Damn if he didn't want to kiss her again. "And then?" she prompted.

"And then..." He blew out a breath and leaned his elbows on his knees. "I don't know."

"Well," she sighed, and rubbed her hands down her thighs. "I guess I should thank you."

He cast a glance at her over his shoulder. "No need to thank me."

She stood from the step and looked down at him. "Isn't there, though? You sensed I was on the verge of losing it, so you found the perfect solution."

Slowly, he pushed to his feet so she had to tilt her face up to his. Yeah, he liked that better than her looking down on him. "I think we both know there was more to the kiss than that."

"Really?" she countered with half a smile. "And what else was there?"

Shit, did she want him to compose a sonnet? He was a guy, and guys usually didn't put that much thought into kissing a woman. Their thoughts usually went from "This is hot as shit" to "What do I need to do to get her clothes off?"

When he didn't answer right away, Audrey lowered her gaze and pursed her lips.

"Good night, Cameron." She opened the door to the guesthouse, the screen door creaking in the quiet night and sounding like a cannon firing his execution. "By the way, the wine was yours."

And just like that, he'd gone from his libido firing off like a rocket to wondering what he'd epically screwed up.

NINE

Audrey woke from a dreamless sleep with a startling jerk, immediately sensing something was off with her surroundings. The early Sunday morning sunshine poured through the open drapes that she'd forgotten to close last night. But it wasn't the shocking brightness that threw her off.

The place was too quiet.

The bedside clock read nine fifteen and Audrey's first thought besides why the hell she hadn't closed the drapes last night was Piper. The kid was always out of bed by seven thirty or eight, with the boundless energy of kids, ready to tackle the day. She'd slide out of bed, then curl up onto the couch to watch whatever cartoons she could find, while she waited for Audrey to get up and make some breakfast.

But Piper wasn't in the guesthouse. Even as Audrey tossed the covers back and jerkily pulled on a pair of flannel pants, she knew the kid was gone. There were no sounds indicating she was anywhere. No singsong sounds of cartoons filling the small space. No sounds of rummaging in the fridge because she was too hungry to wait for Audrey to get up. Not even the noise of her talking to herself as she played some make-believe game in her room across the hall.

No, no, no. A layer of sweat coated Audrey's hands as she frantically searched her mind for where the kid could have gone. Without bothering with shoes or her hair, she darted from Piper's bedroom to the small living space, calling the girl's name.

Nothing.

Not even a giggle.

Her heart pounded erratically in her throat, threatening to choke the life out of her as Audrey imagined every ungodly, horrifying scenario. What if someone had come in here in the middle of the night and snatched Piper right out of her bed? What if Piper had decided to go exploring and wandered off somewhere? Gotten lost? Maybe she was roaming the neighborhood right now, lost, confused, crying?

Even as Audrey knew she was being a tad irrational with her runaway imagination, she'd still never forgive herself if something happened to Dianna's little girl, especially after Audrey had promised to love and take care of Piper as if the child were her own.

And she had. Until this morning.

Until you lost her!

Audrey's bare feet scuffed over the worn carpet in the living room. The front door was open, leaving the screen door to reveal the bright early morning.

There!

She'd gone outside.

Audrey exhaled a shaky breath as she damn near kicked open the screen door and yelled the child's name.

"Piper!"

She was only greeted with silence and the occasional neighborhood sound. A car driving by. A lawn mower in the distance. A couple of dogs barking in unison.

But no six-year-old.

Out of the corner of her eye, she spotted Cameron's dark, shaggy head through the window as he moved around the kitchen. Maybe he'd seen her or heard something. Of course, if he had seen Piper wandering around this morning and hadn't said anything to her, Audrey would kick his cement-hard ass into the next century.

Without thinking about manners or even announcing herself, Audrey opened the sliding glass door with too much force. She barreled into the house, bare feet and all.

"Piper!" she yelled.

Cameron spun around, obviously startled at her appearance. "Whoa, what's with the yelling?"

Audrey didn't have time for his stupid questions. "Have you seen Piper? I can't find her anywhere." And she could only imagine the sight that she made, with her wide eyes, ratty old white tank top, and too big flannel pants.

Cameron stepped aside and revealed the kid perched on the kitchen counter. "Yeah, she's right here."

The breath whooshed out of her lungs at the same time that tears stung the back of her eyes. Dammit, she was way too emotional over this girl. The split-second realization that something really bad could have happened to Piper had Audrey ready to do some serious bodily harm to someone. Including Cameron.

Audrey practically ran into the kitchen.

"We're makin' French toast," Piper announced as her legs swung back and forth.

Audrey would never forgive herself if anything were to happen to Piper. She gripped the girl's arms. "Do you know how freaked out I was when I woke up and you were gone?"

Piper's smile fell as she sensed Audrey's displeasure. "Sorry," she muttered, even though Audrey knew she didn't fully understand.

"The next time you leave the guesthouse, you have to let me know," Audrey added.

Piper's eyes grew wide. "I was hungry, and you were still asleep."

"So then wake me up."

Piper stared at her, then nodded. "'Kay."

Audrey yanked the girl into a crushing hug, telling herself Piper really was fine and in one piece, but her heart was still hammering in her chest.

"Okay," Cameron said in a soothing voice. "You're crushing the kid."

Audrey allowed Cameron to draw her back, drawing on the strength of his warm palms curled over her shoulders. But the tears that had been threatening for the past ten minutes, which now felt like an hour, broke through the surface. She spun around, only to save face, and tried to pull herself together.

"Hey." Cameron's rough palm wrapped around her upper arm.

Audrey swiped at her eyes. "I thought she was gone." And how embarrassing was this? She lost sight of Piper for all of ten minutes, and she was reduced to a sputtering mess.

"But she's not," Cameron reassured her. "She was with me, and she's fine."

Audrey shook her head. "You don't understand. I promised Dianna."

Cameron turned her around and looked in her eyes. "You're being too hard on yourself. Look at her." He turned her toward Piper to see the kid dipping her index finger in the egg mixture. "She's fine. She's a normal six-year-old who's contaminating my egg mixture with her dirty hands."

Despite the situation, a laugh popped out of her. Then she sobered and shook her head. "You don't know what it's like to have someone just disappear from your life." As soon as the words were out of her mouth, Audrey realized she was talking as much about her mom as she was Piper. She also realized her mistake when Cameron's unusually soft expression hardened. "Okay, yeah, you do. Dumb thing to say."

One of his brows lifted. "You're forgiven." His hands rubbed up and down her arms in a hypnotic rhythm that had her heart finally slowing down. "You okay now?"

Audrey gave a small nod, silently battling with the lingering effects of fear, mingling with mild embarrassment for her mini freak-out.

Okay, not so mini. She'd all but barged in here with her crazy morning hair and bloodshot eyes from being up too late.

At the thought of her late night, Audrey slowly took notice of the man in front of her. After all, he'd been the reason for her late-night escapade. Since she refused think about, like an all-out memory block, the kiss that had curled her toes, Audrey was left with him, in the flesh.

Literally.

As in low-slung sweatpants, and the smooth, bronzed skin and taut muscle of his bare chest. Audrey secretly congratulated herself for being dead-on accurate about

Cameron Shaw. As though any man had a right to have such carved lines and a freakin' eight-pack that could put an Olympic athlete to shame. And God, he smelled good. Like freshly showered man.

Seriously unfair.

One side of his mouth quirked, as though to say, *Yeah, I see you lookin', honey*.

"You hungry?" he asked instead of acknowledging the drool coming out of her mouth.

"Um..." She crossed her arms in front of her, suddenly reprimanding herself for not bothering with a bra. So far he'd been a gentleman, keeping his eyes above her chin, which was more than she could say for herself.

Her eyes, which didn't seem to be functioning properly, dropped down again, taking special note of his flat brown nipples.

Cameron's finger touched her chin and nudged her face up. "How about we keep our eyes up here?"

"Easy for you to say," she muttered. At least she had a shirt on.

"Is it?" he countered.

She gave serious thought to smacking him. But that would mean putting her hands on him again, which she was so *not* doing.

"Yeah, I guess I could eat."

"Don't do me any favors," he chided.

Actually, breakfast smelled damn good, like the meals her mother used to make. She'd already learned that Cameron was a good cook. Audrey liked having her own way in the kitchen, and Cameron clearly did too, which had led to some disagreements about food.

Who would've thought two people would argue about how food was supposed to be prepared.

Piper picked up a slice of bread and dropped it in the egg mixture. "Cameron let me crack the eggs," she announced. "But I got shells in them. And when I took them out, my hands were all sticky with egg."

"Let me see." Audrey studied Piper's hands and pretended to be appalled. "Oh, these are disgusting!"

Piper giggled, making her green eyes light up. "No, they're not! I cleaned them," she exclaimed.

Beside her, Cameron chuckled, and the sound did something funny to her insides, like they went all mushy and soft.

Piper picked up Jellybean, who had been sitting on the counter next to her. "Jellybean wants powdered sugar on her French toast. Powdered sugar is her favorite."

Cameron shot a quizzical look at Piper as he removed two slices of browned bread from the pan. "I thought jelly beans were her favorite."

Piper swung her legs back and forth. "Only for lunch and dinner. For breakfast powdered sugar is her favorite."

Yeah, okay. They both knew the stuffed cat was as particular about her food as Piper was. But Cameron didn't argue. He snagged a bag of the white stuff from the pantry and set it on the counter next to Piper. "Powdered sugar it is."

"But don't stick your hand in there," Audrey warned when Piper unzipped the bag and stuck her index finger inside.

"Just a little bit to taste." The tip of her finger came away white, and she licked the stuff off her finger with a soft *smack*.

Cameron finished making breakfast and settled Piper at the counter with her plate. Audrey fixed her own while Cam dumped a pound of syrup over his.

"I didn't mean for us to crash your Sunday morning," she told him. "You could have sent Piper back over to me."

"It's fine." Cameron flicked a glance at Piper, who'd managed to cover the front of her pajama top with white powder. "She just startled me when I heard noise in the living room."

Audrey watched the little girl for a moment, wondering if maybe she hadn't been paying enough attention to her. Had she been neglectful with all her thoughts preoccupied with school, her business back in Boulder, and kissing Cameron? A wave of heat flooded her cheeks. She should have been more focused on Piper, not thinking about the man next to her and how she wanted to give those loose sweatpants a good tug. He was probably commando underneath his pants. All the hottest men usually went without underwear, at least in her experience. Something about them throwing off heat like furnaces and not wanting the extra layers.

She bet his ass was nice and tight…

And there she went again, centering her thoughts on a man who had only kissed her last night to shut her up, then turned around and made Sunday morning breakfast for his niece.

"I don't think she knew what to do with herself," Audrey commented. "She and Dianna used to make breakfast together every Sunday."

Cameron glanced at her with an unreadable expression. Did that make him uncomfortable? Would he have had a woman here if she and Piper hadn't been around?

"She told me," he finally responded.

Audrey almost choked on her French toast. "Piper talked about her mom?"

Cameron nodded and cleaned the rest of his plate with a

final swipe of his fork. He set it down on the counter with a soft clatter. "She said her mom used to make pancakes look like Mickey Mouse. She'd use blueberries for the eyes and a piece of black licorice for the mouth."

Audrey smiled at the sweet memory, grateful to finally think of something other than Dianna frail and bald from cancer. "Dianna wasn't a very good cook. They ate a lot of mac and cheese and hot dogs. But they always cooked together; it was sort of their thing." She slid Cameron a look, hoping he wouldn't see the sorrow on her face. "Dianna was really hands-on with Piper."

Cameron shifted his gaze to Piper again. "I can tell. She's a well-balanced kid."

"What else did she say?" Audrey asked.

"Not much." He crossed his arms, which only emphasized the enormity of his biceps. "Just that Sundays were always her favorite with her mom."

"I should have a talk with her," Audrey said more to herself.

"Why?" Cameron asked.

"Just to make sure she's okay."

"She's fine, Audrey. You fuss over her too much," he added when she shot him a confused look.

"I don't fuss," she argued.

He watched her while leaning against the kitchen counter. "You fuss."

Audrey picked at her French toast, even though it was too good not to inhale. "I just want to make sure she's okay. She's been through a lot."

"So you've said. But the only way she's going to get back to a normal routine is if people stop treating her differently."

Audrey ran her gaze over his strong profile, taking in

his straight nose, unruly dark hair, and early-morning scruff darkening his square jaw. "Sounds like you're talking from experience."

Again with the shoulder shrug, as though it didn't matter to him. "I have a vague idea of what she's going through."

Audrey supposed he would, given how he'd lost his dad. And maybe that was why Dianna had chosen Cameron for Piper. Setting aside the family aspect, she wanted to leave her daughter with someone who could identify with her. Someone who could match his own grief with hers, someone who knew how it felt to be alone. And for the first time since she met him, her apprehension loosened. She hadn't been sure about Cameron, because his reception of them had been lukewarm. Ever since Dianna's death, she'd been obsessed with Piper having the best, so she didn't have to feel another minute of grief.

"It's okay, you know," Cameron commented.

Audrey blinked at him.

"For her to be sad. She needs to be able to grieve without people making her feel like it's not okay."

The comment took her aback. She hadn't made Piper feel like that, had she? She shook her head and placed her plate on the counter next to Cameron's. "I'm not trying to make her feel like that. I just . . . " She blew out a breath. "I just want her to be happy. She deserves that after what she's been through."

"I know," Cameron agreed. "And I'm not saying you're doing anything wrong. But she needs to feel like it's okay to let it out, rather than bottling all her sadness for her mom inside."

"Do you think that's what she's doing?"

Cameron watched Piper feed a bite of French toast to Jellybean. "I think she's trying her best to be a good girl."

"Is that what you did?"

Cameron was silent for so long that she didn't think he was going to answer. "My mom did her best with me after my dad took off. She worked two jobs to make up for the loss of income. But she was...unusually happy. Too happy for a woman whose husband walked out on her and left her with a kid to raise. She was always asking me if I was okay and telling me to smile." He shook his head. "Made me mad."

"Why would that make you mad?" she asked. "She was just trying to protect you."

"Yeah, I know what she was doing. But I wanted to grieve in my own way, and she wouldn't let me."

She watched Piper again, trying to make sense of Cameron's advice. She'd been so sure she'd been doing the right thing with Piper, always making sure she was happy and adjusted, because she couldn't stand to see the shadows in her eyes. No child should have to grieve the way Piper had. She was too special for that.

A warm hand on her arm jerked her out of her thoughts. "I'm not trying to make you feel bad. I know you mean well. But if she wants to be sad, let her be sad. By the way, I'm taking Piper shopping this afternoon."

Cameron was going to shop with a six-year-old? "For what?"

"School stuff," he responded. "She still needs supplies, right?"

"Well, yeah, but..." Actually, she had planned on taking Piper and hadn't expected Cameron to just up and do it himself. Logically she knew he should. It was his place now to take care of these things. "I'll get changed after breakfast and go with you."

Cameron shook his head. "Nope. Just me and her."

"Wait—"

"No arguments, Audrey. You want me to do this, right?"

She blinked at him, still thrown off by the conversation. "Yeah."

"So let me do it. And also, you were right last night."

Huh? His change of subject was so fast, she could only blink. "Right?" she repeated.

"I did kiss you to get you to shut up," he murmured.

Had he moved closer to her? All of a sudden she could smell him. Like, *smell*. And she bet it was the natural smell of his clean skin and not some body wash or cologne. Did he just roll out of bed smelling like an orgasm in a bottle? Because her insides were, like, seriously dancing.

"But I'm not sorry," he told her.

"Um, okay?" What else was she supposed to say? She was too focused on the pulse beating at the base of his strong neck. She bet he smelled really good there too.

"Most people go around apologizing for things like that," he continued, as though she'd asked for more explanation. "But I'm not going to." He stepped even closer and lowered his head. She readied herself for another kiss. Instead, his lips bypassed hers and went to her ear. His nose nuzzled her lobe; then he inhaled a deep breath. "Do know you why?"

Her hand curled into his bare shoulder. Yeah, his skin was as warm as it looked. "Because you're a big tough man who apologizes to no one?"

His throaty chuckle in her ear sent a shiver zinging down her spine. "Because you liked it just as much as I did. And you tossed and turned a lot last night, didn't you?"

Hell, yeah, she had. But she wasn't about to tell him that.

In a hasty and sudden move, he pulled back. "By the way, my mom is coming to dinner next Sunday."

And with that, he was gone, out of the kitchen and taking her quivering stomach with her.

And wasn't that just great? She went from kissing him to meeting his mom.

TEN

The following Monday at practice, Cameron was still thinking about Audrey. To his surprise, his thoughts this morning hadn't centered on kissing her or the way her hungry gaze had left a scorching path over his bare chest. He couldn't stop thinking about the wounded look on her face when they'd talked about Piper.

How could she have known she was smothering the child? Cameron had felt the need to gently point it out to her, then wanted to kick his own ass for making her doubt herself.

Audrey was too special for self-doubt. And she didn't need him heaping onto what was already a world of grief after dealing with Dianna's death. Audrey had been through a lot: the disappearance of her mother, her strained relationship with her brother and father. Starting her own business. Losing a friend.

And then throwing all her energy into Piper, setting

aside her own life to make sure Piper was happy. Audrey gave new meaning to the word *selfless*.

Cameron grinned to himself when he thought about calling Audrey selfless. She'd probably argue with him, because the woman argued *everything* with him. That should annoy him, but Cameron found it an oddly refreshing change from the women who only wanted to get in his pants. They'd come around for a good time, then offer him a satisfied smile as they strolled out the front door.

It was all so...empty.

And it had worked for him. Until Piper had blinked up at him with sad green eyes and forced him to reevaluate his entire existence.

Even though he still wasn't sure what to do with the kid, and still felt a surge of panic every time she looked at him, Cameron knew he couldn't carry on the way he had been. The question was, where did he go from here?

To Denver and drag Piper to another city? Or did he turn his dream offer down and stay in Blanco Valley?

Beside him, Blake blasted his whistle and called the players to huddle. As he approached the team to go over mistakes, Cameron consulted his notes and realized he hadn't written a damn thing.

Brandon nudged him. "You've got that look on your face again."

Shit, he seriously needed to work on his poker face. Maybe he should practice in the mirror. He chose not to say anything, mostly because he didn't trust his voice.

"Would it be so bad to get a little tangled up with her?" Brandon suggested, obviously knowing what Cameron was thinking about.

Cameron watched Blake go over plays with the team.

The kids were sweaty and hot but determined. "Is that what you thought about Stella?"

Brandon moved his shoulders, as though not comfortable with the question. "I didn't think I had any kind of future with Stella."

Cameron snorted and turned to face his friend. "Yeah, and I've got such a bright future with Audrey? We don't even live in the same town."

"What if you end up in Denver? It's not that far from Boulder."

"I haven't decided about Denver. And I owe you an ass kicking, by the way," Cameron added.

"Don't you think she was bound to find out?" Brandon shot back. "How did she take it?"

Cameron kept his focus on Blake and the kids, even though he felt Brandon's intent gaze. Blake ended his instruction, and the team dispersed to run through the play again.

"You haven't even talked to her about it yet, have you?" Brandon questioned. Then he laughed and shook his head. "Have you learned nothing? Women don't like surprises."

Actually, he had been planning on telling her the whole thing. Then her tone had changed, going from casual conversation to tense when she'd sensed he was keeping something from her. He'd suspected it hadn't been the right time to delve into the subject further, so he'd been evasive. Then he'd been possessed with thoughts of pressing his lips to hers, of leaning her back against the wooden steps and slipping his hand beneath her shirt. Then she'd gone and hurled all sorts of accusations at him, like kissing her just to shut her up.

"I don't know," he admitted to Brandon in a low voice.

Brandon shot Cameron a look with lifted brows. "You don't know what?"

Cameron scrubbed a hand down his face, wishing he'd taken the time to shave that morning. "Hell, I don't know that either."

"Sounds like you could use a couple episodes of *Dr. Phil.*"

Cameron rolled his eyes.

"In all honesty, though," Brandon went on.

"Please, let's not," Cameron protested.

"Just talk to her," Brandon suggested.

"Cameron, are you having woman problems?" came a godforsaken voice from behind him.

He kept his focus forward on the players rather than acknowledge Drew's comment.

Drew stopped next to Cam. "Aren't you supposed to be some kind of smooth operator?"

Smooth operator? What decade were they in?

Normally Cameron would throw out some offhand remark to get Drew all riled up. Something like, "Need someone to show you how it's done?"

But Cameron was over that. He was over deliberately baiting Drew until steam puffed out of the man's too-small ears and he'd be out for blood. Pushing Drew to his limit no longer gave him the satisfaction it used to. Now Cameron was just tired and wanted to be left the hell alone.

"Nothing you need to concern yourself with, Drew," was all Cameron said.

"Maybe not," Drew said. "But I just feel like I need to look out for my married friends."

Cameron finally turned to Drew and looked down on the shorter man. "Now, why do you have to go and do that?

Here I am, trying to be a nice guy, and you say stupid shit that makes me want to kill you."

"Just keeping it real," Drew said with a shrug, even though his red ears gave his false confidence away. They both knew Cameron would wipe the field and the bleachers with the guy.

"Why don't you take a step back, Drew?" Brandon suggested.

"Made any decisions about Denver yet?" Drew asked.

"Yeah, I've decided to stay here and see your pretty face every day."

Aaaand there was the familiar shade of red Cameron was so used to seeing. It flooded Drew's face and reminded Cameron why he used to always get in trouble in high school and why he was better off keeping his mouth shut.

Blake headed back to the sidelines, his attention bouncing from Drew to Cameron. "How's it going today, Drew?" Blake asked.

Drew pasted a big, fake smile on his face, and Cameron had to give the guy a smidgen of credit. He knew how to turn it off and on, which was something Cameron had yet to figure out.

"Great. Just came to see how the team's doing," Drew commented. "We're playing a tough one on Friday and wanted to talk your game plan."

He and Blake stepped to the side, but not before Blake tossed Cameron a look that said, *You just can't help yourself, can you?*

No, he couldn't. He had impulse issues.

"What the hell?" Brandon complained.

Cameron held his hands up in defense. "What? I was minding my own business when he came over here and egged me on."

Brandon shook his head. "Yeah, but why do you have to say shit like that to him?"

Because Drew Spalding was an ass who deserved it. Drew Spalding was the type of man who used his own grief as a weapon and had taken things to a level with Cameron they shouldn't have gone. He knew Brandon and Blake suspected there was more to their story than just Cameron screwing Drew's wife.

They were right, but they didn't have a clue why.

And Cameron would keep it that way.

"Do you remember what your teacher's name is?" Audrey adjusted Piper's backpack for the fifth time and smoothed her hand over the child's hair. That morning, after setting her alarm for six thirty, she'd readied Piper for her first day of kindergarten, then spent twenty minutes trying to get Piper's hair to look just right. Piper had scowled at Audrey's reflection because she hated braids, and Audrey had assured her she looked just like a Disney princess, which had lessened the scowl to a mere pout.

Now they were in front of Cameron's house waiting for the bus to pick up Piper. Audrey swallowed back a lump as she took in Piper's pink leggings, matching sweater and boots. They'd picked out the ensemble together last night before putting in a dual effort to make Piper's lunch. Cameron had done a surprisingly good job of shopping for Piper. They'd been gone for four hours, and the entire time Audrey had been tempted to call to make sure they were okay. She'd had to force a distraction upon herself not to invade their time together. Despite her worries, they'd returned intact, full of smiles and shopping bags crammed full of stuff. Cameron had even thought to purchase a lunchbox and two new pairs of shoes.

"Ms. Matthews," Piper answered as she swung her backpack back and forth.

"And do you remember where you're supposed to sit?" Audrey knew she was overworrying, or fussing, as Cameron had accused. But she couldn't help it. Piper had never been to school before and didn't know any of the kids. What if she got lost on her way to the classroom? What if she went into the wrong classroom? What if none of the kids talked to her?

Good grief, is this what parents went through every day? How did they not lose their minds with worry all the time? Cameron had seemed to handle it much better than Audrey as he'd simply ruffled Piper's hair this morning before leaving for work with a muttered, "Have a great day, kid."

Piper nodded and picked at the strap of her backpack. "Yeah, it's the desk with my name on it," she answered, reminding Audrey she was obsessing again and needed to chill. Best to just focus on getting Piper on the bus for now.

But maybe one last question first. "And do you remember where to put your backpack?"

Piper slumped her shoulders, indicating she was tired of all the poking and prodding. "I know, Audrey. It's cubby number twenty-three. That's my student number because Ms. Matthews told me."

Yeah, okay, she needed to stop already and give Piper more credit. She'd be okay. She'd make friends and have a great time and tell Audrey all about it after school.

She heard the familiar sounds of the bus pulling around the corner, and Audrey's heart picked up. Okay, this was it. Time to put Piper on the bus and spend her first day without the child who'd become like her shadow.

Audrey swallowed back a lump as she held Piper's

backpack for her to slip on. "You're going to have a great day, right?"

Piper nodded. "Yeah."

"And remember to eat all the food in your lunch." *Okay, you're fussing again.*

The warning sounded oddly like Cameron, and Audrey shoved the thought away.

"But I don't like those red things you packed," Piper complained.

Audrey knew that was going to be an issue, but she'd packed them anyway. "Those are strawberries, and they're really good for you. They make you run fast."

Piper spun around after securing her *Frozen* backpack over her shoulders. "No, they don't. You're just saying that so I'll eat them."

Audrey squatted in front of Piper as the bus rolled to a stop next to the curb. "Why don't you just give them a try for me?"

Piper didn't answer, and Audrey knew that was her way of saying, "Yeah, fat chance."

The bus doors swooshed open with a soft hiss. Piper turned around, ready to climb on the thing, but Audrey stopped her. She turned the girl around and gave her a fierce hug, willing the tears to hold off at least until Piper was on the bus. It wouldn't do either of them any good for her to turn into a blubbering mess now. Piper needed Audrey to be strong, even though she was crumbling inside at the idea of Piper being gone for the whole day.

For months, it had been the two of them. Piper would turn her big, green eyes to Audrey's, or slip her fragile hand in Audrey's bigger one as though to say, "You've got my back, right?"

The amount of trust Piper had in Audrey was both staggering and unfamiliar. She was unused to someone, especially someone so small and vulnerable, depending on her. For her entire adult life, it had been just her, and for a glimmer of a moment, Audrey understood the apprehension Cameron must have felt when he'd met Piper.

Piper squirmed, indicating the hug was over. "Bye, Audrey." And then she turned and marched up the bus steps.

"Hey," Audrey called out before the driver could close the doors. "I'll be waiting right here for you after school." Piper gave one last nod before disappearing.

The lump that had filled her throat finally burst, and the first tears leaked out. Audrey swiped them away as the bus rumbled down the street and made a left turn to fade from view.

She should be happy for Piper, and she was, actually, but Audrey couldn't help but fight back the emptiness that took place of the little girl that had come to mean so much to her. And the urge to run after that bus wasn't a good sign. If Audrey was this much of a mess just seeing Piper off to school, what would it be like when she had to say goodbye for good?

Just thinking about never waking up to Piper's soft voice in the morning or seeing that ratty stuffed cat she dragged around was even more depressing than seeing the girl off to school.

Maybe she should...

No. Relocating was not an option. Her life was in Boulder. Her business she'd spent so many years building. All her friends. Her town house. Her empty town house.

Still, she couldn't uproot her life and move to the other side of the state for a little girl and her drop-dead sexy uncle.

Piper would be okay with Cameron. She still wasn't

sure Cameron would be okay with Piper. Audrey could still see a thread of uncertainty in his eyes whenever he looked at Piper, as though he thought Piper would shatter.

Audrey turned from the street and headed back to the guesthouse. On her way, she passed her car and noticed the yellow Post-it on her windshield.

Knowing who it was from, Audrey was already grinning. She was like some needy teenager who'd been passed a note in science class by her crush.

Seriously pathetic.

She snatched the note off the car anyway.

I noticed the air in your front tire was low. So I filled it.

C

Just a capital *C*. Not even his full name, because they had grown that comfortable with each other. Audrey didn't even flinch, because she liked that he was comfortable with her. It meant she was on her way to cracking that badass exterior he wanted her to think he had.

She was already convinced he wasn't the hard-ass he wanted people to think. Not when he went around doing things like cooking breakfast with little girls, not calling the police on nosy old ladies, and filling Audrey's tires for her.

Not only had no man ever done anything like that for her, but she also liked that he noticed, then took it upon himself to fix it.

He was a fixer. A doer. Which meant he cared more than he wanted her to think.

Audrey's smile widened as she tucked the note to her chest, like it was some kind of declaration of love.

Yeah, right. She'd guess Cameron Shaw had never made such a declaration to a woman before. He wasn't the type. No, he was the type who showed how he felt rather than wasting his time with words.

She entered the guesthouse and tucked the Post-it note away with the other two he'd left after fixing the porch step and the water line to the house.

Okay, so it was silly, keeping his little notes. But one day, when she was gone and had moved on with her life, she'd be able to look back and remember that Cameron Shaw had a heart, and he hadn't been too proud to show her.

Did that make her special? Audrey wasn't sure yet, but she knew there was something there. Something... different between her and Cameron that she hadn't felt before.

Audrey poured herself another cup of coffee and left the guesthouse for the back door to Cameron's house. He told her, shortly after they'd moved in, that he'd leave his sliding glass door unlocked should she need anything.

She let herself inside his quiet, cool house, inhaling the scent that she'd come to associate with Cameron. The whole place smelled like him. Warm. Manly. A lot like the man himself.

She knew where he kept his Post-its because they'd gone back and forth enough times. She opened the kitchen drawer and snagged a pen and the last little yellow square, making a mental note to grab more.

Thanks for fixing my tire. BTW, you're out of Post-its.

A

She slapped the note on the television screen, where she knew he'd see it because he always watched a quick recap on ESPN in the living room every night before bed.

Not that she'd been learning his habits or anything.

Still, Audrey couldn't help the grin that sneaked along her mouth as she let herself out the back door.

ELEVEN

Audrey returned home fifteen minutes before Piper's bus was supposed to drop her off from school. After an exhausting day of Skyping with her business partner, grocery shopping, then meeting at Annabelle's to discuss her nursery, Audrey was ready to drop with a glass of wine. Or maybe the whole bottle.

Except the last time she'd done that, she'd ended up lip-locked with a man who sent her hormones into hyperdrive. So maybe wine was a bad idea.

She had just enough time to unload all the groceries, which may or may not have included extra cookie dough ice cream and a jar of marshmallow cream. Just for those nights when the urge to slip in Cameron's back door was so strong that her fingers actually itched. Yeah, ice cream was a totally suitable substitute.

But the ice cream would have to do, because it was becoming increasingly hard to keep her cool around him. To keep her sly glances to herself. To control the trembling of her fingers whenever he was in the room. Talk about a massive crush. Audrey couldn't remember the last time she'd crushed this hard.

The bus pulled in front of Cameron's house just as Audrey was walking to the curb. Three kids got off, each running off in different directions. Then Audrey's heart lifted at the sight of Piper, whose hair had become unraveled from the two braids she'd spent twenty minutes on that morning. Piper bounded down the steps with all the energy and enthusiasm of a six-year-old. She turned and waved to the bus driver, causing Audrey's heart to pinch even tighter. Her hair was a mess of baby-fine waves, from the braids. There was a grass stain on her left knee and a funky-looking green spot on the bottom of her pink sweater. Despite the mess, Piper was just about the sweetest thing Audrey had seen all day. She'd missed the squirt like crazy.

But as Piper hopped off the bus, Audrey fought back the wave of sorrow, because Dianna should have been the one to greet her daughter after school. She should have braided Piper's hair and done all the school shopping and packed Piper's lunch with a note to have an awesome day. But she wasn't, and Audrey was assaulted again by the unfairness of the situation. There would be no family dinner around a table tonight, no mother to help her with her homework or tuck her in.

But she has you.

Audrey lifted her chin, determined not to let the thoughts show on her face.

"Hey, kiddo." Audrey picked the girl up, backpack and all, and hugged her little body close. She hadn't expected to miss Piper so much.

Piper jumped up and down when Audrey released her. "I got on green today."

Audrey took Piper's hand and led her to the guesthouse. "Green?"

"Ms. Matthews has three colors on the wall. Green, yellow, and red," Piper explained. "Red is for when you're bad, and Carter got on red because he talked during story time. But I didn't. I got on green because I didn't talk."

Audrey grinned down at her as the entered the house. "Of course, because you tried your best, right?"

Piper nodded and dropped her backpack on the floor. "Yep." She turned and blinked up at Audrey. "I have to go to the bathroom."

"Okay, you know where it is," Audrey responded, even though she knew how Piper was going to respond.

She shook her head, sending her soft waves around her shoulders. "You have to come with me, remember?"

Audrey lifted a brow and jabbed a hand on her hip. "Piper, we've talked about this. You need to start using the bathroom by yourself. How do you go at school?"

"I just go with a friend."

Audrey pondered her options, knowing she didn't have many with a tenacious six-year-old. She blew out a breath. "I'll walk you to the bathroom, but I'm not staying in there with you."

Piper grabbed Audrey's hand. "But I'm scared."

The inflection of emotion in the girl's voice tugged harder on Audrey's heartstrings. She squatted and took both of Piper's small hands in her own. "Honey, the bathroom isn't a scary place. Why are you afraid of it?" she asked, even though she knew the answer. Ever since Dianna had passed away, Piper had been terrified of using a bathroom by herself.

"Just am," Piper said in a low voice. She averted her gaze to her scuffed boots and sniffed.

Audrey resisted the urge to pull Piper into her arms and tell her it was okay. Just give her a little reassurance, that she wasn't alone. Then she remembered Cameron's words about being too fussy, so she held back.

Instead she settled on resting her hands on Piper's tiny shoulders. "Sweetie, you're going to have to get over your fear of the bathroom. I won't always be here to go with you."

"Why can't you?" Piper questioned.

Oh, God, not this again. They'd had this discussion a few times, and Audrey thought Piper understood. She knew Piper wanted Audrey to stay, but how was she supposed to respond to that?

"You know why, Piper," Audrey answered. "Because I have to go home eventually."

Piper blinked at her. "But why can't this be your home?"

Yeah, Audrey. Why?

"Because my home is in Boulder." Yeah, great answer.

"But why can't this be your home?" she asked again. "Don't you like it here?"

If only it were that simple… "Of course I like it here. I love Blanco Valley, and I love being here with you. But my work is in Boulder. I can't just leave my business."

Piper scratched the side of her face. "Why can't you move your business here?"

Okay, she was running out of reasonable excuses here. "Because…" Shit, because why? "Because I have a business partner who I work with, and I can't leave her to do all the work herself."

Piper blinked again, and Audrey knew she didn't understand. And why would she? Her world consisted of cartoons, a stuffed cat, and jelly beans.

"Can she move down here?" Piper asked with all the confidence of someone who thought they'd figured it out.

"No, honey, she can't. Now how about we use the bathroom now?" Audrey pushed, desperate to put an end to the line of questioning. Piper could be relentless when she put her mind to it, as were all kids, Audrey imagined. But it broke her heart to see the confusion written all over her sweet face. Audrey wanted to do everything in her power to make Piper happy, to give her the stable home she'd once had with Dianna. She feared that when she left, she'd rock the girl's world all over again.

They used the toilet, while Audrey waited in the hall, giving Piper an extra reminder to wash her hands.

"Is Cameron here? I wanna tell him about how I got on green today." Piper skipped out of the bathroom and headed for the kitchen.

Audrey followed her, knowing the girl was hungry. "Nope, he's still at work. But he'll be home around dinnertime, and I'm sure he'd love to hear about your day."

As Audrey made Piper a snack of sliced cheese with crackers and grapes, Audrey questioned her own words. How much interest would Cameron really have? Okay, she knew she wasn't giving him enough credit, but her own protectiveness for Piper was coming out and landing square on Cameron. She needed him to be more involved in Piper's life. More important, Piper needed him to be more involved, to know her schedule and her teacher's name and how to pack her lunch.

She made a note to talk to him about it later and went about making Piper's snack.

They spent the remainder of the afternoon hanging around the guesthouse; then Audrey took the time to go through Piper's school folder while Piper went to the back-yard to play. There were a half dozen forms Cameron needed to sign.

Daylight slowly faded into twilight, and Cameron pulled his rumbling Camaro into the driveway around six thirty.

Her traitorous heart did a triple beat when she watched him unfold his long legs from the driver's seat. Piper skipped toward him, but Audrey remained behind the screen door, grateful for the cover so she had a moment to compose herself. He already saw too much when he caught her watching him. She didn't need to be giving the man any advantages.

Lord knew he had too many.

Piper jumped up and down on two feet as she followed Cameron to the front door. Audrey couldn't be sure, but she thought maybe he'd glanced in her direction as though wondering where she was.

Before she could consider it too long, her cell phone rang. Her stomach clenched when she spotted her brother's name on the display. The only time he called was to talk about her mother's disappearance and the case that detectives were still working on. However, as much as Audrey wanted to hear something about what had happened to her mother, she wasn't in the mood to talk to him. Their conversations made Audrey long for the time when she and Paul could laugh and tease and play. Now they just passed along information, like two coworkers who occasionally saw each other at a staff meeting. She allowed the call to go to voice mail. If Paul had important information to relay, she could call him back.

It wasn't supposed to be this way. *Life* wasn't supposed to be this way. At least her life wasn't. When she'd been a kid, she'd received an unreasonable amount of satisfaction planning her future. Her career, husband, kids, and all that. So far, nothing had worked out the way she'd dreamed all those years ago. Everything was upside down and constantly changing, and the element of the unknown placed a throbbing tension in the back of her skull.

Mom gone. Best friend gone. A brother she barely talked to. A father who was emotionally unavailable. A career that was finally thriving, and one that she loved. But was that what she'd been reduced to? That woman who threw herself into her job because she had nothing else going for her? No husband waiting for her, no kids to tuck in at night? No big, overly loud Christmases with family bustling around the kitchen and nephews and nieces running down the halls?

And then there was Cameron. He was everything she'd once wanted. He had a good, stable job. He was a homeowner. Not to mention how softhearted he was with Piper. Smart. Good-looking...

Oh, who was she kidding? The man gave new meaning to "good-looking." It was like looking at Chris Hemsworth and thinking *eh*.

But Audrey had enough experience to know life was more about a checklist. It was about feelings and instinct. Spontaneity and *living*. Not simply going from point A to point B. Sometimes Audrey felt like she'd become one of *those* people.

Only thing was all her instincts about Cameron had been screaming at her since day one.

Be careful with this one.

He's just like the others who've hurt you.

Audrey pulled in a breath as she lifted her head and spotted Cameron on the back porch watching her. The look on his face was peculiar. His brows were knitted in a way that she thought maybe he wanted to go to her, but for some reason he held himself back.

Don't, she wanted to say to him.

"Everything okay?" he called.

"Yeah." Audrey stood from the step, because she needed to do something with her nervous energy.

Audrey reached the top of the steps, but Cameron hadn't moved from his spot behind the railing. He had one lean hip pressed against the wood, his hands folded over his impressive chest. That was another thing Audrey noticed about him. The man leaned a lot, as though *casual* were his middle name. As though he had all the time in the world. He moved with an easy, casual grace of someone who was confident in his own skin. And yet he always watched her with an intensity that made her want to squirm.

"I see Piper found you," she said.

Cameron surprised her by smiling. The action had been unexpected and sent Audrey's hormones into overdrive. "Yeah, she's been telling me about her day for the past half an hour. Some kid named Gavin kept poking her in the shoulder with a purple crayon and was sent to the time-out chair."

Audrey smiled along with him because it was impossible not to smile when talking about Piper. "I think she had a good day."

A look of concern flashed across Cameron's face. "Were you worried she wouldn't?"

"How could I not worry about that?"

He lifted one shoulder. "I guess you can't really help it, can you?"

She narrowed her eyes at him. "What's that supposed to mean?"

"Nothing."

She took a step toward him and tried not to notice how the man towered over her. "No, there was something there. You had a disapproving tone."

"No, I didn't."

"Yes, you did. As though I can't help but to *fuss* over her, as you put it before."

He blew out a breath. "I only meant because you care about her. Not everything has a double meaning, Audrey."

"Oh."

"Yeah, *oh*," he replied.

"You know, if she's ever bothering you, you can just send her back to me," she said.

Cameron's head tilted as though he didn't understand the question. "*Bothering* me?"

Audrey tried not to let his tone get under her skin. She had the feeling she'd insulted him. "Yeah, you know. Piper can be a lot if you're not used to her."

"Meaning?"

Audrey picked at a splinter on the wood railing. "I just don't want her to wear you down before I leave."

"Wear me down?"

She blew out a breath. "Why do you keep repeating everything I say?"

"Because I'm trying to figure out where you're going with this," he told her.

Where was she going? Audrey wasn't sure she knew. The only thing she was certain of was that seeing Cameron look almost concerned for her had thrown her off balance. Audrey didn't like being off balance, despite the fact that it was a permanent condition around this man. So she'd done the only thing she knew how to do.

She was trying to get her bearings back, to get her surroundings back under control. Usually it worked, but around Cameron, her normal methods always seemed to fail her.

She shook her head, knowing Cameron wouldn't understand. "Forget it. So Piper got off the bus at three thirty," she told him.

Cameron blinked as though trying to process the change in subject. "Okay."

Audrey nodded and watched him. Not even a flicker of interest. "Don't you think that's something you should know?"

"And you just told me," he said without skipping a beat.

"Yes, but what if I hadn't told you? How would you know when she got home? And who will be here to meet her after I leave?"

Cameron held his hands up. "Okay, hold on. Why don't you tell me what's really going on?"

Audrey blinked. "What do you mean?" Except she knew exactly what he meant.

He took a step closer to her so that his hand rested next to hers on the railing. Close enough to feel the heat from his body, even though the temperature was in the low sixties. "I mean why you're so hell-bent on picking a fight with me."

"I'm not," she lied. "I just need to make sure we're on the same page—"

He stepped closer. "Audrey..."

"How are you supposed to know these things if I don't tell you—"

"Audrey," he murmured again as he placed his hand over hers on the railing.

His tone stopped her cold, and she dropped her attention to his hand, so much bigger than hers, cradling it with a soft yet firm touch. His hand felt *good*. Like warmth blooming across her belly, toe-curling goodness. Which begged the question...if his warm palm felt this good with just a simple touch, what would it feel like if he were to *really* touch her?

"Holy John Galliano," she muttered to herself.

One side of Cameron's mouth kicked up. "Christ, don't start that again."

"I can't help it. You're so..." Her voice trailed off because she didn't know quite how to explain Cameron, especially to the man himself. Actually, that wasn't true. She had a pretty good idea which words to use. *Smokin' hot. Seriously sexy.*

Yeah, no way was she saying that to him.

The grip on her hand tightened. "So what?"

Audrey opened her mouth, then snapped it shut when her brain almost malfunctioned and forced her to spew out obscenities, like *smoldering* and *tight-as-shit-abs*. No reason to balloon the man's ego any bigger than it already was.

"Don't hold back, Audrey," he said to her. "Tell me what you really think."

How was she supposed to do that when the thumb stroking back and forth over her hand was short-circuiting her wires?

She blew out a breath. "Karl Lagerfeld."

"You're going to have to start using your words, Audrey," he teased.

"You're just..." she started. "Too much."

"Too much," he repeated.

She couldn't help the smile that curled her lips. "There you go again repeating my words."

He shook his head. "And there you go again saying things that don't make sense."

Well, it made sense to her. She just didn't know how to explain it to him. At least other than *I want to jump your bones and bang like rabbits.*

"You're too much for me," she blurted out.

She expected him to pull back. Instead he grinned. A big, sexy, you-know-you-want-me smile that had shivers skating down her spine.

"That wasn't meant to be funny," she scolded.

"I'm not laughing," he said around his shit-eating grin.

"Kind of seems like it," she argued.

His thumb continued back and forth over her knuckles. "Yeah, it's kind of funny."

Lovely to know her torment was so hilarious to him.

He leaned even closer, so that his nose was a breath away from her. She could feel his breath, hot on her skin. She resisted the urge to close her eyes and lean in to him, for just a moment to feel his warmth and strength. Maybe tuck her head in the curve of his neck...

"Because you want me," he stated. As though he were giving her a weather report.

Why was he not as off balance as she was? Why was she the only one who seemed to be affected by... whatever it was between them? The thought left Audrey feeling cold and treading in familiar waters from every other guy she'd been involved with.

"You have a high opinion of yourself," she countered, because that was easier than admitting he was right. Cameron straightened and chuckled. "Yeah, okay." He gave her hand a tug and led her toward the sliding glass door. "Let's get some dinner."

She followed him blindly because his hand felt so damn good wrapped around hers. Protective and fitting. Like their fingers belonged tangled up in each other. The thought startled Audrey as much as it created a warm bubble around her heart.

Just as she was about to follow him through the door, he

surprised her by stopping and pinning her against the door frame. Her brain screamed at her to push him back, to slap away the hands that were creeping over her hips and tugging her to him so that she could feel all the hard goodness beneath his athletic pants.

"But let's get one thing straight, Audrey," he breathed in her ear.

Why was he always whispering in her ear? And why didn't she have the compulsion to stop him?

"Soon you're going to stop saying those ridiculous names," his soft voice said.

Her eyes shuttered closed when his mouth traced the outer shell of her ear. And then her quaking breath turned into a gasp when his lips oh so gently touched the sensitive spot on her neck.

God, the man knew how to use his mouth. Cameron was persistent and tender at the same time, knowing how to draw out the suspense of *just kiss me already* until Audrey wanted to sink her teeth into the bulk of his shoulder.

"And you're going to say mine instead."

The confidence in his voice was almost as unnerving as the reaction her body had to his. She could feel the bulk of his thighs against hers all the way to his hard chest teasing the tips of her breasts.

Finally she gave in to the compulsion to lean into him and press her lips to his jaw. But the moment was cut short and Audrey was left cold when Cameron pulled away and lifted her chin with the tip of his index finger.

"Soon, Audrey."

TWELVE

The next morning Cameron woke up with a stiff neck and a bitch of a headache, not to mention the serious case of blue balls, straining against the fabric of his boxer briefs. He blamed the woman across the way for that, and the habit she'd developed of licking her lips whenever he was around.

He'd thought about knocking on her door last night to finally scratch the itch they'd both been feeling. But it had been midnight when he'd returned home, bordering on homicidal after the Bobcats had lost. He'd come to learn that Audrey sometimes stayed up late, but his hand had hesitated on the sliding glass door at the sight of the pitch-dark guesthouse. Instead he'd gone to bed with sweat beading his temples and a raging hard-on. Normally he'd call Tessa, who'd been texting and calling nonstop about when they were going to "get together." Cameron knew her idea of getting together was what he needed to ease the tension humming through his system. But for some reason the idea of getting sweaty with a woman who enjoyed casual sex as much as he did didn't really light his fire anymore.

The thought should have sent him into a panic. But, Cameron realized as he swung his legs out of bed, he felt...oddly calm, as though a final piece of a puzzle was clicking into place. Strange that he hadn't even realized there was a piece missing.

Or maybe he had known but hadn't cared. He hadn't cared there'd been a hollowness inside him that he'd been content to leave unfilled. He still wasn't sure if Audrey had been the one to fill it or if it was Piper.

Cameron scratched his bare belly as he padded toward the kitchen to start coffee.

"What the fu—" Cameron jumped back at the sight of Piper in his living room, holding some horridly hairless creature that looked like a cross between a giant gerbil and a mutant rat.

Piper's eyes widened as she cradled the squirming creature to her chest. "That's a bad word. You should say 'shoot' instead. Sometimes Audrey says cheese 'n' rice."

Of course she did. Cameron cleared his throat and stayed back, for fear that the um...animal might morph into something else. Or spew hot venom everywhere.

"What is that thing?" he asked the girl.

The mutant in Piper's arms squirmed enough until the kid finally let it go. The thing turned over and started licking its crotch. Wonderful.

"It's a cat," Piper answered as a matter of fact, as though it should have been so obvious with its strangely pink skin and way too big, black eyes.

Cameron cleared his throat again. "That's definitely not a cat."

Piper reached out and ran her hand over the animal's back, because Cameron refused to call the thing a cat, and giggled when it nibbled on her fingers. "Yes, it is. Isn't she cute?"

Cute? It looked like it had been turned inside out.

"Where'd you find it?" Cameron asked.

"In your backyard. She was wandering around by herself." Piper crooned at the thing, telling her what a pretty girl she was. Maybe Piper had swallowed a hallucinogenic. "I think she lost her mommy. I think she's sad."

Cameron was pretty sure the cat wasn't sad. "Why is she bald? Did someone set her on fire?"

Piper's eyes widened as she let out a gasp.

Good going, asshole. You need to learn how to talk to kids.

Cameron took a tentative step into the living room, careful to make sure the thing wasn't going to hiss or…foam at the mouth, or something. "I just mean, why doesn't she have any fur?"

Piper just lifted her little shoulders and ran her hand down the cat's back again. "I don't know. Maybe someone cut it all off."

With what, a lawn mower? Or maybe a blowtorch?

"I'm going to keep her and name her Jellybean Junior," Piper announced.

Was the kid for real?

Cameron didn't know what to sputter out first. That no way in hell were they keeping that sorry excuse for a feline, or could they please come up with a more original name?

But before he could utter either thought, Piper spoke up again. She scooped the real Jellybean off the living room floor and bounced on her knees. "I'm hungry. Can we make some more pancakes? And can I have chocolate chips in them this time?"

"Uh..." Cam kept one eye on the cat, who'd pounced over to the end table and was batting her scrawny paws at the lamp cord dangling over the edge. He used his boot to scoot the cat away, because the last thing he needed was for the lamp to come crashing down on Jellybean Jr. Except...No. He wasn't that heartless. "Why don't we go see what we can find in the kitchen?"

It was strange how he'd started thinking "we" when talking about him and Piper. When had he stopped being an "I"?

Piper ran into the kitchen, dragging her stuffed cat with her. The real cat followed, her sharp claws skidding across the tile. Cameron briefly wondered if he should, like, feed the thing. Maybe give it some water? Cats drank water, didn't they?

Shit, he didn't know. There was no way they could keep it. He was barely fumbling his way around Piper, without adding a deranged cat to the mix. A cat who was currently attacking Cameron's shoes. Without thinking, he scooped the shoes up and plopped them on a barstool.

While Piper helped herself to the pantry, because she had already learned where he kept his food, Cameron snagged his cell off the kitchen counter and snapped a photo of the cat. He texted it to Brandon, with the caption:

Found a buddy for you.

Cameron placed the phone down and scrounged up some breakfast for himself and Piper. His gaze flickered to the guesthouse, briefly wondering if he should check on Audrey. Would she still be sleeping? Showering? The image of her standing beneath the hot spray, water cascading down her damp skin...damn. Cameron needed to pull himself together, lest he embarrass himself in front of his niece.

He and Piper had just started cracking eggs in a bowl when his cell vibrated. Cameron checked it, already knowing what Brandon's response would be.

If you try to leave me with that thing, you'll have to enroll in witness protection. What the hell is it? It looks like a shell-less turtle.

Cameron thumbed his reply. *It's a cat. Just show the picture to Stella.*

His phone buzzed.

No way. She'll bully me into taking it. Sorry, bro, but you're stuck.

Cameron set the phone back down and accepted his reality. He was officially a single guy with a niece he was still unsure about and an alien creature who'd already developed an obsession with his shoes.

Oh, and let's not forget the woman you want to bang and then take out to dinner.

Cameron had never wanted to take a woman out to dinner before, unless he was trying to get into her pants. But with Audrey it was more than that. More than romancing her with an endgame in mind. He wanted to take her somewhere nice so she could put on something other than skinny jeans. Not that her ass didn't look damn fine in denim, but he wanted to see her in a skirt. Or a dress. Either was optimal for sliding his hands up the back of her thighs...

"Can you use chocolate chips to make a smiley face on my pancakes?" Piper asked, interrupting his R-rated thoughts. "My mom used to do that."

Cameron slanted a look at Piper at the mention of her mom. Piper had only mentioned her mom one other time. The conversation he had with Audrey about this very thing came to Cameron's mind. But he also wondered if he should be doing more. More...well, he wasn't sure exactly what. Maybe talking to Piper more about it? Asking how she felt, if she was all right?

"Did your mom used to make you breakfast?" Cameron asked, keeping his tone light.

Piper swung her legs back and forth on the counter. "Sometimes. Mostly she just made me cereal or toast."

Cameron flipped a pancake in the pan. "You said your mom used to make you breakfast every Sunday."

Piper scratched her nose. "Yeah, but just on Sundays. But mostly she was always sick."

His heart gave a painful squeeze at Piper's casual tone. Realistically, he knew Piper was anything but casual about her mother's death, but the way she said it, with such calm acceptance...Cameron was more torn up about it than he thought he'd be.

"Your mom was real sick, huh?"

Piper nodded and kept her attention on the pancakes cooking in the pan.

Cameron wanted to ask more, but the words stuck in his throat. He didn't want to send Piper into a fit of tears, because female tears...damn. He didn't have the faintest clue about that one.

However, she was his niece. Shouldn't he be more comfortable talking to her? He would need to know these things if the two of them had a chance in hell surviving on a long-term basis.

"You know..." Cameron cleared his throat and ordered himself to find his balls. "If you ever want to, you know, talk to someone about your mom, you can come to me."

Piper blinked up at him as though she didn't understand.

Cameron tried for a different angle. "Do you think about her a lot?"

Piper's legs stopped their swinging. "Yeah," she said after a moment.

Cameron scooped three done pancakes off the pan and set them on a plate. "What do you miss most about her?"

"The way she used to read me stories with all the voices," Piper answered. "And her hugs."

Cameron swallowed past the lump in his throat, feeling more emotional than he thought possible. "She gave good hugs, huh?"

Piper nodded and scratched her bare knee.

"What was your favorite story she used to read to you?"

Piper thought for a moment, then answered, "*Pinkalicious.*"

Cameron nodded because he didn't know what the hell that was. "I could read that to you sometime, if you'd like," he found himself saying. "I don't know if my voices would be as good as your mom's, though."

Piper inhaled deeply. "Audrey reads it to me. She does good voices." Her legs resumed their swinging. "She gives good hugs too."

Yeah, he bet Audrey gave good hugs.

Dude, you're talking to a six-year-old. Chill on the sexual innuendos.

"Sounds like you like hugs a lot."

Piper plucked a chocolate chip out of the bag. "Just from my mom and Audrey."

So she had some touchy-feely issues. Cameron could understand that.

He cleared his throat and decided a change in subject was needed. The mood was plummeting downhill fast, and that hadn't been his intention. He'd simply wanted to gauge Piper's emotional stability, and he realized she had some deeply buried sorrow for her mom.

"You ready for some pancakes?" he offered.

The kid perked up, nodding so fast that her uncombed hair fell in her face.

"How about you do the smiley face?"

Piper gladly scooped up a handful of chocolate chips and started rearranging them on the pancakes. Luckily they were cool enough that the chips didn't melt.

"If you're my mom's brother, how come you never came to visit us?" Piper asked. "This boy who I used to live next to had an uncle that came to visit them a lot. He even took them skiing once. But Mom would never let me go skiing because she said I could break my arm."

Cameron blinked his thoughts in order, not expecting that to come out of the kid's mouth. There were so many subjects that he wasn't sure what to address first.

"Well," he started. "I'm a lot older than your mom was, and we lived in different towns, with different parents."

Piper tilted her head. "How can you be her brother if you have different parents?"

Such a logical question that required a complicated answer.

"Your mom and I had the same dad," he answered as he swallowed back the bitterness of even speaking of his old man. "But we had different mothers. And your mom was born a long time after I was."

Another blink. "So you lived far away from her?"

Cameron nodded and shut off the burner. "Yep."

Piper finished placing the chocolate chips, resulting in large eyes and a crooked smile. "But if you had the same dad, how come you guys never saw each other? Didn't you love each other?"

Ah, God. Why did the kid always have to ask such loaded questions? In her little sheltered mind, the situation should have been that simple. And Cameron wished it were. He wished his prick of an old man had stuck around. He wished he'd had an opportunity to get to know his younger half sister. He wished he'd made more of an effort to meet Piper before Dianna had died.

He braced his palms on the counter and looked at his niece. "Piper," he said to her. "If I'd had the chance to get to know your mom better, I'm sure I would have loved her. But we were in a difficult position that neither of us could control. Do you understand?"

Piper pursed her lips, as though in thought. "Yeah."

Her answer was simple, but Cameron knew she didn't really understand. How could she? He wouldn't expect anyone to fully understand the difficult position his father had put both him and Dianna in. Unfortunately, at the time, he'd been a pissed-off, selfish kid who'd had no interest in getting to know his father's love child. But he couldn't tell Piper that.

She dug into her breakfast, chewing slowly and getting chocolate all over her mouth. Cameron had just cut into his own breakfast when his sliding glass door was thrown open.

"Piper?" Audrey called as she burst into his living room with all the urgency he'd come to know her for.

"Uh-oh." Cam set his plate down and gave Piper a pointed look. "You didn't tell Audrey you were coming over here?"

Piper's gaze sobered. "I forgot."

"She's in here," Cameron called to Audrey.

Audrey skidded to a stop in the kitchen, then approached Piper. "Honey, we talked about this," she told the girl. "You have to tell me when you leave the guesthouse."

Piper gazed down at her knees. "I forgot," she said again.

Audrey huffed out a breath in relief and pinned her eyes on Cameron.

Her cheeks were flushed, somehow managing to match the chaotic ponytail that looked like it had been slept in. Her light blue flannel pants were too big and were an odd pairing with the gray, sleeveless, muscle-type shirt she had on. The outfit was the most unsexy thing Cameron had ever laid eyes on, and had more wrinkles than a carelessly folded linen shirt.

Despite the state of Audrey's disarray, and the just-been-thoroughly-fucked hair, Cameron couldn't help the grin that crept along his mouth. He wondered if she even realized what she looked like in front of him and was willing to bet if she had a mirror, she'd run and hide. Oddly, Cameron didn't want her to run and hide. He sort of liked this relaxed side of her and the simplicity of her Saturday morning attire.

It made her look like she belonged, as though she'd just rolled out of his bed and come to join them for breakfast.

"What?" Audrey questioned when she caught him staring.

The break in the silence brought Cameron back to reality. She hadn't emerged from his bed. She wasn't here for breakfast, and she didn't belong.

She belongs more than anyone else you've been with.

Cameron knew that simply telling himself that Audrey didn't belong didn't necessarily make him believe it. Because she was...comfortable here.

And he was comfortable with her being here.

"Nothing," he said with a shake of his head.

She narrowed her eyes as though she didn't believe him. Hell, he wouldn't believe him either.

"Gave you a scare, did she?" he pressed. Because that

was better, safer, than pressing his lips to her bare ones. As though he needed a reminder of how soft they were.

Audrey shook her head, and Cameron remembered how emotional she'd been the last time. Cameron decided to take pity on her.

"Holy God, what is that?" Audrey said with a gasp.

Cameron followed her gaze, already knowing what he'd find.

Yeah, there was Jellybean Jr., aka Satan's Spawn, trotting into the kitchen with one of his socks dangling from its mouth. And wouldn't you know the thing would have picked one that had been discolored from the wash. He glanced at Audrey, but she was too busy processing the hairless monstrosity.

"It's a cat," he answered, while trying to swipe the sock out of the cat's mouth. But he, she, or it was too fast and spun around. "Dammit," he muttered.

"Says who?" Audrey asked.

"That's Jellybean Junior," Piper spoke up.

Audrey offered him a grin. "Aw, you can call him J.J."

"We're not calling him anything. And how do you know it's a him?"

Audrey eyed the cat again, who'd already torn a hole in his sock. "Well, it's certainly not female."

"I don't think it's an actual animal. It looks like a science experiment gone wrong."

"You guys are hurting J.J.'s feelings," Piper complained.

"Where'd she come from?" Audrey asked, ignoring Piper's words.

"Outer space," Cameron muttered.

Audrey gazed at him for a moment. "Not an animal person, are we?"

Cameron placed a hand on his bare chest. "I'm absolutely an animal person." He jabbed a finger at J.J. "That's not an animal."

Audrey watched as the cat went to town on Cameron's sock before turning her half smile on him, and damn if it wasn't like a punch in the chest. "What?" he demanded.

"You have pink socks?"

He resisted an eye roll. "No, smartass. That was a white one that got mixed up with a pile of red clothes."

She tilted her head at him. "You actually separate your clothes by color?"

Why the hell should that surprise her? "Shocked to learn I can do my own laundry? I can even brush my teeth too."

Audrey shrugged. "I kind of figured you'd just spray some Febreze on them. Or maybe beat them over a rock."

"What the hell's Febreze?" he questioned.

She just smiled as though he'd proved her point for her.

Then her mischievous gaze dropped to his chest, as though she just realized he didn't have a shirt on. Cameron had yet to bother with getting dressed, and now he was patting himself on the back for his lack of forethought. In the recent weeks, he'd come to love nothing more than ruffling Ms. Bennett's sexy feathers

His attention shifted back to her, and he added a quirk to his mouth for good measure. As though to say, *Yeah, you're not the only one who can play*.

Audrey cleared her throat, effectively ending the moment. She was good at that: dragging them back to reality. Yeah, Cameron needed a good dose of that. But sometimes he wished she'd let herself go.

Hadn't he told her all she needed to do was say yes?

He thought he'd left the ball in her court, but so far all she'd done was dribble the thing with no intention of returning it. Perhaps he should change that.

"I'm going to go play with J.J.," Piper announced. She hopped off the counter and chased after the cat to where it had dragged Cam's poor pink sock.

"So are you going to keep her?" Audrey asked.

At first Cameron thought she was talking about Piper. Funny how his thoughts automatically went to the little girl.

"I don't know a damn thing about cats," he said.

"But that doesn't really answer the question," she countered.

Yeah, he knew that. He also knew he'd end up keeping the heathen for the simple fact that he/she made Piper smile.

"Listen," he started, trying to find his words without sounding like an ass. "I need to apologize for last night." And then he added for old times' sake, "And I'm not talking about getting your panties in a twist. Because I won't say sorry for that."

The red flaring in her cheeks gave Cameron a healthy amount of male satisfaction. "Don't for one minute think you have any influence on my panties."

They both knew she was full of shit. She was dying to fling said panties at him like he was a rock star.

"I think I do," he argued.

"How are you always so sure of yourself?" she questioned.

He shrugged and feigned more confidence than he felt, especially around this woman. "Just am."

She gazed back at him as her teeth sank into her full lower lip, making Cameron want to lean forward and capture it between his own teeth. Then she'd realize he had every reason to be full of himself. He already knew what she was taking more time to realize: that they'd be really good together.

They'd burn up the sheets for hours, just the kind of physical release he loved best. And she'd love it too.

"You were saying . . . ?" she prompted.

Yes, what had he been saying? Ah yes, he wanted to screw her into the early-morning hours.

Except no! That wasn't what he'd been saying. It had something to do with her taking him seriously. Go figure with how far off track the conversation had gotten.

"Uh, yeah," he said slowly. "I just wanted to say sorry for how I brushed you off last night."

Audrey's brow furrowed in confusion.

"About Piper's schedule," he clarified.

She nodded, but still looked like she didn't understand. Or maybe she did, but simply didn't believe him.

"I don't want you to think that I'm not serious about her," he said. He really had committed himself to learning more about Piper and giving her a permanent home with him.

"Okay," she said slowly. "So what's your plan after I leave?" she pressed as she crossed her arms over her chest.

"My plan?" he repeated. Was he supposed to come up with something to present to her?

"Yes," she answered simply. "What do you plan to do with her in the afternoons while you're still at practice? She gets off the bus at three thirty and you don't get home until six thirty."

"I can probably make an arrangement with a neighbor," he answered. To be honest, he hadn't thought who to leave Piper with while he was still at work. It would be a dilemma, because he couldn't come home, pick her up, and bring her back to the field.

"And you know these neighbors well?" she pressed.

"Well enough."

She nodded, but he could tell her brain was still turning a thousand miles an hour. "Well enough to leave a six-year-old with for three hours?"

He shifted his feet, trying to stuff back his annoyance. "They're not convicted felons, if that's what you're asking."

She took a step toward him, probably trying to intimidate him. The only thing she was accomplishing was turning him on. "I'm asking if they're good enough for Piper."

He matched her closeness, crowding her with his own dominance. She didn't back down, and he had to give her credit for that. The woman knew how to hold her own.

"They are in my book," he told her. Then he tilted his head. "But they're not for you, are they?"

She jerked back as though he'd smacked her. "Not for me?"

"Yeah. I'm beginning to think no one will be good enough for Piper." *Including me.*

"That's not true," she immediately answered.

"I'm kind of thinking it is," he pushed. "You haven't cut me any slack yet."

Her chin lifted. "I'm just trying to make sure we're on the same page."

He stepped closer, crowding himself with her lemony scent. "Audrey, we've never been on the same page."

"That's not true either," she whispered.

He traced the tip of his index finger along the neckline of her shirt, grinning at the sight of her thumping pulse. "Isn't it?"

She sucked in a breath, and Cameron had to fight the urge to kiss the hell out of her, just to show her the only page they occupied together was the combustible attraction between them. But then she'd hate him, if she didn't already. And for some reason, Cameron needed to keep her on his side.

"Cameron, what're you doing?"

Hell if he knew. Torturing himself?

"I just want what's best for Piper," she told him.

Cameron dropped his hand, even though it still tingled from her soft skin. "And I don't?"

"I don't know," she countered. "Do you?"

"Of course I do. Just because I'm not trying to control the situation doesn't mean I don't want what's best for her. She's my niece, for crying out loud."

Audrey took a step back, and Cameron realized his error. He had called her out on one of her deepest insecurities. Not just called her out on it, but thrown it back in her face.

Yeah, good way to get the two of you on the same side.

He reached for her, but she pulled away. "Audrey, I didn't mean—"

"No, I get it. I try to control her too much."

The light in her eyes dimmed, and Cameron wanted to kick his own ass for putting a damper on another conversation.

"That's not what I meant," he tried to clarify.

She smiled, but it didn't reach her eyes. "I think you did," she whispered.

Okay, he did. But he'd only been using it as a defense mechanism for the way she made him feel. An asshole move, sure. But he didn't know what else to do around her.

"Audrey—"

"Okay, I admit I have control issues. But you..." She took a step forward and jabbed him in the chest with her finger. "You have commitment issues. And you know what? I think you're just as controlling as I am."

Say what? "How do you figure that?"

Audrey spread her arms out to encompass their surroundings. "Look around you, Cameron. Who do you see?"

His brow twitched. "Is that a trick question?"

"I don't see anyone," she answered for him.

He shook his head. "Not true. You and Piper are here."

She crowded him again, getting all up in his face. "I'm not talking about me and her. We barged into your life with no warning. I'm talking about other people. A wife, kids, girlfriend. Friends. Family who comes to visit."

Cameron shifted, knowing where she was going and wanting to tell her to shut the hell up. But he didn't, because he knew she was right.

"There's no one." She drilled her point home by poking his chest again. "Because you keep people away. That makes you just as controlling as me."

Cameron wrapped his palm around her hand and tugged it away. "I keep people away because it's safer that way. Because then they can't come in and fuck everything up."

The second the words were out of his mouth, Cameron wanted to yank them back. Of course he didn't mean them, at least not the way Audrey would take them. But when she exhaled a slow breath and moved away from him, Cameron knew she was shutting him out.

"Point made," she uttered. Then she strolled out of the kitchen, leaving Cam to wonder how he'd gone from apologizing, again, to making an ass of himself. Again.

THIRTEEN

Pamela Shaw was a five-foot-five whirlwind of energy with a crop of short chestnut hair and a fierceness that seemed to have Cameron shaking in his boots.

Okay, maybe *shaking* was too strong a word. But, Audrey noticed, the normally gruff, often brusque, six-foot-three scowling man was on much more acceptable behavior. In other words, he wasn't taking swipes at Audrey, nor was he cornering her in the kitchen or, say, the bedroom, and muttering husky words in her ear. In fact, he hadn't said much of anything to her since his mother had swept through the door an hour ago with three sacks full of pork chops, potatoes, and asparagus. Audrey liked to think it was because Pamela brought out the best in her son, and not because of the awkward encounter in his kitchen yesterday. One that left Audrey wanting to jump him while simultaneously punching him in the nose.

Luckily Piper had been blissfully unaware of the tension

skirting between Audrey and Cameron. She'd dragged J.J. over and told Pamela all about how she'd rescued the cat. Pamela had patted Piper on the head and crooned at how nice she was for taking the cat in, while secretly sending Cameron a smile as though congratulating her son for his open-mindedness.

Audrey had just finished cutting potatoes and was reaching for the fridge when Cameron's hand shot out at the same time. She jerked back, then remembered her own rule to not let the man get to her. With a lifted brow, she opened the door and snagged the heavy whipping cream off the top shelf.

Cameron lifted his own brow in response as though to say, *Challenge accepted, Bennett.*

"I like your mom," she blurted out. *You're supposed to be giving each other the silent treatment, remember? Why can't you keep your mouth shut around him?*

Cameron nodded and pulled away from the fridge with an old-fashioned bottle of Coke in his big hand. Audrey tried not to pay attention to those hands, or to remember the way the heat of them melted into her skin whenever he touched her.

"You don't like me getting close to her, do you?" Audrey pressed.

"I didn't say that," Cameron answered as he twisted the cap off his soda, then tossed it on the counter.

Audrey gave herself props for not admiring the strength of his hands. "You don't have to. I can see the annoyance all over your face."

Cameron lifted the bottle to his lips, then paused. "I'm not annoyed."

Audrey resisted chuckling. Barely. "You haven't said two words to me since Piper and I got here."

Cameron took a deep pull of his drink. "I need to apologize for last night."

She hadn't been expecting that. Audrey glanced around the kitchen, trying to gather her thoughts. Piper and Pamela were in deep conversation as Pamela sliced up asparagus. Audrey's potatoes were still sitting in a bowl of water.

"Okay," she acknowledged. "I'm sorry too."

His grin widened. "And you weren't even struck by lightning that time."

"Always looking for ways to be pleased with yourself."

"Who says I have to look?" he countered.

"The rest of us earthlings," she said.

He stepped toward her. "Is that your way of saying I'm special?"

Audrey narrowed her eyes at him. "More like an alien being." She glanced at the space around them. "Why are you always crowding me?"

He came even closer. "Because it makes you sweat."

Immediately her brain conjured up all the ways he could make her sweat. Even more than she already was. She didn't like it, but at the same time she also kind of loved it. When was the last time a man had made her feel alive like this? Made her heart triple beat in her chest? Made her knees tingle?

"And you like intimidating people, is that it?" she pushed.

One of his brows quirked as his gaze dropped to her mouth. "You and I both know intimidation isn't what you're feeling right now. Remember, Audrey, all you have to do is say yes."

Audrey was painfully aware of Pamela and Piper, just feet away.

She placed a hand on his chest, to halt his further crowding. "And then what?"

He blinked. "Huh?"

She tried to move back but was blocked by the fridge. "I say yes. What happens then?"

"Are you saying yes?"

Not quite. But she desperately wanted to. "Hypothetically."

His evil grin was back. "Well, then. Hypothetically, I'd push you against this fridge so you can feel exactly what you do to me. Then I'd put my mouth at that sensitive spot just below your ear..." He dipped his head in demonstration. "Because I think I've already proven just how much you like that."

The man was an evil, masochistic bastard. Audrey would have told him that, but she was too busy being turned on.

"Then," he whispered in her ear, "we'd take things to my king-sized bed, where we'd make love until neither one of us could walk."

Holy Mary, mother of...

"Kate Spade," she whispered.

Cameron chuckled against her neck, then pulled away. "But since we're just talking in hypothetical..." The tip of his index finger skimmed across her collarbone, driving home his point with painful clarity.

"Sorry I asked," she whispered.

"No, you're not." His smug grin widened. "You're too busy picturing it."

Hell, yeah, she was picturing it, which was why she was sorry for asking, because she'd go to bed with the images of Cameron pinning her to the mattress, his big thighs holding hers down as he drove into her...

No, it couldn't happen.

Yes, it could. He said all you have to do is say yes...

And it would be so good too. But she couldn't keep her wits about her and leave with an objective heart if she gave in to her impulses. She was stronger than that and needed to remember why she was here.

Cameron must have sensed the moment she shut her mind off, because he stepped back and reached for his soda again. He took a long, casual sip, while carefully watching her.

"Cameron, will you leave that poor girl alone so she can finish the potatoes?" Pamela called from the stove. "The pork chops are almost ready."

That's right. She'd left the potatoes sitting in a pot of water. Then Cameron had come along with his apologies and bedroom eyes and seductive suggestions and thrown her agenda out the window.

She should go, like, cook. Or something.

She straightened from the fridge, attempting more confidence than she felt, returning Cameron's cocky gaze with one of her own. At least she hoped it was cocky. For some reason she felt questionable.

"I know you don't want me to get to know your mom," she told him. "But you're going to have to get over it. Because I like her, and she's good with Piper."

Cameron's arm shot out and stopped Audrey's retreat. "She gets attached to people easily."

"And what?" she asked with a lifted brow. "You think she'll get attached to me, then I'll crush her heart when I leave?" Cameron opened his mouth to argue, but she stopped him. "I know that's exactly what you think."

"My mother likes you," he said in a low voice.

Audrey had another retort all ready, but something

stopped her. Something in Cameron's gaze that closely resembled pleading. Then she got it. Pamela had been hurt before when someone she loved and cared about left. But how could Cameron compare Audrey to his father?

Audrey turned back to him so Pamela wouldn't overhear them. "Not everyone is a selfish ass like your dad," she told him. "I know you're trying to protect her, but give her some credit. She seems like she's a strong woman. And I doubt my leaving will faze her much, since I'm not anything to her."

Dinner had been an uncomfortable affair that was a mixture of tension between him and Audrey and easy banter between her and his mother.

They liked each other. It was obvious with the easy smiles Audrey kept flashing and the infectious laughter at the stories his mom kept telling. About him. Like that time he'd wet the bed at a friend's house and had to come home in the middle of the night.

Yeah, thanks for that one, Mom.

Audrey and Piper found this story to be hilarious.

Then Pam had moved on to Cameron's awkward tween years and the time he'd been caught with a "naughty" magazine and in a compromising position in the bathroom.

Seriously, why did his mother hate him?

"Honey, are you all right?" his mother asked.

"Are you sure you're not constipated? This kid at school couldn't poop all day and his face was all red. Kind of like yours," Piper said to Cam.

Yeah, that was awesome. He resembled a red-faced kindergartener who needed to take a shit.

"Piper, you know that talk isn't appropriate. Do you need to be excused?" Audrey asked in her authoritative tone.

Across the table, Pamela hid a grin from behind her napkin.

Cameron bit back a smile, because it was kind of funny, and looked at Piper. "I'm fine, kiddo. But thanks for asking."

"Can I have some more mashed potatoes?" Piper asked Pamela.

"Of course, sweetie." His mom got up from the table and returned shortly with the bowl of potatoes. She gave Piper a healthy scoop and set the bowl down.

Piper stabbed her spoon into the food, then proceeded to dump it on the floor. Cameron opened his mouth to ask what the hell she was doing, when Jellybean Jr. scampered over and inhaled the potatoes in one bite.

"Piper!" Audrey exclaimed. "Why did you do that?"

"J.J. was hungry," Piper answered with the calm casualness of a six-year-old.

Audrey scooted her chair back so she could clean the mess up. "Well, J.J. has a bowl of food in the kitchen. We don't give cats people food."

"But that food has eyeballs in it. She doesn't like it," Piper added with a pout. "This kid at school says they grind up eyeballs and put them in cat food. He says it's because everyone hates cats."

Christ. It was probably the same kid who hadn't shit all day.

Audrey masterfully hid a grin. "Piper, not everyone hates cats. And there's no eyes in her food. It's just regular cat food."

Cameron placed his palm on Piper's skinny arm. "If it'll make you feel better, we can go to the pet store and I'll let you pick out different food. You can get whatever kind you think she'll like."

Cameron kept his gaze on Piper and ignored the proud look on Audrey's face, like he'd just announced that he'd ridden his bike without training wheels for the first time. Piper slowly blinked; then her gaze rounded even more.

"You mean I can keep Jellybean Junior?" she asked in a soft voice.

And dammit, his heart wasn't supposed to go all squishy when she looked at him like that. He shouldn't care about pleasing her and wanted to put that sweet smile on her face. The one that lit her up from the inside out and made Cameron want to beat his chest in pride.

"Yeah, you can keep the cat," he told her.

Piper jumped out of her seat and threw her little arms around Cameron's neck. He barely managed to stay upright in his seat. He hadn't expected her to pack such a punch behind such a simple gesture. She'd thrown her whole body into the hug, and Cameron had to grit his teeth against the lump in his throat.

"Thank you, Uncle Cameron!" she exclaimed into his neck. She let go and jumped up and down. "I can't wait to get her her own bed, and toys and a leash so I can take her for walks."

"One condition, though," Cameron said, choosing not the address the walking the cat thing. "We have to change her name. Something that's more fitting to a cat." Especially one that didn't have fur. Like, say, Skeletor?

Piper scrunched her face in thought. "How about Pinkie Pie? Like from *My Little Pony*."

Sure. Or that.

"I love that name," his mother chimed in. "It suits her perfectly."

Were they looking at the same cat?

But Cameron didn't say anything because, you know,

picking your battles and stuff. He'd heard from parents it was important to let the little things go.

Parent.

Shit, was that what he was now?

The familiar panic tried clawing its way back, and Cameron tried desperately to shove it down. He should have been over that by now. Right?

He glanced at Audrey and saw she'd placed one hand over her chest and the other was holding on to his mom.

"What?" he barked.

"We're just so proud of you," Audrey gushed.

Yeah, if she knew what was going on in his head, she wouldn't be so proud.

"Don't go giving me a gold star or anything," he told them.

Pam shook her head. "Oh, honey, we wouldn't do that. A pat on the head would probably be sufficient."

Audrey stifled more laughter.

Cameron ignored the sarcasm because she was his mother and he loved her, no matter how obnoxious she could be. The woman meant well. She had been his whole world after his dad took off.

And now you have Piper. And Audrey.

Except he didn't really have Audrey. She wasn't his to keep. The thought startled him more than it should.

To hide his discomfort, Cameron got up from the table and took his empty plate to the kitchen. They'd all but finished eating, and Piper had already scampered off to play with Jellybean Jr. Oh, wait, *Pinkie Pie.*

Because that was such a better name.

Cameron was at the sink rinsing his dish when his mother approached. Instantly he tensed, because he knew what she was going to say to him.

"You okay, honey?" she questioned.

"Yeah. Why?"

"I don't know," she responded as she set her dish in the dishwasher. "You seem...tense."

Cameron rolled his shoulders as though the mention of the word brought even more tension to his muscles. Hell, yeah, he was tense. Soon Piper would be solely dependent on him. And he was coming to realize that he didn't want Audrey to leave.

Cameron gritted his teeth and sloshed the sponge around the plate harder than he needed to. Water splashed over the edge of the sink and landed on his shirt.

"Honey." Pamela placed her calm hands over his and stilled his movement. "Why don't you take a step back from the plate?"

Cameron did as instructed and dried his hands on a dish towel.

"You like her," his mom calmly stated. Everything about the woman was calm.

Perhaps he should take a page from her book. "Yeah," he acknowledged.

"She's good for you." Pam placed her cool palm over his forearm. "And just so we're clear, I'm talking about Audrey. Though I think Piper is good for you too."

He slanted his mother a look. "Yeah, I got that. But she can't stay here."

Pamela tilted her head. "Why not?"

Cameron braced his hands on the counter behind him and sneaked a peek into the living room to make sure Audrey wasn't close by. She'd moved from the table to the living room, where she and Piper were playing with the cat.

"Because she lives in Boulder," he told his mom.

Pam waved that away as though it were such an easy problem to fix. "Oh, and people never move."

"Why would she?" he countered.

His mother paused before answering. "That's a good question."

He heaved a long sigh. "Mom, why don't you just say what you want to say?"

She smiled as though he was so amusing to her. "What I'm trying to say is, you like each other. And you both love Piper. Maybe you should give her a reason to stay. Make your move already."

Make his move? Seriously?

He opened his mouth, but his mom beat him to the punch. "Why are you afraid of her?"

Okay, wait a minute... "Afraid?"

His mom laughed. "Honey, men never change. You all are the same at sixteen as you are at sixty."

He didn't think that was entirely true, but whatever.

"I'm not afraid of her," he clarified.

"Okay, then you're afraid of what she represents. And don't pretend like you don't know," his mother went on as though reading his mind. "She's different. She makes you uncomfortable."

Cameron shook his head. "Why are you saying that like it's a good thing?"

His mom came closer. "Because uncomfortable means there's something there. Something you don't want to acknowledge. And probably because you've never felt it before."

Another sigh left him. "Mom..."

She held her hands up in defeat. "Okay, I'm officially butting out."

Thank God.

Then Pam pointed an index finger at him, to drive her point home one last time. "But let me just say this. It's rare to find someone who brings us out of our comfort zone. And, honey, I think you could use a little of that in your life."

And she was gone, out of the kitchen as swiftly as she'd delivered her cryptic message. Or not so cryptic. Because Cam got what she was saying.

He liked it, his comfort zone. He supposed that was the point, but still...it kept him safe. Safe from commitment. Safe from getting hurt.

Cameron rubbed a hand along the back of his neck and spotted the woman who had his stomach tied up in knots. She was standing in the doorway of the kitchen, balancing plates in both her hands.

"Sorry," she said with a blink. "You looked sort of... tense."

Cam's scowl deepened. "Why does everyone keep saying that to me?"

"Um...because it's true?" Audrey ventured.

Cameron took the plates from her hands as she approached. "I'm not that tense."

She offered a comforting smile. "You're practically vibrating."

"Yeah..." he started, and then forgot what he was going to say. Audrey blinked at him, and Cameron realized he'd been staring at her. How could he not when her hair kept brushing over her shoulders every time she moved? Or the way her enticing lemon scent kept making him think about summer afternoons and cuddling in a hammock.

"Cameron?" Audrey prompted.

"Yeah?" He gazed down at her, momentarily distracted by how her teeth kept stabbing into her lower lip.

"You sounded like you were going to say something else."

Oh. Right. Except he couldn't remember what.

"I just wanted to apologize for earlier," he blurted. Because why not? He'd gotten so good at it.

Audrey's brow furrowed. "For what exactly?"

Shit, she was going to make him spell it out. Of course she would.

"I didn't want to imply that you and my mom couldn't be friends," he told her.

Audrey nodded. "So you're apologizing for being an ass?"

He narrowed his eyes at her.

She held her hands up in defense. "Just trying to be clear. And just so you know, I don't need your permission to be friends with your mom."

Yeah, Cameron had already learned that about Audrey. She did as she liked, and screw it if Cam didn't like it. "Okay, yeah, I was an ass." He placed the dirty dishes on the counter and opened the dishwasher.

"Apology accepted. So, that was a nice thing you did for Piper," Audrey told him. "Letting her keep the cat."

Cameron snorted. "Do you really think I'd make her get rid of it? Even if it does look like an alien life-form?"

Audrey leaned against the counter and crossed her arms. "Actually, no. You wouldn't do that to her."

Cameron snorted. "Good to know you don't think I'm that much of a dirtbag." He hadn't meant for the words to slip out. But there they were, hanging between the two of them like some insecure confession. Only Cameron had never had issues with being insecure. Some would say he was cocky. He'd call it confident. But with Audrey... something about her perceptive gaze made him feel like he was under a microscope. She was always watching him, making him feel like he needed to sit straighter or . . . something.

"Cameron," Audrey said. She took a step closer and placed a hand on his arm. "Is that really what you think?"

His gaze dropped down to her slim, cool palm, cupping his forearm in a soft grip that he was sure was meant to be comforting. Except her touch didn't comfort him. It was damn hard to be reassured when all he wanted to do was pin her against the counter and shove his tongue down her throat, maybe slip his hands underneath her baggy sweater so he could mold his palms over her plump breasts.

Audrey must have sensed the direction of his thoughts, because she snatched her hand away.

"Anyway . . ." She cleared her throat. "I know it's something Piper is really excited about."

"Yeah, well." He cleared his throat too. Because damn. "I don't want to make the kid cry or anything."

She slid him a look as she started grabbing dirty pots off the stove. "Oh, I'm sure that's why."

"Why what?" Cameron asked, momentarily distracted by how her pants curved over her round ass.

She shot him a look over her shoulder. "Why you secretly love Piper."

Cameron absently grabbed a clean pot Audrey had just washed and ran a dishtowel over it. Secretly loved Piper? Did he love Piper? If so, was he trying to keep it a secret? Not only did he not know the answer to any of those questions, but he kind of had the feeling Audrey was right.

"Well, don't shut down on me," Audrey teased.

Cameron set the dry pot aside and accepted another one from her.

"She loves that cat," Audrey whispered. "Dianna would never let Piper have a pet."

"Why?" Cameron asked.

Audrey ran the soapy sponge in circles over a frying pan, before rinsing it. "She worked all the time. And then she got sick."

Cameron noted the way her hands tightened on the frying pan and the clenching of her jaw. "You loved her," he observed.

For a second, he thought she wouldn't respond, or maybe she would toss out one of her quick-witted responses that she seemed so good at to throw him off. Then she sniffed, and Cameron realized how way off base he was. He'd touched on a nerve.

Then she nodded, a tiny movement of her head that he almost missed when he set another dry pot aside.

"I'm sorry," he told her.

Audrey washed the last pan and shut the water off. "For what?" she asked without looking at him.

"For your loss."

Cameron waited for her to say something like "Thanks," or "Yeah, it was hard." But she just looked at him. She gazed at him in a way that was like someone sticking an ice pick through his heart.

It was your loss too.

That was what he saw when he looked in her eyes. She was pleading with him to open up, to admit that the loss of a sister he never knew had affected him in some way, that he wasn't a robot who slept around and kept people at a distance so they couldn't hurt him.

And yeah, he supposed that it had been his loss too. He'd never made an attempt to get to know Dianna. His anger and resentment toward his father had created a selfish, sullen kid who'd had no interest in his little sister.

Cameron wanted to hang his head in shame. He wanted to kick his own ass for allowing all those years to go to waste.

"Stop," Audrey said, clearly sensing his inner battle.

"I never cared to get to know her," he admitted.

Audrey's gaze softened. Suddenly he wanted her to touch him again, to feel her soft skin against his.

"That wasn't your fault," Audrey told him.

Cameron leaned back against the counter. "Wasn't it?"

"No. And Dianna understood that."

Cameron glanced at Audrey. "She told you that?"

Audrey shrugged. "Dianna wasn't like that." A small smile tilted the corners of her mouth. "She saw the good in everyone. Gave everyone the benefit of the doubt." Audrey paused and glanced at her feet. "The world lost a good one with her," she added quietly.

Without thinking, Cameron touched Audrey's chin, which he'd meant to be a brief moment of contact. But his hand lingered, going from a soft brush to gripping her chin and turning her face to his. "She was lucky to have you."

Audrey's eyes darkened, then glossed over with the typical telltale signs of tears. Cameron felt a moment of panic because, shit, he didn't do tears. Like, at all. Just the sight of them made his muscles tense and his mouth clamp shut. But Audrey pulled herself together, and Cameron felt a smidge of regret.

Why?

Because tears from Audrey would have given him a reason to pull her to him. To soothe her, to run his hands down her back.

"Actually, I was the lucky one," she finally said. "As corny as that sounds," she added with a stiff laugh. "Dianna was one of those friends that don't come around very often."

"Must be why Piper is such a good kid," Cameron added.

Audrey gave him half a grin and poked him in the stomach. "I knew you secretly loved her. It's okay, I won't tell anyone, lest I offend your man card."

He leaned closer to her. "Honey, there's not much that could offend my man card."

One of her brows arched. "I wouldn't be so sure about that," she taunted. "You have a hairless cat living in your house named after an animated pony."

He narrowed his eyes at her. "You planted that cat, didn't you?"

She offered him a smug smile. "Yep. It was all a part of my diabolical plan. To find the ugliest, most pathetic-looking animal, then sneak it into your house so Piper could fall in love with it. You totally figured me out."

"I knew you had a naughty side," he said.

Audrey's smile slipped as her gaze slid to his mouth. "Don't you wish."

He edged closer to her, ignoring the sounds of his mother and Piper in the living room. "Don't tempt me, Audrey," he warned.

She tilted her head at him. "Whatever do you mean?"

Closer, he moved until their hips were nearly touching. Hadn't they been in a position similar to this before? And hadn't it led to some seriously awesome kissing? "Yeah, you pretend you're all innocent. But you're not, are you?"

She stayed decidedly mum, keeping that sassy mouth shut, when all he wanted to do was kiss the shit out of her, to lick away the look of triumph on her face whenever she thought she'd one-upped him.

Her hand came up to his chest. Cameron wasn't sure if she meant to push him away or just wanted to feel if his heart was pounding as hard as hers. Didn't matter, because he wasn't going to let her push him away. There was something explosive between the two of them, and it was only a matter of time before it brought both of them down.

"You want to say yes," Cameron whispered.

Audrey pulled back and crossed her arms over her chest. "And then what?"

Um...Did she need him to spell it out for her? Surely she wasn't that inexperienced.

"We have some seriously hot sex," he answered.

Audrey glanced into the living room as though worried his mother and Piper would overhear. "Okay. Then what?"

Cameron opened his mouth, then shut it again. He blew out a breath and scrubbed a hand down his face. "Damn, Audrey. I don't know."

She jabbed him in the chest again. "See, that right there. That's what I'm talking about."

"What the hell *are* you talking about?" he demanded.

She rolled her eyes like he was completely daft. "The fact that you don't know what would happen next. You wouldn't even know what to do, would you?"

"How the hell would I?"

She came closer and got in his face. Why was she always doing that? "Because there is no *next* with you, is there?" He opened his mouth to argue, but she beat him to it. "And I'm not talking about a next time in bed, either."

"I don't know what you want from me, Audrey," he said to her.

"I just want you to be honest," she responded. "I want you to admit that what you want is the conquest. The chase, the mystery, or maybe another notch in your bedpost."

He shook his head. "That's not fair."

"Oh, come on," she went on. "You're going to tell me that you don't have a string of satisfied women strolling around town?" When he didn't answer fast enough, Audrey pushed away from the counter. "That's what I thought."

He snagged her elbow before she could abandon him, needing to set her straight. "What bothers you more, Audrey?" he said in a low voice. "The fact that I have a string of satisfied women, or the fact that you're not one of them?"

Her eyes flared at him, and her arm jerked. For a moment, Cameron thought she was going to hit him, knowing full well that he deserved it for being an ass. Again.

"You want me to be honest?" he went on. "Then you need to start being honest too."

She opened her mouth, probably to argue, and Cameron tightened his grip on her elbow to snag her attention. "I need to hear you say you don't want me."

Her breath huffed out of flared nostrils, which matched her dilated pupils and the fluttering pulse at the base of her neck.

"On second thought, don't answer that," he decided. Then he lowered his head and slammed his mouth over hers.

Cameron wanted to shout in triumph when Audrey melted against him and parted her lips. She just *knew* what he wanted.

Smart girl.

Someone squealed, and Audrey jerked away from him as though they'd been caught necking behind the bleachers. Cameron had done his share of necking in various places, and none of those experiences came anywhere close to this.

Audrey touched her lower lip, and Cameron couldn't

help a sly grin at how her fingers trembled. He'd done that to her. Not some other bastard who didn't appreciate how beautiful and responsive she was.

"You don't impress me," she told him.

Whaaaaat?

Cameron lifted a brow to mask the incredulity coursing through his system. His ass, he didn't impress her.

"I've dated men like you my whole adult life," she went on. "You're all the same."

He took a step toward her. "I doubt that."

She chuckled, but it was void of humor. "Do you? Because so far you haven't done anything to show me you're any different from dozens of other men who are too good-looking and only care about having a good time." Her gaze ran over him. "You get what you want; then you move on to the next willing woman."

He continued his advance on her, keeping one eye on his mother and Piper, just to make sure they still had privacy. "I won't deny I like women," he told her. "I like the way they smell. I like the way their hips always fit perfectly against mine." He allowed his gaze to travel down her body. "And I like how they feel beneath me in bed." He savored the intake of her breath with a growing smile. "And yeah, I like to have a good time. I get what I want from a woman, and I move on because it suits me." He lowered his head to her ear and gripped her waist with a firm palm. "I like sleeping around and have always done so because none of them were worth any staying power." He nuzzled her ear with his nose, his grin widening when she gasped. "Do you understand what I'm telling you, Audrey?"

He pulled back to make sure she got his message loud and clear: that *she* could be that woman.

FOURTEEN

Audrey had to drink two cups of coffee that morning and had gone through the rest of her concealer. Even three days after Sunday dinner, she still wasn't sleeping. Every time she closed her eyes, she felt Cam's lips on hers. How his hand on the back of her head had almost brought her to tears. The man was good. Too damn good for her, and each time she succumbed to his charm, she was reminded why she'd made a vow to stay away from men like him.

Only she wasn't sure she wanted to stay away from him anymore. The more she was around him, the more she fell into those deep blue eyes, the more her resolve continued to crumble. Only a thin layer was left after last Sunday. After he'd kissed her senseless, joked around with his mother, and played with that damn cat.

Cameron Shaw was a good man. It chapped Audrey's ass to even admit that, because it had been his initial self-centeredness that had made it easy to stay away from him. But she could no longer tell herself that he was nothing more than a pretty face with a cement-hard ass and hands that could bring a woman into oblivion. There was helluva lot more to Cameron than he wanted people to see.

After their encounter in the kitchen, she'd had the feeling whatever it was between them had shifted. It had gone from being a game to something more real—with real feelings, real consequences. Yes, falling for Cameron would bring disastrous consequences for her.

Except she wasn't falling for him. Nope, couldn't happen.

She didn't even like the guy.

Cough, bullshit, cough.

Maybe she should buy a vibrator.

Audrey thunked her head against the steering wheel as she arrived back home.

Home.

There was that word again. It kept slipping in there with other ridiculous thoughts that made too much sense, yet she didn't want to hear.

She'd been out all day, picking things up for Annabelle's nursery, desperately trying to take her mind off...well, anything Cameron Shaw.

It was hard to do when she was staying in such close proximity to him and Piper was constantly yammering on about the guy, about how much she liked him, how he made good pancakes, and used funny voices when he read her stories.

The man read Piper stories.

And he used voices.

As if Audrey wasn't conflicted enough. Turned on enough. Confused enough. He had to go and be a good uncle, and all that.

Charming.

Audrey snorted as she exited the car.

"Asshat," she muttered to herself, only because throwing a derogatory comment about Cameron every once in a while helped to keep her in balance, centered her chi. Or something.

And just that morning, he'd made Piper breakfast. Not Audrey. Piper had run over to the main house so she could have breakfast with Cameron before the bus had picked her up for school. Pinkie Pie had pounced along too, and Audrey had gotten a glimpse in the kitchen window of Cameron holding the cat.

Not only hugging it but snuggling it like the cat was a damn golden retriever—only way uglier and with talons the size of a bald eagle's.

The man was such a fraud. So much for hating that damn cat.

Audrey had finished her first mug of coffee, and while pouring herself another one, she furiously shoved back the feeling that she'd been missing out on something, a moment that should have included her. Having breakfast together like a family. Only they weren't a family. Cameron and Piper were. But Audrey was . . .

What was she?

Horny. Horny is what you are.

Yes. Yes, that was true, but not the word she'd been looking for.

Audrey unloaded her stuff for Annabelle and brought everything into the guesthouse.

What she needed was some more caffeine. But not coffee because, damn, it's not like she was an addict.

Much.

Only there wasn't any soda left, Audrey realized after

opening the fridge door. And she didn't have time to run back out before Piper got off the bus.

She shut the fridge door and looked over toward Cameron's house.

Yeah, he totally wouldn't mind.

And even if he did mind, she was taking one anyway. Served him right for making her discombobulated all the time.

As she opened the door, a jingling from behind her caught her attention. Last week, Audrey had purchased a collar for Pinkie Pie with a bell on it; that way she would know where the creature was wreaking havoc. The cat came running out of Audrey's room, with one of her bras dangling from her mouth.

"What the hell?" she demanded.

Pinkie Pie tripped over the straps, which were flapping all over the place, but somehow managed to stay on four feet.

She yanked her pink-and-black Victoria's Secret bra from the cat's mouth. "This was in a drawer," she said to the animal. "How did you even get this?"

But Pinkie Pie didn't get it because, well, she was a cat. She only jumped up and down, batting her paws at the dangling straps.

Audrey held the bra out of reach. "No. Bad cat," she chastised. "Bad Pinkie Pie. Go play with the cat toys I bought you."

But Pinkie Pie didn't even glance in the direction of the basket of cat toys. She only gazed up at Audrey with her big green eyes as though to say, *"But those don't have straps and underwire."*

"This bra cost more than you're worth," she said to the cat. "Go...catch a mouse or something."

Audrey held on to the bra, not trusting Piper's pet for one second, and made a quick trip to Cameron's house for soda. She snagged the last Dr Pepper, then scribbled a quick apology on a Post-it for taking his last soda and slapped the thing on the fridge. A small smile turned up the corners of her mouth at the thought of continuing their Post-it conversations. She certainly hadn't meant it to become their thing, but Audrey found herself looking forward to seeing the little yellow squares with Cameron's signature *C* on the bottom.

Just last week she'd found one on the windshield of her car saying he'd replaced her wiper fluid. It wasn't a big deal. It was wiper fluid, for crying out loud. But Audrey had been unable to stop the little pang in her chest at his thoughtfulness. The man was a constant paradox of irritating and sweet. Audrey had exhausted herself trying to figure him out, and she realized that maybe she never would. She'd already accepted the fact that Cameron didn't want to be figured out.

As Audrey reentered the guesthouse, she recalled a conversation she'd had with Piper, that she'd stay until the girl was comfortable with her uncle.

Was that time already here? Even though she'd given Cameron until the end of the football season? That was only four weeks away, much sooner than she was ready for. Over that last week or so, Audrey had stopped thinking about her departure. Her thoughts had slowly turned to other things, like finishing Annabelle and Blake's nursery, attending the class Thanksgiving party at Piper's school, getting Pinkie Pie her shots.

Maybe she needed to call Stevie. Touching base with her business partner should help Audrey realign her priorities to returning home. Her business had always been her baby, and perhaps she needed to focus on that, instead of Thanksgiving parties and cats.

And the man and little girl she didn't want to leave.

Audrey shook her head as she dialed Stevie's cell.

Her business partner answered on the second ring with her typical short and professional greeting.

"Hey, stranger," Stevie said after Audrey said hello. "Shagging the hot uncle yet?"

She lounged back on the couch and propped her feet on the coffee table even as a ribbon of heat curled through her belly. "You've been watching *Austin Powers* again, haven't you?"

"Those movies never get old," Stevie said with a smile in her voice. "And no answering questions with questions. Tell Auntie Stevie all about it. Did he rock your world? Curl your toes? Does he have any good tricks you can tell me about?"

"Okay, first of all, chill," Audrey interrupted. She'd been having a hard enough time tuning out those kinds of visions without such vivid descriptions. "Second of all, no."

"No, what?" Stevie demanded. "No, you're not shagging him? Or no, he didn't rock your world? Because I have a hard time believing the last one."

"You must stop using the word *shagging*," Audrey ordered. "And how would you even know?"

"Know what?" Stevie repeated. "That he would rock your world? Something tells me he's that type."

Audrey scowled into the phone. How had their conversation steered to this? "But you've never even met the guy."

"He has a sexy name. It's strong and alpha."

Audrey couldn't help but laugh. "He has an alpha name? That's your reasoning? What if his name was Sheldon?"

"Then we probably wouldn't be having this conversation." Stevie replied easily. "Could you imagine yelling 'Oh, Sheldon!' in bed? I'm sorry but, ew."

Her friend had a point. Not only did Cameron's name fit him perfectly, but Audrey had no issues imagining yelling Cameron's name. Or moaning it...whichever.

A shiver wracked her body. "No, I'm not shagging him."

"Hmmm," Stevie responded. "Maybe you should. You sound...rigid."

"I'm not rigid."

"You sound like it."

Okay, so maybe she'd been a bit...tense lately. Not sleeping. Because every time she closed her eyes, she saw Cameron. Felt him. Heard his deep voice in her ear, telling her how good she smelled, how she fit perfectly against him.

But rigid?

"Just have relations with the guy already," Stevie announced.

Audrey smiled. "Relations?"

"Well, *shagging*'s been banned."

Audrey picked at the hem of her shirt. "It would be inappropriate." And who was she trying to convince?

"Why?"

"Because he's Piper's uncle."

Stevie snorted. "Yeah, but he's not your uncle. Just bone the guy already." Stevie paused.

"I was just calling to see how things are," Audrey said, deliberately changing the subject. "Are you totally drowning yet?"

"Hmm, subject change. Okay I get it." Stevie chuckled. "Things have been crazy, but luckily my sister's been here helping. Picking up the slack so I can focus on the jobs."

Audrey frowned into the phone. "I thought Suzanne worked as a pharmacy technician."

"She did, but they recently laid her off," Stevie explained. "I brought her in to help manage clients and book appointments and things like that."

"Oh," Audrey commented, not sure how she felt about outside help being brought in without Audrey being consulted. Even if it was Stevie's twin sister. "Does Suzanne have experience with interior design?"

Stevie rattled some papers on the other end of the phone. "No, but she's not doing any of the creative stuff. I was just so overwhelmed with doing it all while you're gone, and Suzanne was available. She's just acting as my assistant basically."

"Sounds like she came at the right time," Audrey answered, forcing back the strange feeling in the pit of her stomach. *Stevie is not replacing you. She's just getting some help until you come back.* "I was thinking about making a quick trip back for a few days," she blurted out. "Just to play catch-up and help you out until things are settled here."

"Sure," Stevie answered easily. "If you feel you need to. But there's no rush. You can take your time down there until you're ready to return for good."

For good. That sounded so...final.

"I just figured you could use some extra days of my help," Audrey went on, as though she felt Stevie needed the extra convincing.

"Well, if you have some things you need to work on, then yeah. But Suzanne's been enough help for me here," Stevie explained.

A few minutes later, they hung up. Audrey stayed on the couch, watching Pinkie Pie run back and forth across the living room with one of Audrey's already torn-up socks hanging from her mouth.

Did Stevie really not need her? Audrey figured her business partner would be all but begging Audrey to return. A small part of her had thrived on being needed, on knowing she had a role waiting for her at home. Okay, she still had a role, and Stevie still needed her. She couldn't run that entire business on her own. It took two of them for things to run smoothly.

Didn't it?

But it sounded like things were running smoothly without her.

It stung. Just a little.

So maybe she didn't need to take a trip home after all. Maybe she would anyway, just to prove their business needed Audrey there, to show Stevie that her sister Suzanne wasn't a suitable replacement.

Now you're just being childish and overreacting.

Piper eventually got off the bus, and Audrey spent the next two hours going through her school folder, helping her study spelling words, and listening to Piper complain how reading logs were sooooo boring. Audrey eventually got the kid to read for twenty minutes with the promise of taking Pinkie Pie out for a walk, meaning they'd let the cat traipse across the backyard.

"Piper, you like being here with your uncle Cameron, right?" Audrey asked as Piper was dragging a string of yarn for Pinkie Pie to chase.

"Yeah," she answered without looking up.

Audrey was looking for a little more than a one-word answer, but she didn't push. "Do you think you'd be okay with him for a few days by yourself?"

"By myself?" the kid asked as she looked up. "You mean without you here?"

Audrey's heart constricted at the look of confusion on

Piper's face. "Yes, but Uncle Cameron will be here with you. And Pinkie Pie."

The cat in question batted her paws at the string. One of her claws got caught, prompting a giggle from Piper. "Sure. But you're coming back, right? Cause you live here now?"

Oh, God. Not this. Audrey knew Piper wouldn't understand, and she had had a feeling that her extended stay in Blanco Valley would confuse the girl and make her think Audrey was staying for good.

"Yes, I'm coming back," she answered, avoiding the part about living here.

Piper grinned and returned her attention to Pinkie Pie. "I hope Uncle Cameron will make me some more chocolate chip pancakes. He makes the best pancakes."

Audrey had to agree that Cameron was a good cook. She was surprised at how much she enjoyed cooking together—despite all the bickering. Piper would take her spot on the counter and help, and Audrey and Cameron would commence fighting over how to shred chicken or when exactly to salt the water before adding pasta. The whole thing infuriated her, yet she always found herself seated at dinner with a smile on her face.

It was so...normal. At the same time, she was out of her comfort zone.

Piper squealed, and Audrey glanced up, ready to attack Pinkie Pie for scratching Piper. Only it wasn't the cat who had captured Piper's attention. It was her uncle. A six-foot-whatever beast of a man looming at the top of the porch and bracing himself against Piper's enthusiastic hug.

"Can you make me popcorn?" Piper asked him.

Audrey stood from the grass. "Piper, give him a minute to settle after working all day."

But Cameron's gaze was fixed on his niece, who'd wrapped herself around Cameron's long legs. "Sure, squirt. You want kettle corn or movie theater butter?"

And wait a second... Piper hadn't once asked Audrey for a snack. Had she been waiting for Cameron to get home?

"I can get her something," she spoke up. "You don't have to bother."

Cameron finally lifted his deep blue gaze to Audrey, pinning her with an intense look that made her think of something other than popcorn. "It's no bother," he told her. "I bought it just for her."

Piper jumped up and down as though she'd won a victory.

Cameron grinned, and Audrey's heart shifted some more. He really was good with her, and Piper loved him.

"Can I have both?" Piper asked, jumping up and down.

"Why don't you come inside and pick a flavor?"

Piper abandoned Cameron's legs and ran into the house without awaiting further instruction. Audrey thought she saw Cameron smile and shake his head, but the gesture was so minimal that she wasn't sure.

He followed the kid and held the sliding glass door open. "You coming?" he asked Audrey.

She paused before answering because the warnings were back. The ones that always flashed right before he kissed her. Naturally, she ignored them again and walked into Cameron's house. The sneaky bastard remained by the door so she'd be forced to brush past him. For a second, she thought about waiting for him to move, letting him know she was on to him and she wasn't about to partake in his little game.

But... the hell with it. The games were kind of fun, the

most fun she'd had in years, even if they did leave her panting.

"You're spoiling her, you know," Audrey told him as she followed him to the kitchen. Piper was already there, climbing the pantry shelves to get to her snack. "Giving her popcorn before dinner."

"Don't say anything," Cameron said with a wink. "Or she'll be on to me."

Audrey glanced at Piper, who'd climbed onto the counter and retrieved a bowl. "I think she's already on to you."

Cameron paused in the act of opening the popcorn bag. "Is this the part where you warn me about spoiling her diet? Or not giving her snacks past five o'clock?"

Audrey opened her mouth to agree. Yes, she'd been keeping Piper on a much stricter eating schedule; otherwise the kid would be snacking twenty-four seven. She wanted to open her mouth about the importance of giving Piper boundaries and rules, which Cameron always seemed much less concerned with. And yeah, it rankled with Audrey's controlling side. But...as Audrey glanced at Piper and saw her ear-to-ear grin, she held back.

This was a special thing with her and her uncle, and Audrey didn't want to mess with it.

"No," she answered. "Have a bowl of popcorn with her, if you want."

Cameron opened his mouth, then narrowed his eyes at her. "Really?" he asked. "That's all you're going to say?"

"Yep."

"You're not going to suggest I give her apple slices in the shape of a smiley face? Or maybe some gluten-free raisins?"

"Pretty sure raisins don't have gluten," she answered.

Cameron glanced at the clock. "And you're not going to tell me this is spoiling her dinner? That I'm doing it all wrong?"

"I—" She didn't do that, did she?

Cameron tapped her chin with this index finger. "Yeah, you do that sometimes," he told her as he ripped open the plastic and unfolded the popcorn bag. "But I understand, so it's cool." He placed the bag in the microwave and set the timer. Piper was standing at the kitchen counter with her hands wrapped around the metal bowl. Cameron absently ran his hand over Piper's curls. Audrey briefly wondered if he realized he'd done it.

He shrugged as he turned to face her. "You can't help but tell people what to do. I'm kind of thinking maybe you should have been a teacher. Or a prison warden," he added with a grin.

Audrey opened her mouth to argue, as always seemed to be her first instinct with this man, when she realized what he was doing. "I thought maybe you were going to say it's because I care about Piper."

"Well, yeah," he agreed. "But that wouldn't have made your cheeks go all red."

Audrey resisted the urge to place her palms over her face, just to ward away the heat that always crept up when Cameron teased her. "My cheeks aren't red."

"Pretty red."

They stared at each other for a moment as the seconds ticked away on the microwave. She knew was he was doing: trying to get a rise out of her. Ruffle her feathers. Turn her on. And just because it was stupid easy for him to make her pant didn't mean she had to give him the satisfaction of letting him know how he affected her.

He probably already knows.

Yeah, he was that confident. And that correct.

Audrey crossed her arms over her chest. "Okay, but you do know this is going to spoil her dinner, right?"

Cameron shrugged again. "So? The kid's not going to waste away because she eats popcorn for dinner instead of a balanced meal of chicken nuggets and jelly beans."

"I only gave her jelly beans with her dinner that one time," Audrey pointed out.

"Hey, I'm not judging," he told her as the microwave dinged. "I get why you do it."

Audrey watched as he tugged the bag open, steam billowing up, and poured the buttery popcorn into the metal bowl. Piper bounced up and down, then ran out of the kitchen with her pseudo-dinner.

"I'm going to let her eat that whole thing," Cameron said. "And you know what else?" He lowered his voice to a whisper and leaned closer. "I'm even going to let her eat it in the living room."

Audrey ignored the way he smelled. The way he *always* smelled: like clean man and musky and hot.

"Cameron," she said as he chuckled and followed Piper into the living room, "you know she'll get it everywhere."

"Probably," he stated without turning around. "And I may or may not clean it up, either. Maybe I'll even leave the little kernels and dirty bowl for the morning."

Audrey stared at him as he retrieved his cell phone, car keys, and wallet out of his jeans and tossed them on the coffee table. Then he reached behind his head and yanked his hooded sweatshirt off. The movement caused the black T-shirt underneath to lift, revealing a slice of skin that was offset by a strip of white elastic. Yeah, Cameron Shaw was a briefs guy. She'd already known that, having barged in on him a few Saturday mornings, earning herself an eyeful of bronzed, sculpted, holy-cow-chiseled chest. He caught her staring, of course, and flashed her a grin.

A grin of triumph. Of yeah-I-caught-you-checking-me-out.

Audrey cleared her throat. "Seriously, you..." She gestured toward Piper on the living room floor, who was sharing popcorn with Pinkie Pie. "You're not going to leave that for the morning, are you? For the love of God, clean it up tonight."

His grin widened as he threw himself down on the couch. "Yeah, I don't think so." He twisted around and glanced up at her. "I think I'll leave it out. Just knowing that it'll keep you up tonight will make the ants worth it."

Audrey glared at him as she took a seat on the couch next to him. "You're evil."

Cameron jerked his head toward Piper. "But look how happy she is."

"She can be just as happy in a clean living room."

Cameron switched his attention back to her, and Audrey resisted the urge to squirm. The man kicked back like he had no plans to move any time soon. His long legs spread apart, his arms resting on the back of the couch. A man at ease. Except she knew Cameron was rarely at ease. And also...

His lap looked like it would be perfect for her to crawl across and straddle.

She shifted, and Cameron's grin widened as though he'd gotten a peek at her thoughts.

"What did you mean earlier?" she blurted out.

"You mean the thing about you being a prison warden?" he questioned.

Audrey sent him a droll look.

"The gluten-free raisins?" he tried again.

This time Audrey glared. "When you said you got why I do it."

"Ah," Cameron said with a nod. "That."

He knew what she was talking about. The man was just messing with her again.

"Just that I get why you fuss over her. You feel guilty," he stated.

Audrey immediately opened her mouth to argue, then shut it. Did she feel guilty? What would she have to feel guilty of?

"Guilty," she repeated.

Cameron gazed at Piper on the floor as she shoved handfuls of buttery popcorn into her mouth. He grinned when half the kernels landed on the floor.

"I'm not criticizing you, Audrey," he replied with a glance at her. "I said I understood why."

"And what about you?" Audrey said, needing to turn the conversation away from her.

"What about me?"

"You once said that you identify with her. You understand her loss."

Cameron was silent a moment as he watched Piper and Pinkie Pie on the living room floor. Audrey hoped it was because he was remembering his own experiences and not taking the time to formulate the right answer, what he thought she'd want to hear.

"Yeah," he finally said. Then he looked at her. "But you already knew that."

Yeah, she did. But she still felt like she hadn't been given the entire story.

"And you still think you're not right for her?" Audrey pushed.

Cameron rubbed his chin, calling attention to the dark

stubble shadowing his jaw. A shiver ran down her spine as she imagined how it would feel to get a little whisker burn from the guy. Maybe some on her neck. A little on her thighs. She barely held back a sigh.

"I—" He broke off when he looked at her, and his mouth quirked. "Audrey." When she forced herself to make eye contact with him, her breath shuddered. "You're not thinking dirty thoughts, are you?"

She opened her mouth, then shook her head. "Don't change the subject."

Cameron scooted closer on the couch. "Oh, but let's." The rough pad of his thumb stroked the hammering pulse at the base of her neck. "Let's talk about what's going on right here."

She swatted his hand away and thought about moving away from him. "Let's not."

He lowered his head, and Audrey braced herself for contact, even though they were already touching on the couch. But his lips bypassed hers and went for her ear, where he nuzzled and breathed and drove her out of her mind with his warm breath and soft lips.

Audrey tried to pull back, but stopped. Not because Cameron was holding her down, but because she didn't want to. "Do you enjoy torturing me?"

He grunted, then slid a chunk of her hair over her shoulder. "You owe me another pack of soda," he said against her ear.

The bastard was smiling. She could feel it against her skin, and every feminist bone in her body wanted to tell the man off. "How do you know that was me?" she whispered. "Maybe Pinkie Pie grew a set of opposable thumbs."

"Audrey," he muttered against her ear, causing another

wave of shivers, "I know it was you. You're the only soda fiend in this house."

She grinned despite herself. "Says the guy who keeps his fridge stocked with them."

He pulled back and grinned at her, and she wanted to yank him closer. "Because I know you'll come sneaking."

"So why don't you just buy them and put them in my fridge?"

Cameron brushed his hand along her collarbone. "Maybe I like knowing you've been sneaking around my house."

Audrey placed a hand on his chest, ignoring the fact that he not only knew she'd let herself in here when he wasn't home, but he also knew that she loved her some soda. She also knew the man was observant and wasn't surprised at the little things he'd picked up about her. A month ago, it would have terrified her, but now...now she'd grown used to it. Not only that, but she sort of liked it. Liked knowing he paid enough attention to her. That he watched her. Made her feel all hot from the inside out.

Cameron glanced at her hand on his chest, as though waiting for her to push him away. Instead, she tightened her grip and leaned closer.

"Cameron..." Audrey licked her lips and summoned her courage. "I don't have a great history with men," she admitted. "I've been with guys like you before, and it never ends well."

"That's not the first time you've compared me with some douchebag ex of yours," Cameron pointed out. "Why don't you try explaining that one?"

She pulled in a deep breath. "Men who...like to have a good time. And don't tell me you're not one of those guys," she added with a rush before he could argue with her. "You've already admitted as much to me."

"Okay," he answered slowly. "I won't." He brushed his thumb over the back of her hand. "So what're you afraid of?"

She focused her attention on his hand covering hers, because looking into his deep blue eyes was too much. It was too much to see that he cared, that he got her, when she didn't really want him to. Because then she was left defenseless, when she'd basically just admitted she wanted to jump in bed with him.

"I'm afraid of having my heart broken again," she admitted.

"Fair enough," he said after a moment.

"So?" she asked, looking at him. "Are you going to break my heart, Cameron?" Maybe she didn't want to go home to Boulder, after all. Maybe her quick trip home was less about checking on her business and more about talking to Stevie. About maybe leaving the business with her. Possibly going into business for herself here.

"That's the last thing I want, Audrey," he told her, and she believed him.

FIFTEEN

I wanna do the merry-go-round again," Piper announced as she tugged on Audrey's hand and bounced up and down.

Audrey stifled a groan because they'd ridden the thing three times already. Wasn't it enough?

Apparently not, because Audrey found herself in front of the merry-go-round for the fourth time, watching Piper climb on the same horse.

So far, Cameron had been decidedly absent from this carnival fund-raiser for the football team.

He was probably off doing his thing with the players and their parents. Certainly he wouldn't go off with some other woman.

Just because other guys had done that to Audrey before didn't mean Cameron would. After all, he did say he'd find them and take Piper to play some games. But she and Piper had been here for almost two hours, and still no sign of him.

Seriously, you must stop obsessing.

He'd find them. Hadn't they turned a corner three nights ago in his living room? When she'd given him a semi-green light? Whatever the hell that was. Audrey still hadn't figured out yet what she'd agreed to. She'd assumed he'd come knocking on the guesthouse door after Piper had gone to bed and slowly peel her clothes off. Instead, she'd gotten a polite text.

Still think you'd make a good prison warden.

Okay, so not so polite. But it had still made her smile. And then she'd texted back, *stop texting me already!*

Piper squealed, and Audrey was jerked back to the present. She grinned at the girl and waved as the merry-go-round spun around again. Her heart lightened to see the youthful joy on Piper's face, and it was yet another reminder that Audrey didn't want to leave. She could easily relocate here and start another business. Then she wouldn't have to go through the gut-wrenching pain of saying goodbye to a little girl who'd stolen her heart. Her dearest friend's daughter who was the personification of light and practically defined the phrase "starting over."

Maybe Audrey ought to take a page out of Piper's book.

The merry-go-round ended, and Piper came running off the ride. Then she grabbed Audrey's hand and started rattling on about games and winning some giant pink giraffe. Because the kid didn't have enough stuffed animals.

"How about another ride?" Audrey suggested instead.

Piper jumped up and down. "I wanna go win a prize. Please, please, please, please—"

"All right," Audrey interrupted. "What game do you want to play?"

"I want to go shoot the ducks," Piper said as she pointed to the game.

Audrey glanced over and stifled a shudder. Ugh, guns. "You want to shoot those poor ducks?"

Piper grinned up at her. "They're not real ducks. They're just pretend for the game."

"How about the ring toss?" Audrey didn't have the guts to admit how awful her aim was.

Piper made a face. "That's for babies. I wanna shoot ducks." Piper pointed a long, skinny arm at the game in questions. "'Cause look, you can win that giant cowboy hat."

Audrey slanted the girl a look. "I thought you wanted the pink giraffe?"

"No, I want the hat. 'Cause I can wear it to school, and everyone will think it's cool."

Audrey resigned herself to her fate and made their way to the game. "I don't think you can wear a hat that big to school."

Piper bounced on her feet as they stood in front of the booth. "I can on hat day."

Oh. Hat day. Well, then, she'd get Piper the damn hat.

The kid behind the booth handed Audrey the fake rifle and gave instructions. Basically shoot the ducks with...whatever this gun shot out.

It wasn't, like, real bullets, was it?

Audrey raised the gun as the ducks came to life and spun around in circles. She missed the first two shots and felt an actual trickle of sweat slide down her spine. After all, she only had three shots to win the stupid hat, and Piper was watching with growing concern.

"That's just about the worst shooting I've ever seen."

Audrey's hand jerked at the sound of the deep voice behind her. Luckily her finger hadn't been on the trigger, otherwise she would have wasted her last shot. Then she'd have been in deep water with an expectant six-year-old.

She turned and clapped eyes with Cameron, and tried not to react at how he looked in his dark gray sweater and blue jeans.

"You think you can do better?" she taunted.

Cameron wagged his fingers at her. "Give me that thing."

She passed over the gun and stepped aside. The game was still going, the ducks still spinning in circles like little yellow maniacs.

Beside her, Piper was practically bursting with energy. "You have you to win that prize, Uncle Cameron," Piper quipped.

"Yeah, watch how it's done," he told Piper, but his gaze was on Audrey.

She shivered at his low tone and how the fake gun looked cradled in his big hands—as though the thing belonged there, and he'd done it before. "Those ducks are demonic," she warned him. "Look, they're laughing at you."

Cameron slid her a look as he set the gun in place. "Pretty sure that's quacking."

She leaned closer and whispered, "Laughing."

Cameron chuckled and set his sights on his target. "Sore loser, much?" Then he squeezed the trigger and one of the ducks was knocked over, signaling a bell, indicating he'd won.

When Piper realized what her uncle had done, she jumped up and down and held her hands out for the giant hat. The attendant behind the booth plopped the thing on her head, and it immediately slid down and covered her face.

Cameron picked the hat up and settled it more firmly on Piper's head. "Looks good on you, kid," he told her.

Audrey snorted. "It's ridiculous."

Cameron grinned as Piper adjusted the hat. "I think you're jealous that you don't have one of your own. Want me to win you one?"

Audrey rolled her eyes. "I think you've shown off enough for one night."

"Thanks for my hat, Uncle Cameron," Piper exclaimed. "Can we go win the giraffe now?"

"I'm all out of cash, squirt. How about another ride?"

But Piper didn't even hear Cameron's offer. "I see my friend Anna from school." Piper looked up at them and pointed off in the distance. "Can I go ride the bumper cars with her?"

"Sure," Cameron told her, and the three of them made their way from the games back to the rides.

Once there, Piper handed over her hat, because the thing kept slipping over her eyes, and ran off to join her friend. The two girls squealed as they were led into the riding zone and got to pick their cars.

"Don't you think she's too small to sit in one of those by herself?" Audrey questioned. "Maybe I should ride with her."

Cameron leaned toward her. "You're fussing again," he said in a low voice.

Audrey blew out a breath as she watched a giant grin light up Piper's face. "You're right."

Cameron leaned his forearms on the railing. "First time at a fair?"

"No, she's been before," Audrey answered.

Cameron's mouth quirked. "I meant you."

She narrowed her eyes at him. "Funny." Audrey sobered as she watched Piper. "The first fair she went to was with her grandfather."

Cameron watched her for a moment. "My father?"

Audrey nodded, knowing she had be careful when broaching the subject of Cameron's family life. All this time she'd spent with him, and she still didn't know much about his relationship with his dad or Dianna. She wanted to know more, because she had a feeling that past was what made the man tick.

"Actually, Piper doesn't remember," Audrey added. "She was just a baby. Your dad had come to town to visit, and he took Dianna and Piper to some fall fair in Denver." She risked a glance at him, but he was watching Piper. "It was one of the last times they were together."

Cameron grunted. "The old man was never much into family time." He looked at her briefly, but it was long enough to see the tumult in his gaze. "It was more than he ever did with me."

"Dianna always thought he was trying to absolve his guilt," Audrey said. "Trying to spend time with her to make up for what he did to you."

"Good of him," Cameron muttered.

Audrey ran her finger along the edge of the railing. "If it makes you feel better..." But her voice trailed off, because she and Cameron had seemed to find a temporary reprieve and she didn't want to spoil it.

"What?" he asked as he looked at her.

Audrey pulled her gaze away from his long lashes. "Dianna and your dad were never that close. I don't think he made much of an attempt with her. Or Piper."

His brow furrowed. "Why would that make me feel better?" he asked, as though insulted.

"I don't know," she admitted. "I just meant...you weren't the only one who was abandoned by him."

Cameron was silent a moment, and Audrey thought she'd lost him. That she'd said too much and he was mentally slamming the door on her. Then he surprised her by responding. "My dad wasn't really father material. He'd been having an affair with Dianna's mom for a year before he walked out on us."

"I'm sorry," she said lamely. "Your poor mom."

But Cameron just shrugged. "She handled it pretty well. I don't think I ever saw her cry."

"I bet that was more for you, trying to be strong and all that."

"I wish she wouldn't have."

Audrey watched as Piper got off the bumper cars, then followed her friend back around to the line so they could ride again. "What do you mean?"

"Just would have been nice to see some emotion from her. Instead of forcing false happiness all the time."

Audrey immediately thought of herself and how she'd continually smiled for Piper in the days and weeks following Dianna's death. How she was always so worried about how Piper was adjusting. "She probably thought she was doing what was best for you. Maybe she saved her tears for when she was alone."

Cameron shook his head. "I'm not so sure. My dad was an even worse husband than he was a dad. He and my mom had been growing apart, and I think the only thing she missed was the income he brought in. After he left, she had to find a second job so we wouldn't lose our house."

Audrey placed a hand on his arm. "She did that for you."

A muscle in his jaw ticked. "Yeah," he said after a moment. "She's the strongest woman I know."

"It's obvious how close the two of you are," Audrey agreed. "And she was really good with Piper."

Cameron smiled for the first time since mentioning his dad. "I think she sees Piper as a pseudo-granddaughter. She's pretty much lost hope of getting any grandkids out of me."

Something inside Audrey twisted at his words. *Don't ask. It's none of your business.* But then her mouth disconnected from her brain. "You don't want kids?"

His shoulders moved, and Audrey wondered if it had more to do with restlessness. "Sure, someday."

"But it's not a priority for you," she added, because she was masochistic like that.

He turned his head and winked at her. "Got to have a wife first."

She nudged his shoulder with hers. "Look at you being all traditional."

His grin widened. "Surprised?"

She shook her head. "No, just..." Then she laughed. "Actually, yeah."

His look sobered. "Just because I like to have a good time doesn't mean I don't want to settle down one day. I meant it when I said I haven't met a woman worth settling down for."

Audrey ignored the sharp pain in her stomach. "Think you ever will?"

His gaze dropped to her mouth. "Maybe."

She licked her lips and did a mental happy dance when his blue eyes darkened. "What if you've already met her and you haven't realized it?"

Stop baiting him. Stop pushing his buttons.

Cameron angled his body toward her and rested one elbow on the railing. "What're you saying, Audrey?"

Yes, Audrey. What are you saying?

"I just mean..." She cleared her throat. "That what if in the middle of all your..." She broke off, searching for the right term. "Good timing, the woman for you was already there? Only you didn't notice her, and she moved on to someone else?"

Cameron seemed to think this over for a moment, although Audrey wasn't so sure, because he moved closer and fixed his attention on her lips again. They actually tingled. "I don't think so," he finally said.

"But how do you know?" Did she have to sound so breathy?

The corners of his mouth turned up, and he trailed one finger along the edge of her jaw. "I just do."

"Always so sure of yourself," she whispered.

"On this? Yeah."

She tilted her head at him. "That cockiness works on a lot of women, doesn't it?"

His voice dropped an octave. "Obviously."

"How is that supposed to be obvious to me?" *Really? You need him to show you?*

"Oh, Audrey," he chastised. "Your naïveté would be sweet if you weren't such a big faker."

Cameron shifted, and then his lips were just there, touching hers, and Audrey didn't have time to wonder how that had happened so fast. One second she'd been trying to talk herself out of kissing him, and the next she was clutching his shoulders and sliding her tongue along his.

She shouldn't have been surprised at how good it was. After all, they'd kissed a few times already, and each time it knocked the breath from her lungs. So Audrey was surprised at how, well...surprised she was. Cameron really was a skilled kisser. Each time he made it feel like it was the first time, and every time he knocked her off her feet.

He changed the angle of the kiss without breaking contact, using his hand to cradle the back of her head and guide her. Audrey went with the flow and allowed him to maintain the control, even though she wanted to climb his body. Cameron must have sensed her desperation because he grinned against her mouth and kissed her harder, as though he suspected she wanted to pull back. Maybe he'd taken her gasp of breath as hesitation, but the feeling coursing through her system was anything but.

Audrey couldn't help feeling a sense of rightness. Like they belonged. Like she'd been born to kiss *this* man, feel *his* fingers biting into her hips. To place her hand over his heart and wonder if she was the one who made it beat faster.

Yes.

The word whispered in the back of her mind, sounding strangely like Cameron's, as though offering confirmation to her own musings. Audrey spared about a second trying to push the thought away, then gave up. Surrendering to the knowledge that whatever was between them was real and not going away anytime soon was easier than her continued denial, than her fruitless efforts to push the man away with childish games.

So she pressed closer, needing to feel more of him, needing to know how she affected him. The evidence was there, nudging her belly and causing another wave of shivers to snake down her spine.

Then something flashed out of the corner of her eye, followed by a yelp.

Cameron slowly lifted his head. "Don't hold me responsible for what I may do to these women."

Audrey blinked. "What?"

But Cameron had already shifted his attention to whatever had interrupted them. Audrey followed his line of sight and bit back a grin at the four women gawking at the two of them. Their signature beehives left no doubt as to who they were and what they were doing with their camera phones. Someone seriously ought to start reporting these ladies.

"I got a good one, girlies!" Lois shouted as she waved her phone in the air. "This one's going on the Instagram."

"How many times do we have to say it, Lois?" Lois's friend piped up. "There's no *the*. It's only Instagram. Not *the* Instagram."

"I still think I got the better shot," another one chimed in. "I have here a prime picture of Cameron palming the woman's ass."

Audrey couldn't help the heat that flamed her cheeks. She wasn't sure if it was from hearing the word *ass* leaving a seventy-something-year-old's mouth or the fact that they'd so easily noticed Cameron's firm grip on her derriere.

Cameron pinched the bridge of his nose. "Lois, if you post any pictures you just took to any social media site, I'll sic Brandon's dog on you." Then he jabbed a finger at her friend. "Same goes for you, Beverly."

"Already uploaded mine," Beverly announced. Then she beamed at the rest of them. "Told you my phone was faster. The three of you need to get the new iPhone already."

Virginia rolled her eyes and leaned heavily on her cane.

Cameron blew out a heavy breath and shook his head. "Son of a mother's whore."

"You watch your tongue, young man. We may be progressive, modern women, but we're still ladies."

Cameron narrowed his eyes at them. "Somehow I doubt that, Patty."

Beverly gripped Lois's skinny arm. "Let's go get funnel cakes before they run out. I want hot fudge and powdered sugar on mine."

The four women walked away, with Cameron's gaze never leaving them. "I know where you live," he called after them. Then he placed his attention on Audrey, and his gaze further darkened. "What're you laughing at?"

"Nothing," she immediately said. "But I think maybe you secretly love them."

"*Love* them?" he questioned. "They're a public menace. They need to be committed."

"They also make you smile," she pointed out.

Cameron turned toward her and gripped her elbow. "That's not a smile. It's a grimace of pain."

Audrey held back another grin as she allowed him to lead her to... "Where are we going?"

"The bumper cars," he answered. "I need to bash my frustration out."

The ride that Piper was on had just ended, and the girl came running around to the line again.

"I wanna ride with Uncle Cameron," she announced.

Cameron glanced down at the girl as he passed over ride tickets to the attendant. "Just be sure to hold on tight." Then he winked at Audrey and she had a feeling that maybe he was talking about both of them.

SIXTEEN

L ater that night, Cameron was digging around in the fridge while simultaneously nursing a serious case of blue balls. He thought about jumping in the shower and giving himself some relief, but the thought didn't hold much appeal. Then, as he'd been sniffing his way through leftovers, his phone dinged with another text from Tessa. The woman had been trying to get in touch with him for weeks. Normally, Cameron would have told her to come on over. But now...now Tessa didn't interest him.

What he and Tessa had was casual anyway, and both agreed to stick with it as long as it was working. Well, now it was no longer working for Cameron.

That's because she doesn't have blond hair and make you hard as a rock.

Yeah, there was that.

Tessa had to know things would end between them

sooner or later. In fact, Cameron was surprised she'd stuck around this long.

Cameron finally found something to zap in the microwave as his phone pinged again. With a sigh, he picked the device up and thumbed the message.

Busy tonight? I can be there in ten.

The one before that said something about missing him and how some guy she'd met while visiting her sister hadn't come close to satisfying her the way Cameron could. The thought that she'd been with some other guy, and was now trying to get a booty call out of him, should have caused at least some jealousy. But nothing.

The microwave dinged as he typed his reply.

Tired tonight. Getting ready for bed.

He wondered for a minute if she'd see that as an invitation. But Tessa knew better than to show up unannounced.

You didn't exactly put up a fight the last time she showed up unannounced.

But that was before Audrey.

He'd never talked about his father to anyone. Not even his mother. Not Blake and not Brandon either. But tonight, he had found himself spilling his guts to her, and all Audrey had to do was bat those long lashes at him, and he felt as though he could tell her anything, that she wouldn't judge or make him feel like an insensitive prick for ignoring his sister all those years. She'd simply listened and comforted him.

Cameron blew out a breath as he gathered his leftovers from the microwave. After a second thought, he set them back down and picked up his phone again. He needed to send a clearer message to Tessa so she understood.

I think our arrangement has run its course, Tessa. We should probably go our separate ways.

Was that clear enough? Too abrupt? Shit, he didn't want to come off as an insensitive ass. Normally he ended relationships in person, but what he and Tessa had wasn't really a relationship, so...

Yeah, he supposed it would have to do.

Having Audrey here, and Piper too, had made him take stock of his life. It had made him wonder if he'd been truly happy before the two of them had come along.

A knock sounded at his door just as Cameron cut into his leftover grilled chicken. With a resigned sigh, he placed his dish on the kitchen counter and went to the door.

When he opened it, Tessa breezed past him in a cloud of perfume and determination that had once turned him on. Now he just wanted to scratch his head and ask himself what he ever saw in her.

"When you said you were going to bed, I figured I'd join you," she told him as she kicked off her shoes and dropped her purse.

See? Invitation.

He should have listened to his own warnings.

"Tessa," he said on a tired breath. "I really am going to bed."

She smiled at him. "I know. And I'll join you."

"I don't think you understand." He gripped her shoulders. "I'm going to bed *alone*. And did you not get my second text? This needs to end."

She blew out a breath and took a step back. "I met someone," she said.

Cameron waited to feel something. A flicker of jealousy, betrayal, anything. But nothing.

"That's great," he told her.

She blinked at him. "You don't care."

He shrugged. "I'm happy for you." When she didn't

respond, Cameron ran a frustrated hand through his hair. "Tessa, you're the one who wanted this casual. No questions, no commitments. Remember?"

"Yeah, I just..." She broke off and looked around. "I thought maybe you'd feel something."

"Tessa, what're you doing here if you've got a guy waiting for you?"

"We haven't made anything exclusive yet," she answered with a shrug.

"So you thought you'd stop by for one last booty call?"

Tessa made an impatient noise. "You never seemed to mind before."

He crossed his arms over his chest. "Well, I mind now. You need to go."

She laughed. "Why, you have a woman stashed in the back?"

Audrey's face immediately flashed across Cameron's mind, but he shoved it away.

"Ah, shit," Tessa muttered, obviously taking his silence the wrong way. Or maybe she took it exactly as he'd wanted her to. Either way, he didn't care. He just needed her gone.

Cameron shook his head. "There's no one here," he told her, not really sure why he felt the need to correct her assumption.

Her eyes dropped closed for a second. "Can you just be straight with me for a minute? What's going on? You've never shoved me out the door like this before."

He blew out another tired breath and wrestled with whether or not to be straight with her. Despite how pushy she could be, Tessa was a good woman. She was nice and fun to be around and could offer some other guy a lot. Just not him.

"We've run our course, Tessa," he told her.

"Really?" she asked, as though she didn't believe him.

"Yeah," he confirmed.

She came closer, and Cameron automatically recognized the look in her eye. It was the one she'd shown him when they'd first met and all he'd been able to focus on was her long legs and come-hither smile. And damn if his body didn't react. He was still a man, after all, even if his thoughts were on Audrey and finishing that kiss.

Cameron lifted his hands to hold her away, but somehow he found himself gripping her shoulders. Tessa must have taken the gesture as an invitation because her smile grew.

"I don't think so," she muttered.

"Tessa," he warned.

She either didn't hear him or chose to ignore the edge in his voice. Her hands crept up and slid over his chest. His body reacted further, and Tessa's grin widened when she felt the evidence pressing against her thigh.

Her gaze dropped to his erection. "You're still going to ask me to leave? Come on, Cameron."

His back teeth gritted together in agony as she pressed a soft kiss to his neck.

Push her away. Put her in her place. You're trying to be a better man for Audrey.

His hands tightened around her shoulders, but his movements were halted when he felt her tongue.

She's doing that thing you like, his evil side whispered.

What would Audrey have to say about this? his more sensible side countered.

Ultimately, Cameron found the strength to shove Tessa back. He was just about to tell her enough already, when a movement out of the corner of his eye caught his attention.

Cameron held his breath, because he knew what he'd find before he even turned his head.

Audrey's expression was full of disappointment and hurt, and a thousand other things he couldn't name.

He opened his mouth to explain, anything to chase away the disgust darkening her whiskey eyes. But nothing came out, because deep down he knew he'd lost her. He'd lost whatever trust he'd managed to gain in the past few days. Then she was gone, pivoting on her heel and disappearing into the moonless night.

Tessa made a noise behind him. Cameron really didn't care, because his heart was currently plummeting to the bottom of his stomach.

When he turned, she was slipping her shoes on. She offered him a sad smile. "We're not all that different," she told him. Then she scooped her purse off the floor and slung it over her shoulder. "I'll see myself out."

He watched her walk out, his gaze dropping to the perfectly round ass that had attracted him in the first place. Yeah, Tessa was beautiful. She was ambitious and aggressive and outspoken and good in bed. But she wasn't the one who squeezed his heart whenever he looked at her. The honor belonged to a blond, pushy, gorgeous woman that he'd let slip from his grasp.

Audrey's hand trembled as she splashed a healthy amount of red wine into a glass. She still shook as she raised the glass to her lips, and the sweet liquid rolled over her tongue and burned all the way to her stomach. She immediately pulled another sip, before the first one was able to fully settle in the pit of her stomach. After the first glass she poured another, thinking the alcohol would have steadied her hand by now. But the damn thing still shook like a leaf in a storm. Like . . .

Like someone jealous.

The word burned across her mind, furthering her anger and disrupting the peace she'd finally settled into.

For the first time in a long time, she'd felt a sense of peace with her life. That things were finally clicking into place. That maybe...

Maybe she'd finally settled where she was supposed to be.

Then reality had come smacking down and reminded her that no.

There would be no peace for her. No comfort. No settling down.

And, really, it was her own fault. As much as she'd like to blame Cameron, Audrey knew she shouldered some of the responsibility. The man was who he was, and she couldn't change him. No amount of wishing and daydreaming could mold him into the man she wanted him to be.

On the other hand, the scene she'd walked into...that woman's lips on Cameron's neck. His hands gripping her shoulders. Audrey had been hit with a blinding white numbness she'd never felt. She'd been unable to do anything other than stand there and watch, because she'd been unable to identify the foreign feeling coursing through her system. Then she'd stubbed her toe on the edge of the door as she'd been trying to back out, and the gig had been up.

Cameron had been able to see every emotion swirling through her eyes. She'd wanted to smack herself for being so predictable, for thinking that slinking over there at eleven o'clock at night had been a good idea. For thinking that he'd welcome her with another one of his soul-searing kisses and drag her to bed. And it figures that the one time she'd conjured some boldness with a man, it would come back to bite her in the ass.

And why would he want her anyway? The woman who'd been draped all over him and sucking on his neck was the opposite of Audrey. Tall, elegant. Gorgeous. Polished. Not that Audrey was a slouch. She knew she was attractive and maybe even beautiful if she made enough effort. But that woman...with her size C's and slim legs. She was the type of woman Cameron belonged with.

Audrey poured herself another hefty glass and smiled to herself when the tremble had lessened.

Behind her, the door to the guesthouse opened, letting in the cool midnight air. The moon was absent tonight, leaving the backyard an inky mass so Audrey hadn't seen him come. But she'd known he'd eventually show up.

Audrey lifted the wineglass to her lips. "Go away, Cameron." She downed another healthy sip, just so she'd have something to occupy herself.

He approached, but didn't say anything. Audrey didn't turn around, couldn't face him and show just how much he'd hurt her.

"Audrey," he said in a low voice.

She ignored him and continued to sip her wine.

"That wasn't what it looked like," he told her.

It's not me, it's you. Your check is in the mail. Yeah, she'd heard them all.

"I was trying to get her to leave," he went on.

A laugh popped out of her. "Yeah. Looked like it."

He sighed and reached around her to pluck the wineglass from her hands. She almost turned to demand to know what the hell he thought he was doing, but found she didn't have the strength. She was tired, defeated, and confused.

Audrey bit her lip as Cameron set the glass down, then wrapped both hands around her shoulders and turned her to face him. But the second she clapped eyes with his, she remembered how he'd held that other woman the same way, and she shrugged out of his hold. He immediately dropped his arms and held his hands up in defeat.

"Okay," he said. "I get it."

"I don't think you do," she whispered.

"So why don't you tell me?" he suggested.

She laughed, even though it was far from funny. "You want me to explain to you why I'm upset over what I just walked in on?"

Cameron nodded. "Okay, dumb question." He gazed at her for a moment. Then he tilted his head as though a thought had just occurred to him. "On second thought, explain."

Audrey resisted the urge to smash the bottle of wine over his head. "You want *me* to explain?"

"Yeah," he said without hesitation.

She jabbed a finger at herself. "I'm supposed to explain when you're the one who—"

"I'm the one who what?" He crossed his arms over his chest. "Why were you sneaking into my house at eleven o'clock at night?"

She opened her mouth to answer, then shut it. They both knew why, and they both knew she had no defense. But how had he managed to turn the discussion around on her?

"What if I told you that was exactly what it looked like?" Cameron countered.

"You just told me it wasn't," she argued.

He stepped closer. "But what if it was?"

She shook her head and laughed at herself for what an idiot she was. She snagged the wineglass off the counter and tossed back another sip.

"It doesn't matter," she told him.

He came up behind her so she could feel the heat of his chest against her back. "I think it matters to you."

Her eyes dropped closed, and instantly her mind replayed the scene again. Audrey sliding the glass door open, stepping foot inside Cameron's dark house. Feeling the nerves skitter through her system at the thought of what she was about to do. Then the blood in her veins turning to ice when she caught sight of Cameron and the woman. The dinner churning in Audrey's stomach at the intimate scene before her, and wondering how she could have been so horribly wrong.

She whirled on him. "Okay, you know what? Yeah, it matters," she spat out. "It matters when you're about to be the only person in Piper's life and your house is a revolving door of women. It matters when you kiss me like you did tonight, then three hours later you've got some other chick climbing all over you." She jabbed him in the chest. "It matters when that's the worst way possible for me to find out how wrong I was about you."

Audrey hadn't realized how hard her heart was pounding or how close to tears she was when Cameron wrapped his hand around her finger and drew it away from his chest.

"I'm sorry," he muttered.

She blinked, because it was the last thing she expected him to say. She'd grown so used to his taunts and firing questions at her just to throw her off.

"Tessa is a woman I used to be involved with," he admitted.

Even though Audrey had figured as much, hearing the words from his mouth still created a sick feeling in the pit of her stomach.

"She just showed up tonight, and I was trying to explain to her that she can't do that," he went on.

Audrey ordered her breathing to slow down so she could hear him out.

"I ended things with her, Audrey."

"Why didn't you just tell me you had a girlfriend?" *And what were you doing kissing me?*

One of his brows arched. "She wasn't really my girlfriend."

Oh.

"I just explained to her that we needed to go our separate ways," he explained. "She didn't want to take no for an answer. That's when you walked in."

"So then why didn't you tell me that you have other women you're involved with?" she pushed. "Why make me feel like I was it for you?"

He gripped her shoulders again, and this time she let him. Maybe it was the tightness of his fingers around her arm, but she felt like he needed her to listen. "Because I haven't been involved with anyone else since you moved in here. The thing with Tessa was just casual and not even exclusive." His hold on her tightened. "And you *are* it for me, Audrey."

She blinked and tried to process his words, but they were foreign to her. She'd never been it for anyone before. "What d'you mean?"

"I mean..." He shook his head and cursed. "I mean I don't want there to be anyone else. Casual or otherwise."

Was she supposed to take that to mean that he wanted...something with her? But what? A fling until she went home? Was he going to ask her to stay in Blanco Valley so they could have something more permanent? Part of Audrey shivered at the thought that a man could want her that much. That Cameron could want her that much. The other part...was terrified that she wouldn't know how to answer him, that she'd allow her fear to cloud her opportunity to be happy.

"What are you saying, Cameron?"

"I'm saying…" He scrubbed a hand over his head. "I don't know what the hell I'm saying. Just that maybe…" He cleared his throat. "Maybe you don't have to rush home after the football season is over."

"I've already stayed too long," she pointed out.

"I'm sure you have," he agreed.

"And I need to get back to my business."

"Also agreed," he said with a nod.

Audrey chewed her lower lip. "And you don't really need me anymore. Piper's settled in here, and you've picked up the hang of things. It makes sense for me to go back."

"Right. Except it doesn't make sense."

Audrey shook her head. "I'm going to need you to be a little clearer, Cameron."

"How can it make sense for you to leave, when your being here makes more sense?"

It was so close to what she wanted, and needed, to hear from him, yet Audrey couldn't help the frisson of unease that snaked through her system.

"Because of Piper?" she pressed.

He cleared his throat again, which she'd learned was a nervous habit. "Yeah, and—"

"Audrey?"

The little voice coming from the darkness behind her put a stop to whatever Cameron was about to say. For the first time, Audrey wished she didn't have a six-year-old depending on her. As selfish as that sounded, she needed another minute to sort out whatever this was with Cameron, because as soon as Cameron locked gazes with

Piper, she knew the moment was over. Who knew if she'd get it back?

What had he been about to say?

She turned and pasted a smile on her face for Dianna's daughter. "Yeah, sweetie?"

"I had a bad dream." Piper clung to the doorframe of her room, her curls a wild mess around her face. "And I have to go to the bathroom."

"Okay." She turned back, but Cameron was gone. He'd slipped out as silently as he'd slipped in, leaving her to wonder if the door had been shut completely.

SEVENTEEN

Audrey found herself looking forward to Sunday dinner with Cameron's mom, Pamela. Not only was the woman a breath of fresh air who wasn't afraid to give her son a hard time, but also her presence gave Audrey a reprieve. Ever since their strange talk the night before, Audrey found she didn't know what to say around Cameron or how to act around him. She felt like a high schooler who'd just admitted she had a crush on a boy.

To make matters worse, Cameron had spent the better part of the afternoon giving her lingering looks and teasing the panties off her. Figuratively, of course.

Since Pamela had cooked the last time, Audrey had insisted on making the dinner. Cameron looked like he'd been about to have a heart attack when Audrey announced she was going to make pot roast with potatoes and carrots. Their bickering about how to cook had started that morning when Cameron insisted the roast would be better in the oven so it could be basted in a Dutch oven. Since Audrey didn't even know what the hell a Dutch oven was, and scolded her hormones for jumping all over the place, she'd placed the meal in a Crock-Pot. The vein in Cameron's forehead looked like it had been about to burst when she'd refused to let him "check" on the meal. And by "check" she knew he meant take over because he didn't trust anyone else in the kitchen.

"You should probably check those vegetables," he told her as he began the preparations for the gravy.

The only reason she was allowing him to help was because he'd insisted. She hadn't been able to stop him from clattering a skillet on the stove and making the stuff.

"The vegetables are fine," she reassured him, but gave the Crock-Pot a peek just in case. Yeah, they still looked good.

"How long has it been since you've basted the roast?" he asked her.

"Cameron, will you leave the woman alone?" Pamela scolded her son. "I'm sure she's capable of cooking her own meal without your interference."

Audrey resisted the urge to stick her tongue out and swore she heard him mutter, "Not happening" under his breath.

"That gravy doesn't look like it's thick enough," she told Cameron.

Pamela hid a smile behind her wineglass.

Cameron lifted a brow. "It'll be plenty thick. You're not supposed to add the flour all at once."

"And you haven't put enough drippings in it," she pressed, because... well, because she wanted to.

Cameron set his spoon down and turned to face Audrey. Behind them, Pamela muttered, "Uh-oh."

"You want to come over here so I can show you how it's done right?"

Audrey opened her mouth, then had the feeling he wasn't talking about gravy. His question had too much of a seductive tone. For a second she thought about taking him up on his offer, but with an audience, she knew it would be a bad idea. She didn't want to give Pamela the wrong impression about their relationship. She didn't want to give her false hope.

Or maybe you're more worried about giving yourself false hope?

No, that definitely wasn't it.

She gestured toward the gravy. "Just make sure it has plenty of flavor. I like my gravy meaty."

Cameron lifted a brow as though to say, *Thought so.*

"I see you finally patched up the curtains, Cam," his mother said.

Cameron tossed another spoonful of flour into the gravy. "Actually, Audrey fixed those," he said casually, as though she had the right to go around mending his things.

"How nice," Pamela beamed. "And I'm assuming you sewed up the pillows too?"

The throw pillows on Cameron's couch had been coming apart at the seams. The only reason why Audrey had fixed them was because she got tired of hearing him complain about constantly having to restuff them.

Yeah, that's why.

"Just trying to show my gratitude for Cameron letting us stay here."

Cameron snorted and muttered, "Bullshit" under his breath.

Pamela nodded, but Audrey had the feeling she didn't buy Audrey's lame reason. Hell, Audrey didn't buy it either.

"And are you also responsible for the ceiling fans suddenly being dust free?" Pamela prodded.

Okay, Audrey had spent a day over here doing some housework. So sue her. Piper had been at school, and Audrey had had a few hours to herself. So she'd let herself in the back door, sewn the tear in the curtains, patched the throw pillows, and dusted the fans. She'd also vacuumed, mopped, and polished the furniture. Cameron may have been wicked in the kitchen, but he was a lousy housekeeper. Audrey hadn't minded; tidying up Cameron's house had felt so domestic.

"Yeah, that was me," she finally answered. When both of Pamela's brows lifted, Audrey rushed to explain more. "I was just giving the place some TLC. No big deal."

Out of the corner of her eye, Audrey saw Cameron slant her a look, but she refused to glance his way. She didn't want him to see how important it had been for her to show her gratitude even though she'd still been pissed at him.

"Well, I think the place looks good," Pamela commented instead of calling Audrey out on her bullshit. "Who knows what Cam will do without you when you leave."

Audrey paused with her water bottle halfway to her mouth. She forced herself to drink just as Cameron cleared his throat while he stirred the gravy. Yeah, he wasn't the only one who didn't know what to say, or how to look, or how to act.

The impulsive side of her wanted to stroke a hand over his shoulder and reassure him that he didn't need to be tense around her, that he hadn't screwed anything up, that she wanted to finish their conversation and maybe explore things further. But she didn't want to scare him off, so she decided to wait a few more days.

"By the way, you're out of soda," Pamela announced. "Do you have a grocery list I can add it to?"

"There's a pad of paper in the drawer," Audrey jumped in. She barely resisted slapping a hand over her mouth as Pamela stared at her and Cameron smirked. Funny how she'd come to know Cameron's house so easily, how she moved from one room to the next, picking up his shoes and placing them by the front door so he wouldn't forget them, making sure the newspaper got brought in before it rained, because she knew he liked to read it at the kitchen counter.

When had they fallen into such a comfortable routine?

"Okay," Pamela said slowly. "Thanks." But when she opened the drawer, her actions froze. "Um, Cameron?" she said, and she reached a hand in the drawer and pulled out about a dozen yellow Post-it notes. Every single note Audrey and Cameron had left for each other over the past two months. "Are you planning on doing some scrapbooking?"

Audrey damn near spit out her water and just barely managed to get the stuff down. She noticed Cameron only offered his mom a quick glance, then went back to his gravy. He probably thought he could shrug off the fact that he'd saved every Post-it she'd written him, but the way his hand tightened around the spoon gave him away.

He hadn't wanted anyone to find those. But if not, why had he placed them in a drawer that he knew she sometimes opened?

"Audrey insists on leaving me notes everywhere," he explained, though it wasn't much of an explanation.

Pamela dropped the notes and continued her search for the pad of paper. "Yes, but why have you saved all of them?"

The kitchen was silent for a moment, with Audrey staring into her bottle of water and Cameron stirring the gravy to a slow death. Pamela bounced a look between Audrey and Cam, slowly picking up on…whatever the hell was going on in here.

She shut the drawer. "I think I'll go outside and check on Piper."

Pamela slipped out the back door, leaving the two of them alone.

"I think the gravy needs more flour," Audrey said in an attempt to lighten the atmosphere.

"Don't start," Cameron warned.

Audrey bit back a grin when she saw him toss a pinch of flour into the pan. She silently sipped her water for a moment while listening to Piper squeal in the backyard. "So, are we going to talk about it?" she pressed.

Heat bloomed across her stomach when Cameron grinned. "You mean the fact that I saved every note you've ever written?"

She pointed at him. "Yeah, that."

"I only did that because I knew people wouldn't believe me when I tell them you only communicate via Post-its."

"Funny."

Cameron set the spoon down and turned to face her. "Okay, you want to know why?" When she nodded while swallowing past the lump in her throat, he went on. "I wanted to have something to remember you by when you leave."

Oh. *Oh.*

"I was thinking maybe I could cradle them in my lap while I watch *The Notebook*."

She lifted her eyes to the ceiling. What had she expected? "Now you're just being an ass."

He turned back to his gravy. "Yep."

She came closer and set her water bottle on the counter. "No, but seriously. Why did you save all those?"

"I just told you," he said with a shrug.

She snorted. "You're not going to sit down and watch a Nicholas Sparks movie."

"Maybe I am," he told her. "*The Notebook* was pretty damn good."

She crossed her arms over her chest and stared at him. "You've actually seen *The Notebook*."

He jabbed his gravy spoon at her. "Only because I was forced. I want to go on record with that. I don't sit around and watch Nicholas Sparks movies by myself."

"Why, not enough blood and guts in them?"

"Now you're getting it," he answered with a grin, and her heart flipped again.

Yeah, she could totally picture him sprawled out on the couch watching *Rambo* or maybe one of the *Terminator* movies. And maybe she'd be curled up next to him with a soft blanket and Piper lying across their laps...

"Okay, but truth time," she said. "Why do you have all those?"

Cameron continued to stir the gravy before turning the burner to low. Then he pierced her with a look that sent shivers down Audrey's spine. "Okay, you want the truth? They make me smile. I don't get enough of that in my life."

Her insides just about cracked open at his confession. How could he not have enough in his life to make him smile? Everyone needed to smile every once in a while. Cameron had a great one; too good to not be flashing it at everyone he met. Audrey considered it a travesty that more people didn't get to enjoy that heart-melting grin.

Except Piper. He smiled a lot around Piper. But it was impossible not to be happy around that little girl.

"Okay," she said.

"That's it? Just 'okay'?"

"Did you expect me to mock you?" she questioned.

He scrubbed a hand down his face. "Actually . . ."

Audrey was about to give him the mocking he was looking for when she realized he was kidding. The grin tugging at the corners of his mouth gave him away.

See, he smiles for you too.

"They're quirky and different," he went on. "I like that about you. It's refreshing."

Heat flared across her cheeks at his roundabout compliment. And she'd gotten to know him enough to acknowledge the fact that his words were genuine.

Just tell him. Tell him you don't want to leave.

But Cameron wouldn't want to settle down, even if, just last night, he'd told her she was it. He wasn't that type of guy, and she feared it would only be a matter of time before he tired of her. Hadn't every other one of her boyfriends done that very thing? Tired of Audrey and moved on to the next hot thing?

"I was just going to say the gravy needs more flour," she blurted out. Because she couldn't help herself. Because she was a coward who couldn't admit to her biggest fear.

"No, it doesn't," he responded without even looking at the gravy. "And don't use my food control issues to distract me."

"It usually works," she muttered to herself.

"Not this time," he muttered back and took a step closer to her. "Now, tell me what's wrong before I have to coax it out of you."

Make him coax it out of you. She narrowed her eyes.

"You're blushing," he said.

He was close. Too close. As in close enough for her to see the brown flecks in his eyes.

"It's just hot in here," she said.

His mouth curled further. "Yeah, it is." His hungry gaze dropped from her face down her body, touching on all the places where she wanted his hands. Her breasts, her stomach, her thighs. Basically everywhere.

"I think the question you should be asking isn't why I saved all those notes," Cameron told her. "It should be why you still haven't said yes to me. What're you afraid of, Audrey?"

Everything.

She opened her mouth, but the words were stuck in her throat. She was afraid of what he could do to her, and afraid of admitting she was afraid. She'd never opened herself up to a man before, not like the way Cameron was demanding.

She lifted her hand and toyed with the neckline of his T-shirt, momentarily distracted by the strong column of his throat.

"I... don't really know how to do this," she admitted.

"Do what?" he pressed.

"Leave myself vulnerable for someone. Especially a man."

Cameron's brows lowered a fraction. "Who hurt you?"

She shook her head, then forced the words out. "No one in particular. I just don't have the best track record with men. Men who..." How could she explain it in a way that she was sure he'd understand?

"Men like me," he finished for her.

Had she thrown that accusation out at him before? Yeah, she was pretty sure she had. Thinking back now, Audrey realized it had been an unfair thing to say to him. It was a defense mechanism to keep him away, keep him from seeing how vulnerable and scared she was.

"I didn't mean it the way you think," she said.

"Yeah, you did." His hand found its way back to her

hair, threading through the strands. "But it's okay. You've been burned in the past by guys like me, so you're gun-shy. Nothing wrong with that."

She dropped her gaze to this throat. "That's why I had such a hard time when I saw Tessa here. I was brought back to every other guy I'd been with. It opened a wound I thought had closed."

"Understandable," he agreed. Then he lowered his head so he could see her eyes. "And maybe a little jealous?" he asked, as though hopeful.

"Don't push it," she warned.

He pinched her chin. "Come on, you know you were a little jealous."

"Do you want me to be?" she countered.

"You're the one who said it was truth time."

"Yeah, but we weren't talking about this," she pointed out. *You can't expect him to be brutally honest, if you're going to hold back.* Audrey wanted to smack her inner voice upside the head for being so damn sensible. She blew out a breath and admitted defeat, something she did a lot around this man. "Okay, maybe a small part of me wanted to scratch her eyes out."

Cameron's half grin became full-blown. "There it is."

"Do I get a gold star now?" she teased.

"How about a kiss instead?" he murmured.

His mouth hovered just above hers, close enough to feel his hot breath, and Audrey had to hold herself back from jumping on him, from sliding her tongue in his mouth before she had a chance to second-guess herself.

"I think I'd rather have the gold star instead," she whispered back.

His mouth slid along hers; then he grinned against her. "Liar."

Audrey's lips parted just slightly, inviting him in, when the sliding door was thrown open. Piper came running in, wild hair flying around her face, shoes untied and cheeks pink.

Cameron had already moved back before Audrey even realized they'd been interrupted.

"Audrey, guess what Pinkie Pie just did?" the little girl asked. "She saw a bird, then climbed up the tree to try and catch it."

"Is she stuck?" Cameron wanted to know, as though he hadn't been about to shove his tongue in Audrey's mouth.

Piper switched her attention to her uncle and shook her head. "No, she jumped down. But she's all dirty with leaves and bark and stuff."

"She *jumped*?" Audrey repeated.

Piper hopped on both feet. "Yeah, and she landed on all four of her feet. Isn't that cool?" Then Piper was gone, running out the door as fast as she'd appeared.

She and Cameron exchanged a glance, but his expression didn't mirror her amused one. His eyes were hot and dark and the pulse at the base of his neck was hammering. Audrey's smile slipped as she remembered the way he'd been about to kiss her.

One of these days they weren't going to stop at just kissing. And then she wasn't sure if she'd be able to save herself.

EIGHTEEN

The fall afternoon was crisp and cool, perfect weather for the extra sprints the players were doing to make up for their piss-poor attitudes. Blake had little patience for their whining and moaning about how tired and overworked they were. He'd blown his whistle and told them to start running and not to stop until he felt like they'd had enough.

"They think they're tired now," Blake muttered. "I'll give them something to whine about."

Cameron grunted as the players sprinted from one side of the field to the next. They knew better than to give it less than their all. If even so much as one kid slowed down, Blake would make them pay. Cameron understood they were nearing the end of the season, but the kids knew the drill by now. Prima donna attitudes didn't go unnoticed or unpunished.

Of course, the end of the season also meant something

else that Cameron didn't want to think about. Being without Audrey had been keeping him up at night. She was distracting him at work, sucking the breath from his lungs. Every time he looked at her, every time he was around her and heard her soft laughter, he wanted to beg her to stay, tell her to think about Piper and how much the girl loved her.

Not just Piper.

But Cameron didn't have the right to ask that of Audrey, especially after she'd caught him with Tessa. He was surprised she hadn't yanked Piper and run for the hills.

She has faith in you.

Now he had to show her that faith was justified. But first he needed to make a decision about Denver. Over the past few weeks, the offer had become less important, less urgent. Every time he looked in the backyard and watched Piper play with her psychotic cat, Denver held less appeal. Every meal he shared with Audrey, or Post-it note he found, he wanted to burn the offer letter. Problem was, he hadn't been able to bring himself to even tell her about the offer. He'd made the decision to turn it down before Audrey had a chance to put all the pieces together.

Blake whistled again and ordered the players to take a breather. They slowed to a stop, sweat dripping down their faces, chests heaving with exhaustion.

"Take a water break, gentlemen," Blake told them.

Cameron was about to have a word with the offensive line when he spotted Drew Spalding exiting the field house. He wasn't alone. An older man with thinning hair, a white polo, and a belly that spilled over the waistband of his khakis shook Drew's hand.

Cameron elbowed Blake. "Hey, who's that guy with Drew?"

Blake blew out a breath. "I'll tell you, but you have to promise to be chill."

A feeling of unease curled Cameron's stomach. "What the hell does that mean?"

"Apparently he's expressed interest in your job. Drew's showing him around the facilities."

"He's interviewing candidates for my job?" Cameron glanced at Blake. "I haven't given my notice yet."

"But you're going to," Blake pointed out. "It's only a matter of time, right?"

Cameron glared. "Says who?"

"Um…" Blake scratched his chin. "You?"

"Bullshit." Cameron turned to confront the athletic director and put the man in his place, when Blake's hand shot out and latched on to Cameron's arm.

"Hey," Blake warned. "When I said be chill, I specifically meant don't go over there and beat the shit out of Drew."

Cameron pulled his arm free. "I only did that once," he pointed out, then stalked away.

Cameron's long legs ate up the ground beneath him, his irritation growing with each step. In all honesty, Cameron was irritated with himself for allowing Drew to think he'd just bow out, that he'd give the smug bastard the satisfaction of getting rid of Cameron Shaw that easily.

And the man still deserved an ass beating for almost ruining Cameron's squeaky-clean reputation at his previous school.

Cameron had never told anyone what Drew had done on the sly, mostly to protect those he loved the most. He hadn't wanted to put his mother through the agony of thinking her son was a homewrecker, especially having lived with a cheating spouse. To this day, Cameron wanted to kick his own ass for getting involved with Drew's wife. It had been the biggest mistake he'd made, and Drew had seen to it that Cameron continued to suffer.

He reached the two men just as Mr. Potbelly said his thanks, then turned to leave. Drew popped a bubble with his gum, then gave Cameron an openmouthed grin. Cameron wanted to knee the guy is his too-small balls.

"How's it going today, Shaw?" Drew asked.

Cameron gritted his teeth together. "Yeah, don't start with that bullshit. What's with you interviewing someone for my job?"

"Technically that wasn't an interview," Drew explained. "I was just showing the guy around. His actual interview isn't until next week."

Cameron blew out an impatient breath. "I haven't turned in my resignation yet, Drew."

Drew waved a hand in the air. "A technicality. It's a matter of time now."

Cameron took a step closer to the guy and tried desperately to remember Blake's warning not to kick Drew's ass. "I know you think you can push me out of here, but it won't work."

Drew's smile grew even more smug. "I'm not pushing you out of here, Cameron. You're leaving on your own."

"No, I'm not," Cameron corrected him. "Because I turned Denver down."

A flicker of doubt shadowed Drew's eyes. But it was gone quickly. "No, you haven't. You want your own team too badly to turn that down."

"I changed my mind," Cameron said with a shrug. "I've decided to stay."

Drew ran his gaze up and down Cameron. "Bullshit."

Cameron patted Drew's face. "Nah." He leaned closer

and dropped his voice low. "I know you think you won this round, but I'll never give you the satisfaction, Spalding." He turned and walked away, mentally giving himself a pat on the back for not smashing his fist into the other man's smug grin.

"Hey, is that lady friend of yours single?" Drew called out, but Cameron kept walking. "The blond one with the kid?"

Cameron immediately halted, but he didn't turn around. He counted to ten and gritted his back teeth and willed his feet to keep moving, knowing that Drew was only bringing Audrey up to piss him off. Hell, it was working, but Cameron closed his eyes and gave himself a healthy pep talk. Behind him, he heard Drew approach, but Cameron still didn't turn around. He knew he was being too generous by giving the man a chance to save his own skin by keeping his big mouth shut.

When Cameron opened his eyes, he saw Blake watching carefully, shaking his head in silent warning.

Then Drew spoke again and broke through Cameron's waning calm.

"I was thinking of giving her a call," Drew said in a low voice.

Cameron cracked his knuckles.

The man stepped closer and lowered his voice again. "She seems real . . . sweet," Drew added with a chuckle.

Cameron didn't give himself time to think. He spun around and landed a blow to Drew's jaw. The man's head was jerked back, but he recovered quickly and got his own punch in, square in Cameron's eye. Fire exploded across his skull, drowning out Blake's curses and hollers from the players.

Cameron knew he'd pay for his action later, but he'd

been unable to stand there and listen to the prick taunt him about Audrey. Drew laughed as Cameron staggered back. Seeing the evil grin breaking across the man's mouth, even as it dripped with blood, only fueled Cameron's blood-lust for the other man. He lunged and tackled Drew to the ground, landing on top of him with a loud grunt. Drew struggled, but Cameron was able to hold the man back with another punch across the face, adding to the blood already decorating his jaw. Somehow Drew wriggled an arm free and clocked Cameron again, this time getting him across the jaw. The taste of blood immediately filled his mouth, but Cameron was too focused on the asshole beneath him to tend to his pounding eye and already swollen lip.

"Get off me, you animal," Drew grunted as Cameron punched him again.

Behind him, he heard Blake coming to stop Cameron, but he ignored him and everyone else. The red haze cloud-ing his vision wouldn't allow him to do anything else but vent years of anger and hatred for the man who had made Cameron's life a living hell.

"You'll fucking pay for this," Drew muttered around a mouthful of blood and an already black eye.

Cameron shrugged Blake's hands off as he tried to pry Cameron off Drew. He grabbed a handful of Drew's pretentious-as-shit polo and lifted the man's head off the ground. "You ever mention Audrey again, I'll end you," he said in Drew's face through gritted teeth. "You hear me? I'll fucking end you."

"Cameron!" Blake barked. This time he managed to haul Cameron to his feet, leaving Drew sprawled on his back, his head lolling to one side.

Cameron ignored the gawkers and whispers from the players and other coaches as he shoved Blake's hands off.

He stood over Drew and jabbed a finger at him. "Don't ever forget that."

"What part of *don't beat the shit out of him* did you not get?" Blake questioned.

Cameron ignored the question and swiped a hand across his mouth, not surprised to see the smear of blood. His left eye was blurry and swollen and dripping with something. Probably more blood. Cameron had underestimated Drew's agility, but he hadn't cared because he'd gotten the last word. The whole thing had been worth it to see his nemesis lying on the ground like a defeated contender, face covered in blood, eye just as swollen as Cameron's.

"Go get that checked out by the school nurse," Blake told him.

Cameron shot him a *get real* look and kept walking.

Blake held his hands up. "Sorry for giving a shit." Then he let out a humorless laugh and scrubbed a hand down his face. "*Fuuuuck*, Cameron."

"Don't start." He kept walking until he was off the field, not glancing back to see if Drew was still pissing and moaning on the ground like a baby.

Audrey was attempting to make meatballs while simultaneously listening to Piper's rambling stories about school. Audrey had already screwed up once by putting in too many breadcrumbs while Piper had been throwing math equations at her. She'd never thought that hearing "What's two plus three?" would throw off her concentration while reading a recipe, but it had.

Of course, Cameron would probably tell her not to use breadcrumbs anyway. The man had an annoying habit of interfering with her cooking and dictating her recipes. She knew how to cook, thanks very much.

On the other hand, she'd grown used to his controlling ways in the kitchen. It was actually kind of cute the way he'd salt pasta water when he thought she wasn't looking. The kitchen had gotten rather quiet after Piper had run down to friend's house for dinner, and Audrey realized how late Cameron was tonight. He was usually through the front door by six thirty. It was seven fifteen and he still wasn't home.

Should she call him?

No, that would be too needy. She wasn't that person.

But what if something had happened? What if he had car trouble and his cell phone was dead?

He's a grown man and can take care of himself.

Audrey forced herself to relax as the front door opened, then shut. Her pulse automatically sped up, and she chastised her own predictability. All he had to do was enter the premises and her skin got all hot and itchy and her heart did that triple-beat thing.

She braced herself for his appearance, forced her breathing to slow, but there was no sign of him. His footsteps faded as he made a detour to his bedroom. Okay, maybe he just needed to change his clothes first. Just because he hadn't come running straight to her didn't mean anything. It didn't mean she was all hot and bothered for nothing.

Audrey rolled her shoulders and waited for the simmering tension to ease, but it didn't. It never did with Cameron.

She finished assembling the meatballs on a platter and slid them in the oven to broil. After setting the timer, she set off to find Cameron to let him know how long until dinner.

The back of the house was silent. She'd expected to hear the shower running and had a moment's hesitation. The last thing she needed was to walk in on the guy with no clothes on. Or standing beneath the steamy spray.

Actually...

Bad Audrey!

She pulled herself together by the time she reached Cameron's room. The shower wasn't running, but she decided to announce herself anyway. You know, just in case.

"Cameron?" But he didn't answer, and she didn't let his silence deter her.

She stepped into his room, ignoring the messed up bed and the images *that* created.

When she came to the bathroom door, she stopped. There he was, in his typical coaching attire of athletic pants and hooded sweatshirt, leaning over the bathroom counter as he dabbed a wet washcloth to the corner of his mouth.

Audrey dragged her gaze away from his perfectly round ass and was about to ask him how his day had been, when she had a good look at his face.

His left eye was a swollen mess, decorated with a deep purple and red. And his mouth...Audrey gasped as Cameron touched the washcloth to the side of his mouth, trying to wipe away blood that oozed from a cut.

"What the hell happened to you?" she blurted out.

Cameron swiped at the cut. "I fell" was his curt answer.

"Off a cliff?"

His eyes dropped closed as a weary sigh escaped him. "Not now, Audrey."

"At least reassure me that the other guy looks as shitty as you," she said.

He cut her a glance. "He looks worse." He might have been smirking, but it was hard to tell with half his lip bloody and swollen.

"Of course he does," she muttered, and shouldered her way into the room. The place smelled like him, like his shampoo and minty toothpaste. His stuff was all over the place, a stick of deodorant on the counter and a towel hanging crookedly on the towel rack.

She ignored the intimacy of being in Cameron's bathroom, of getting an eyeful of a pair of black boxers on the floor, and pushed him away from the counter.

"Audrey..." he said again with a sigh.

She squatted and opened the cabinet under the sink. "Hush," she told him. "Someone needs to teach you some organization skills," she said more to herself as she shoved past an unopened bottle of hair gel. When did he ever plan on wearing that stuff? And a box of...condoms?

Okay, don't think about that.

Cameron sighed again. "Out," he told her.

Audrey continued to ignore him as she finally spotted a first-aid kid. She actually hadn't been sure he'd have one of these. At first she'd just been going to look for some Band-Aids. She stood with a victorious smile, but her grin slipped when she was confronted with his deep scowl.

She'd learned quickly that Cameron Shaw scowled *a lot*. But paired with the black eye and split lip, it was downright scary.

"You're not putting anything on me," he told her.

She set the kit on the bathroom counter. "Don't be such a drama queen. It'll get infected if you don't treat it." She actually wasn't sure about that, but she needed something believable so he didn't kick her out.

They were both silent as Audrey dug around the box and found some antiseptic wipes. She started on his eye first. "So this cliff," she said as she dabbed the towelette to his bruise, "did it have fists and an ego as big as yours?"

Cameron's brow furrowed as he attempted to narrow his eyes at her. At least that's what Audrey assumed he was doing, because he winced and closed his eyes. The smartass in her wanted to chastise him, but the softie in her felt bad. Kind of.

"Sorry," she muttered. "You don't have to tell me about it if you don't want to."

Cameron cleared his throat, and Audrey attempted to back up, to give the man some space. But she soon realized there was nowhere to go. Her butt rested against the counter, because Cameron had refused to give her extra room, so she'd squeezed in as best as she could. Unfortunately, that left them standing closer than she wanted. Close enough to pick out the purple among the blue in the bruise coloring his left eye.

And to count the stubble shadowing his jaw, which still managed to look sexy with a cut lip and puffy eyebrow bone. Even so, Audrey steadied her breathing, because if she inhaled too hard, her breasts would brush against his chest. Bad enough they were in his bathroom, with a box of supersized condoms.

No joke, the man wore supersized condoms.

Because life was just that unfair.

She hadn't really been able to tell, but the box had only felt about half full.

She blew out a breath. "Oscar de la Renta," she muttered to herself.

"What's that?" Cameron asked, his voice all husky and stuff.

"I said your eye's all red," she lied.

His deep blue gaze bore into hers from beneath half-lowered lids. "I didn't ask you to come in here."

"Quiet," she ordered.

They were both silent for a moment while Audrey snagged another wipe for his eye.

"Where's Piper?" Cameron asked.

Audrey carefully dabbed the bruise. "Eating dinner at a friend's house."

Cameron's response was a grunt, a sound that was more a rumbling from deep within his chest.

"His name's Drew," Cameron stated.

Audrey shook her head as she set aside another wipe and moved to his mouth. "What is it with you and this guy?"

"He's an ass."

Audrey gave Cameron a droll look as she rewet the washcloth. "Lots of people are assholes. I don't see you getting into fights with all of them." She wrung the excess water from the cloth and dabbed away the dried blood on his mouth. "Hold still," she told him when he winced.

"We don't like each other."

Audrey snorted. "Ya think?"

Cameron successfully narrowed his eyes this time. "Most nurses aren't this rude."

Audrey held the washcloth from his mouth and smiled at him. "I never claimed to be a nurse." She touched the cloth to his mouth again. "I knew you wouldn't do a good enough job cleaning this, and my OCD couldn't handle it."

"That's the only reason, huh?" he countered.

"Yep." After she finished cleaning away the dried blood, she dug for more antiseptic wipes to disinfect the cut. "So you got into a fight with this guy Drew," Audrey concluded.

Cameron snorted. "You could say that."

"Isn't he, like, your boss?"

Cameron's hand whipped up and snagged Audrey's. "If you're going to take his side, I'll pick you up and toss you out of here."

Audrey held her breath as Cameron's fingers held her wrist in a tight grip, the damp washcloth dangling from her fingers. "Calm down," she reassured him. "I'm just trying to understand."

"Maybe I don't want you to understand," he muttered.

She felt an inexplicable need to help him, to soothe whatever war was battling behind those blue eyes of his. He looked like shit, sounded like shit, and she wanted to comfort him. But she knew when to back away, and Cameron was at a breaking point.

She held her hands up, dropping the washcloth to the floor. "Fine. Clean your own wounds, then."

He muttered a curse as she turned and stalked out of the bathroom, trying to squash the hurt that unfurled in her belly. Audrey would be the first to admit that she could be a little meddlesome sometimes, and seeing Cameron hurt had touched her in a deep place that she couldn't name. A place she'd locked away when she'd decided to keep people at a distance.

She bit back the sting of tears as she cleaned the dinner dishes while the meatballs continued to cook. Hell, she wasn't even hungry anymore. Maybe she'd leave the dinner to Cameron and retreat to the guesthouse.

Then she heard him coming into the kitchen. She felt him standing behind her as she washed a bowl and set it on the rack to dry.

"I'm sorry," he told her.

Audrey didn't acknowledge him, because she wasn't entirely confident she could keep herself together.

"There are things about me I haven't told people," he continued. "And I'm not used to someone caring so much." When she still didn't respond, he sighed. "I feel like I've spent half my time apologizing to you."

"Maybe you should stop being an ass," she blurted out. Okay, she hadn't meant that to sound so harsh. But, damn, he'd hurt her.

"Yeah," he agreed.

His agreement somehow still didn't make her feel better. Cameron approached her and shut the water faucet off. Then he grabbed the sponge from her hand and set it down. "Will you stop for a minute so I can talk to you?"

"Talk or grumble?" she asked.

He went to the fridge and snagged a bottle of beer. "Want one?" he asked her.

She shook her head and waited for him to talk.

First, he popped the top off the bottle and pulled a long sip. After lowering it, he crossed the kitchen again and leaned against the counter next to her. "I had an affair with Drew's wife."

Well, then. That she hadn't been expecting, even though that tidbit Lois told her about the married woman had never been far from her mind. Audrey opened her mouth, to find some appropriate response, but nothing came to mind. "You slept with a married woman?" she blurted, probably not doing a good enough job of keeping the disappointment out of her voice.

Cameron must have sensed it because he slid her a dark look. "I didn't know she was married."

"But didn't you, like, go to high school with this guy, or something?" she wanted to know. "How could you not know the woman was his wife?"

"We both went away to different colleges, and at the time I was coaching football for a high school in a different town. I hadn't seen or spoken to Drew in years."

Audrey watched Cameron take another sip of his beer, suspecting he needed the moment to gather the details of the story. "And you saw no wedding ring, and she made no mention of a husband?"

Cameron lowered the bottle and stared down into it. "No. She was in pharmaceutical sales and traveled all over. We met at lunch when she accidentally picked up my sandwich instead of hers. I'd never seen her before, and she told me her last name was Jones." Cameron looked at her and, for the first time, seemed more exhausted than angry. "I had no reason to believe she was married."

Damn. Okay, so simple mistake. But still. Sleeping with another man's wife. That was *no bueno*.

Audrey leaned back against the counter next to him. "So how did you eventually find out?"

Cameron blew out a heavy breath. "About a month later, Drew showed up at my house and landed a right hook to my jaw. Told me to stop banging his wife or he'd make me pay."

"Make you pay?" Audrey repeated.

Cameron tossed back some more beer. "Apparently he'd been suspicious of Lauren for a while and hired a private detective to follow her around. The guy followed her to my house and snapped pictures of us through a window."

Audrey swallowed and decided not to ask what the pictures were of. Her imagination was doing the work for her. She held back a shudder.

"Drew tossed a manila envelope at me and said if I didn't quit my job as head coach, he'd send copies of the photos to every newspaper in the area. He wanted everyone to know what a home-wrecking bastard I was."

"And you saw the pictures he had?" Audrey asked. "That's what was inside the envelope he gave you?"

Cameron nodded. "Yeah. So I left my job, even though the school district had offered me another contract."

Audrey stared at him. "You just quit your job?"

Cameron was silent for a moment. "I didn't want my mom to find out. Bad enough she had to deal with a cheating husband. I didn't want her to think her son turned out the same way."

Something inside Audrey twisted at his words. She wanted to reach out to him and soothe the tension away from his brow, to take the pain away from the cut on his mouth. But she wasn't sure he'd accept the comfort, so she kept her hands to herself.

"Your mom has no idea this happened," she guessed.

"Nope."

Audrey inhaled. "Does anyone know?"

"Blake and Brandon know about the affair. Nobody knows about the photos or the real reason I left my other coaching job."

And yet he'd told her. Audrey squashed back the glimmer of hope that burst inside her. He'd confided in her, a very deep and painful thing for him. He told her something he kept buried from others. But it may not mean anything. Of course she wanted it to mean something. She wanted it to mean that he felt enough for her to share that part of his life.

"That was kind of a shitty thing for him to do. Bullying you like that."

Cameron just shrugged. "I did a shitty thing to him."

"Yeah, but not intentionally," she pointed out.

"Didn't matter to him. His marriage had ended, and he blamed me."

Audrey watched Cameron peel the label from the beer bottle, noticing how his knuckles were bruised and covered with dried blood. "Sounds like it wasn't much of a marriage if his wife was running around on him."

Another shrug as he lifted the bottle to his lips.

"So how did you end up working for Drew?" Audrey wanted to know. "Seems to me like he'd never hire you after all that."

Cameron laughed, but it lacked humor. "Now that's a funny story. When Blake retired from the NFL, Drew hired him, and then Blake asked me if I'd be interested in being his assistant coach. Told Drew he'd only take the job if I came on board too."

Audrey scratched her chin. "And you had no problem coming here and working for Drew?"

"I don't really work for Drew. To be honest, I don't see him that much. But yeah, part of me wanted to accept the job just to piss the guy off."

"So you've just been one big, happy family?" Audrey asked.

Cameron snorted. "Hardly. But we've turned the team around, so Drew knows to keep his mouth shut."

Audrey nodded and ran her gaze over Cameron's bruised face. "Except for tonight."

"Yeah, that," he agreed.

"So you took this job just to rub your presence in Drew's face?"

Cameron glanced at her. "Well, I took the job because I'd have a chance to work with my best friend. The Drew thing is just a bonus."

She smiled, despite the situation. "How have you managed not to kill each other so far?"

"I usually have better restraint," he answered.

"So what did he say to piss you off?"

Cameron opened his mouth, then touched the tip of his finger to his swollen eye. "Nothing out of the usual," he finally answered. "I just lost it, I guess."

Audrey finally gave up her restraint and rubbed the pad

of her thumb over the cut bisecting his lower lip. "He must have deserved it, then."

He gazed at her, and for a moment Audrey thought he was going to kiss her. But she didn't want to hurt his lip any more than it already was, no matter how badly she wanted to soothe away his pain. "Why are you always defending me? I don't need anyone to fight my battles."

She offered him a smile. "You may not need it. But sometimes it's nice for someone to have your back. Don't you think?"

The way he looked at her, the way his eyes darkened, told Audrey she'd touched a nerve, something he hadn't wanted her to see.

She cleared her throat when she realized Cameron wasn't going to answer her. She'd made him uncomfortable, and she didn't want to scare him away. "I have to take a few days in Boulder next week," she announced. "I need to catch up on some work; then I'll be back."

One of his brows lifted. "You're going to leave me here alone with a six-year-old?"

She offered him a teasing grin. "Consider it practice for when I go home for good." Just saying the words was like swallowing glass. But Audrey needed to start accepting the reality that her time here would be over soon. No matter how much it killed her to leave, she couldn't live in Cameron's guesthouse forever.

"I don't know," Cameron said. "I think I might end up killing that cat."

Audrey nudged his shoulder with hers. "I think you love that cat."

"Love her?" he repeated with a horrified look. "The thing has chewed up every pair of socks I own. And two of my belts."

"You're telling me Pinkie Pie climbs into your hamper and pulls out your dirty socks?"

He narrowed his gaze at her. "Sometimes I leave them on the floor."

Audrey merely looked at him.

"Okay, so I'm not the best housekeeper," he admitted.

"It's okay," she said with a shrug. "We can't all be perfect. Just make sure Piper's in bed when the ladies come calling."

A muscle in Cameron's jaw ticked.

"Kidding," she reassured him. "I know you have better judgment than that."

"Do you?" he questioned in a low voice.

"Of course," she stated, knowing she'd touched a nerve. She didn't want him thinking she looked down on him. "You and Piper will be fine."

"That's not what I'm worried about," he muttered.

The oven dinged, effectively ending the moment.

She pushed away from the counter. "Dinner's done."

NINETEEN

For a moment, Cameron had been worried he'd completely ruined things with Audrey, that she'd shrink in horror after learning about his darkest secret. But she'd taken it in stride, surprising him again by her resilience and acceptance. He was sure he'd seen disappointment in her eyes when he'd finally told her the sordid truth, but she'd masked it well. Then she'd gone on by trying to imply the whole thing hadn't been his fault. Like he was supposed to believe that. That he'd been blameless for ruining Drew's life. Yeah, Drew might be an ass—that dated back to high school. But Cameron wasn't a heartless shit. No man deserved to have a cheating, deceptive wife. Cameron knew firsthand what that did to a family, and he hadn't wished that on Drew.

Unfortunately, he'd inadvertently played a part, and he'd carried the guilt, buried underneath his contempt for the man. And yeah, it was why he kept his relationships strictly casual. Despite the fact that his fling with Drew's wife had been casual, he'd started to develop feelings for Lauren, only to have the rug yanked from under him when he'd found out she had a husband. Cameron had never confided in anyone how much her deception had hurt him. He'd shrugged it off as a yeah-well-we-were-just-fooling-around-anyway type of thing. Sure, it had started as that at first. But after a few weeks, at least for him, it had become something more. He'd looked forward to her coming to town, to seeing her, hearing about her week. Then Drew had shown up and literally punched the reality into him. He'd grieved in private and tried to move forward as best he could.

Since then he'd yet to meet a woman who was worth him exposing that hidden place. Until Audrey. Until her smile, her laughter, and her goodness, and bringing a little girl into his life who was afraid of toilets, befriended hairless cats, and made him see life differently.

Piper had returned home after eating dinner at her friend's house. She'd come running through the front door and rambled to him and Audrey about how she'd had cut-up hot dogs, apples, and green peas. Then she'd gone straight to the backyard to play with her cat.

Cameron had attempted to help clean up the dinner dishes, but Audrey had shooed him outside. He suspected maybe she realized that he needed a moment to process some things. He'd gratefully slipped out the door and watched Piper roll around the grass, getting her clothes and hair filthy. He smiled at her lack of inhibition, wondering when the last time was that he'd allowed himself to be as carefree as she was, to smile and laugh like she did.

"Uncle Cameron, will you play catch with me?"

Cameron blinked and realized Piper had found the old

football that had been left in the yard. He ambled down the porch steps and took the ball from her. "Do you know how to throw a football?"

"Sure," she announced. She took the ball back, arched her arm over her head, and let the thing loose. It landed right in front of her and rolled to a stop. "See?"

Cameron chuckled and picked the ball back up. He palmed it in his hand, allowing himself to revel in the feel of the soft leather. "Not a bad try, but there's a secret in throwing one of these things." He glanced at her. "Want me to tell you what it is?"

Her eyes grew wide. "Yeah," she whispered.

Cameron squatted in front of her and held the ball out. "See these white laces here?" He ran the tip of his index finger over them.

Piper touched them. "Is that where they sewed the ball to keep it from falling apart?"

Cute, but also an interesting observation. "No, this is to guide you on where to put your hands." He showed her by demonstrating with his own fingers. "See, you palm the ball like this and line your fingers up with the laces. Then you can throw it."

Piper watched the ball fly across the yard. She got up and ran for it. "I want to try it now." She skipped back toward him, holding the ball in both hands. She attempted to palm the ball like he had, but her hand was too little. "Am I doing it right?"

Cameron made an adjustment to her fingers. "Now throw it. But don't bring your arm back too far. And let the ball go about here," he instructed as he demonstrated how to move her arm.

She gave it a shot, with a huge grin breaking across her face. Of course, she didn't execute exactly how he'd shown

her, but it was pretty damn close, and the ball flew a lot far-
ther. She jumped up and down and ran to the ball.

"I wanna throw it again," she announced. "Can I throw
it and you catch it?" she asked him.

He stood from his crouch. "Sure." He made sure not to
go too far, knowing she wouldn't be able to cross the whole
yard with one throw.

She jumped up and down again and clapped her hands
when he caught her throw. "Now you throw and I'll
catch it."

Cameron waited for her to stand still before he let the
ball fly. He arched it too high and the thing went flying
through her hands, even after she jumped to try to catch it.

"You're supposed to let me catch it," Piper chastised
him. She snagged the ball from the grass and threw it back
to him. "Like that."

Was she instructing him on how to throw the ball, after
he just showed her? He grinned and shook his head.
"Thanks for the pointer," he told her. "I'll see if I can do
better."

This time he underhanded it, and Piper held her arms
out, but the ball bounced out of her hands and landed on
the ground. "That's not how you showed me to throw it."

Damn, kid.

She threw the ball at him, and he caught it. "Okay,
let's try it again," he said to her. "This time I want you
to watch the ball and try to cradle it in your hands when
you catch it."

Piper tilted her head to one side. "You mean like a
baby?"

Cameron opened his mouth, then burst out laughing.
"Not really. I mean like this." I tossed the ball in the air and
caught it the way he described. "Understand?"

Piper nodded and swiped a strand of hair out of her face. The whole time Pinkie Pie had been running back and forth, as though she were trying to catch the ball too. Cameron had been tempted to drop the thing on her.

Cameron held the ball up with one hand. "Ready?"

The kid nodded again and held out her hands.

This time she caught it and jumped up and down. They played for a few more minutes, when Piper stopped and glanced toward where Audrey had stepped onto the back porch.

"Audrey, come play catch with us. Uncle Cameron taught me how to throw."

Cameron glanced at her and allowed his gaze to appreciate the way her leggings showed off her slim legs. And damn if he didn't want them wrapped around his hips.

"Yeah, I don't really do the football thing," she told them.

He arched a brow at her and silently winced at the pain it caused in his eye. "You are if you're going to stay in this house," he replied. "Get down here."

She came down the steps. "I don't suppose I have a choice in this?"

"No." He snagged her wrist and yanked her in front of him. "It'll be fun."

"I doubt that," she complained. "I don't like football."

"Bite your blasphemous tongue," he warned, then placed the ball in her hands.

She took it, but held it out in front of herself like she didn't know what to do with the thing. He rolled his eyes and readjusted her grip.

"It's not going to bite you," he soothed.

She slanted him a look over her shoulder. "Says you."

He chuckled and placed her hand on the football and

moved her fingers to rest on the laces. Yeah, he may have touched her more than he should have. Brushed the tops of her hands with his fingers longer than necessary. Stood a little too close, maybe made sure his hips nudged hers. Audrey cleared her throat, and Cameron told himself she was trying to cover up a moan. Because he sure as hell was.

"Make sure your fingers align with the laces like this," he said as he showed her.

Her breath shuddered, and if Piper hadn't been watching them, he would have spun her around and kissed the hell out of her. Cut and bruises be damned. His face was already throbbing. What was a little more pain?

"And don't throw it too high," Piper added as she watched them. He hoped she wasn't watching the hard-on growing beneath his athletic pants.

"Maybe I should have Piper show me how to do this," Audrey suggested when his erection nudged her rear end.

"Not on your life," he growled in her ear.

"Are you masochistic?" she asked

Cameron paused and thought about it. "Probably. Now, pay attention, because there'll be a quiz." He raised her arm and demonstrated. "Let it go right about here," he said as he showed her. "And you want the ball to have a spin."

Audrey snorted. "Yeah, sure. I'll make that happen."

Cameron stepped away from her and crossed the yard.

"You expect me to throw this thing that far?" she asked him.

Beside her, Piper patted her leg. "Don't worry, it just takes practice. Want me to show you?"

"Yeah, have at it, kid."

Cameron narrowed his eyes at Audrey when she handed the ball to his niece. "Chicken," he called out to her.

Audrey simply shrugged and stepped aside for Piper.

The little girl raised her arm and sent the ball flying. But she threw it toward the ground and the ball hit and rolled lopsidedly toward a tree.

Audrey patted Piper on the back. "Wow, that was great," she gushed at the girl, then gave Cameron a sly grin. "Your uncle's a great teacher."

Cameron picked up the ball and pointed it toward her. "You're not getting out of this."

"You have to cradle it like a baby," Piper instructed. "Like this." She held her hands out to show Audrey.

Audrey glanced back and forth between Piper and Cameron. "Um…"

But he didn't give her time to reconsider or pass off to Piper. He arched a gentle throw, making sure it went right to her and wouldn't smack her in the face. Audrey held her hands up, but it was to block the ball instead of catch it, and the ball hit her open hands and fell to the ground.

"You call this fun?" she questioned, then scooped the ball up. "Why does it have to be such a weird shape? Don't you have any baseballs?"

Cameron sent her a dark look. "Baseball is for sissies. Now throw the thing already."

Audrey muttered something, which sounded suspiciously like "stubborn ass." Cameron kept his mouth shut and figured she'd probably toss the ball at his head if he pushed her much further. She arched her arm back and sent the thing sailing. It actually wasn't a bad throw, just slightly off with the aim.

Cameron channeled his college playing days and stretched his arms to the side and had to practically dive for the thing.

"Whoa, that was a cool catch!" Piper gushed.

"You did that on purpose," he accused Audrey.

But Audrey just shrugged and curled her mouth up in a half smile. Yeah, she'd thrown it shitty on purpose. Cameron was starting to suspect she was better at football than she wanted him to think.

Without warning, he let the ball fly, putting a full spin on it. Audrey's reaction to catch it was so automatic that she didn't even hesitate to cradle the thing and tuck it under her arm.

Cameron strolled toward her and yanked the ball from her grip. "You're just a big, fat faker, aren't you?"

She touched the tip of her index finger to the bruise on his eye. "You just seemed so eager to teach me that I didn't want to crush your ego any more than it already was."

His gaze dropped to her mouth. "Thoughtful of you."

Pinkie Pie came running over and batted at the laces on Cameron's shoes. He nudged the cat away. "Back away if you know what's good for you, cat."

"Come here, Pinkie." Piper picked the animal up and cradled her close. "I think she wants to rock on the swing." The two of them climbed the steps to the swing and plopped down. The cat squirmed to try to get away, but Piper had a tight grip on her.

"Can we be done with this lesson now?" Audrey asked.

Cameron grinned. "Why, because you don't need lessons?"

Audrey yanked the ball back from him. "No." She tossed the ball in the air and caught it again. "My dad taught us how to play. And then...when everything fell apart, we stopped."

"And now it's too painful for you to play?" he guessed.

She shook her head. "No. I just never really liked football to begin with."

"Hmm." He snatched the football back from her and

bounced it back and forth between his hands. "I guess you're forgiven, then."

She smiled. "Kind of you."

He moved to sit on the porch steps and motioned her to join him. "It's a shame, because I could have had someone to toss the ball around with." Why did he admit that? Like she cared.

"Well, who do you usually play with?"

Cameron shrugged and palmed the ball. "No one, really. Sometimes Brandon, but he works a lot. And now that he's married and his son is off at college, he's all about Stella. Selfish bastard," he muttered.

Audrey grinned. "You're not jealous, are you?"

He tossed her a confused look. "Of Brandon?"

"Yeah," she answered with a shrug "Well, maybe not of him exactly. But what he has. A family. Someone to share his time with, or toss the ball around with."

Actually, yeah. Sometimes he was a bit envious. "I never really thought about it like that," he lied.

"It's okay to admit it. I won't tell anyone." She paused a moment. "So why are you still single?"

He snorted. "It's not like I can just run out and pick up a wife from the hardware store."

"Maybe you just haven't tried hard enough."

The cool breeze that kicked up wrapped her lemony scent around him, and he wanted to bury his face in her hair. "Or maybe I hadn't met anyone worth the effort." Hadn't he told her that already?

Her brow furrowed as she studied him. Busted. "Why did you say it like that?"

"Like what?" Yeah, totally believable.

"*Hadn't.* It's past tense, like you're no longer looking."

Cameron gazed over the lawn, listening to Piper croon

to her cat, telling her what a pretty girl she was. He knew he had three choices. He could deny, which was his first instinct because he'd been doing it for so long. It would be easy to throw her off.

No, it wouldn't, because she always sees right through you.

Yeah, so that probably wasn't a good idea.

Then there was his personal favorite: distraction. He could just kiss the hell out of her, which he knew worked every time. But that would only be a temporary reprieve. It was truth time, and not only that but he also needed to start being honest with himself. From the second he'd met Audrey, he'd stopped being interested in other women.

"Yeah, you caught me," he admitted. "I'm not really looking anymore."

Audrey's face fell, but only for a moment, because she gathered herself quickly. "You gave up that easily, huh?"

Cameron picked up the ball again, needing something to do with his hands, lest he tear her clothes off. "No, I haven't given up." He looked at her and held her gaze for a moment. "I stopped looking when I met you. Actually," he continued with a shrug, "I don't think I was ever really looking, because I didn't care."

Audrey's throat worked as she swallowed. Her mouth opened, then snapped shut, followed by a laugh that sounded more nervous. "What're you saying, Cameron?"

He cupped her chin and tugged her face closer to his. "I'm saying I haven't cared about any other woman since I met you. I'm saying you're the one who would make me..." His words trailed off, because his brain couldn't seem to find the right ones to describe how he felt. Because he'd never felt like this before, and putting those feelings into words was way harder than he thought it would be.

Audrey's tongue swiped across her full lower lip. He'd made her nervous. But at least she wasn't running through her weird lists of names again. "Make you what?"

He cleared his throat and continued to hold fast on to her jaw. "Be better."

She offered him a small smile. "Maybe I don't want you to be better. Maybe I like you just the way you are."

"*I* want to be better," he corrected.

She shook her head, and he finally let go her. "But you don't need me for that."

He grabbed her shoulders, needing her to understand. "Hell, yes, I do."

She licked her lips again, and damn, he was *this* close to kissing her. "Cameron—"

"Don't go back to Boulder," he interrupted.

Her eyes grew wide. "I have to."

He shrugged that off. "Okay, fine go back and tie up loose ends. But come back and don't leave again."

One of her brows arched. "Is that an order?"

"You know what I mean," he answered.

"Actually, I'm not sure I do."

He blew out a breath, getting the feeling he was blowing this. He was stumbling over his words too much, or not using enough finesse to get his point across. And what was his point? He wanted her to stay in Blanco Valley. He wanted her to move all her shit to his house and sleep in his bed. He wanted to turn the guest room into a girly, pink room for Piper. Hell, he'd even buy the damn cat her own bed.

But how could he make Audrey understand that? He'd never been good with words, and he knew that's what she was waiting for.

He shoved a hand through his too-long hair. "I got a job offer in Denver," he told her. "To be the head coach for a high school up there."

She gaped at him for so long, Cameron wasn't sure she was going to answer. "Congratulations," she finally said.

He wanted to grab her and shake her. "That's all you're going to say? You're not going to get all pissy for not telling you or possibly uprooting Piper again?"

"Do you want me to get pissy?" she asked.

He stood from the steps and glared down at her. "I want you to be honest. I want you to stomp your foot and yell at me for not thinking of Piper first. I want you to tell me to stay."

She stood on the bottom step, so they were eye level. "If I tell you to stay, will you?"

Damn, this conversation wasn't going as planned. "I haven't decided yet."

She jerked as though he'd stuck her. "Then why did you ask me?"

"Jesus," he muttered to himself. He always felt like he was talking in circles with this woman. "I don't know. I thought I did, but..." His words trailed off because, dammit, he didn't know anymore.

Her eyes searched his, looking dangerously close to welling up. "But what?" When he didn't answer, she went on. "I can't tell you what to do, Cameron."

"But you want to," he guessed. Actually, it wasn't a guess. He knew she was dying to blurt out all her feelings.

"What, are you waiting for me to tell you what to do? You won't make a decision unless you know how I feel about it?"

Was that what he was doing? Was that why he'd waited so long to have this discussion? Her opinion mattered to him, and yet he knew the decision was solely his. So why was he having such a hard time?

Audrey glanced over her shoulder as though looking for someone else. "You don't even know what you want, do you?"

That wasn't true. He knew he wanted her and Piper. Hell, he wanted the whole family thing. But was he willing to give up his dream offer?

"Audrey—"

"You can't have it all, Cameron," she interrupted. "I can see the wheels turning in your mind. You're trying to figure out a way to tie the whole package together the way you want it."

That wasn't what he was doing. Was it?

With a frustrated groan, Cameron ran a hand over his head. "Audrey," he said again. He opened his mouth to tell her...Hell, he didn't know what he wanted to tell her. Yeah, he wanted this job. He wanted Audrey too. But he didn't know how to do both. She didn't even live here, and he couldn't bring himself to ask her to give up her life for him. Especially when he didn't even know where he was going.

Audrey shook her head. "You know where to find me when you've made up your mind."

Audrey inhaled a shaky breath and looked like she was about to say more when they both heard a snort from behind them. Piper was curled up on the swing, fast asleep with the cat curled into a tight ball at her feet.

"I'll carry her to bed," Cameron said.

TWENTY

Cameron knew Audrey was mad at him, and he didn't blame her.

You've scared her off.

Of that, he was reasonably sure. But why was she spooked? Okay, he got that she had trust issues. He of all people understood trust issues. But he figured after he'd opened up that whole can of worms that was Drew Spalding, she'd see it as an act of faith and realize that he was trying, trying more than he had with any other woman.

After she'd snuck back into the guesthouse, he'd left Piper on the couch for a little while before carrying her to her bed. He'd tucked her in, expecting Audrey to show herself and put Piper in her pajamas. But her bedroom door had been closed with no sound, so he'd assumed she'd gone to bed, even though it had been just shy of nine o'clock.

An hour later, he was still pacing around the living room, trying to figure out how to make things right with her. He knew they were off. Audrey was vivacious and opinionated. She rarely hid from him, and the fact that she'd slipped away so suddenly didn't sit well with him.

His indecisiveness freaked her out. Hell, it freaked *him* out. He'd been so sure of what he'd wanted. Of where he was going. Now he didn't know up from down. And what scared him more than anything was for the first time, a woman was worth giving up what he thought he'd always wanted. Damn, he was no good at this, and being left to his own thoughts probably wasn't the best thing. He was going to think himself into insanity.

He tossed a look at his bedroom, thinking he ought to just go to bed and sort things out with Audrey in the morning. But he knew if he lay down right now, he wouldn't sleep. He'd spend the entire night replaying their conversation over and over again, wondering where he'd gone wrong, what he could have done differently.

Not let her out of his sight.

That had been a mistake. He should have forced her to come clean before giving her a chance to escape.

Cameron took one more turn around the room, then shoved a hand through his hair.

Screw it.

He'd just have to go over there and demand they talk this out.

He let himself out the back door and tromped across the damp grass. The night was chilly and overcast, and Cameron wished he'd left his sweatshirt on. Without knocking, because he knew she wouldn't answer, he let himself through the front door. Luckily the screen door was already open, because the thing tended to squeak, and he didn't want to give Audrey any warnings.

The inside was dark and quiet. It smelled good, like

cinnamon and *Audrey*. Plus she'd done an amazing job of keeping the place clean and making it homey. There were a couple of pictures Piper had colored stuck to the fridge with magnets. A blanket was tossed over the back of the couch, and a vase of flowers sat on the kitchen counter. Cameron had never taken the time to do much with the place, because no one ever stayed here. But he knew he'd never be able to step foot inside without thinking of her.

Cameron glanced around one more time and was about to leave when he did a double take down the hallway. A slant of light spilled out from underneath the bathroom door.

Gotcha.

The corner of his mouth curled. She thought she could hide from him.

With silent footsteps, he crossed the small living space and came to a stop at the bathroom. He pressed his ear to the door, trying to listen for any sound. The shower. Crying. Humming.

Nothing.

Then, a splash of water.

Was she in the tub? Cameron tried to chase the image away, but his mind was tricky. The image formed faster than he could stop it. Suds clinging to her damp skin. One leg propped up on the edge, perfect for him to slip in between...

Okay, this isn't why you're here.

Quietly he knocked.

He braced himself for silence, which was what he got.

He knocked again. "Audrey," he said quietly so as not to wake Piper.

"You can come in," she told him.

Wait, she wanted him to come in? What if she was all

naked and stuff? And soapy? How was he supposed to stand there with her naked in the bathtub?

Maybe she was just running water in the sink and that was the splashing he'd heard. But Cameron knew he couldn't possibly be that lucky, and the second the turned the knob he knew he was right.

Yep. Naked in the bathtub.

"Uh...I can come back."

The only saving grace was the giant mound of bubbles that covered everything but her head, which was leaned back. Her eyes were closed, and her hair was piled in a loose knot on top of her head.

"No need," she said without looking at him.

But Cameron just stood there, imagining things that he shouldn't be, like what was underneath the bubbles and how she'd managed to wash her back. Because, you know, he could, like, wash it for her. Or something.

He cleared his throat.

Say something intelligent, dumbass.

"No, really. I think I should come back." *Okay, that's not intelligent.*

She lifted her head and pinned him with her brown eyes. "What's the matter? Never seen a woman in a bathtub before? Because I would find that hard to believe."

Was she for real? "Is that a trick question?"

She tilted her head as though in thought. "Actually, no." She ran her palm over the top of the bubbles. "What're you doing here, Cameron? Besides destroying my relaxation."

"You're the one who told me to come in," he pointed out.

"Because I knew you wouldn't just go away."

Okay, that was true.

He leaned against the bathroom counter. Was it just him, or were the bubbles diminishing? "We need to finish our earlier conversation," he told her. Kudos to him for keeping his mind on track. When she didn't respond, he glanced at her. "Audrey—"

"Cameron," she interrupted in a quiet voice. "I can't have this conversation right now."

"Okay," he responded, because he wasn't sure what else to say. "Look, I know I have a lot of thinking to do, and to be honest I'm..." He blew out a breath. "I'm confused."

"I get that. And maybe..." She glanced at him quickly, but then her gaze skittered away. "Maybe you just need some time alone. To think about things."

"So where does this leave us?" he asked. Time alone? Like without her? Cameron didn't want that. He wanted her here, with them. Him and Piper. The three of them, like...like a family.

She was silent a moment, then blew out a breath. "I'm not sure."

Cameron crossed his arms over his chest and stared at the gray bath rug. "I don't think I'm the only one who doesn't know what they want."

She looked at him. "Okay, maybe I don't know what I want right now. But you have someone else looking to you for stability. You have to give that to Piper now."

His brow furrowed. "You think I don't know that?"

Audrey sat straighter in the tub, sending water sloshing over the sides. "How the hell should I know? You don't even know what you want, so how should I know?"

He blew out a frustrated breath. "I didn't come in here to fight with you. I..." Cameron ran the words through his mind, knowing what he wanted to say, but unsure how to say it. "What if you moved down here?"

Audrey blinked at him as though unable to comprehend his words. "Cameron, be serious."

"I am being serious."

"We were just talking about how you need time to think," she told him. "Because you don't know what you want."

"I know I want this," he stated with confidence.

"This what?" she pressed. "What exactly will this be?"

He looked her dead in the eye. "This will be you and me. You, me, and Piper." Because that was what he wanted. Set aside the job and Drew and everything else, and all that mattered were Audrey and Piper.

"And how am I supposed to believe that you're ready to settle down?" she countered. "You've always had this carefree lifestyle of women coming and going, and now all of a sudden you want to do the family thing? What if you decide it's too much?" she questioned. "What if one day you can't handle it anymore, and you check out? You leave me and Piper to handle things ourselves because this isn't what you signed up for—"

"Audrey," he interrupted, knowing where her fears were coming from. He squatted next to the bathtub, inhaling the fresh scent of her soap and the bubbles. "I'm not your father," he told her. "I won't just quit on you when it becomes inconvenient for me. I know everyone else in your life has done that, but that's not me."

She offered him a sad smile of understanding. "I know, I just…" Her gaze skittered away again. "I have a hard time separating the two. Nothing in my life has ever been permanent."

Cameron couldn't stand to hear any more, because Audrey had so much to offer people. It was a horrible waste to know a person of her warmth and giving nature would intentionally isolate herself.

"Look, this whole thing is new for me too," he admitted.

"I'm not saying I'm perfect and I won't disappoint you. And yeah, I'm unsure about the job. I won't lie by saying the offer doesn't mean anything, because it does. But I'll try, and that's what should matter." Right? But when she didn't respond, he pushed her. "Audrey—"

"Could you hand me a towel?" she interrupted.

Um... sure? Or how about no towel?

But seriously, he was trying to have a conversation, and here she was trying to make his brain explode.

He stood and yanked the towel off the bar and held it out to her. Before he had a chance to react or, say, turn around, she stood from the tub, water and soap running down her trim body, clinging to her round breasts, soft tummy, and lean thighs.

Cameron swallowed, almost taking his tongue with it, and turned around. He figured taking the initiative to give her a moment of privacy would be the gentlemanly thing to do. Instead of, you know, ripping the towel out of her hands and carrying her to the bedroom.

Yeah, gentlemanly.

She didn't say anything as he stared at the bathroom wall, closing his eyes against the sounds she was making behind him. The soft fibers of the towel rubbing against her skin. Water dripping off her body and landing on the floor. The sight of her bare feet just inches from his.

"You can turn around now," she told him.

He held his breath and slowly turned just in time to get an eyeful of her left breast before she covered it up. Plump, rosy nipples. Creamy skin. *Fuuuuuuck.*

"Jesus, Audrey," he muttered.

"You've had your tongue down my throat several times," she pointed out.

"Yeah, but..." He scrubbed a hand through his hair

and willed his fingers to stop trembling. He hadn't been this worked up since his freshman year of high school when Carly Dowd had given him his first blow job in the backseat of her daddy's car. He laughed. Actually fucking laughed.

"But what?" she asked innocently as she scrubbed a hand towel over her head.

He gestured toward her barely covered body. "You act like kissing and...this is the same thing."

She dropped the smaller towel on the counter and clutched the one wrapped around her body tighter. "And what is this?"

"Shit if I know, Audrey," he admitted. "I came in here to finish our conversation, and you're..." What was she doing? Really, all she'd been doing was bathing, and he'd intruded on her. "You're...naked."

She took a step toward him. "And?"

He narrowed his eyes and gritted his teeth. "Don't push me."

Audrey lifted her hand and touched the tension between his eyes. "You take yourself too seriously, Cameron."

He grabbed her hand and held her to him, so she wouldn't have a chance to get away. In the past, he'd been too easy on her, giving her ample opportunity to escape when all he wanted to do was finish what they'd started. Multiple times.

"I'm not letting you run away this time," he warned.

Her gaze dropped to his mouth.

Without giving himself time to think, or giving Audrey time to hide, he yanked the towel from her and tossed it over his shoulder. He grinned as she gasped, then allowed his gaze to touch every naked inch of her.

Yeah, well worth the wait.

The woman was something of fantasies, like those Greek goddesses who lay around in togas and sip wine all day, then bathed naked in a stream. Her skin was pale and creamy, with full breasts, probably enough for a healthy handful, a pinched waist, and curvy hips. Her legs were long and her small feet were accented by glittery golden nail polish.

His gaze slowly traveled back up her body, lingering on the dark patch of curls at the juncture of her thighs, taking in her small navel, then her puckered nipples. Cameron's mouth watered at the thought of taking a tight nub in his mouth. He was about to tell her that, to announce everything he intended to do to her, when the look in her eyes stopped him.

She was afraid. Afraid of putting herself out there. Afraid that he'd hurt her.

His gaze softened, and he cupped her face with his hand. "Do you trust me?" he asked.

She licked her lips, then gave him a small nod. Something inside softened as relief made his knees week.

Without giving her time to reconsider or call the whole thing off, he hooked his hands under the backs of her thighs and hoisted her up.

She yelped and grabbed on to his shoulders.

"This would work a whole lot better if you'd wrap your legs around me," he told her as he backed out of the bathroom.

Her pupils filled her beautiful brown eyes, and she hooked her legs around his. Cameron didn't bother biting back a groan as he finally had Audrey's lush nude body pressed all over his.

"We're finally finishing this," he told her as he entered the dark bedroom and kicked the door closed behind him.

She clung to his neck as he set them both on the bed. "Seems to me we're just starting."

Much later, Audrey lay in the dark, willing herself to sleep, but her mind wouldn't settle down long enough to give her peace.

The man next to her took up most of the twin-sized bed with his big body, which threw off heat like a Colorado summer. He hadn't given her a moment's rest for the better part of three hours, moving inside her body, pinning her to the mattress and staring down at her like he'd been seeing her for the first time. Even now, after her heart had slowed, she shivered, thinking how right it had felt to be beneath him. To feel his thighs forcing her legs apart and his hot breath on her neck as he came inside her.

It had been the most intense moment of her life. Intense, but just as precious. Just as sweet and tender and *different*. Because *he* was different. The way he looked at her, kissed her, touched her. Made love to her. It had been nothing like she'd ever experienced, and it frightened her. She was even more frightened than she already had been of possibly uprooting her entire life for a man who, until just a few months ago, was happily single. A man who, for all she knew, wanted her to move here because it's what he knew. Maybe being left alone with Piper scared him. Okay, she got that. It was natural to feel some trepidation at the thought of being solely responsible for another human being. But did he want Audrey here because her presence brought him comfort? Comfort in all the uncertainty that came with raising a little girl? Or did he want her here because he *wanted* her here? Because he couldn't live without her?

Because he loved her?

The situation was about as clear as a foggy San Francisco day. Audrey wasn't sure if she could change her entire life for a man who didn't even understand his own motives.

"I can't," she whispered into the dark. Cameron's breathing had changed, so she knew he was awake.

He rolled over and looked at her.

Audrey kept her gaze on the ceiling because it was safer that way. If she looked into his blue eyes, she'd cave. She'd give in to her desires, and she needed to stay strong.

"I can't move here to be with you, Cameron." Just saying the words was like swallowing glass, but she had to get them out. "It's better this way," she said, finally looking at him.

His gaze was shadowed, but she felt his eyes cutting straight through her.

"Better for who?" he countered.

"I can't give up my entire life for a man who doesn't even know what he wants," she said, ignoring his question.

He shifted under the covers, pushing up on an elbow. "What about what Piper's given up?"

His words were soft, but they were like an ice pick to her heart. She tossed an angry look his way. "Don't you dare." She sat up, mirroring his pose. "I know damn well what she's given up. I watched her mother waste away for months, then held her shaking body as she sobbed over Dianna."

"And yet here she is," Cameron said. "As resilient as ever."

"What the hell's that supposed to mean?" she demanded as she scrambled off the bed, searching for something to cover herself up. "That I don't have it in me?" After spotting a hooded sweatshirt on the floor, Audrey scooped it up and pulled it over her head. "That I'm scared or something?"

Cameron stood up from the bed also, but more slowly than she had and completely uncaring about his nudity. "I'm not saying anything, Audrey."

She jabbed an index finger at him. "Yes, you are. You're saying I'm too scared to take a chance." Dammit, she wasn't.

"I'm not saying it, Audrey. You are. And there's nothing wrong with being afraid," he pointed out.

"I'm not afraid," she reiterated. "I'm just trying to protect myself."

One side of Cameron's mouth kicked up. "That's what you're calling it? Protection?" He shook his head as he yanked his boxers over his hips. "At least I admit that I'm not sure what I want." He tugged his shirt over his head then reached for his jeans. "But you? You think you know exactly what you want. You think you have it all planned out, but you really don't have a clue."

She watched him grab his shoes as fear fisted in her heart. "I was never part of the deal, Cameron," she reminded him. "It was just supposed to be you and Piper. None of this"—she waved her hand around the bedroom—"was supposed to happen."

"But it did happen," he said after he put his shoes on. He came toward her and took her chin in his hand. "But you go back to Boulder. Go on back, if that's what you really want."

TWENTY-ONE

Cameron dragged himself through the door at eleven o'clock that Friday night. The Bobcats had played a hard game, pushing it until the last second and barely squeaking out a six-point victory over the Alamosa Maroons. But he'd returned home with a heavy heart because Audrey wasn't there.

She'd left early that morning and driven back to Boulder, taking a piece of his soul with her. As he'd watched her put Piper on the bus, running her hands over the girl's ponytail, knowing that Audrey was minutes away from hopping in her car and leaving, he tried telling himself that it would be okay, that he knew it would be okay. But he didn't know shit. And he was just as pissed at her as he was himself. He was pissed at her for running away, for thinking she knew what was right. And he was pissed at himself for completely botching the conversation, for demanding that she admit she was just as scared as he was, but maybe they could figure it out together.

But the sinking feeling in his chest had worsened when she'd pulled out of the driveway and disappeared down the street. She hadn't said goodbye, and he'd tried not to take it personally. But how could he not, when the night before last he'd been inside her. Several times. But something had felt off as he'd stared at the empty driveway, and it wasn't just the knowledge that she wouldn't be here when he returned home.

She was just going to use the time away as an excuse to find a reason why being with him wouldn't work. He knew because he'd used the tactic before on just about every woman he'd been with. And to be honest, it stunk.

Like yesterday's garbage left in hundred-degree heat.

But okay, fine. He'd give her space. She needed it, and he got that. He just hoped she didn't use the time to talk herself out of something that could be really good.

The house was quiet when he shut the door. The porch light had been left on, as well as the lamp on the hall table. Last night Audrey informed him that she'd made arrangements with his neighbor Zoey to come and stay with Piper after school until after the game. Yeah, that was all good and stuff. He knew Zoey. He liked her and trusted her.

She was twenty-five and lived with her grandfather, who was showing early signs of dementia. She was a good kid. Responsible and sweet.

But she wasn't Audrey. She didn't have brown eyes and she didn't irritate the shit out of him with her cooking skills and kiss like sex on a stick.

Zoey was in the living room watching some old Clint Eastwood movie with the volume turned way down. She turned when the floor creaked beneath his feet.

"Hey," she greeted with a warm smile.

Cameron set his bag down and pulled his cap off his head. "Sorry I'm so late."

Zoey just shrugged. "Hey, I went to every Bobcat game in high school. I get it." She stood from the couch and slipped her tennis shoes on. "Think we'll make state this year?"

"Better believe it," he answered. They just needed to win one more game to clinch a spot in the playoffs.

"I had a hard time getting Piper to settle down," Zoey admitted. "It was almost ten o'clock before she got in bed."

Cameron just waved that away. "That's all right. She's usually pretty wound up on Fridays."

Zoey gave him a cheeky grin. "To be honest, I think she was waiting for you. She kept saying she couldn't fall asleep until you read to her."

Hello, ice pick? Meet heart.

"She's a sweet girl," Zoey added.

"Yeah," Cameron agreed easily. "Where'd the little monster end up?"

Zoey laughed, obviously knowing he was talking about Pinkie Pie. "On the bed with Piper. Though she did get a hold of one of Piper's tennis shoes and chewed it up pretty good." Zoey sent him an apologetic look. "Sorry about that."

Cameron walked her to the front door. "I can't keep the cat out of trouble either, so don't worry about it."

He opened the door and handed her sixty dollars, but Zoey just waved it away. "Oh, I don't want to be paid. Audrey tried to offer me money too, but I wouldn't take it." Zoey slipped her coat on and walked down the steps. "She said you'd try to pay me too but not to take a dime from you. She also said she'd text me your phone number and that you'd be proud of her for not wasting anymore Post-its." Zoey shrugged as though she didn't understand why.

But Cameron knew why. As he shut the door, he found himself glancing around as though expecting to find a little yellow square waiting for him. Of course there weren't any. Audrey had no reason to leave one for him.

He blew out a breath as he turned the television off in the living room and headed toward his bedroom. But at the last minute, he detoured to the guest room, where he knew Piper had been set up for the night. The light had been left on, but Cameron wasn't surprised. He knew she sometimes slept with the light on because she got scared.

He stepped into the room and watched Piper sleep. Luckily Pinkie Pie didn't even stir when he sat on the edge of the bed. The thing merely flicked an ear and kept on sleeping. Or plotting a world takeover.

Piper sighed when Cameron ran his hand over her soft hair. As he sat there, he tried to summon a memory of Dianna as this age, to see if Piper resembled her mother. He knew Dianna had been blond, and the two of them shared the same deep green eyes of their father. But Piper's lips were fuller and her chin pointier. Other than that, he couldn't tell if Piper really resembled her mother all that much.

For the first time, Cameron felt a pang in his chest. Piper would probably ask questions like that one day, wouldn't she? She'd want to know more about her mother, what she was like, her favorite stuff. And Cameron wanted to kick his own ass for not taking the time to get to know his own sister well enough. He hadn't cared. And now he wouldn't be able to tell Piper everything she'd want to know about her mom.

But Audrey would know.

One more reason for Audrey to stay. For Piper and the bond the two of them had. She could tell the little girl all about her mother and what sort of person she'd been.

Piper stirred in her sleep, and Cameron turned the light off before leaving the room. All he wanted to do now was crash, but he stopped in the hallway. Actually, that wasn't all he wanted to do, but it was late. She probably wasn't still up.

But if she was...

Yeah, she probably was.

Despite their tumultuous night together and the uncertain way they'd left things, Cameron still wanted to talk to her. To know...Oh, hell he wasn't sure what he needed to know. That she was still there. That she hadn't completely shut him out.

Cameron pulled his cell out of his pants pockets and entered his darkened bedroom. He dialed Audrey's number and collapsed back on the bed, listening as it rang once, twice, then three times. He was about to hang up when her sweet hello brought a smile to his face.

"I didn't wake you, did I?" he asked her.

He listened while he heard the rustling of bedding on the other end. Cameron gritted his teeth against the image of her lying beneath the sheets. "No," she answered. "I've been awake."

A smile tugged at the corners of his mouth while he stared at the dark ceiling. "Couldn't sleep without me there, huh?"

"Wouldn't you like to think so?" she teased.

Cameron folded one arm behind his head. "I know so."

"Okay, you caught me," she agreed. "I was lying here, pining for you."

His grin grew. "I knew it. You can't live without me."

"Don't let it go to your head or anything."

"Too late," he admitted. "And we won tonight, so thanks for asking."

Her chuckle was soft in his ear. "You haven't given me a chance. You've been too busy stroking your ego."

"I'd rather you do the stroking," he murmured.

"I'm sure you would."

Cameron shoved back the disappointment when she hadn't agreed. "How was your drive up there?"

"Long and uneventful."

He paused before asking his next question. "When're you coming back?" Desperate much?

She sighed. "I just got here, and you're already desperate for me to come back? Is Piper driving you that crazy?"

"She always drives me crazy," he admitted, deliberately ignoring her first question.

"I think you love the crazy," she teased.

Yeah, he did. Never thought it possible, but there it was.

They were both silent a moment, Cameron listening to the night sounds and to Audrey's easy breathing from the other end.

"I miss you," he finally admitted. "I...I want you to come back."

She didn't respond right away, and Cameron's heart started to sink. "Cameron," she said on a sigh. "We both need time before we have this conversation again."

She was right. He knew she was right. But he didn't want time to think. He just wanted *her*.

"Of course I miss you," she said after a moment of silence. "I have no one here to show me the incorrect way to throw a football."

He narrowed his eyes, even though she couldn't see him.

"One more word like that out of your mouth and I'm hanging up."

She got quiet a moment. "I missed you the second I pulled out of the driveway this morning."

Her admission created a knot in his stomach.

"But I still need time to think," she went on. "And you need the time to think too."

He pulled the phone away from his ear and glared at the screen, as though she could see him. "What the hell would I need time to think about?"

"Whether this is what you really want," she answered.

He clenched his teeth. "I already told you it was."

"People change their minds, Cameron."

Damn it, she still didn't trust him. "I already told you, I'm not going to."

Her deep sigh was like a fist around his heart. "I know you said that, but..."

He waited for her to finish, but she didn't. "But what?"

"I have a history of people deciding not to stick around," she explained. "Things get a little tough and they check out. I'm trying to protect myself."

He got the need to protect oneself, but damn. "I'm not your father, Audrey. Haven't I told you that?"

"I know you did," she agreed quickly. "And I believe you. I do."

"But what?" he pressed when he suspected there was more.

"But I just need this time," she answered, "to put some things in perspective."

"All right," he agreed slowly. "Whatever you decide, Piper and I will be here. We're not going anywhere."

She paused longer than Cameron was comfortable with. "I know."

But did she?

* * *

Audrey had ended her second day in Boulder by FaceTiming with Cameron and Piper. They'd talked for almost an hour, keeping Audrey in the loop while they cooked meat loaf and mashed potatoes. Cameron had made a big show of using heavy whipping cream in the potatoes instead of half-and-half, smirking at her the whole time because he knew it would bug the shit out of her. Meanwhile, Piper had talked her ear off about Pinkie Pie, the French toast they'd made for breakfast, and a trip to some video arcade.

Audrey had listened to Piper's rambling storytelling as best she could, while watching Cameron in the background. She'd wanted to reach into the screen and run her fingers through his hair. The past few days, her thoughts had been occupied with the night they'd spent together. How right it had felt and, at the same time, how it had scared her, because she'd known there had been no going back. And she'd gone into it with her eyes wide open, knowing there was a good possibility of getting hurt.

At the time, she hadn't cared. All she kept thinking about was how much she wanted him. But in the mix of all those thoughts had been their argument, an argument that had left her even more confused than before. Cameron had brought up a lot of really good points. Did she know what she wanted?

She wanted the dream. The home, the family, the house full of noise. Maybe even a golden retriever. But could she have that with Cameron? How was she supposed to think she could, when he'd told her to go back to Boulder?

Audrey was sure, in the back of her mind, that he wasn't kicking her out. Maybe it was a test? Or perhaps he was giving her permission.

Hell, she was so confused Audrey didn't know which way was up.

She'd decided to have Sunday brunch with her best friend. Roxy always had a way of putting things into perspective, and Audrey needed to talk things out.

She and Roxy had planned to meet at a café that served the best breakfast croissants and vanilla lattes. Calories be damned, because she planned to indulge.

Her friend was already waiting for her, having snagged a table outside. Dark sunglasses covered her eyes and her legs were crossed.

"I ordered for you," Roxy announced as Audrey sat down.

"Thanks," she breathed, and immediately reached for her latte.

Roxy just grinned. "Maybe I should have ordered something stronger," she joked.

Audrey set the drink down and placed a napkin in her lap. "The last thing I need is something to rev me up even more."

Roxy wagged her fingers in a "give it to me" gesture. "Okay, spill. Why're you here?"

Audrey blinked at her friend. "Because we're having brunch," she stated.

"No," Roxy responded with a sigh. "I mean here in Boulder."

Okay, that. "To catch up on some work," Audrey responded, avoiding Roxy's gaze.

Roxy chuckled. "Try the truth this time. Why did you rush back here? You know Stevie's handling things."

"Yeah, she and her sister," Audrey muttered.

Roxy tilted her head to one side. "Doth I detect some resentment?"

"No," Audrey insisted. Then her shoulders sagged in defeat. "I don't know. Maybe."

"You think you're being pushed out," Roxy concluded. "That you're not needed."

Audrey picked up her drink. "Well, I hadn't really thought that until you said it," she muttered grudgingly.

Even though her friend had sunglasses on, Audrey could still detect an eye roll. "Yes, you were. Admit it."

"Okay, yeah. I feel a little strange about someone else stepping into my shoes in the company I helped build," Audrey admitted.

"And that's a totally normal reaction," Roxy soothed. "But maybe Stevie's not trying to fill your shoes."

Audrey knew her business partner and friend would never deliberately push Audrey out. Still, she couldn't help but feel slighted.

"Maybe Stevie knows you don't really want to come back," Roxy went on.

Audrey sighed as their food was delivered. "How can *she* know that when I don't even know that?"

"But I think you do," Roxy pushed softly as she picked up her fork.

Audrey grabbed her own fork, but hesitated before cutting into her breakfast croissant.

"You haven't been happy since Dianna died," Roxy continued. "Her death changed you."

What had changed her more than anything was seeing how Piper had been left alone. Left to wonder why she had no other family. Why her only grandparent, Dianna and Cameron's father, had no interest in her. Left to wonder why she had no dad, no siblings. Audrey had seen a bit of herself in the six-year-old and had vowed to protect the girl, to make sure Piper was never left to wonder why no one cared enough to bother.

"Why shouldn't you change things up a bit?" Roxy asked as she cut into her own food. "There really isn't anything here for you, anyway."

Audrey stabbed her fork into her croissant. "That's not true. I have my business. And you."

"You can build another business somewhere else." Roxy reached across the table and covered Audrey's hand with her own. "And you'll always have me." She shrugged. "Besides, you barely talk to your father, and you have virtually no relationship with your brother. Go make new memories somewhere else."

Audrey gazed at her food before shoving the bite in her mouth. After chewing and swallowing, she responded, "You make it sound so easy."

"Why should it be hard?" Roxy countered. She jabbed her fork toward Audrey when Audrey opened her mouth to argue. "And don't start coming up with excuses. You always do that."

Audrey snapped her mouth shut. "I don't *always* do that."

"And what about this guy?" Roxy went on. "You find the one man in forever that lights you up, and you'd consider walking away from that?" Roxy shook her head. "Girl, you need your head examined."

"Hey," Audrey tried protesting, but they both knew she didn't have a leg to stand on. "I'm trying to be cautious."

"Why?" Roxy questioned. "For God's sake, woman, stop being your own worst enemy. You like this guy, yes?"

Audrey blew out a breath. "Yeah," she whispered.

Roxy waved a hand in the air. "Actually no. You love him." Audrey opened her mouth, but Roxy was faster. "I don't want to hear anything out of your mouth besides how right I am."

Audrey leaned back in her chair. "I'm thinking maybe I should have had brunch with Stevie."

Roxy just shrugged. "I like Stevie, but she doesn't tell it like it is the way I do." Roxy stated her words with a small grin.

Audrey grinned back and picked up her fork again. "You're right about that. But at least with Stevie I could have a peaceful meal."

Roxy leaned across the table and whispered, "What fun would that be?" Her expression grew serious. "I refuse to let you get in your own way. Go be with Piper. Be with Cameron. Give it a shot and see where it goes."

"What if it doesn't work?" she found herself asking.

Roxy just shrugged that away and stuffed more food into her mouth. "Then at least you can say you tried. And maybe I'll come visit you up there just to see what all the fuss is about."

TWENTY-TWO

Audrey had decided to stay one extra day in Boulder. Last night on the phone, she'd thought she'd seen a cloud of doubt in Cameron's eyes when she'd told him. Instinctively she'd wanted to reassure him, to remove the insecurity her delay had caused him. But she'd kept her thoughts to herself, knowing she needed to take care of some things before she could clue him in. He'd agreed to get Piper ready for school this morning, and Audrey told him she'd be home by the time the girl got off the bus, so he wouldn't have to find someone to stay with her after school.

Home.

It felt right, and Audrey wondered how she could have ever doubted. Roxy had been correct when she'd said that Audrey needed to get out of her own head.

Audrey had timed her arrival for the middle of the day, so she could have some time to think before she had to face Cameron.

She drove past the high school, barely managing to keep her gaze from wandering to the parking lot to search for his car.

Finally, she reached Cameron's house and was surprised to spot his car in the driveway.

Why wasn't he at school?

She wasn't ready for this. If she didn't have time to prepare herself, the minute she saw those wide shoulders and lean hips, all she'd want to do would be to thread her fingers through his hair and kiss him, beg him to drag her to bed, and then she'd forget everything she wanted to say to him.

Maybe she could slip into the guesthouse without him noticing she was home.

There was no sign of him outside, so Audrey parked her car behind his and edged her way to the guesthouse in the back. She shoved away the feeling that she was deliberately being sneaky and used her key to open the door.

But the door was already unlocked.

She supposed that wasn't so strange since all of Piper's stuff was here...

Audrey paused in the doorway and looked around. The place seemed the same. Clean. Quiet. Quaint.

And yet...something felt off. The place felt empty.

Too empty. Which was strange because all the furniture was there. The couch, the small coffee table, the barstools. Everything looked and felt exactly as it had when she and Piper and first moved in.

Then Audrey figured out why.

All the personal touches were gone. The throw over the couch. The vase of flowers on the kitchen counter. Even Piper's drawings had been removed from the fridge.

Audrey set her keys and purse on the bar top and

glanced around. Everything she'd added to the place had been taken away.

Had Cameron lost faith in her after all and boxed up all her stuff? Did he expect her to collect it and be on her way?

She swallowed past the lump in her throat and made her way to Piper's room.

Just like the main living area, all the furniture was still there. The bed and nightstand, but that was it. All of Piper's stuff was missing. Her alarm clock, her snow globe collection. The framed photograph of her and Dianna that had been next to the bed. Even Pinkie Pie's bed was gone.

Okay, so clearly Cameron had moved Piper to the main house. Wasn't he supposed to do that? It was where Piper belonged and what Audrey had been pushing for from the beginning. So why wasn't she happier?

Turning, she moved to what had been her room, knowing what she'd find. Or what she wouldn't find. Furniture? Check.

Personal belongings? Nada.

No scented candles, no stack of magazines. And the closet was empty.

Audrey's heart plummeted to the bottom of her stomach as she stared at the space where her clothes had hung just a few days ago.

All gone.

What the hell?

Audrey ran through every conversation they'd had while she was away, trying to figure out a clue.

Cameron and Piper had been their normal selves and they'd talked about normal things. Cameron hadn't clammed up like he always did when he had something on his mind.

Well, now she had something on her mind, and she wanted answers.

Everything she'd originally planned to say flew from her mind as she stalked out the screen door and across the back lawn.

Just who did he think he was, cleaning out all her stuff like that? Without even giving her a chance to say what she wanted to say? He'd said he understood her need for some time to sort through her thoughts. Had he lied? Changed his mind?

Well, Audrey wasn't going to give him a chance to weasel or kiss his way out of this without explaining himself.

She let herself in the back door and looked for signs of him. When she saw none, she walked through the eating area, then stopped short.

Her eyes narrowed on the pair of drawings on the fridge in the kitchen. The same drawings that had been in the guesthouse. Audrey glanced around and did a double take on the flowers decorating the breakfast table.

Why would Cameron get rid of all her stuff, but keep the flowers she'd bought?

She opened her mouth to call his name when he found her first.

And all the accusations she'd wanted to hurl at him faded. Why did he have to look so good? Why did she want to throw herself at him and tuck her head in the curve of his shoulder? Her heart filled with so much love that it almost knocked the breath out of her.

"I wasn't expecting you back for a few hours," he said to her.

She shifted her feet and searched for something to say. "I made better time than I thought," she lied.

"Uh—"

"Where's all my stuff?" she blurted out.

His eyes widened. "Now, don't get mad—"

"You removed all my things from the guesthouse and I'm not supposed to be mad? You could have just waited until I got back, and I would have done it myself."

Cameron took a step toward her. "I wanted to surprise you. Though I wasn't really expecting you to be angry."

She laughed, because if she didn't she might start crying. "Not mad? You're throwing me out before we even have a chance to talk, and I'm not supposed to be mad?" She jabbed her index finger toward the table. "And, by the way, those are my flowers."

"That's why I brought them over here," he answered her.

Audrey jerked the vase off the table, ignoring the water that splashed on her shirt. "You can't throw all my things out and keep the flowers I bought. I'm taking these with me." And why was she so hung up on the damn flowers?

"Audrey..." Cameron gently took the vase from her tight grip. "I haven't thrown your things out. I just moved them."

She watched as he set the flowers back on the table. "Yeah, moved them to some storage unit outside of town, probably."

He blew out a breath and grabbed her hand. She tried to resist as he tugged her along, but he was too strong, too determined.

"Let go. I'm mad at you," she said as she fought.

"Will you be quiet a minute?" he said without looking back at her.

Dammit, tears started stinging the backs of her eyes.

But she fought them because, hey, she had some dignity. "Cameron, please. If you want me to go, just say so. We don't have to go through this big production of humiliating me."

One tear fell just as he stopped outside his bedroom and turned toward her. Using his thumb, he brushed the tear away and smiled at her.

The sick bastard.

"Will you just wait a minute and look, please?" he asked her.

Audrey waited a moment before looking into his bedroom, afraid to see whatever he'd wanted to show her. She hadn't pegged him as the type to play sick games with her, but the twisting in her stomach wouldn't stop. Another tear spilled as she inhaled a shuddering breath.

Cameron swiped that one away too and stepped out of the doorway so she could see whatever he'd wanted to show her.

She blinked and shook her head. "I think it would be better if I just go—"

The rest of the declaration caught in her throat as her gaze connected with the stack of magazines on the nightstand.

Cameron didn't subscribe to *Cosmo*.

Those were her magazines.

"You like to keep them on the nightstand, right?" Cameron questioned.

She swallowed at the uncertainty in his voice. "Um…"

He shook his head. "That's okay, you can keep them somewhere else. There's a magazine rack in the bathroom." Then he gave her hand another tug.

Audrey tried digging her heels in the carpet when she spotted a mess on the bed: a large picture frame that had been taken apart, along with all the Post-it notes they'd written to each other. They were strewn all over the bed. But she didn't get a chance to ask what that was all about, because Cameron didn't stop pulling her until they were in the closet.

"I put some old junk in storage to make room for all your things," he was telling her as he flipped the closet light on. He kicked a pair of running shoes out of the way.

That was when Audrey noticed her things. *All* of her things. They took up half the closet where half his clothes had once hung.

All her jeans, sweaters, and dresses. Her shoes had been arranged neatly on a shoe rack on the floor, and he even had her belts and scarves neatly organized.

Audrey's breath held in her throat as she ran her gaze over the clothes, back and forth, trying to make sense of what he'd done. Everything was there, hanging next to his as though they'd been there for years. As though they belonged and fit perfectly.

"Cameron..." she whispered.

"I thought you'd want to go back and rearrange everything the way you want it," he told her. "I just wanted to get it all in here."

She finally looked at him and almost choked at the doubt on his face. From the moment she'd met him, Cameron Shaw had been the most confident, cocky man she'd ever met, sure of himself with the way he swaggered and kissed and teased her.

But as he gazed at her as though he expected her to start hurling stuff across the room, Audrey's heart broke a little.

She licked her lips. "Cameron, what's going on? Why have you done all this?"

"I think you know, Audrey."

She supposed, in some tiny corner of her mind, Audrey knew what she was looking at. But years of disappointments had conditioned her always to think the worst, not to get her hopes up. She'd conditioned herself to no longer believe in happy endings, at least her own happy ending. Her mind had automatically tried to come up with alternative reasons for why Cameron had moved all of her things to his house.

"You want me to stay here with you?" she questioned.

He tucked a strand of hair behind her ear and offered her a sympathetic smile. "I want you to live here with me. And Piper. We talked about it over the weekend, and we decided we're not going to let you leave."

"You talked about it over the weekend," she repeated. "You and Piper?"

"Yes, ma'am. So last night the two of us took it upon ourselves to move all your stuff over here. We didn't want you to come home and pack everything up."

"Just because it's all here doesn't mean I can't pack it all up," she pointed out, even though that was rather a worthless argument.

"Yeah, but you won't."

She nodded and glanced at her shoes arranged neatly on the rack. "You're sure of that, huh?"

"Pretty darn."

"There's one thing you got wrong, though," she pointed out.

The muscles in Cameron's throat worked as he swallowed. "What?"

"My sweaters go in a dresser," she told him. "The hangers stretch them out."

He chuckled his relief. "Yeah, I actually knew that. But I didn't have any extra space in my drawers."

She crossed her arms over her chest. "Well, that's going to be a problem. Because you'll have to buy another piece of furniture, and I don't know if your room has the space."

Cameron tugged her back into the bedroom. "I'll just get rid of some of my stuff then. I care more about you than I do all my clothes."

Audrey wasn't sure how to react to his admission, so she walked to the bed and picked up one of the Post-its. This one read, *Fixed the broken porch step.* It had been one of the first notes he'd left her, and even then she'd cherished it. Not only the act of the repair itself, but also the note and his strong handwriting. She'd read the thing over and over again before tucking it away in a drawer, just as he had hers. Audrey had no clue how he'd found them all, or when he'd found them.

"What're you doing with all these?"

"Ah..." Cameron ran a hand over the back of his neck. "You actually weren't supposed to see it until it was finished."

She slid him a look. "What's it going to be?"

Cameron picked up the empty frame. "A sort of collage, I guess. See, they're going inside this matting; then I'm framing it." He looked at her and held up one of the notes. "See, these mark a critical time in my life, and I wanted to preserve them. They don't belong in the garbage. They're too precious for that."

Audrey tried to formulate a response in her mind. *Thank you* was so inadequate, and everything else got caught in her throat. She did the only other thing she could think of. She grabbed him and yanked his mouth down on hers. He stumbled toward her in surprise, but then immediately joined her in the kiss.

Her lips parted and her tongue tangled with his, signifying the days they'd spent apart and the emotion that still hadn't been spoken between them. She knew Cameron wasn't good with words, so she let the kiss do the talking.

Audrey's knees went weak when Cameron tunneled his hand into her hair and held her mouth harder to his. She'd only meant the kiss to be a quick show of her love, of how much his gesture meant to her. It had quickly turned fierce, just as all their other kisses had. But before it could be taken further, because she still had things to say, Audrey pulled away and took a deep breath.

Cameron tried hauling her back, but she shook her head.

"I think it should be hung in the entryway," she suggested. "That way everyone can see it when they come in."

"I don't want everyone to see it," he argued. "It goes in the bedroom." He held up a note for her to see. "These are between you and me, and I don't want anyone else intruding."

His admission melted her heart even more, further confirming that she'd made the right decision to leave her old life behind and start anew with him. How could she have thought this was a bad idea? That Cameron was a risk? Staying away from him had been the risk. Second-guessing herself had been the only danger to herself, not opening her heart to Cameron.

He tossed the note on the bed and crossed his arms over his chest. It was a classic defensive move she'd seen a dozen times, and she braced herself.

"Okay, now I'm just waiting for you to say it," he announced.

Audrey blinked in confusion. "Say what?"

"How much you love me and can't live without me," he said without hesitation. Then he took a step toward her and settled his hands on her hips. "How much you pined for me when you were away. That you cried yourself to sleep each night and that the possibility of letting a stud like me slip away would be crazy."

Audrey grinned and toyed with the collar of his shirt. "That's a bit extreme. And I've met studlier guys than you."

He pinched her ass. "Okay, then I'll settle for you just telling me you love me."

"I don't know, it may go to your head."

He nuzzled her neck. "Honey, it's already gone to my head. And my heart."

She wrapped her arms around his neck. "Well, in that case I guess I do love you. But I'm only saying it because you told me to."

He pulled back and scowled at her. "Since when have you done anything I've told you to?"

"Maybe you should try saying please every once in a while."

He set her away from him. "I'll try and work on that. In the meantime, I was saving this note for last. I thought you could put it in after all the others."

Audrey's brow furrowed as she accepted the note from him, trying to remember if there was another one she'd forgotten, because she'd pretty much memorized every single one they'd written to each other.

But when she took in the four words, her eyes filled, and Audrey knew why she hadn't seen this note before. She didn't bother asking how he would know to write *I love you too*.

But he'd known, just as she'd known that he'd sealed her fate with the first look. The first kiss. The first smirk. The only thing that surprised Audrey was how long it had taken her to realize it.

With a smile and another kiss, she handed the note back to Cameron.

He let the thing flutter to the bed as he took her in his arms and showed her what he'd already told her.

Love Always Wins in Champion Valley!

Coach Blake Carpenter and physical therapist Anabelle Turner need to keep things professional for the good of the team. But when the score is this close—and the passion this fierce—it's anybody's game...

Keep reading for an excerpt of *Winner Takes All*.

Available now!

ONE

"Half these kids don't know a blitz from a fumble."

Blake Carpenter had to admit his assistant coach wasn't wrong. Most of these kids couldn't pass for shit. The kicker couldn't find the goalposts if they had flashing lights on them. And these boys couldn't take the Colorado heat without bitching like a bunch of little girls. Damn, Blake hated it when his best friend was right.

How had his life come to this?

A year ago he'd been playing pro football, something he'd dreamed of since he was a little kid. Making more money than he knew what to do with and enjoying every advantage and privilege a multimillion-dollar contract could throw his way.

Yeah, life had been good.

Great, actually.

Until it had all come crashing down after multiple knee surgeries and an early retirement due to a positive drug test. Testing positive once had been bad enough. But after his coach had warned him that his second test would most likely be positive, Blake had taken matters into his own hands and retired. He'd warned his trainers to not give him that "medication" they kept injecting because of his torn ACL. He should have known better.

It had cost him everything he'd worked for. His contract. His career.

His passion.

And no football organization in their right mind would hire someone who had a history of using performance-enhancing drugs, not even for a front office job. So he'd left football and returned to Colorado, where he'd grown up, fully intending to live out the rest of his life in peace. That had lasted about a year before he'd been bored out of his mind, since there was only so much solitude and hiking a person could do before that got old real fast.

It was only after watching the high school football team die a slow death of humiliation and defeat, ending their eighteenth losing season, that Blake ended his pity party.

Now here he was, a week into his new job of coaching a high school football team that hadn't seen a winning season since the Clinton administration.

Needless to say, it had been a pride-swallowing moment.

He had no one to blame but himself for his fall from being a football god to a thirty-four-year-old high school coach who'd received more wary looks from parents than a stripper at confession.

Apparently some moms and dads didn't want the likes of him coaching the children they felt could be the next Aaron Rodgers or Peyton Manning.

Whatever.

Blake didn't have the heart to tell them the only way these kids could be Aaron Rodgers was if they stole the guy's identity.

In other words, not gonna happen.

In other words, he had his work cut out for him.

And you've only got one season to make it happen, pal.

That was another little tidbit that chapped Blake's ass. If he couldn't pull off a winning season, then he'd be shown the door faster than he could call his next play.

The school district's athletic director had made that point very clear when he'd hired Blake. Bring the team to the playoffs this season or find another job.

Sure.

Piece of cake.

"What the hell is number twenty-four doing?" Cameron muttered. Cam's blue eyes were hidden by a pair of dark sunglasses, despite the overcast day. But Blake could feel his best friend's gaze, analyzing and scrutinizing each move the kid on the field made.

Cameron Shaw was a play-calling genius who could turn a ballerina into the next Heisman winner. He and Blake had played ball in high school together, then in college, and Cam had been coaching high school ever since. Blake had agreed to do the job only if he could have Cam by his side.

"Strickland!" Cameron bellowed to number twenty-four, whom he'd had a close eye on since practice started. Cam crooked his finger for the kid to approach.

Brian Strickland, a junior with the heart of a lion but the talent of a ten-year-old, whipped his helmet off and ran toward them.

"Yeah, Coach?" Brian asked with a noticeable tremor to his voice.

"You decide to take a nap out there, or what?" Cameron barked.

Brian's gaze flickered to Blake's, then back to Cameron at the same time that his Adam's apple bobbed up and down like a buoy in a storm.

"No, sir," the kid answered as he licked his lips and cleared his throat because his voice had cracked. Actually cracked.

"You got some hot rally girl on your mind?" Cam asked.

A pink flush filled the kid's cheeks. Oh yeah. There was definitely a rally girl.

Brian shook his head, then swiped the back of his hand across his sweaty brow. "No, sir. I mean, she's not really my rally girl but—"

"Yeah, okay," Cameron cut him off. "I'm just trying to figure out why you're not running the play I gave you."

Brian shook his head, as though not sure how to answer the question. Probably because he didn't know. Probably the kid thought he had been running the play, only the play in his head wasn't the play Cam had given them.

Blake kept silent while Cameron did his thing with the player.

"Remember, ninety percent of the game is in here," Cameron said as he tapped the kid on the forehead with his knuckle. Then he slapped Brian on the shoulder. "Now get your ass back out there."

Instead of responding, Brian replaced his lid and sprinted back on the field. Blake hooked his hands on his hips, blew his whistle, and clapped his hands three times. The kids, recognizing the signal to lend their undivided attention to their coach, snapped their heads toward Blake. Some of them removed their helmets; others tried to get their labored breathing under control.

"You expect to win games with that half-assed display you just showed me?" Blake called out to his players. The kids alternated between panting and shifting their feet on the grass. "If you expect people to spend their hard-earned money on tickets to watch you play, you've got to do a hell of a lot better than that. Otherwise all they're going to get is a bunch of sorry-ass pansies who couldn't outplay a pee-wee league."

The team stared back at Blake with wide eyes, reminding him he was dealing with a bunch of kids who didn't have the hardy exterior of professionals. Were they not used to a coach who told them like it was? Blake rolled his shoulders, attempting to loosen his muscles and the tension that came with the enormous responsibility of whipping these kids into shape.

"I didn't hear a 'yes, Coach'!" Cameron called out.

The kids responded with a "yes, Coach" that sounded like a bunch of defeated rejects, bringing Blake back to the reality of their situation. Seeing their faces, looking into the eyes of kids who'd never tasted victory, who'd never known the exhilaration of having the town at their backs, stands filled with screaming fans, was like someone letting the air out of Blake's balloon. Having experienced that firsthand, Blake knew how walking around on cloud nine could fuel a player's motivation to exceed to the next level. To elevate the game even higher so the fans knew they could depend on them to bring them another win.

These poor kids didn't have the first clue what that was like, and they deserved to feel it, even for just a brief moment. Blake swore to himself they would have that for more than just a moment.

"Again!" Cameron demanded. "Make them hear you in Pagosa Springs! Remind those guys that we're still here!"

This time their collective "yes, Coach" was loud enough to be heard on top of Chimney Rock.

Blake blew his whistle again. "Y'all will keep running that play until you can execute it in your sleep!"

The grunts and smacking of helmets that followed brought a fresh wave of nostalgia over Blake. There wasn't quite anything like the sounds and smells of the game. The feeling was something only someone with a passion and drive for football could understand. For years it was all Blake had known. All he had cared about and he had never wanted or imagined doing anything else with his life.

He only had himself to blame for effing it all up. Knowing how things ended, would he have done anything differently?

Hell yes, he regretted the use of illegal drugs to enhance his body. And, sure, he could've outed the trainers. But ultimately, he was the one responsible for his own body. Ultimately, he'd allowed them to do whatever it took to win.

Blake turned his attention back to the kids on the field as Matt West, his cousin's son, executed some serious blocking, paving the way for Scott Porter to move forward and receive the ball.

"Now that's the kind of passion I like to see."

Blake gritted his back teeth when Drew Spalding sauntered up next to him. The school district's athletic director managed to radiate cockiness and charm all at the same time.

"Something I can help you with, Drew?" Blake asked as he kept his focus on his players, hoping Drew would take Blake's not-so-subtle hint and go the eff away.

"Just thought I'd stop by for a few minutes and watch the first practice of the season," the guy answered.

Invaded was more like it, because they both knew Drew was there to see the coaching staff more than the kids. Drew and Cameron had a rivalry that went back to high school, and things had only gotten worse from there.

Drew pointed toward the end of the field. "Why is Cody doing push-ups over there? Seems to me he ought to be running the play with his team."

The muscle in Blake's jaw clenched even tighter. "He mouthed off to Cameron." Damn, was this guy going to question everything he did?

"You shouldn't overwork your quarterback," Drew scolded. "He could pull a muscle."

He shot the athletic director an impatient look. "Then he shouldn't be talking back to his coaches. The kid needs to understand that he's not in Texas anymore."

Cody Richardson was one of the few kids on the team with real talent. The problem was he had a chip on his shoulder the size of Rhode Island and an entitled attitude to go along with it. In Blake's world, respect had to be earned. Apparently Cody had gotten used to it being handed to him.

Blake whistled and motioned for Cody to rejoin his team. He tugged on the bright red practice jersey and jogged toward the huddle.

"Maybe Cameron was being too hard on the kid," Drew commented.

"Cameron was doing his job," Blake shot back. He jerked his head toward the benches behind them. "Why don't you take a step back and let me coach my team, Drew."

Drew looked as though he wanted to argue. Knowing the guy, he probably did. Blake didn't give a shit. Drew might be Blake's superior, but on the football field, Blake always had the final word. The kids needed to know that just as much as Drew did.

"This isn't high school anymore, Blake, so you don't need to keep one-upping me," Drew commented in a hard voice.

Blake turned to face the athletic director. "I'm not trying to one-up you, Drew. I'm trying to do the job you hired me to do."

The guy held his hands up in surrender, but the slight tilt of his mouth contradicted the benign gesture. "I just wanted to see how the team looks." He lowered his hands and took a few steps backward. "It might be too early to tell, Carpenter, but one season may not be enough time for you to get the job done."

One season was more than enough time, but Blake kept the argument to himself as Drew walked away. Let the cocky asshole think he had the upper hand. Blake would prove himself on the field; then Drew would have to keep that trap of his shut. The play ended and Cameron signaled for the kids to run it again. They got halfway through when a shadow appeared beside him. A long, slender, and curvy shadow, followed by the scent of . . . something flowery and feminine. Blake didn't know the distinction between the smell of a rose and a carnation, but whatever it was was damn good. Like attention-getting, hair-standing-on-the-back-of-his-neck good.

And the soft voice that followed was the perfect match to the knock-you-on-your-ass scent messing with his concentration. "Coach Carpenter?" the woman asked.

Blake kept his attention on his players. "If you have a problem with the way I talk to your kid, then I suggest you don't come to the practices," he told the woman.

"Uh...," she started, clearly taken aback by his abrupt statement. "No, I'm not related to any of the players, Mr. Carpenter."

The play finished and Blake blew his whistle. "Water break, gentlemen," he called to his players. He waited a moment before turning to the woman who'd interrupted his practice. When he did, the hazel eyes that blinked back at him just about knocked him on his ass. And yeah, she was way too young to be the mother of a high schooler.

So what the hell was she doing here?

Besides clouding his thinking with whatever the hell she sprayed on herself.

"What can I do for you, Miss..." He waited, arching a brow above his sunglasses.

She blinked at him, then stuck her hand out. "Turner," she answered. "Annabelle Turner."

Her full lips curved into a small but oddly seductive smile, which was like a punch to Blake's gut.

What the hell?

He took her hand, noting how much smaller and softer it was than his. Her petite fingers curved around his palm, but instead of shaking her hand, he just held on to it. As though he were some jackass who had never gone through a hand-shaking ritual before.

"Again, what can I do for you?" he wanted to know.

She withdrew her hand from his and rubbed it up and down the top of her thigh, which was covered in some kind of black spandex. As though she'd just come from the gym. Probably had considering how lean she was.

"I wanted to come and introduce myself before we started working together," she answered.

His brow twitched in confusion. "Working together?" he repeated.

"With the players," she clarified with a wave of her hand toward the field.

"I'm not following you, Ms. Turner."

"I'm the physical therapist," she explained. Her teeth stabbed into her full lower lip when he didn't respond to her announcement. "Drew Spalding hired me to work with the kids," she went on. "Do you know Drew? He's the athletic director—"

"I know who Drew is," he interrupted. Out of the corner of his eye, he saw Cameron walk onto the field to speak to the players.

Annabelle smiled, creating a shallow dimple in her right cheek. "Sorry, but you were looking at me like you didn't know what I was talking about."

He turned to face her, noting how her long thick hair kept teasing her jawline when the wind blew. The strands were dark on top, the color of a rich Tennessee whiskey, which slowly faded to a brighter blond on the ends, curling slightly into a perfect outward flip.

"That's because I don't, Ms. Turner," he explained.

Her brow crinkled at his abrupt tone. Excuse him for being an asshole, but he had a team to coach and this woman, with her provocative scent and legs for days, was pulling his thoughts off of play calling and onto lazy afternoon sex.

"Drew hired me last season to work with the players," she explained, which still wasn't much of an explanation. "Since the team doesn't have an official doctor, he thought I could help them."

"Help them with what?" Yeah, he knew what physical therapists could do for football players. As a professional, he'd been treated by some of the top PTs in the country. What he didn't know was why she was here, with a high school football team. He'd never heard of a high school football program hiring their own therapists and doctors, unless it was a wealthy 5A school, which Blanco Valley wasn't.

"Stretching," she answered. "Conditioning. Treating old injuries that might hinder their abilities."

Blake hadn't been made aware of a physical therapist working with the team. That sort of practice was unorthodox and unnecessary in Blake's mind. Professional football teams had all sorts of trainers and doctors to make sure the players were kept in the best shape possible.

But this was high school, for crying out loud. What the hell did they need a physical therapist for?

"Talent is what these kids need, Ms. Turner. Not stretching exercises."

Her mouth opened to say something, then shut again. "Drew thinks I can—"

He crossed his arms over his chest. "Last I checked, Drew Spalding wasn't this team's head coach. I am. I don't know you from Adam, so I'm not about to let you walk in here and step on my toes." He turned from her and walked onto the field, determined to get his mind back on his players and off this woman.

But the tenacious little thing had other plans because she grabbed his forearm, digging her sharp fingernails into his flesh, giving him an impression of delicate, soft skin, which was odd given the firm grasp she had on his arm.

"Are you dismissing me, Mr. Carpenter?" she demanded.

He spared the hand on his arm a quick glance, noting how trim and neat her fingernails were. Unpainted. Practical. Then quirked a brow at her. "Beautiful and insightful. Quite a combination."

She stared at him for a moment, drilling her greenish-brown eyes into his and touching a place deep inside that hadn't been touched in a long time. The one that had to do with arousal and reacting to a beautiful woman. Then the angelic look on her face was replaced with a firm set of her full mouth, a look she no doubt mastered.

"You can't just shrug me off, Mr. Carpenter. Even though you didn't hire me, I can be helpful to your players." She took a step toward him. "You haven't even seen what I can do yet."

He allowed his gaze to drift over her lithe body, touching on her flat stomach, then skimming down her toned legs. As a football player, Blake had mastered the art of intimidation, often being able to get inside his opponent's head with a simple searing look.

But he had to give this five-foot-nothing sprite some credit. She held her ground almost as well as some of the fiercest players he'd gone up against.

"I don't need to see what you can do, Ms. Turner." He ended the conversation by turning his back on her and walking the rest of the way to the center of the football field. Whether or not she actually left, he had no idea. But he could have sworn he heard the words *impossible asshole*.

Yeah, he was that.

About the Author

Erin Kern lives in north Texas with her husband, two kids, and their dog. She loves barbecue, Texas sunsets, antiquing, and high school football games. The first book in the Champion Valley series, *Winner Takes All*, was published in August 2016, and was inspired by Erin's love of Texas football, small towns, and happy endings.

When she's not at the computer working on her next tale, she can be found spending time with her kids or curled up with a good book.

You can learn more at:

ErinKern.com
Twitter @erinkern04
Facebook.com/ErinKernAuthor

Fall in Love with Forever Romance

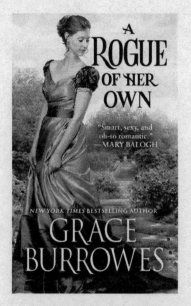

A ROGUE OF HER OWN
By Grace Burrowes

From Grace Burrowes comes the next book in the *New York Times* bestselling Windham Brides series! All Charlotte Windham needs to maintain her independence is a teeny, tiny brush with scandal. What she doesn't count on is that one kiss will lead her straight to the altar with a brash, wealthy upstart she barely knows.

Fall in Love with Forever Romance

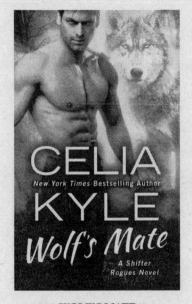

WOLF'S MATE
By Celia Kyle

From *New York Times* bestselling author Celia Kyle comes the first book in the Shifter Rogues series! Cougar shifter Abby Carter *always* plays it safe. That's why she's an accountant—no excitement, no danger, and no cocky alpha males. But when Abby uncovers the shady dealings of an anti-shifter organization, she'll have to trust the too-sexy-for-her-peace-of-mind werewolf Declan Reed...or end up six feet under.

Fall in Love with Forever Romance

AS THE DEVIL DARES
By Anna Harrington

Lord Robert Carlisle never backs down from a challenge, but finding a husband for the captivating Mariah Winslow seems impossible. Mariah knows Lord Robert is trying to secure a partnership in her father's shipping company, a partnership that is rightfully hers. She'll play his game, but she won't be tempted by this devil—even if she finds him wickedly irresistible. Fans of Elizabeth Hoyt, Grace Burrowes, and Madeline Hunter will love the newest book in the Capturing the Carlisles series.

Fall in Love with Forever Romance

CHANGING THE RULES
By Erin Kern

The next stand-alone novel in Erin Kern's Champion Valley series! Cameron Shaw knows how to coach high school boys on the football field, but caring for his six-year-old niece, Piper, is a whole different ballgame. Audrey Bennett wasn't planning to stick around once she delivered Piper to her new guardian, but the gruff former football star clearly needs help. And the longer she stays—watching Cameron teach Piper to make pancakes and tie her sparkly pink shoelaces—the harder it is to leave.

THE SWEETEST THING
By Jill Shalvis

Now featuring ten bonus recipes never before seen in print! Don't miss this new edition of *The Sweetest Thing*, the second book in *New York Times* bestselling author Jill Shalvis's beloved Lucky Harbor series!

The *New York Times* Bestseller

JILL SHALVIS
The Sweetest Thing

A Lucky Harbor Novel

"My go-to read for humor and heat."
—SUSAN MALLERY

INCLUDES
10 BONUS
RECIPES